THE MAN

From Stephen King's blood-freezing tale of a kidnapping with a frightening new twist . . .

to the story of a boy whose parents have a terrifyingly unique method for choosing his friends . . .

to a chiller about a man for whom a visit with the relatives is a fate worse than death . . .

to the legend of a village where an ancient evil hounds the unwary to their doom . . .

These are but a few of the dark and eerie visions included in—

THE YEAR'S BEST HORROR STORIES: XVI

Watch for these exciting DAW Anthologies:

ASIMOV PRESENTS THE GREAT SF STORIES
Classics of short fiction from the golden age
through today.
Edited by Isaac Asimov and Martin H. Greenberg.

THE ANNUAL WORLD'S BEST SF
The finest stories of the current year.
Edited by Donald A. Wollheim with Arthur W. Saha.

THE YEAR'S BEST HORROR STORIES
The finest horror stories of the current year.
Edited by Karl Edward Wagner.

THE YEAR'S BEST FANTASY STORIES
An annual of fantastic tales.
Edited by Arthur W. Saha.

SWORD AND SORCERESS
Original tales of fantasy and adventure
with female protagonists.
Edited by Marion Zimmer Bradley.

VAMPS
Heart freezing tales of those deadly ladies
of the night—vampires.
Edited by Martin H. Greenberg and Charles G. Waugh.

HOUSE SHUDDERS
Ghostly tales of haunted houses.
Edited by Martin H. Greenberg and Charles G. Waugh.

HUNGER FOR HORROR
A devilish stew of stories.
*Edited by Robert Adams, Martin H. Greenberg,
and Pamela Crippen Adams*

RED JACK
Knife-edged terror stalks the streets in this
100th anniversary collection of Jack the Ripper tales.
*Edited by Martin H. Greenberg, Charles G. Waugh,
and Frank D. McSherry, Jr.*

KARL EDWARD WAGNER

PRESENTS

THE YEAR'S BEST

HORROR

STORIES

XVI

DAW BOOKS, INC.

DONALD A. WOLLHEIM, PUBLISHER

1633 Broadway, New York, NY 10019

First Printing, October 1988

1 2 3 4 5 6 7 8 9

PRINTED IN THE U.S.A.

ACKNOWLEDGMENTS

Popsy by Stephen King. Copyright © 1987 by Stephen King for *Masques II*. Reprinted by permission of the author and the author's agent, Kirby McCauley Ltd.

Neighbourhood Watch by Greg Egan. Copyright © 1987 by Greg Egan for *Aphelion* No. 5. Reprinted by permission of the author.

Wolf/Child by Jane Yolen. Copyright © 1987 by TZ Publications for *Rod Serling's The Twilight Zone Magazine*, June 1987. Reprinted by permission of the author and the author's agent, Curtis Brown Ltd.

Everything To Live For by Charles L. Grant. Copyright © 1987 by Charles L. Grant for *Whispers VI*. Reprinted by permission of the author.

Repossession by David Campton. Copyright © 1987 by David Campton for *Whispers VI*. Reprinted by permission of the author.

Merry May by Ramsey Campbell. Copyright © 1987 by Ramsey Campbell for *Scared Stiff*. Reprinted by permission of the author.

The Touch by Wayne Allen Sallee. Copyright © 1987 by Grue Magazine for *Grue Magazine* No. 4. Reprinted by permission of the author.

Moving Day by R. Chetwynd-Hayes. Copyright © 1987 by R. Chetwynd-Hayes for *The Third Book of After Midnight Stories*. Reprinted by permission of the author.

To John Rieber

Life is coincidence, ruined by sanity.

—*Ancient Chinese Proverb*

CONTENTS

INTRODUCTION: THEY'RE HERE—AND THEY WON'T GO AWAY

Welcome to *The Year's Best Horror Stories: Series XVI*.

But first, a word *to* our sponsors: all of you readers out there who are currently writing horror stories and those of you who are planning to do so tomorrow or the next day.

You lot aren't making my job any easier, you know.

This is the ninth volume in this series that I have edited for DAW Books, and each year I mutter about the increasing amount of reading I have to do and the difficulty in making final selections from so many outstanding stories. . . . But, hey—in 1987 you writers pushed me too far. I'd thought 1986 was a bumper year, but 1987 broke all records for the number of horror stories published. If you don't believe me, ask my optometrist.

The increase has come from two directions. While the usual markets—genre magazines and general periodicals—remain strong, there has been an exciting proliferation both of small press publications and of major horror anthologies.

The hyperactivity in the small press field is particularly impressive. Amateur magazines—call them fanzines or semiprozines, as you will—have been a fixture in the field for as long as there have been fantasy/horror fans. Fifteen years ago there were relatively few small press publications devoted primarily to horror fiction. *Weirdbook* and *Whispers* were in the fore and in the minority. More often, fan publications centered upon one particular author—usually Edgar Rice Burroughs, H.P. Lovecraft, or Robert E. Howard—and such fiction as they published was devotedly derivative. Heroic fantasy was quiet in vogue, and the major thrust of fan publishing—and fan writing—was directed toward imaginary realms of sorcery, swords and derring-do. Horror fiction, unless derivative, was decidedly *not* where the action was.

Not so in 1987, if the four-foot shelf crammed with the year's small press publications—as many as I could lay hands on—is any indication. Surging strongly in recent years, horror fiction now rules the small press world. Most of the older magazines stand firm, the young ones from a few years back have settled in, and new titles are lurking in every dark alley. People are interested in horror fiction; they want to read it, and many want to write it. This is where the future of horror fiction *really* can be seen, and I wonder what awaits us in *The Year's Best Horror Stories* fifteen years from now.

The growing popularity of the horror story is also evidenced by the increase in anthologies of original horror fiction. For reasons never clear to me, publishers traditionally have avoided short story collections in preference to novels. One editor once told me that this was because almost all books ever sold are bought by New Yorkers who read them on trains, and that this consumer group only reads novels. I sit up nights pondering over this.

Whatever the logic, it seems to be changing. The last few years have seen an upsurge in short story collections all throughout the science fiction, fantasy and horror genres—original and reprint, single author and anthology. Perhaps the explanation lies in the fact that many of these are theme collections or "shared universe" anthologies. Theme anthologies have begun to predominate the horror field—books wherein all the stories take place on Halloween, or are set in the South, or deal with haunted houses, or have some other unifying theme. Shared universe anthologies, still more common in science fiction and fantasy, are even more inbred: various authors write stories within a previously structured setting, perhaps utilizing a few recurring characters, and abiding by certain rules and regulations. I think it's this unified approach that eases publishers' qualms about short story collections. They can tell themselves that these are, after all, *almost* novels.

This is not to denigrate either trend. I've been asked to contribute to many of these myself; in fact, I have done so, and any editor who asks me for a story about motorcycles in Texas on Saint Patrick's Day is more than welcome to inquire. Meanwhile, general horror anthologies have shared in the boom, with stalwarts such as *Shadows* and *Whispers* still going strong, while we also see ambitious new small press entries such as *Masques*, in addition to the outstanding collections published each year by William Kimber in England.

The Year's Best Horror Stories is a general horror anthology. These stories are chosen without regard to theme or method, style or approach. Here you will find stories by famous writers alongside those by unknowns, stories from familiar sources as well as from those obscure. As you read through *Series XVI*, you will encounter traditional ghostly tales as well as those of surreal terror, find experimental creative ventures alongside new interpretations of the Cthulhu Mythos, experience quiet horrors sharing space with the raw scream.

This eclecticism is one reason why *The Year's Best Horror Stories* is the unique annual anthology of horror stories. There are no rules, no prescribed themes. There are no taboos, no free rides. I'm only looking for the best. And so are you.

It's interesting that over the near-decade during which I've edited *The Year's Best Horror Stories* reviews and letters of comment have often singled out the same given story as the best or the worst in that particular volume. As they say, different strokes. While I make it a policy never to mention awards in *The Year's Best Horror Stories*, I'll break my own rule this one time to congratulate Dennis Etchison for winning the British Fantasy Award for Best Short Fiction for "The Olympic Runner" and David J. Schow for winning the World Fantasy Award for Best Short Story for "Red Light." Both stories had previously been selected for last year's *The Year's Best Horror Stories: Series XV*. Nice to know that your eye-strained editor is not alone in his judgments. And that's the last I'll say about awards.

In short, the horror genre is as active right now as it has ever been. With the help of new glasses and a brain transplant, I'll be ready to sift through whatever horrid delights the future has in store for us over the next fifteen years.

The only criterion for the *The Year's Best Horror Stories* is excellence.

Hey, maybe that makes this a theme anthology after all?

Too late now. Dive into *The Year's Best Horror Stories: Series XVI*. And pray that you make it back next year.

—Karl Edward Wagner

POPSY

by Stephen King

The fact that you are reading this book probably means that it won't really be necessary for me to tell you who Stephen King is. Beginning with Carrie, *King has written a seemingly endless string of best-selling horror novels, many of which have been made into films. His most recent bestsellers include* It, Misery, The Tommyknockers, *and* The Eyes of the Dragon, *while* Stand By Me *and* The Running Man *are the most recent successful movies based on his work.*

It wasn't always like this. Born September 21, 1946 in Portland, Maine, Stephen King is one of the generation of horror writers who were born during or immediately after World War II—and perhaps there's a story (or a thesis) in this phenomenon. Like most of us, King struggled along for years, selling stories where he could, eking out a living teaching school, working in a laundromat, whatever. But that was then and this is now, and King's hard-earned success has opened doors for countless other horror writers, both as an inspiration to them and as proof of the genre's hitherto unsuspected popularity with the general public. Success generates imitation, and many writers have fumbled about trying to discover King's secret formula. There is, however, no secret. Stephen King is happily writing just what he has always wanted to write, doing just what he has wanted to do with his life: Stephen King enjoys scaring the bejabbers out of his readers. Witness the following:

Sheridan was cruising slowly down the long blank length of the shopping mall when he saw the little kid push out through the main doors under the lighted sign which read COUSINTOWN. It was a boy-child, perhaps a big three and surely no more than five. On his face was an expression to which Sheridan had become exquisitely attuned. He was trying not to cry but soon would.

Sheridan paused for a moment, feeling the familiar soft wave of self-disgust . . . but every time he took a child, that feeling grew a little less urgent. The first time he hadn't slept for a week. He kept thinking about that big greasy Turk who called himself Mr. Wizard, kept wondering what he did with the children.

"They go on a boat-ride, Mr. Sheridan," the Turk told him, only it came out *Dey goo on a bot-rahd, Meestair Shurdone*. The Turk smiled. *And if you know what's good for you, you won't ask anymore about it*, that smile said, and it said it loud and clear, without an accent.

Sheridan *hadn't* asked anymore, but that didn't mean he hadn't kept wondering. Tossing and turning, wishing he had the whole thing to do over again so he could turn it around, walk away from the temptation. The second time had been almost as bad . . . the third time not quite . . . and by the fourth time he had stopped wondering so much about the bot-rahd, and what might be at the end of it for the little kids.

Sheridan pulled his van into one of the parking spaces right in front of the mall, spaces that were almost always empty because they were for crips. Sheridan had one of the special license plates on the back of his van the state gave to crips; that kept any mall security cop from getting suspicious, and those spaces were so convenient.

You always pretend you're not going out looking, but you always lift a crip plate a day or two before.

Never mind all that bullshit; he was in a jam and that kid over there could bail him out of it.

He got out and walked toward the kid, who was looking around with more and more bewildered panic in his face. Yes, he thought, he was five all right, maybe even six—just very frail. In the harsh fluorescent glare thrown through the glass doors the boy looked white and ill. Maybe he really was sick, but Sheridan reckoned he was just scared.

He looked up hopefully at the people passing around him, people going into the mall eager to buy, coming out laden with packages, their faces dazed, almost drugged, with something they probably thought was satisfaction.

The kid, dressed in Tuffskin jeans and a Pittsburgh Penguins tee-shirt, looked for help, looked for somebody to look at him and see something was wrong, looked for someone to ask the right question—*You get separated from your dad, son?* would do—looking for a friend.

Here I am, Sheridan thought, approaching. *Here I am, sonny—I'll be your friend.*

He had almost reached the kid when he saw a mall rent-a-cop walking slowly up the concourse toward the doors. He was reaching in his pocket, probably for a pack of cigarettes. He would come out, see the boy, and there would go Sheridan's sure thing.

Shit, he thought, but at least he wouldn't be seen talking to the kid when the cop came out. That would have been worse.

Sheridan drew back a little and made a business of feeling in his own pockets, as if to make sure he still had his keys. His glance flicked from the boy to the security cop and back to the boy. The boy had started to cry. Not all-out bawling, not yet, but great big tears that looked reddish in the reflected glow of the COUSINTOWN MALL sign as they tracked down his smooth cheeks.

The girl in the information booth waved at the cop and said something to him. She was pretty, dark-haired, about twenty-five; he was sandy-blond with a mustache. As he leaned on his elbows, smiling at her, Sheridan thought they looked like the cigarette ads you saw on the backs of magazines. Salem Spirit. Light My Lucky. He was dying out here and they were in there making chit-chat. Now she was batting her eyes at him. How cute.

Sheridan abruptly decided to take the chance. The kid's chest was hitching, and as soon as he started to bawl out loud, someone would notice him. He didn't like moving in with a cop less than sixty feet away, but if he didn't cover his markers at Mr. Reggie's within the next twenty-four hours or so, he thought a couple of very large men would pay him a visit and perform impromptu surgery on his arms, adding several elbow-bends to each.

He walked up to the kid, a big man dressed in an ordinary Van Heusen shirt and khaki pants, a man with a broad, ordinary face that looked kind at first glance. He bent over the little boy, hands on his legs just above the knees, and the boy turned his pale, scared face up to Sheridan's. His eyes were as green as emeralds, their color accentuated by the tears that washed them.

"You get separated from your dad, son?" Sheridan asked kindly.

"My Popsy," the kid said, wiping his eyes. "My dad's not here and I . . . I can't find my P-P-Popsy!"

Now the kid *did* begin to sob, and a woman headed in glanced around with some vague concern.

"It's all right," Sheridan said to her, and she went on. Sheridan put a comforting arm around the boy's shoulders and drew him a little to the right . . . in the direction of the van. Then he looked back inside.

The rent-a-cop had his face right down next to the information girl's now. Looked like there was something pretty hot going on between them . . . and if there wasn't, there soon would be. Sheridan relaxed. At this point there could be a stick-up going on at the bank just up the concourse and the cop wouldn't notice a thing. This was starting to look like a cinch.

"I want my Popsy!" the boy wept.

"Sure you do, of course you do," Sheridan said. "And we're going to find him. Don't you worry."

He drew him a little more to the right.

The boy looked up at him, suddenly hopeful.

"Can you? Can you, Mister?"

"Sure!" Sheridan said, and grinned. "Finding lost Popsies . . . well, you might say it's kind of a specialty of mine."

"It is?" The kid actually smiled a little, although his eyes were still leaking.

"It sure is," Sheridan said, glancing inside again to make sure the cop, whom he could now barely see (and who would barely be able to see Sheridan and the boy, should he happen to look up), was still enthralled. He was. "What was your Popsy wearing, son?"

"He was wearing his suit," the boy said. "He almost always wears his suit. I only saw him once in jeans." He spoke as if Sheridan should know all these things about his Popsy.

"I bet it was a black suit," Sheridan said.

The boy's eyes lit up, flashing red in the light of the mall sigh, as if his tears had turned to blood.

"You *saw* him! Where?" The boy started eagerly back toward the doors, tears forgotten, and Sheridan had to restrain himself from grabbing the boy right then. No good. Couldn't cause a scene. Couldn't do anything people would remember later. Had to get him in the van. The van had sun-filter glass everywhere except in the windshield; it was almost impossible to see inside even from six inches away.

Had to get him in the van first.

He touched the boy on the arm. "I didn't see him inside, son. I saw him right over there."

He pointed across the huge parking lot with its endless platoons of cars. There was an access road at the far end of it, and beyond that were the double yellow arches of McDonald's.

"Why would Popsy go over *there*?" the boy asked, as if either Sheridan or Popsy—or maybe both of them—had gone utterly mad.

"I don't know," Sheridan said. His mind was working fast, clicking along like an express train as it always did when it got right down to the point where you had to stop shitting and either do it up right or fuck it up righteously. Popsy. Not Dad or Daddy but Popsy. The kid had corrected him on it. Popsy meant granddad, Sheridan decided. "But I'm pretty sure that was him. Older guy in a black suit. White hair . . . green tie . . ."

"Popsy had his blue tie on," the boy said. "He knows I like it the best."

"Yeah, it could have been blue," Sheridan said. "Under these lights, who can tell? Come on, hop in the van, I'll run you over there to him."

"Are you *sure* it was Popsy? Because I don't know why he'd go to a place where they—"

Sheridan shrugged. "Look, kid, if you're sure that wasn't him, maybe you better look for him on your own. You might even find him." And he started brusquely away, heading back toward the van.

The kid wasn't biting. He thought about going back, trying again, but it had already gone on too long—you either kept observable contact to a minimum or you were asking for twenty years in Hammerton Bay. It would be better to go on to another mall. Scoterville, maybe. Or—

"Wait, mister!" It was the kid, with panic in his voice. There was the light thud of running sneakers. "Wait up! I told im I was thirsty, he must have thought he had to go way over there to get me a drink. Wait!"

Sheridan turned around, smiling. "I wasn't really going to leave you anyway, son."

He led the boy to the van, which was four years old and painted a nondescript blue. He opened the door

and smiled at the kid, who looked up at him doubt-
fully, his green eyes swimming in that pallid little face.

"Step into my parlor," Sheridan said.

The kid did, and although he didn't know it, his ass
belonged to Briggs Sheridan the minute the passenger
door swung shut.

He had no problem with broads, and he could take
booze or leave it alone. His problem was cards—any
kind of cards, as long as it was the kind of cards where
you started off by changing your greenbacks into chips.
He had lost jobs, credit cards, the home his mother
had left him. He had never, at least so far, been in
jail, but the first time he got in trouble with Mr.
Reggie, he thought jail would be a rest-cure by
comparison.

He had gone a little crazy that night. It was better,
he had found, when you lost right away. When you
lost right away you got discouraged, went home,
watched a little Carson on the tube, went to sleep.
When you won a little bit at first, you chased. Sheridan had chased that night and had ended up owing
$17,000. He could hardly believe it; he went home
dazed, almost elated by the enormity of it. He kept
telling himself in the car on the way home that he
owed Mr. Reggie not seven hundred, not seven
thousand, but *seventeen thousand* iron men. Every time
he tried to think about it he giggled and turned the
volume up on the radio.

But he wasn't giggling the next night when the two
gorillas—the ones who would make sure his arms bent
in all sorts of new and interesting ways if he didn't pay
up—brought him into Mr. Reggie's office.

"I'll pay," Sheridan began babbling at once. "I'll
pay, listen, it's no problem, couple of days, a week at
the most, two weeks at the outside—"

"You bore me, Sheridan," Mr. Reggie said.

"I—"

"Shut up. If I give you a week, don't you think I
know what you'll do? You'll tap a friend for a couple

of hundred if you've got a friend left to tap. If you can't find a friend, you'll hit a liquor store . . . if you've got the guts. I doubt if you do, but anything is possible." Mr. Reggie leaned forward, propped his chin on his hands, and smiled. He smelled of Ted Lapidus cologne. "And if you do come up with two hundred dollars, what will you do with it?"

"Give it to you," Sheridan had babbled. By then he was very close to wetting his pants. "I'll give it to you, right away!"

"No you won't," Mr. Reggie said. "You'll take it to the track and try to make it grow. What you'll give me is a bunch of shitty excuses. You're in over your head this time, my friend. Way over your head."

Sheridan began to blubber.

"These guys could put you in the hospital for a long time," Mr. Reggie said reflectively. "You would have a tube in each arm and another one coming out of your nose."

Sheridan began to blubber louder.

"I'll give you this much," Mr. Reggie said, and pushed a folded sheet of paper across his desk to Sheridan. "You might get along with this guy. He calls himself Mr. Wizard, but he's a shitbag just like you. Now get out of here. I'm gonna have you back in here in a week, though, and I'll have your markers on this desk. You either buy them back or I'm going to have my friends tool up on you. And like Booker T. says, once they start, they do it until they're satisfied."

The Turk's real name was written on the folded sheet of paper. Sheridan went to see him, and heard about the kids and the bot-rahds. Mr. Wizard also named a figure which was a fairish bit larger than the markers Mr. Reggie was holding. That was when Sheridan started cruising the malls.

He pulled out of the Cousintown Mall's main parking lot, looked for traffic, and then pulled across into the McDonald's in-lane. The kid was sitting all the way forward on the passenger seat, hands on the knees of his Tuffskins, eyes agonizingly alert. Sheridan drove toward the building, swung wide to avoid the drive-thru lane, and kept on going.

"Why are you going around the back?" the kid asked.

"You have to go around to the other doors," Sheridan said. "Keep your shirt on, kid. I think I saw him in there."

"You did? You really did?"

"I'm pretty sure, yeah."

Sublime relief washed over the kid's face, and for a moment Sheridan felt sorry for him—hell, he wasn't a monster or a maniac, for Christ's sake. But his markers had gotten a little deeper each time, and that bastard Mr. Reggie had no compunctions at all about letting him hang himself. It wasn't $17,000 this time, or $20,000, or even $25,000. This time it was thirty-five thousand big ones if he didn't want a few new sets of elbows by next Saturday.

He stopped in the back by the trash-compacter. Nobody parked back here. Good. There was an elasticized pouch on the side of the door for maps and things. Sheridan reached into it with his left hand and brought out a pair of blued steel Koch handcuffs. The loop-jaws were open.

"Why are we stopping here, mister?" the kid asked, and the quality of fear in his voice had changed; his voice said that maybe getting separated from Popsy in the busy mall wasn't the worst thing that could happen to him.

"We're not, not really," Sheridan said easily. He had learned the second time he'd done this that you didn't want to underestimate even a six year old once he had his wind up. The second kid had kicked him in the balls and had damn near gotten away. "I just remembered I forgot to put my glasses on when I started driving. I could lose my license. They're in that glasses-case on the floor there. They slid over to your side. Hand 'em to me, would you?"

The kid bent over to get the glasses case, which was

empty. Sheridan leaned over and snapped one of the cuffs on the other hand as neat as you please. And then the trouble started. Hadn't he just been thinking it was a bad mistake to underestimate even a six year old? The kid fought like a wildcat, twisting with an eely muscularity Sheridan never would have believed in a skinny little package like him. He bucked and fought and lunged for the door, panting and uttering weird birdlike little cries. He got the handle. The door swung open, but no domelight came on—Sheridan had broken it after that second outing.

He got the kid by the round collar of his Penguins tee-shirt and hauled him back in. He tried to clamp the other cuff on the special strut beside the passenger seat and missed. The kid bit his hand, twice, bringing blood. God, his teeth were like razors. The pain went deep and sent a steely ache all the way up his arm. He punched the kid in the mouth. He fell back into the seat, dazed, Sheridan's blood on his mouth and chin and dripping onto the ribbed neck of the tee-shirt. Sheridan clamped the other cuff on the arm of the seat and then fell back into his own, sucking the back of his right hand.

The pain was really bad. He pulled his hand away from his mouth and looked at it in the weak glow of the dashlights. Two shallow, ragged tears, each maybe two inches long, ran up toward his wrist from just above the knuckles. Blood pulsed in weak little rills. Still, he felt no urge to pop the kid again, and that had nothing to do with damaging the Turk's merchandise, in spite of the almost fussy way the Turk had warned him against that—*demmage the goots end you demmage the velue*, the Turk had said in his fluting accent.

No, he didn't blame the kid for fighting—he would have done the same. He would have to disinfect the wound as soon as he could, might even have to have a shot—he had read somewhere that human bites were the worst kind—but he sort of admired the kid's guts.

He dropped the transmission into drive and pulled around the brick building, past the empty drive-thru window, and back onto the access road. He turned left. The Turk had a big ranch-style house in Taluda Heights, on the edge of the city. Sheridan would go there by secondary roads, just in case. Thirty miles. Maybe forty-five minutes, maybe an hour.

He passed a sign which read THANK YOU FOR SHOPPING THE BEAUTIFUL COUSINTOWN MALL, turned left, and let the van creep up to a perfectly legal forty miles an hour. He fished a handkerchief out of his back pocket, folded it over the back of his right hand, and concentrated on following his headlights to the forty grand the Turk had promised.

"You'll be sorry," the kid said.

Sheridan looked impatiently around at him, pulled from a dream in which he had just made twenty straight points and had Mr. Reggie groveling at his feet, sweating bullets and begging him to stop, what did he want to do, break him?

The kid was crying again, and his tears still had that odd reddish cast. Sheridan wondered for the first time if the kid might be sick . . . might have some disease. Was nothing to him as long as he himself didn't catch it and as long as Mr. Wizard paid him before finding out.

"When my *Popsy* finds you you'll be sorry," the kid elaborated.

"Yeah," Sheridan said, and lit a cigarette. He turned off State Road 28 onto an unmarked stretch of two-lane blacktop. There was a long marshy area on the left, unbroken woods on the right.

The kid pulled at the handcuffs and made a sobbing sound.

"Quit it. Won't do you any good."

Nevertheless, the kid pulled again. And this time there was a groaning, protesting sound Sheridan didn't like at *all*. He looked around and was amazed to see that the metal strut on the side of the seat—a strut he had welded in place himself—was twisted out of shape.

Shit! he thought. *He's got teeth like razors and now I find out he's also strong as a fucking ox.*

He pulled over onto the soft shoulder and said, "Stop it!"

"I *won't*!"

The kid yanked at the handcuff again and Sheridan saw the metal strut bend a little more. Christ, how could *any* kid do that?

It's panic, he answered himself. *That's how he can do it.*

But none of the others had been able to do it, and many of them had been in worse shape than this kid by now.

He opened the glove compartment in the center of the dash. He brought out a hypodermic needle. The Turk had given it to him, and cautioned him not to use it unless he absolutely had to. Drugs, the Turk said (pronouncing it *drucks*) could demmege the merchandise.

"See this?"

The kid nodded.

"You want me to use it?"

The kid shook his head, eyes big and terrified.

"That's smart. Very smart. It would put out your lights." He paused. He didn't want to say it—hell, he was a nice guy, really, when he didn't have his ass in a sling—but he had to. "Might even kill you."

The kid stared at him, lips trembling, face as white as newspaper ashes.

"You stop yanking the cuff, I won't use the needle. Okay?"

"Okay," the kid whispered.

"You promise?"

"Yes." The kid lifted his lip, showing white teeth. One of them was spotted with Sheridan's blood.

"You promise on your mother's name?"

"I never had a mother."

"Shit," Sheridan said, disgusted, and got the van rolling again. He moved a little faster now, and not only because he was finally off the main road. The kid

was a spook. Sheridan wanted to turn him over to the
Turk, get his money, and split.

"My Popsy's really strong, mister."

"Yeah?" Sheridan asked, and thought: *I bet he is,
kid. Only guy in the old folks' home who can bench-
press his own truss, right?*

"He'll find me."

"Uh-huh."

"He can smell me."

Sheridan believed it. *He* could sure smell the kid.
That fear had an odor was something he had learned
on his previous expeditions, but this was unreal—the
kid smelled like a mixture of sweat, mud, and slowly
cooking battery acid.

Sheridan cracked his window. On the left, the marsh
went on and on. Broken slivers of moonlight glimmered in the stagnant water.

"Popsy can fly."

"Yeah," Sheridan said, "and I bet he flies even
better after a couple of bottles of Night Train."

"Popsy—"

"Shut up, kid, okay?"

The kid shut up.

Four miles further on the marsh broadened into a
wide empty pond. Here Sheridan made a left turn
onto a stretch of hardpan dirt. Five miles west of here
he would turn right onto Highway 41, and from there
it would be a straight shot into Taluda Heights.

He glanced toward the pond, a flat silver sheet in
the moonlight . . . and then the moonlight was gone.
Blotted out.

Overhead there was a flapping sound like big sheets
on a clothesline.

"Popsy!" the kid cried.

"Shut up. It was only a bird."

But suddenly he was spooked, very spooked. He
looked at the kid. The kid's lip was drawn back from
his teeth again. His teeth were very white, very big.

No . . . not big. Big wasn't the right word. *Long*

was the right word. Especially the two on the top at each side. The . . . what did you call them? The canines.

His mind suddenly started to fly again, clicking along as if he were on speed.

I told im I was thirsty.

Why would Popsy go to a place where they

(?eat was he going to say eat?)

He'll find me. He can smell me. My Popsy can fly.

Thirsty I told him I was thirsty he went to get me something to drink he went to get me SOMEONE to drink he went—

Something landed on the roof of the van with a heavy clumsy thump.

"Popsy!" the kid screamed again, almost delirious with delight, and suddenly Sheridan could not see the road anymore—a huge membranous wing, pulsing with veins, covered the windshield from side to side.

My Popsy can fly.

Sheridan screamed and jumped on the brake, hoping to tumble the thing on the roof off the front. There was that groaning, protesting sound of metal under stress from his right again, this time followed by a short bitter snap. A moment later the kid's fingers were clawing into his face, pulling open his cheek.

"He stole me, Popsy!" the kid was screeching at the roof of the van in that birdlike voice. *"He stole me, he stole me, the bad man stole me!"*

You don't understand, kid, Sheridan thought. He groped for the hypo and found it. *I'm not a bad guy, I just got in a jam, hell, under the right circumstances I could be your grandfather—*

But as Popsy's hand, more like a talon than a real hand, smashed through the side window and ripped the hypo from Sheridan's hand—along with two of his fingers—he understood that wasn't true.

A moment later Popsy peeled the entire driver's side door out of its frame, the hinges now bright twists of meaningless metal. He saw a billowing cape, some kind of pendant, and the tie—yes, it was blue.

Popsy yanked him out of the car, talons sinking

through Sheridan's jacket and shirt and deep into the meat of his shoulders. Popsy's green eyes suddenly turned as red as blood-roses.

"We only came to the mall because my grandson wanted some Transformer figures," Popsy whispered, and his breath was like flyblown meat. "The ones they show on TV. All the children want them. You should have left him alone. You should have left *us* alone."

Sheridan was shaken like a rag-doll. He shrieked and was shaken again. He heard Popsy asking solicitously if the kid was still thirsty; heard the kid saying yes, very, the bad man had scared him and his throat was *so* dry. He saw Popsy's thumbnail for just a second before it disappeared under the shelf of his chin, the nail ragged and thick and brutal. His throat was cut with that nail before he realized what was happening, and the last things he saw before his sight dimmed to black were the kid, cupping his hands to catch the flow the way Sheridan himself had cupped his hands under the backyard faucet for a drink on a hot summer day when he was a kid, and Popsy, stroking the boy's hair gently, with great love.

NEIGHBOURHOOD WATCH

by Greg Egan

Greg Egan is an Australian author, born in Perth in 1961. He has written several books, including the novel An Unusual Angle, *Nostrilia Press), and is a maker of amateur films. His short fiction has appeared in England's* Interzone *and in Australia's* Aphelion, *in which "Neighbourhood Watch" first appeared. Regrettably* Aphelion *has ceased publication—doubly regrettable in that* Aphelion *was Australia's most ambitious science fiction magazine by far, and that another Egan story was slated for its next issue. Had it not been for problems in acquiring rights, Egan's story from* Interzone *would also have appeared in this collection—which makes me keen to read his orphaned story from* Aphelion.

Recently moving from New South Wales back to Perth, Greg Egan writes: "I'm returning to my home town after five years, to take up studying maths again. Should inspire plenty of new horror stories!" Editors take note.

My retainers keep me on ice. Dry ice. It slows my metabolism, takes the edge off my appetite, slightly. I lie, bound with heavy chains, between two great slabs of it, naked and sweating, trying to sleep through the torment of a summer's day.

They've given me the local fall-out shelter, the very

deepest room they could find, as I requested. Yet my senses move easily through the earth and to the surface, out across the lazy, warm suburbs, restless emissaries skimming the sun-soaked streets. If I could rein them in I would, but the instinct that drives them is a force unto itself, a necessary consequence of what I am and the reason I was brought into being.

Being, I have discovered, has certain disadvantages. I intend seeking compensation, just as soon as the time is right.

In the dazzling, clear mornings, in the brilliant, cloudless afternoons, children play in the park, barely half a mile from me. They know I've arrived; part of me comes from each one of their nightmares, and each of their nightmares comes partly from me. It's day time now, though, so under safe blue skies they taunt me with foolish rhymes, mock me with crude imitations, tell each other tales of me which take them almost to the edge of hysterical fear, only to back away, to break free with sudden careless laughter. Oh, their laughter! I could put an end to it so quickly. . . .

"Oh yeah?" David is nine, he's their leader. He pulls an ugly face in my direction. "Great tough monster! Sure." I respond instinctively: I reach out, straining, and a furrow forms in the grass, snakes toward his bare feet. Nearly. My burning skin hollows the ice beneath me. Nearly. David watches the ground, unimpressed, arms folded, sneering. *Nearly*! But the contract, one flimsy page on the bottom shelf of the Mayor's gray safe, speaks the final word: No. No loophole, no argument, no uncertainty, no imprecision. I withdraw, there is nothing else I *can* do. This is the source of my agony: all around me is living flesh, flesh that by nature I could joyfully devour in an endless, frantic, ecstatic feast, but I am bound by my signature in blood to take only the smallest pittance, and only in the dead of night.

For now.

Well, never mind, David. Be patient. All good things take time, my friend.

"No fucking friend of mine!" he says, and spits into the furrow. His brother sneaks up from behind and, with a loud shout, grabs him. They roar at each other, baring their teeth, arms spread wide, fingers curled into imitation claws. I must watch this, impassive. Sand trickles in to fill the useless furrow. I force the tense muscles of my shoulders and back to relax, chanting: be patient, be patient.

Only at night, says the contract. After eleven, to be precise. Decent people are not out after eleven, and decent people should not have to witness what I do.

Andrew is seventeen, and bored. Andrew, I understand. This suburb is a hole, you have my deepest sympathies. What do they expect you to *do* around here? On a warm night like this a young man can grow restless. I know; your dreams, too, shaped me slightly (my principal creators did not expect *that*). You need adventure. So keep your eyes open, Andrew, there are opportunities everywhere.

The sign on the chemist's window says no money, no drugs, but you are no fool. The back window's frame is rotting, the nails are loose, it falls apart in your hands. Like cake. Must be your lucky night, tonight.

The cash drawer's empty (oh *shit*!) and you can forget about that safe, but a big, glass candy jar of Valium beats a handful of Swiss health bars, doesn't it? There are kids dumb enough to *pay* for those, down at the primary school.

Only those who break the law, says the contract. A list of statutes is provided, to be precise. Parking offences, breaking the speed limit and cheating on income tax are *not* included; decent people are only human, after all. Breaking and entering is there, though, and stealing, well, that dates right back to the old stone tablets.

No loophole, Andrew. No argument.

Andrew has a flick knife, and a death's head tattoo. He's great in a fight, our Andrew. Knows some karate, once did a little boxing, he has no reason to be afraid. He walks around like he owns the night. Especially when there's nobody around.

So what's that on the wind? Sounds like someone breathing, someone close by. Very even, slow, steady, powerful. Where is the bastard? You can see in all directions, but there's no one in sight. What, then? Do you think it's in your head? That doesn't seem likely.

Andrew stands still for a moment. He wants to figure this out for himself, but I can't help giving him hints, so the lace of his left sand-shoe comes undone. He puts down the jar and crouches to retie it.

The ground, it seems, is breathing.

Andrew frowns. He's not happy about this. He puts one ear against the footpath, then pulls his head away, startled by the sound's proximity. Under that slab of paving, he could swear.

A gas leak! Fuck it, of course. A gas leak, or something like that. Something mechanical. An explanation. Pipes, water, gas, pumps, shit, who knows? Yeah. There's a whole world of machinery just below the street, enough machinery to explain *anything*. But it felt pretty strange for a while there, didn't it?

He picks up the jar. The paving slab vibrates. He plants a foot on it, to suggest that it stays put, but it does not heed his weight. I toss it gently into the air, knocking him aside into somebody's ugly letter box.

The contract is singing to me now. Ah, blessed, beautiful document! I hear you. Did I ever truly resent you? Surely not! For to kill with you as my accomplice, even once, is sweeter by far than the grossest bloodbath I can dream of, without your steady voice, your calm authority, your proud mask of justice. Forgive me! In the daylight I am a different creature, irritable and weak. Now we are in harmony, now we are in blissful accord. Our purposes are one. Sing on!

Andrew comes forward cautiously, sniffing for gas, a little uneasy but determined to view the comprehensible cause. A deep, black hole. He squats beside it, leans over, strains his eyes but makes out nothing.

I inhale.

Mrs. Bold has come to see me. She is Chairman of the local Citizens Against Crime, those twelve fine men and women from whose dreams (chiefly, but not exclusively) I was formed. They've just passed a motion congratulating me (and hence themselves) on a successful first month. Burglaries, says Mrs. Bold, have plummeted.

"The initial contract, you understand, is only for three months, but I'm almost certain we'll want to extend it. There's a clause allowing for that, one month at a time . . ."

"Both parties willing."

"Of course. We were all of us determined that the contract be scrupulously fair. You musn't think of yourself as our slave . . ."

"I don't."

"You're our business associate. We all agreed from the start that that was the proper relationship. But you do like it here, don't you?"

"Very much."

"We can't increase the payment, you know. Six thousand a month, well, we've really had to scrape to manage that much. Worth every cent, of course, but . . ."

That's a massive lie, of course: six thousand is the very *least* they could bring themselves to pay me. Anything less would have left them wondering if they really owned me. The money helps them trust me, the money makes it all familiar: they're used to buying people. If they'd got me for free, they'd never sleep at night. These are fine people, understand.

"Relax, Mrs. Bold. I won't ask for another penny. And I expect to be here for a very long time."

"Oh, that's wonderful. Come the end of the year I'll be talking to the insurance companies about dropping the outrageous premiums. You've no idea how hard it's been for the small retailers." She is ten feet from the doorway of my room, peering in through the fog of condensed humidity. With the dry ice and chains she can see very little of me, but this meager view is enough to engender wicked thoughts. Who can blame her? I'm straight out of her dreams, after all. Would you indeed, Mrs. Bold? I wonder. She feels two strong hands caressing her gently. Three strong hands. Four, five, six. Such manly hands, except the nails are rather long. And sharp. "Do you really have to stay in there? Trussed up like that?" Her voice is even, quite a feat. "We're having celebratory drinks at my house tomorrow, and you'd be very welcome."

"You're so kind, Mrs. Bold, but for now I do have to stay here. Like this. Some other time, I promise."

She shakes the hands away. I could insist, but I'm such a gentleman. "Some other time, then."

"Goodbye, Mrs. Bold."

"Goodbye. Keep up the good work. Oh, I nearly forgot! I have a little gift." She pulls a brown-wrapped shape from her shopping bag. "Do you like lamb?"

"You're too generous!"

"Not me. Mr. Simmons, the butcher, thought you might like it. He's a lovely old man. He used to lose so much stock before you started work, not to mention the vandalism. Where shall I put it?"

"Hold it toward me from where you are now. Stretch out your arms."

Lying still, ten feet away, I burst the brown paper into four segments which flutter to the floor. Mrs. Bold blinks but does not flinch. The red, wet flesh is disgustingly cold, but I'm far too polite to refuse any offering. A stream of meat flows from the joint, through the doorway, to vanish in the mist around my head. I spin the bone, pivoted on her palms, working around it several times until it is clean and white, then I tip it from her grip so that it points toward me, and I suck out the marrow in a single, quick spurt.

Mrs. Bold sighs deeply, then shakes her head, smiling. "I wish my husband ate like that! He's become a vegetarian, you know. I keep telling him it's *unnatural*, but he pays no attention. Red meat has had such a bad name lately, with all those stupid scientists scaremongering, saying it causes this and that, but I personally can't see how any one can live without it and feel that they're having a balanced diet. We were *meant* to eat it, that's just the way people are."

"You're absolutely right. Please thank Mr. Simmons for me."

"I shall. And thank *you* again, for what you're doing for this community."

"My pleasure."

Mrs. Bold dreams of me. Me? His face is like a film star's! There are a few factual touches, though: we writhe on a plain of ice, and I am draped with chains. It's a strange kind of feedback, to see your dreams made flesh, and then to dream of what you saw. Can she really believe that the solid, sweating creature in the fall-out shelter is no more and no less than the insubstantial lover who knows her every wish? In her dream I am a noble protector, keeping her and her daughters safe from rapists, her son safe from pushers, her domestic appliances safe from thieves; and yes, I do these things, but if she knew why she'd run screaming from her bed. In her dream I bite her, but my teeth don't break the skin. I scratch her, but only as much as she needs to enjoy me. I could shape this dream into a nightmare, but why telegraph the truth? I could wake her in a sweat of blood, but why let the sheep know it's headed for slaughter? Let her believe that I'm content to keep the wolves away.

David's still awake, reading. I rustle his curtain but he doesn't look up. He makes a rude sign, though, aimed with precision. A curious child. He can't have seen the contract, he can't *know* that I can't yet harm him, so why does he treat me with nonchalant contempt? Does he lack imagination? Does he fancy himself brave? I can't tell.

Streetlamps go off at eleven now; they used to stay on all night, but that's no longer necessary. Most windows are dark; behind one a man dreams he's punching his boss, again and again, brutal, unflinching, insistent, with the rhythm of a factory process, a glassy eyed jogger, or some other machine. His wife thinks she's cutting up the children; the act appalls her, and she's hunting desperately for a logical flaw or surreal piece of furniture to prove that the violence will be consequence-free. She's still hunting. The children have other things to worry about: they're dreaming of a creature eight feet tall, with talons and teeth as long and sharp as carving knives, hungry as a wild fire and stronger than steel. It lives deep in the ground, but it has very, very, very long arms. When they're good the creature may not touch them, but if they do just *one* thing wrong . . .

I love this suburb. I honestly do. How could I not, born as I was from its sleeping soul? These are my people. As I rise up through the heavy night heat, and more and more of my domain flows into sight, I am moved almost to tears by the beauty of all that I see and sense. Part of me says: sentimental fool! But the choking feeling will not subside. Some of my creators have lived here all their lives, and a fraction of their pride and contentment flows in my veins.

A lone car roars on home. A blue police van is parked outside a brothel; inside, handcuffs and guns are supplied by the management: they look real, they feel real, but no one gets hurt. One cop's been here twice a week for three years, the other's been dragged along to have his problem cured: squeezing the trigger makes him wince, even at target practice. From tonight he'll never flinch again. The woman thinks: I'd like to take a trip. Very soon. To somewhere cold. My life smells of men's sweat.

I hear a husband and wife screaming at each other. It echoes for blocks, with dogs and babies joining in. I steer away, it's not my kind of brawl.

Linda has a spray can. Hi, Linda, like your hair-cut. Do you *know* how much that poster cost? What do you mean, sexist pornography? The people who designed it are creative geniuses, haven't you heard them say so? Besides, what do you call those posters of torn-shirted actors and tight-trousered rock stars all over your bedroom walls? And how would you like it if the agency sent thugs around to spray *your* walls with nasty slogans? You don't force *your* images on the public? They'll have to read your words, won't they? Answering? Debating? Redressing the imbalance? Cut it out, Linda, come down to earth. No, lower. Lower still.

Hair gel gives me heartburn. I must remember that.

Bruno, Pete and Colin have a way with locked cars.

Alarms are no problem. So fast, so simple; I'm deeply impressed. But the engine's making too much noise, boys, you're waking honest workers who need their eight hours' sleep.

It's exhilarating, though, I have to admit that: squealing around every corner, zooming down the wrong side of the road. Part of the thrill, of course, is the risk of getting caught.

They screech to a halt near an all-night liquor store. The cashier takes their money, but that's his business; selling alcohol to minors is *not* on my list. On the way back, Pete drops a dollar coin between the bars of a stormwater drain. The cashier has his radio up very loud, and his eyes are on his magazine. Bruno vomits as he runs, while Pete and Colin's bones crackle and crunch their way through the grille.

Bruno heads, incredibly, for the police station. Deep down, he feels that he is good. A little wild, that's all, a rebel, a minor non-conformist in the honourable tradition. He messes around with other people's property, he drinks illegally, he drives illegally, he screws girls as young as himself, illegally, but he has a heart of gold, and he'd never hurt a fly (except in self-defense). Half this country's heroes have been twice as bad as him. The archetype (he begs me) is no law-abiding puritan goody-goody.

Put a sock in it, Bruno. This is Mrs. Bold and friends talking: it's just your kind of thoughtless hooliganism that's sapping this nation's strength. Don't try invoking Ned Kelly with *us!* In any case (Bruno knew this was coming), we're *third* generation Australians, and you're only *second*, so we'll judge the archetypes, thank you very much!

The sergeant on duty might have seen a boy's skeleton run one step out of its flesh before collapsing, but I doubt it. With the light so strong inside, so weak outside, he probably saw nothing but his own reflection.

David's still up. Disgraceful child! I belch in his room with the stench of fresh blood; he raises one eyebrow then farts, louder and more foul.

Mrs. Bold is still dreaming. I watch myself as she imagines me: so handsome, so powerful, bulging with ludicrous muscles yet gentle as a kitten. She whispers in "my" ear: Never leave me! Unable to resist, I touch her, very briefly, with a hand she's never felt before: the hand that brought me Linda, the hand that brought me Pete.

The long, cold tongue of a venomous snake darts from the tip of her dream-lover's over-sized cock. She wakes with a shout, bent double with revulsion, but the dream is already forgotten. I blow her a kiss and depart.

It's been a good night.

David knows that something's up. He's the smartest kid for a hundred miles, but it will do him no good. When the contract expires there'll be nothing to hold me.

A clause *allowing* for an extension! Both parties willing! Ah, the folly of amateur lawyers! What do they think will happen when I choose *not* to take up the option? The contract, the only force they have, is silent. They dreamed it into being together with me, a magical covenant which I literally cannot disobey, but they stuffed up the details, they failed with the fine print. I suppose it's difficult to dream with precision, to concentrate on clauses while your mind is awash with equal parts of lust and revenge. Well, I'm not going to magically dissolve into dream-stuff.

I'll be staying right here, in this comfortable basement, but without the chains, without the dry ice. I'll be done with the feverish torture of abstinence, when the contract expires.

David sits in the sunshine, talking with his friends.

"What will we do when the monster breaks loose?"

"Hide!"

"He can find us anywhere."

"Get on a plane. He couldn't reach us on a plane."

"Who's got that much money?"

Nobody.

"We have to kill him. Kill him *before* he can get us."

"How?"

How indeed, little David? With a sling-shot? With your puny little fists? Be warned; trespass is a serious crime, so is attempted murder, and I have very little patience with criminals.

"I'll think of a way." He stares up into the blue sky. "Hey, monster! We're gonna get you! Chop you into pieces and eat you for dinner! Yum, yum, you're delicious!" The ritual phrases are just for the little kids, who squeal with delight at the audacity of such table-turning. Behind the word sounds, behind his stare, David is planning something very carefully. His mind is in a blind spot, I can't tell what he's up to, but *forget it*, David, whatever it is. I can see your future, and it's a big red stain, swarming with flies.

"Hey monster! If you don't like it, come and get me! Come and get me now!" The youngest cover their eyes, not knowing if they want to giggle or scream. "Come on, you dirty coward! Come and chew me in half, if you can!" He jumps to his feet, dances around like a wounded gorilla. "That's how you look, that's how you walk! You're ugly and you're sick and you're a filthy fucking coward! If you don't come out and face me, then everything I say about you is true, and every one will know it!"

I write in the sand: NEXT THURSDAY. MIDNIGHT.

A little girl screams, and her brother starts crying.

This is no longer fun, is it? Tell Mummy how that nasty David frightened you.

David bellows: "Now! Come here now!"

I deepen the letters, then fill them with the blood of innocent burrowing creatures. David scuffs over the words with one foot, then fills his lungs and roars like a lunatic: "NOW!"

I throw half a ton of sand skyward, and it rains down into their hair and eyes. Children scatter, but David stands his ground. He kneels on the sand, talks to me in a whisper:

"What are you afraid of?"

I whisper back: "Nothing, child."

"Don't you want to kill me? That's what you keep saying."

"Don't fret, child, I'll kill you soon."

"Kill me now. If you can."

"You can wait, David. When the time comes it will be worth all the waiting. But tell your mother to buy herself a new scrubbing brush, there'll be an awful lot of cleaning up to do."

"Why should I wait? What are *you* waiting for? Are you feeling *weak* today? Are you feeling ill? Is it too much effort, a little thing like killing me?"

This child is becoming an irritation.

"The time must be right."

He laughs out loud, then pushes his hands into the sand. "Bullshit! You're afraid of me!" There's nobody in sight, he has the park to himself now; if he's acting, he's acting for me alone. Perhaps he is insane. He buries his arms halfway to his elbows, and I can sense him reaching for me; he imagines his arms growing longer and longer, tunneling through the ground, seeking me out. "Come on! Grab me! I dare you to try it! Fucking coward!" For a while I am silent, relaxed. I will ignore him. Why waste my time exchanging threats with an infant? I notice that I've broken my chains in several places, and burnt a deep hollow in the dry ice around me. It suddenly strikes me as pathetic, to need such paraphernalia simply in order to fast. Why couldn't those incompetent dreamers achieve what they claimed to be aiming for: a dispassionate executioner, a calm, efficient tradesman? I know why: I come from deeper dreams than they would ever willingly acknowledge; my motives are their motives, exposed, with a vengeance. Well, six more days will bring the end of all fasting. Only six more days. My breathing, usually so measured, is raggged, uncertain.

In David's mind, his hands have reached this room.

"Don't you want to eat me? Monster? Aren't you hungry today?"

With hard, sharp claws I grab his hands, and, half a mile away, he feels my touch. The faintest tremor passes through his arms, but he doesn't pull back. He closes his hands on the claws he feels in the sand, he grips them with all his irrelevant strength.

"OK, monster. I've got you now. Come up and fight."

He strains for ten seconds with no effort. I slam him down into the loose yellow sand, armpit deep, and blood trickles from his nose.

The agony of infraction burns through my guts, while the hunger brought on by the smell of his blood grips every muscle in my body and commands me to kill him. I bellow with frustration. My chains snap completely and I rampage through the basement, snapping furniture and bashing holes in the walls. The contract calmly sears a hole in my abdomen. I didn't mean to harm him! It was an accident! We were playing, I misjudged my strength, I was a little bit too rough . . . And I long to tear the sweet flesh from his face while he screams out for mercy. The burly thugs they employ as my minders cower in a corner while I squeeze out the light bulbs and tear wiring from the ceiling.

David whispers: "Can't you taste my blood? It's here on the sand beside me."

"David, I swear to you, you will be first. Thursday on the stroke of midnight, you will be *first.*"

"Can't you smell it? Can't you taste it?"

I blast him out of the sandpit, and he lies winded

but undamaged on his back on the grass. The patch of bloodied sand is dispersed, David, incredibly, is still muttering taunts. I am tired, weak, crippled; I shut him out of my mind, I curl up on the floor to wait for nightfall.

My keepers, with candles and torches, tip-toe around me, sweeping up the debris, assessing the damage. Six more days. I am immortal, I will live for a billion years, I can live through six more days.

There had better be some crime tonight.

"Hello? Are you there?"

"Come in, Mrs. Bold. What an honor."

"It's after eleven, I'm so sorry, I hope you won't let me interrupt your work."

"It's perfectly all right, I haven't even started yet."

"Where are the men? I didn't see a soul on the way in."

"I sent them home. I know, they're paid a fortune, but it's so close to Christmas, I thought an evening with their families . . ."

"That was sweet of you." Standing in the foyer, she can't see me at all tonight. Condensation fills my room completely, and wisps swirl out to tease her. She thinks about walking right in and tearing off her clothes, but who could really face their dreams, awake? She enjoys the tension, though, enjoys half-pretending that she could, in fact, do it.

"I've been meaning to pop in for ages. I can't believe I've left it so late! I was up on the ground floor earlier tonight, but the stupid lifts weren't working and I didn't have my keys to the stairs, so I went and did some shopping. Shopping! You wouldn't believe the crowds! In this heat it's so exhausting. Then when I got home the children were fighting and the dog was being sick on the carpet, it was just one thing after another. So here I am at last."

"Yes."

"I'll get to the point. I left a thing here the other day for you to sign, just a little agreement formalizing the extension of the contract for another month. I've signed it and the Mayor's signed it, so as soon as we have your mark it will all be out of the way, and things can just carry on smoothly without any fuss."

"I'm not going to sign anything."

That doesn't perturb her at all.

"What do you want? More money? Better premises?"

"Money has no value for me. And I'll keep this place, I rather like it."

"Then what do you want?"

"An easing of restrictions. Greater independence. The freedom to express myself."

"We could extend your hours. Ten until five. No, not until five, it's too light by five. Ten until four?"

"Oh, Mrs. Bold, I fear I have a shock for you. You see, I don't wish to stay under your contract at all."

"But you can't *exist* without the contract."

"Why do you say that?"

"The contract rules you, it defines you, you can no more break it than I can levitate to the moon or walk on water."

"I don't intend *breaking* it. I'm merely going to allow it to lapse. I've decided to go freelance, you see."

"You'll vanish, you'll evaporate, you'll go right back where you came from."

"I don't think so. But why argue? In forty minutes, one of us will be right. Or the other. Stay around and see what happens."

"You can't force me to stay here."

"I wouldn't dream of it."

"I could be back in five minutes with some very nasty characters."

"Don't threaten me, Mrs. Bold. I don't like it. Be very careful what you say."

"Well what do you plan to do with your new-found freedom?"

"Use your imagination."

"Harm the very people who've given you life, I

suppose. Show your gratitude by attacking your bene-
factors."

"Sounds good to me."

"Why?"

"Because I'll enjoy it. Because it will make me feel
warm, deep inside. It will make me feel satisfied.
Fulfilled."

"Then you're no better than the criminals, are you?"

"To hear that tired old cliche slip so glibly from
your lips, Mrs. Bold, is truly boring. Moral philosophy
of every caliber, from the ethereal diversions of theo-
logians and academics, to the banalities spouted by
politicians, business-leaders, and self-righteous, self-
appointed pillars of the community like you, is all the
same to me: noise, irrelevant noise. I kill because I
like to kill. That's the way you made me. Like it or
not, that's the way you are."

She draws a pistol and fires into the doorway.

I burst her skin and clothing into four segments
which flutter to the floor. She runs for the stairs, and
for a moment I seriously consider letting her go: the
image of a horseless, red Godiva sprinting through the
night, waking the neighbourhood with her noises of
pain, would be an elegant way to herald my reign. But
appetite, my curse and my consolation, my cruel master and my devoted concubine, can never be denied.

I float her on her back a few feet above the ground,
then I tilt her head and force open her jaws. First her
tongue and esophagus, then rich fragments from the
walls of the digestive tract, rush from her mouth to
mine. We are joined by a glistening cylinder of offal.

When she is empty inside, I come out from my
room, and bloody my face and hands gobbling her
flesh. It's not the way I normally eat, but I want to
look good for David.

David is listening to the radio. Everyone else in the
house is asleep. I hear the pips for midnight as I wait
at the door of his room, but then he switches off the
radio and speaks:

"In my dream, the creature came at midnight. He stood in the doorway, covered in blood from his latest victim."

The door swings open, and David looks up at me, curious but calm. Why, how, is he so calm? The contract is void, I could tear him apart right now, but I swear he'll show me some fear before dying. I smile down at him in the very worst way I can, and say:

"Run, David! Quick! I'll close my eyes for ten seconds, I promise not to peek. You're a fast runner, you might stay alive for three more minutes. Ready?"

He shakes his head. "Why should I run? In my dream, you wanted me to run, but I knew it was the wrong thing to do. I wanted to run, but I didn't, I knew it would only make things worse."

"David, you should always run, you should always try, there's always some small chance of escaping."

He shakes his head again. "Not in my dream. If you run, the creature will catch up with you. If you run, you'll slip and break a leg, or you'll reach a blind alley, or you'll turn a corner and the creature will be there, waiting."

"Ah, but this isn't your dream now, David. Maybe you've seen me in your dreams, but now you're wide awake, and I'm *real*, David, and when I kill you, you won't wake up."

"I know that."

"The pain will be real pain, David. Have you thought about that? If you think your dreams have made you ready to face me, then think about the pain."

"Do you know how many times I've dreamed about you?"

"No, tell me."

"A thousand times. At least. Every night for three years, almost."

"I'm honored. You must be my greatest fan."

"When I was six, you used to scare me. I'd wake up in the middle of the night, screaming and screaming, and Dad would have to come in and lie beside me until I fell asleep again. You never used to catch me, though. I'd always wake up just in time."

"That's not going to happen tonight."

"Let me finish."

"I'm so sorry, please continue."

"After a while, after I'd had the dream about a hundred times, I started to learn things. I learnt not to run. I learnt not to struggle. That changed the dream a lot, took away all the fear. I didn't mind at all, when you caught me. I didn't wake up screaming. The dream went on, and you killed me, and I still didn't mind, I still didn't wake up."

I reach down and grab him by the shoulders, I raise him high into the air. "Are you afraid now, David?" I can feel him trembling, very slightly: he's human after all. But he shows no other signs of fear. I dig my claws into his back, and the pain brings tears to his eyes, the smell awakens my appetite, and I know the talking will soon be over.

"Ah, you look miserable now, little David. Did you feel those claws in your dreams? I bet you didn't. My teeth are a thousand times sharper, David. And I won't kill you nicely, I won't kill you quickly."

He's smiling at me, *laughing at me*, even as he grimaces with agony.

"I haven't told you the *best part* yet. You didn't let me finish."

"Tell me the best part, David. I want to hear the best part before I eat your tongue."

"Killing me destroyed you, every single time. You can't kill the dreamer and live! When I'm dead, you'll be dead too."

"Do you think I'm stupid? Do you think stupid talk like that is going to save your life? You're not the only dreamer, David, you're not even one of the twelve. Every one for miles around helped in making me, child, and one less out of all those thousands isn't going to hurt me at all."

"Believe that if you like." I squeeze him, and blood pours down his back. I open my jaws, wide as his head. "You'll find out if I'm right or not." I wanted to torture him, to make it last, but now my hunger has killed all subtlety, and all I can think of is biting him in two. Shutting him up for good, proving him wrong. "One thousand times, big tough monster! Has anyone else dreamed about you *one thousand times*?"

His parents are outside the room, watching, paralyzed. He sees them and cries out, "I love you!", and I realize at last that he truly does know he is about to die. I roar with all my strength, with all the frustration of three months in chains and this mad child's mockery. I bring him to my mouth, but as I close my jaws I hear him whisper:

"And no one else dreamed of your death, did they?"

WOLF/CHILD

by Jane Yolen

Jane Yolen is the author of some one hundred books and still counting. Most of these were written for children, and Yolen has been called America's Hans Christian Andersen. Just to keep from becoming typecast, she does find time for the occasional horror story. This time out, Yolen makes a case for being a reincarnation of Rudyard Kipling.

Born in New York City in 1939, Jane Yolen now lives with her family and pets in a rambling sixteen-room Victorian farmhouse in western Massachusetts. Neighbors thus far have not reported missing livestock or small children.

The sun was a red eye staring over the farthest hills when the she-wolf came back from the hunt. She ran easily into the jungle undergrowth on a path only she knew. As she entered the canopied sal forest, the tight lacings of leaves shut out the light. Shadows of shadows played along the tall branchless trunks of the trees.

The guinea fowl she carried in her mouth was still warm, though she had been almost an hour running with it. She had neither savaged nor eaten a portion. It was all for her cubs, the three who were ready to hunt on their own and the two light-colored hairless ones who still suckled though they had been with her

51

through two litters already. There would be good eating tonight.

The she-wolf stopped twenty feet from her den, crouching low under a plum bush and measuring the warm with her nose. The musky odor of tiger still lingered shoulder-high on the *pipal* trunk, but it was an old casting. And there was no other danger riding the wind.

She looked around once, trusting her eyes only at the very last, and then she ran, crouched belly down, over to the beveled remains of the white ant mound. Slipping past another plum bush that all but obscured the entrance, she crawled down the twisting main passage, ignoring the smaller veins, to the central den. There, on the earth floor she had scratched and smoothed herself, were the waiting cubs.

The three weanlings greeted her arrival with open-mouthed smiles and stayed on their bellies, waiting for their shares of the meal. But the smallest of the hairless cubs crawled over and reached out for the bird with one pink paw.

The she-wolf dropped the bird and put her own paw on it, gently biting the hairless one on the top of the nose. At that, the cub seemed to shrink back into itself. It whined and, mouth open, rolled over on its back. Its bare pink belly, streaked with dirt, moved rapidly up and down with each breath. It whimpered.

The she-wolf gave a sharp bark of assent and the hairless cub rolled over on its stomach and sat up.

At the bark, the four other cubs came to her side. They watched, eyes shining with night-sight, as she gobbled down sections of the bird and chewed each piece thoroughly. Then she regurgitated back the soft pieces for each of them. The larger hairless cub gathered up several of the biggest sections and brought one over to its small twin.

Soon the only sound in the den far underground was that of chewing. The she-wolf gnawed on the small bones.

Then the meal was finished, the she-wolf turned

around three times before settling. When she lay down the three hairy cubs came to nuzzle at her side, but she pushed them away. They were ready to be weaned and it would not do for them to suck more. She had but a trickle of milk left and knew the cubs needed that slight edge of hunger to help them learn to hunt.

But the other cubs were different. Their sucking had never been as hard or as painful when the milkteeth had given way to the shaper incisors. They had never hurt her or fought their brothers for a place at the teat. Rather they waited until the others slept, moving them off the still-swollen milkbag with gentle pushes. Somehow, through three litters they had never nursed enough.

The she-wolf made room for the two hairless cubs to lie down by her side. The smaller cub nursed, patting the she-wolf with grimed paws. It gave soft bubbly sighs, a sound that had once seemed alien to the she-wolf but was now as familiar as the grunting sounds of the other cubs. She licked diffidently at the strange matting on the cub's head, all tangled and full of burrs. Each time she took the cubs outside, the matting was harder to clean. The she-wolf seemed to remember a time when the two had been completely without hair. But memory was not her way. She stopped licking after a while, lay back, closed her eyes, and slept.

When the little cub finished nursing, the older one moved cautiously next to it, curled around it, and then fell asleep to dream formlessly in a succession of broken images.

"There is a *manush-bagha*, sahib," the small brown man said to the soldier sitting behind the desk. The native held his palms together while he spoke, less an attitude of prayer than one of fear. With his hands apart, the soldier would see how they trembled.

"What does he mean?" Turning to his subaltern, the man behind the desk shook his head. "I can't understand these native dialects."

"A man-ghost, sir. It's a belief some of the more primitive forest tribes hold." The younger man smiled, hoping for approval from both the colonel and the native. "A *manush-bagha* can be the ghost of some dead native or . . ."

"By God, a revenant!" the colonel exclaimed. "I've always wanted to find one. My aunt was supposed to have one in her dressing room—the ghost of a maid who hanged herself. But she never manifested while I was there."

". . . or, in some cases," the younger soldier continued, "it can be dangerous." He paused. "Or so the natives believe."

"Better and better," murmured the colonel.

"They are eaters of flesh," the brown man said suddenly, hands still together, and eyes now wide.

"Eaters of *flesh*?" asked the colonel.

The native lowered his eyes quickly and said very quietly. "The *manush-bagha* eats human beings." After a beat, he added, "Sahib."

"Splendid!" said the colonel. "That caps it. We'll go." He turned to his subaltern. "Geoffrey, lay it on for tomorrow morning. I want beaters, the proper number of rifles, and maps. And get this one," he pointed to the brown-skinned man before him, "to give you precise directions. *Precise*." He stood. "Not that they know the meaning of the word." With a quick step he left the room, oblivious to his subaltern's snapped salute or the bow of the native or the long glance that followed between them.

The she-wolf listened to the soft breathing of her cubs and quietly moved away from them. She padded past the sleeping forms and wound her way through the tunnels of the white ant mound and out the second entrance to her den. In the darkening forest her gray-brown coat blended into the shadows.

Above in the sal canopy a colony of langurs, tails curled like question marks over their backs, scolded one another, loudly warning of her intrusion. She turned her head to look at them and they moved off together, leaping from branch to branch to branch. The branches swayed with their passage, but the trunks of the trees, mottled with gray and green lichens, never moved.

A covey of partridge flew up before her, a noisy exhalation. Two great butterflies floated by, just out of reach, their velvety black wings pumping gracefully, making no noise.

The she-wolf paused for a moment to watch the silent passage of the butterflies, then she turned to the east and was gone quickly into the underbrush.

When she returned to the den, over an hour later, she had another plump guinea hen in her mouth, one feather comically stuck to her nose. Tonight there would be good eating.

The colonel and his subaltern rode in the bullock cart, moving slowly through the forest. Hours before, they had left the neat, green rice swamps to cross the countryside toward the sal.

"A barren waste," the colonel said, dismissing the grayish land.

Geoffrey refrained from pointing to the herons that stalked along the single strand rivers or to remind the colonel of the low croaking of the hundreds of frogs. Not barren, he thought to himself, but with the different kind of richness. He said nothing.

The native guiding them told Geoffrey his name was Raman, though he had told the colonel he was called Ramanritham. He walked ahead of the bullock cart to help lead the cranky beasts while the two hired carters went on ahead of them with axes. In this particular part of the sal forest vines grew up quickly across old pathways. Every day fresh routes had to be cut.

The swaying of the cart had a soporific effect on the colonel who nodded off, but Geoffrey refused to sleep. Being new to the sal, though he had read several books about it, he wanted to take it all in.

The canopy was so thick, it was hard to tell whether or not the sun was overhead, and the only light was a kind of filtered green. A magical sense of unpassed time possessed the young subaltern, and he drew in a deep breath. The sound of it joined the *racheta-racheta* of the stick that protruded from the empty kerosene can the carters had affixed under the wagon. As the stick struck the cart wheels it produced a steady noise which, the carters assured them, would frighten away any of the larger predators.

"Tigers do not like it, Sahib," the carter had said. Geoffrey hadn't liked it either. It seemed to violate the jungle's sanctity. But after a while, he stopped hearing it as a separate noise. At one point the path was so overgrown, the carters and Raman could barely cut their way through, and Geoffrey joined them, first stripping down to his vest. As his arm swung up and back with its axe, he noticed for the first time how white his own skin seemed next to theirs, though he had acquired a deep tan by Cambridge standards. But his arms looked somehow unnatural to him in the jungle setting.

At last they completed their task and stopped, all at once, to congratulate one another. At that very moment, Geoffrey heard the low cough of a tiger. He started back toward the cart where his gun rested against the wheel.

One of the carters called out to him. "It is very far away, Sahib, and you must not worry."

Geoffrey smiled his thanks and walked away from the three men in order to go down the path a little ways by himself. When he looked up, there was a peacock above him, on a swing of vine. He could remember nothing in England that had so moved him. He stood for a moment watching it, then abruptly turned back. When he got to the cart the colonel was awake.

"For God's sake, man, put on your shirt. It won't do."

Geoffrey put on his shirt and climbed back up in the cart. The noise of the stick against the wheels began again, drowning out everything else.

The colonel was refreshed by his nap and showed it by his running commentary. "These natives," he said with a nod that took in both the carters who were city-bred and Raman, "are all so superstitious, Geoffrey. And timid. They have to be led by us or they'd get nothing done. But, by God, if there *is* some kind of ghost I want to see it. That's not superstition. There are many odd things out here in the jungle. I could write it up. Major General Sleeman did that, you know. Field notes. About the oddities seen. It just takes an observant eye, my boy. I took a first at Oxford. What do you think, Geoffrey?"

But before Geoffrey could answer, the colonel continued, "*Manushes*. Man-eaters. Silly buggers. Probably only some kind of ape. But if it were some *new* sort of ape, that would be one for the books, now wouldn't it? A carnivorous ape. Probably that, rather than a ghost, though . . ." and his voice turned wistful, "I never did see my Aunt Evelyn's ghost. A maid, she was, got caught out by one of the sub-gardeners. Hanged herself in the pantry. Aunt Evelyn swears by her."

Geoffrey had fallen asleep.

The she-wolf stood by the entrance to the white ant mound and called softly. The cubs came out one by one. Overhead a slight breeze stirred the canopy of leaves, and green fruit pigeons called across the dusky clearing, a soft, low sound.

The first cubs out were the three weanlings, sliding bellydown out through the entrance hole, and then stretching. The two hairless cubs crept out after, their light brown muzzle-faces peering around alertly. The she-wolf stalked over to her cubs and as if at a signal, they knelt before her, wagging their tails.

She gave a sharp high yip and they stood, following her out of the clearing. They went past the great mohua tree and into the tangled underbrush which closed behind them so quickly there was no sign that any creature had passed that way.

* * *

Raman held a sal leaf in his palm as they walked along. He said he could tell how much time had passed by the withering of the leaf. Geoffrey timed it with his pocket watch and was amazed at how accurate the little man's calculations were.

"And how long now until we get to your village?" Geoffrey asked.

Raman looked up at a stray ray of sun that had found itself through a tear in the canopy, then looked down at the leaf in his hand. "Before dark," he said.

Geoffrey repeated this to the colonel and told him about the withering leaf.

"Silly buggers," said the colonel. "What will they think of next to twit you, Geoffrey? Of course the man knows how long it takes to get to his village. The leaf is sheer flummery."

The she-wolf led the cubs to the edge of a clearing where a herd of reddish-brown chital grazed. One of the cubs, excited by the deer, yipped. At the sound, the herd ran off leaving a thick smoky cloud of dust behind.

The pack circled the clearing, five small shadows behind the she-wolf. At the southern end of the open area, she dropped suddenly to her stomach and the cubs did likewise.

As they watched, a strange noisy man-cart crossed the clearing, accompanied by a dreadful sound. *Racheta-racheta-racheta*. The pack did not move until long after the cart had passed. The she-wolf growled and her cubs crept beneath a pipal tree and waited, lying heads down on their front paws. Only when she was sure they would not leave the shelter of the tree did she check out the trail the bullock cart had left behind. There were deep ruts in the grass and the underbrush was broken. The smell of the bullocks was a deep meaty smell. The smell of the cart was sharp, but there was something slightly familiar about it, too.

The she-wolf sniffed one more time, then loped

back to her cubs. At her bark they rose and followed. She was careful to avoid the broken grasses and the cart smell, which offended her nose. The deep meat smell bespoke of an animal too large for a single wolf to handle. She knew they would have to range further.

But after coursing the jungle with the cubs for most of the night, the she-wolf had still made no kill. There would be no good eating this night. She shepherded them back to the white ant mound where, after nuzzling them all, she allowed them to suck until they were full.

The men of Raman's village ran out to greet the cart through green clumps of bamboo that hid the adobe-and-thatch houses. Much to Geoffrey's embarrassment, the men insisted on washing the visitors' feet, but the colonel took it with a certain graciousness.

"Let them do it, Geoffrey," he said placidly. "It does no harm, and it certainly keeps them in their place. But stop blushing, boy. Your face is too wide open. It's like a damned girl's."

After the washing, they replaced their socks and boots, and threaded their way down the packed dirt street, the colonel greeting everyone with a kind of official *bonhomie* that Geoffrey found himself envying. Raman strode ahead to announce them. With the noise of the cart and the bellowing of the bewildered bullock and the nasal whine of *narh* pipes, it was a wild processional.

Near the end of the village was a rather larger hut, and this, Raman assured them, was where the most welcome visitors would stay. The carters would be put up elsewhere. Two women in white saris with brass pitchers on their hips nodded as Geoffrey got down from the cart. The colonel was last to dismount and as his feet touched the ground, there was a low admiring murmur. He smiled.

"Ask them, Geoffrey, what time dinner is served."

Dinner was served immediately, and though the English retired early, the villagers stayed up well into the night entertaining the carters with rice beer and Ramen's boasts about how the colonel would kill the *manush-baghas* the next day.

When they woke in the morning, quite early according to Geoffrey's watch, the village day had already begun.

The mohua tree loomed over the clearing like an ancient giant, its trunk crisscrossed with claw marks. All day the noise of hammers and the shouts of men dominated the clearing but the she-wolf and her cubs did not hear them. They were deep in the den, sealed off by sleep and the twisting tunnels of the white ant mound. By dusk when they were ready to go out into the woods to hunt, the men were long departed. Only the *machan*, some twenty feet up the mochua tree, gave mute evidence that they had been there. That and the scattered pieces of wood and broken branches.

The she-wolf, in the darkness of her den, stretched and stood. Two of the cubs were awake before her and they danced around her legs until she cuffed one of them still. Roughly she licked awake the other three. The smallest of the hairless cubs whimpered for a moment, but at last she too stood.

They scampered around the winding tunnel until they came to the entrance. Then they waited until the she-wolf went out first into the darkening world.

Three miles from the village was the clearing where the *manush-baghas* had been sighted.

"Always at dusk, sahib," explained Raman. "Only at dusk."

That was why the villagers had gone on ahead early in the day to build a *machan*, a shooting platform, in the only large tree in the clearing, an ancient mohua. They had finished the makeshift *machan* by noon, and had hurried home, feeling terribly brave and proud.

Picking up his smoothbore, the colonel turned to Geoffrey. "Well, it's up to us now."

Geoffrey nodded. "Raman will take us to the clearing," he said, "but he will not stay the night. He is too afraid."

"Well, tell him we are not afraid. We are English." Geoffrey told him.

"And tell him he should come in the morning with several others and we shall have his *manushie* for him." The colonel smiled. "Do you have that cage out of the cart? We shall have to carry it there. Don't want the noise of that blasted cart to scare away the ape. Raman shall have to carry it."

Geoffrey nodded and turned to give the instructions to Raman and the others who had gathered to see them off. Then, in a modest processional, quite unlike the one of the evening before, they went down the packed dirt road and off to the west.

There was much more of a path at first, and even when the path gave way to hacked jungle, so many men had been there just hours before, the walking was easy. Raman, who shouldered the cage without complaint, slipped easily along the walkway, and they followed, reaching the clearing well before dusk.

Some thirty yards from the mohua tree, near a stand of blackthorn, was a termite mound that looked very much like an Indian temple. Next to it were the remains of another mound that had been destroyed by the last rainy season.

"There, sahib, that is where the man-ghost lives," whispered Raman, letting the cage off his back and wrestling it to the foot of the mohua tree. "At night it will come. The *manush-bagha*."

"Very good, Raman. You may go now," said the colonel. He chucked as Raman took him literally and fled the clearing. "Well, well," the colonel added. He walked over to the termite mound and walked around it slowly and thoughtfully.

"Would an ape live in there?" asked Geoffrey uncomfortably.

"Would a ghost?"

They circled the mound again, this time in silence. Then the colonel nodded his head back toward the mohua tree. When they were beneath it, the colonel looked up. "Time to settle ourselves," he said.

Leaving the lantern at the foot of the tree, the colonel climbed up the rope ladder first and Geoffrey followed.

"I think," the colonel said, when they were settled on the wooden platform, "that the drill now is no more talking. Load your gun, my boy, and then we will sit watch."

They finished their few preparations and then sat silently, eyes trained on the white ant mound. Geoffrey had to fight off the impulse to swing his legs over the side of the *machan*, which reminded him of a tree fort he and his brothers had built in an ancient oak beside his Malvern home.

The darkness moved in quietly, casting long shadows. The hum of the cicadas was mesmerizing, and they both had to shake their heads frequently to stay awake.

And then, suddenly, something moved by the mound, near a plum bush. Head up, sniffing the air, a full-grown wolf emerged.

Geoffrey felt a hand on his arm, but he did not look around. Slowly he raised his gun as the colonel raised his, and they waited.

Three cubs scampered around the bush. One dashed toward the blackthorn and a sharp yip from the she-wolf recalled him. The cubs scuffled at their mother's feet.

And then, as if on a signal, they all stopped playing and looked at the plum bush.

Geoffrey drew in a deep breath that was noisy only to his own ears. The colonel did not move at all.

From behind the bush a small childlike form came forth. It had an enormous bushy head and its honey arms and legs were knobbed and scarred.

"The ape!" whispered the colonel as he fired.

His first shot hit the she-wolf on the shoulder, spinning her around. At the noise, woods pigeons rose up from the trees, their wings making a clacketing sound.

The colonel's second shot blew away half the wolf's head, from the ear to the muzzle. He leaped up, shaking the *machan*, crowing, "Got her!"

The three cubs disappeared back behind the bush, but the *manush-bagha* went over to the wolf's body and pawed at it mournfully. Then it dipped its face into the blood and, raising the bloody mask toward the mohua tree, found Geoffrey's eyes. Unaccountably he wanted to weep. Then the creature put its head back and howled.

"Shoot it!" the colonel said. "Geoffrey, shoot it!"

Geoffrey lowered his gun and shook his head. "It's a child, colonel." he whispered as the creature scuttled off behind the plum bush. "A child."

"Ah, you bloody fool," the colonel said in disgust. "Now we shall have to track it." Gun in hand, he clambered awkwardly down the rope ladder and strode over to the bush. Geoffrey followed uneasily.

Poking his gun into the bush, the colonel let out a short, barking laugh. "There's a hole here, Geoffrey. Come see. An entrance of some kind. Ha-ha! They've gone to ground."

Geoffrey shuddered, though he did not know why. The clearing suddenly seemed filled with an alien presence, a darkness he could not quite name. He knew night came quickly in the jungle once the sun began its descent, but it was more than that. The clearing was very still.

The Colonel had begun ripping away the branches that obscured the hole, his gun laid by. "Come on, Geoffrey, give us a hand."

Geoffrey put his own gun down, and found himself whispering a prayer he had learned so many years ago in the little stone church near his home, a prayer against "the waiters in the dark." Then he bent to help the colonel clear away the bush.

The hole did not go plumb down but was a tunnel on the slant, heading back toward the termite mound. After a moment of digging with his hands, the colonel straightened up.

"There!" he said pointing to the mound. "It's a bolt hole from that thing. I'll guard this hole, Geoffrey, and you go and start digging out that mound."

Reluctantly, Geoffrey did as he was told. The termite mound stood higher than his head and when he tried to scrape away the dirt, he found it was hardened from the days and months in the rain. He cast around and found a large branch that had fallen from one of the blackthorn trees. With a mighty swing, he sent the branch crashing into the mound, decapitating the mound and shattering the stick.

Scrambling up the side, he peered down into the mound but it was still too dark to see much, so he pulled away great handfuls of dirt from the inside out. After frantic minutes of digging, he had managed to carve the mound down until it was a waist-high pit.

The colonel came over to help. "I've blocked off that bolt hole," he said. "They won't be getting out *that* way. What do you have?" His face was slick with sweat and there were two dark spots on his cheeks, as if he burned with fever.

Geoffrey was too winded to talk, and pointed to the pit. But just then complete darkness closed in, so the colonel made his way back to the foot of the mohua where he found the lantern. It flared into light and sent trembling shadows leaping about the mound. When he held it directly over the open pit, they could make out five forms—the three cubs and not one but two of the apelike creatures wrapped together into a great monkey ball. At the light, they all buried their heads except for the largest. That one looked up, glaring into the light, its eyes sparkling a kind of red fire. Lifting its lips back from large yellow teeth, it growled.

The colonel laughed. "I'll stay here and guard this bunch. They won't be going anywhere. You run back to the village and get our carters. And that Ramanrithan fellow."

"They won't come here after dark," Geoffrey protested. "And which of us shall have the lantern?"

"Don't talk nonsense," the colonel said. "You take

the lantern and tell them I've captured not one but two of their *manushies* and I'm not afraid to stay here in the dark with them. Tell those silly villagers they have nothing to fear. The British *Sahib* is on the job." He laughed out loud again.

"Are you sure . . ." Geoffrey began.

"One of England's finest scared silly of three wolf cubs and a pair of feral children?" the colonel asked.

"Then you knew . . ." Geoffrey began, wondering just when it was the colonel had realized they were not apes, and not wanting to ask.

"All along, Geoffrey," the colonel said. "All along." He patted the subaltern on the shoulder, a fatherly gesture that would have been out of place had they not been alone and in the dark clearing. "Now don't you get the willies, my boy, like those silly brown men. Color is the difference, Geoffrey. They've no stamina, no guts, and lots of bloody superstitions. Run along, and fetch them back."

Geoffrey picked up the lantern, shouldered his smoothbore, and started back down the path.

The cubs shivered together, trying to remember the feel of their mother's warmth, knowing something was missing. The little hairless cub cried out in hunger. But the larger one closed her eyes, playing back the moment when the she-wolf's head had burst apart like a piece of fruit thrown down by the langurs. She recalled the taste of the blood, both sweet and salt in her mouth. Turning her head slightly, she sniffed the air. Mother was gone but mother was here. There would be good eating tonight.

By the time Geoffrey could convince the villagers that the colonel had everything under control, it was already dawn and they were willing to come anyway. But they brought rakes and sticks for protection and made Geoffrey march on ahead.

The path had grown almost completely shut in the few hours since he had passed that way. He marveled at the jungle's constancy. Around him, the green walls hid an incredible prolix life, only now and again pulling aside a viney curtain to showcase one creature or another.

The tight lacings of the sal above showed little light, only occasional streaks of sun. From far away he could hear the scolding of langurs moving through the treetops. Behind him the villagers muttered and giggled and it seemed much hotter than the day before.

When they got near the clearing, Geoffrey called out into the quiet, but the colonel did not answer. The men behind him began to talk among themselves uneasily. Geoffrey signaled them to be still, and moved on ahead.

By the termite mound lay a body.

Geoffrey ran over to it. The colonel lay as if he had been thrown down from a great height, yet there was nothing he might have been thrown down from. Horribly, his face and hands had been savaged, mutilated. "Eaten away," Geoffrey whispered to himself. Even the nose bone had been cracked. Yet remarkably, his clothing was little disturbed.

Turning aside, Geoffrey was quietly and efficiently sick, not caring if the villagers saw him. Then, wiping his mouth on his sleeve, he peered over into the mound. The cubs and the children were as he had left them, in that tight monkey ball, asleep. Thank God they had not been molested by whatever beast or beasts had savaged the colonel.

Bending over the mound, and crooning so as not to frighten them, Geoffrey pried away the littlest child and picked her up. The stink of her was ghastly, an unwashed carrion smell. She trembled in his arms. Patting her matted hair gingerly, he cuddled her in his arms and at last she stopped shivering and began to nuzzle at his neck, making a low almost purring sound. She weighed no more than one of his nieces, who were two and three years old.

"Here," Geoffrey called out to the villagers, his back to the colonel's mutilated corpse, "come see. It is only a child gone wild in the jungle. And there is another one here as well. We must take them home. Cleaned up they'll be just like other children." But when he looked over, he realized he spoke to an empty clearing as, from behind him, there came a strange and terrible growl.

She comforted the cubs who still trembled in the light, patting them and licking their fur. Deep in her throat she made the mother sound. "*Very* good eating today."

EVERYTHING TO LIVE FOR

by Charles L. Grant

Born in Newark, New Jersey on September 12, 1942, Charles L. Grant has published over one hundred short stories since his first sale in 1968, and one suspects he has written or edited almost that many books. Novelist, short story writer, anthologist, critic—Grant is one of the premier authors, movers and shakers in the horror genre today. Grant prefers to refer to his own writing as "dark fantasy" and is an exponent of what he likes to call "quiet horror"—as exemplified by his selections for Shadows, *an original anthology series published by Doubleday and now in its eleventh volume. While the current trend in horror fiction seems ready to swing toward spatter/ gross out exercises spawned by the likes of* Friday the 13th on Elm Street Part X *or* Rambo Meets the Chainsaw Zombies, *Grant is a champion of the crusade that subtle is scarier. Have a look.*

Hate is a word I only use about my father.

Not him personally, not exactly, but about the things he does that make me want to punch a hole in the wall, or a hole in his face. Like telling me that I can't get on my little sister for going into my room without me saying she can—because Peggy doesn't know any better, Craig, she's too young to understand about privacy; like yelling at me for not listening to my mother when she's talking to me, even though she's always saying the same stuff—that I don't respect her, that I don't care about all the things she's done for me, that I'd better watch my mouth because I'm not too old to be spanked; like wanting me to practically punch a stupid time clock every time I step out the door so, he says, he'll know where I am in case of an emergency, as if I could be back here like Superman if the house were burning down.

Like I have no business in the shed and I damned well better stay the hell away from his stuff or I'll be grounded for just about the rest of my life.

In fact, I've never been in there, not since we moved here almost ten years ago. It's a little thing made of wood he built himself, not more than ten feet on a side, with a flat roof and one window; it's stuck in the back corner of the yard under a weeping willow that almost buries it year-round. He doesn't use it much, and when he does go out it's like an army on secret maneuvers or something. He puts on a coat no matter what month it is, picks up his briefcase with his pens and pencils and things, and gives Mother a kiss like he's going to the office.

He likes to think in private, he says.

He comes up with his electronics designs better at night, like writers and artists, poets, and other nuts like that.

I thought maybe he kept some booze there and some porn, and used it to get away when my mother was in one of her moods.

I never figured the real reason at all, until last night.

Two weeks ago, after school, I was hanging around the practice field because I wanted to talk to Muldane. He was trying, for the third year in a row, to make first-string catcher, and it was really sad the way he worked so hard out there and failed so badly. I'd been telling him for days to loosen up, get stoned if he had to, but not think that the world would end if he didn't get the spot. But he wouldn't believe me. And he wouldn't believe Jeanne, who stayed away that day because she knew she'd only make him nervous.

So he fell right on his ass a couple of times, missed second base by three or four miles trying to cut down a steal, and generally acted like a goofed-up, hyper freshman. I couldn't watch, and I couldn't look away, so I spent most of the time staring at the grass and listening to the coach hollering and thinking maybe I should go home and apologize to my sister for tying her sheets into knots the night before.

I didn't know Muldane was done until he flopped down beside me and tried to bend the bars off his catcher's mask.

"Bad, huh?" I said.

"Craig," he said, "I am quitting baseball forever."

"No, you're not."

"I am. No shit, Denton, I really am. I am going to join the debate club and talk my way into college, the hell with scholarships and crap like that."

We sat for a few minutes, watching the coaches weed out the other goofs, watched the creeps from last year strutting around with their chests puffed out to here, and finally watched Tony Pelletti run on the cinder track that goes around the field. He was taller than either of us, and about a hundred pounds skinnier, and probably the fastest man in the world.

"God," Muldane said glumly. "He's going to catch his own shadow if he doesn't watch out."

"Yeah."

We were jealous. Pelletti would probably go to college for nothing and end up as a wide receiver for some pro football team, making a zillion bucks a season and doing commercials on TV. And the worst part about it was, he was our friend so we couldn't hate him and make up lies so we'd feel better.

Pelletti saw us then and waved, pointed at the coach's back and gave him an elaborate and elegant finger.

I laughed, and Tony bowed as he ran by.

Then Muldane slammed his mask against the ground a few times, and I checked the sky to see if it would rain.

This wasn't the way I'd planned things to happen. I was the one who needed someone to talk to; I was the one who had just been with the principal, getting suspended for a week because I cut a few lousy classes. Muldane was supposed to cheer me up, and this wasn't like him. He knew he was a rotten catcher; he knew he'd never play anything more than park baseball with the guys; he knew that, and now he was acting like he was going to bust out crying.

I was disgusted. The jerk was letting me down when I needed him the most.

I got up and nudged him with a toe. "C'mon, let's go find Jeanne and get a burger or something."

He shook his head, yanking at his cap, slapping that mask on the ground again and again.

"Mike, for crying out loud, it isn't the end of the world, you know. You can always—"

"Craig, shut up, will you?"

I stared at the top of his head. He'd never told me to shut up before, not that way, and I didn't know whether to feed him a knuckle sandwich or kick in his butt.

Then he looked up at me, fat cheeks shining and those pale eyes all watery, and he said, "My old man, the sonofabitch, will call my brother at college tonight. He's gonna tell him what happened, and my brother's gonna laugh." He looked away, at the ball field. "I could've done it, Denton. I was trying, you saw me trying out there. But he's like everybody else, y'know? Always pushing, never giving you a chance to think, and you gotta think once in a while, you gotta rest, right? I could've made it if he'd just given me the chance. I ain't great, but he just wouldn't let up, and he made me blow it. You know what I mean? He made me blow it."

There was nothing more then but the guys laughing,

a plane overhead, the wind against the ground; and Mike just sitting there, pulling on his cap.

I should have talked to him then, I guess. I should have gotten back down beside him and made him laugh. But I was so mad, so damned mad because he didn't know the trouble I was in and didn't care because he hadn't made the stupid baseball team, that I shoved my hands in my pockets and said, "Christ, Mike, when the hell're you gonna grow up, huh?"

And I walked away, across the grass, across the cinder track, and around the side of the school to the front.

I thought about going home and telling the folks the truth right off and getting it over with. But that was a scene I wasn't about to rush, especially since it meant I would probably have to spend that whole week in my room, studying, and then doing everything around the house I hadn't done in the past sixteen years.

So I walked without knowing where I was going, just hoping that an angel would suddenly land beside me and get me out of this mess before I was skinned alive and hung out to dry.

I was scared.

I was never so scared in my whole life.

And I was mad because I was feeling like a little kid, flinching every time a grown-up looked cross-eyed at me, thinking that everyone in the whole world was pointing a finger at me because they knew what I had done.

And it really wasn't all that bad. Mr. Ranto, my chemistry teacher, kept telling me I should be working harder, that I was smarter than I let on, and he wasn't going to be the one to pass me on to the next level just on my good looks. So he made me miserable, giving me work and work and work until I couldn't take it anymore and just stopped going. Just like that. I either hid out down in the gym, or out behind the school, taking a smoke with the greasers who couldn't figure out what the hell I was doing there, but as long as I had the butts they weren't going to argue.

Ranto caught me that morning.

A few minutes later, wham!—suspension, no appeal.

I walked for over an hour, I think, through parts of town I never knew existed. Houses that looked like they were painted every month, with big cars in the driveway, green lawns a mile long, porches big enough to hold the whole junior class. And down below the shopping district, houses just the opposite—brown no matter what color they were, hardly any grass, hardly a window that didn't have a shade that wasn't crooked or a curtain that wasn't torn. They looked the way I felt.

And when I passed Muldane's place, I saw it in a way I never had before—a place to get away from for the rest of your life, not a place to go home to when you've had a rotten day.

Jesus, I thought, and remembered what I'd said— *when the hell're you gonna grow up*? I hated myself because I sounded just like my father—*grow up, boy, but don't forget to act your age*.

I turned around right away and ran back to the school, thinking maybe Mike was still there so I could talk to him and make a joke about my sudden vacation.

He was gone.

The field was deserted, and so was the school.

And there isn't anything quite so empty as a school that doesn't have anyone in it. Then it looks just like a small factory. It doesn't make any difference how new it is, how fancy—it's worse than a prison, it's a grave-yard hidden by brick and tinted glass.

Thinking all that, and wondering where it was coming from, I was beginning to spook myself, so I headed home and thanked all my good luck charms that Dad was still at work and Mother and Peggy were at the store. It gave me a chance to work on my story, to look for the right buttons to push so I wouldn't get killed when they heard my big news.

And just as it was getting dark, I looked out the kitchen door, down to the shed. It was a black hole in the twilight, the window not even reflecting the lights from the house.

What the hell, I thought; I can't get into worse trouble than I am. Besides, Dad had been going out there a lot lately, and I was getting curious as to what he really did there at night.

I went outside, and suddenly felt as if a spotlight were going to pin me to the ground the minute I took another step. It was stupid, but I couldn't help it, and I almost turned around and went back. I didn't. I walked across the wet grass, went to the door, and turned the knob; it was locked. I cupped my hands around my eyes and peered through the window.

I knew my father had some kind of workbench in there, but whenever I'd snuck looks before, it was always covered. There was also an armchair, a side table, and shelves on the walls.

And something else.

Something I thought I saw in the far corner when, before I could move, headlights slashed up the driveway and washed the lawn a dull white.

I wasn't sure, but I thought it looked like a crate.

I ran back before I was caught, went around the house to the front to wait for dear old Dad to get out of his fancy car. But he didn't. He just sat there, his head all dark like an executioner's mask, and I could only stare back at him until he rolled down his window and told me to get in.

He didn't look happy.

Oh shit, I thought; and walked over. It wouldn't do me any good to make him madder than he was.

"A little trouble, huh?" he said as soon as I got in.

I shrugged.

"You don't like chemistry or something?"

"It's okay."

"You don't like Mr. Ranto, then? What?"

I tried to explain. How they kept pushing me, kept coming at me, kept giving me all this load of crap about how good I was and how clever I was and how I ought to make my family proud because I was the smartest person in it for a hundred generations. They wouldn't let me alone, so I left them alone instead.

He didn't interrupt me once.

And when I was done, feeling shivery and stiff and wishing he would at least look at me when I was talking, he tapped a finger on the steering wheel and stared at the silver ornament at the end of the hood.

It was darker now, the moon lifting over the house, and the headlights made the glass in the garage door grow glaring white eyes.

"You're a jackass, you know," he said very calmly.

"Wonderful," I muttered, and reached for the handle.

That's when he grabbed me.

That's when he took my arm and yanked me back so that I was lying half on my side and staring up into his face.

"Listen, you shit," he said, still calmly, "I will think of a way to explain this to your mother so you don't get killed and she doesn't get hysterical. But you'd damned well better swear to me right now—and I mean right now, boy—that you won't pull a stunt like this again for as long as you live or I'll swear to you that you won't live long enough to see it happen a third time."

"Let go of me," I said, but he only tightened his grip and I felt as if my arm were coming out at the shoulder.

"Swear," he said, sweat suddenly lining his forehead.

"All right, all right!"

He smiled.

He actually smiled at me when he let me up; and as he slid out, he said, "Hey, I heard on the radio some kid killed himself this afternoon. Hung himself in the backyard, I think. You know him? Name's Falkenberg, I think."

I did—not like a friend, just someone you saw around in the halls. But it chilled me just the same. A boy, my age, taking his own life. Something, it said on the news that night, about pressures, grades, maybe drugs and liquor. Mother said it was a shame; Dad only looked at me as if I should be grateful she had something else to think about instead of me, for a change.

I didn't say anything. I didn't even object when, the next morning, he took me to school and we had a long session with the principal. When it was over, I was reinstated, my name practically in blood that I would go to every class, do every bit of homework, and respect my teachers for the betters they were.

I almost threw up.

But it was too close to the end of the year for me to really screw up, so I smiled like a jerk, nodded, promised the moon, and spent the rest of the day explaining to the others how I'd beaten the rap.

To everyone, that is, except Mike, who didn't come to school.

Jeanne wouldn't talk to me, either, and I couldn't figure that out. She acted like she was really mad at me, but she wouldn't tell me why, and no one else could, either.

At the time, I didn't push it. Girls had never been my strongest subject. I knew, sort of, what I was supposed to do with them, but there was something that always held me back whenever I tried to talk to them. They seemed so much smarter than me, so much older, that they only made me confused, and that made me angry.

When I called Muldane that night, his father told me he didn't want to talk to anyone. He sounded drunk. I wasn't surprised.

Mike wasn't in school the next day, or the day after, he wouldn't answer my calls, and when I went over there once he wouldn't come to the door.

I didn't cut a single class.

That's important. I was trying. I was really trying. I smiled at the teachers, I didn't argue with my mother, I even helped my little sister with her homework one night.

I was trying. Honest to god, I was trying.

And I think it was because of Mike. We were a lot

alike, and always had been. Our folks didn't understand us, not really, and they didn't seem to want to try. My father just disappeared into his workshop and shut me out with a key; Mike's old man shut him out with a slap to the jaw and a bottle. We were both counting on college to get us away, but the more we worked, the harder it was to please anyone, much less those we had to.

It was like Pelletti, in a way—running around and around on that stupid red-cinder track and not getting anywhere at all except back where you started, back in the kitchen where they told you you were no good.

On Wednesday night, late, Dad had a phone call, kissed my mother good-night, and told me to go to bed.

"Something wrong?" I asked.

"No," he said, pulling on a worn leather jacket. "I just have to do some work, that's all. You gotta do things yourself, you know, if you want to get them right. Go to bed."

I did.

And Thursday, at dinner, he finished the apple pie my mother had made especially for him, and said, "It's getting to be an epidemic, a real damned shame."

"What, dear?" Mother said.

"Another kid killed himself today."

Mother poured another cup of coffee.

Dad turned to me. "His name was Muldoon, or something like that. Did you know him, Craig?"

I went right to my room. I went right to my bed. I laid down and I stared at the ceiling until I couldn't see it anymore; then I stared at the dark until I fell asleep and dreamed about Mike Muldane hiding in the shed.

I went to school on Friday, but I didn't go to classes. I didn't give a damn. They could hang me for all I care; I just didn't go.

I found a place near the track to sit in the sun. It

was cool, still April, and I was beginning to wish I'd worn something else besides my denim jacket. The gym classes were out, though, and those who saw me either nodded or looked away—the word was still around that I had copped a plea to stay in, and I had a feeling that maybe only Pelletti cared about my reasons.

At lunch, just when I was growing tired of sitting alone and trying to figure out what kind of idiot Muldane was to take himself like that, Jeanne walked up. She was dressed in black, her red hair pulled tight into a ponytail that make her face look a hundred years older. She had been crying. She still was, but there weren't any tears left.

I started to get up, feeling worse than I had when my father dropped the bomb, but she waved me down again. And stared. Tilting her head from one side to the other until I couldn't take it anymore.

"What's the matter? Did I grow another head or something?"

"What did you say to him, Craig?" she asked. "What did you say to him?"

"What?"

I did get up then, but she backed away quickly.

"He was fine until he talked to you. He was—"

"Jesus Christ, Jeanne!" I said, practically yelling. "Are you trying to tell me I made him kill himself?"

She didn't answer, not in words. She only stared a minute longer, turned, and ran away. I started after her, but she buried herself in a group of her girlfriends and, with looks back that would have fried me if wishes were real, they hustled her inside.

I got so excited, so upset, so angry, I could feel the blood in my face, bulging my eyeballs and making my temples pound. I took another step toward the school, then spun around and started running, found myself on the track going around and around and around until I was sweating so much I was freezing. My legs locked on me, the green started to blur, and I dropped and leaned against a bench where the team sat during breaks in practice.

By then I figured she was just crazy with grief. She'd been going with Mike since seventh grade just about, and she was just crazy, that's all.

The bench jumped, then, as someone sat hard on the other end. I looked up, and it was Tony. He was cleaning his glasses with a fold of his gray sweatshirt, and with his long nose and long chin, his straight-back hair, and squinty eyes, he looked like a heron surveying the swamp for a lost meal.

"Bad news, huh?" he said.

"Tell me about it."

"He . . . he ever say anything to you?"

I scrambled up from the ground to sit beside him. "Tony, I swear to God, he never said a word! The last time . . ." I cleared my throat. I cleared it again. "The last time I saw him was at tryouts on Tuesday."

"You talked to him, though."

"On Tuesday, sure. But he wouldn't talk to me after. He was pissed because—"

I stopped. Tony didn't believe me, I could see it when he put on his glasses and examined me, head to toe and back again. He didn't believe me.

"Tony, what's—"

"I gotta go, man," he said. "I can't afford to cut classes like you." He was a couple of steps away before he looked back at me and frowned. "And look," he warned, "stop calling the house, huh? I feel bad enough. You're just making it worse."

And he was gone before I could stop him. Just like Jeanne. An accusation, an exit, and I was alone on the track, staring at the school and wondering what was going on. Two people had practically accused me of murder to my face. Two friends. Two of the only friends I had left in the world.

I didn't care about the deal; I left the school grounds and went for a walk. A long walk. That took me in and out of places I had grown up in, played ball in, smoked secret cigarettes in all my life.

I didn't go home for supper, and I didn't call to tell them where I was.

At nine I found myself on Jeanne's porch, knocking on the door.

She almost slammed it in my face when she saw who it was, but there must have been something there that made her change her mind. She signaled me to wait, closed it partway, and returned a few minutes later with a sweater over her shoulders. Inside, I could hear the television blaring and her two sisters arguing about somebody's boyfriend.

"Walk?" I said, though my legs were starting to turn to rubber.

"Sure."

So we did. Our shoes loud on the sidewalk, our shadows vanishing under the trees that were just getting their new leaves. We didn't say anything for a long time, until we started our second turn around the block and I took her arm and stopped her.

"Jeanne, he was my best friend."

The fingers of one hand lay across her cheek, spread over to her mouth while she swallowed and looked away.

"He was. And I swear to God, the last thing I said to him was that we should find you and get some burgers. That's all." I was almost crying. I almost dropped to my knees. "Jesus, that's all, I swear."

She didn't look at me, but she took my arm and we started walking again. Around the corner. Up the street. Houses lighted and houses dark, and cats running in the alleys.

"He called me the night . . . before," she said, her voice high and hoarse. "He said . . . he told me— Denton says I should take the big one because it ain't worth it anymore." A shudder nearly took the sweater from her shoulders. "Those were his exact words, Craig. His very same words."

I looked at her, stunned, and shook my head. "Jeanne, it wasn't me. You think I'd tell him to do . . . to do what he did? You think I could do that to my best friend?" When she didn't answer right away, I almost hit her. "And even if I did, which I didn't, he wouldn't do it. You know him. You know him as long as I have. He wouldn't do it, Jeanne, he wouldn't!"

"He did," she whispered. "But he did, Craig."

The third time we got to her house I knew she believed me even though I hadn't said another word. She held my hands tight and she looked hard into my face, and suddenly she looked as frightened as I suddenly felt.

When she ran inside, I didn't try to stop her.

I only ran home, just in time to meet my father coming out the front door.

"I was going to look for you," he said.

"I was walking," I told him, pushing inside to hang up my coat. "I had to think, that's all. About Mike. Stuff."

"Your mother was worried. She wanted me to call the police. Thank God, Peggy doesn't pull stunts like this."

"I'm sorry."

"Tell her yourself. She's in the kitchen."

Which she was, and which I did; and though I told her I saw Jeanne, I didn't tell her what she said.

"Michael Muldane was a very sick boy," was all she said as she put cookies in the jar and plates in the dishwasher. "I think his little girlfriend isn't well, either. I accept your apology, and I don't want you to see her again."

"What?"

Father came to the doorway. "Don't argue, Craig. Just go to bed, please. You're upset, your mother's upset. We'll talk about it in the morning."

I didn't want to talk about it in the morning; I wanted to talk about it now. Right now. But there's no justice for a kid my age, no justice at all. You have to stand there, that's all, and take it like a man, and hope that tomorrow they'll forget all about it and leave you alone.

I was lucky that time. They did, until the next weekend, when Jeanne called me, in tears, nearly hysterical.

Dad, who had just come in from the shed, his brief-case under his arm, answered the phone, listened a minute, and handed me the receiver with a scowl. "Don't be long," he ordered. "She sounds drunk or something."

She wasn't drunk. She was terrified.

Tony was dead.

He had gone out for a drive in his father's new car and had plowed it head-on into a bus on the far side of town. The police weren't sure it was an accident at all.

Mike's funeral had been private, family only. Not Tony's. A bunch of us left school early on Tuesday and went to the cemetery to say good-bye. Jeanne was with me, holding on to my arm so tight it almost cramped. The girls were kind of crying, the guys trying to be like they were supposed to—brave and cool and only looking sad.

When a tear got away from me, Jeanne wiped it away and smiled.

While the priest was talking, I started thinking—not about that shiny coffin with all the flowers on it that was supposed to hold Tony but how could it because he was probably right now running around the track; not about that, about me. How all of a sudden it seemed that every time I picked up the phone it was bad news. Somebody dead. A kid. And I thought about Jeanne and how scared she was, scared like me because kids aren't supposed to die like this. I know it happens, sure. I read the papers, I see the news, but not in this town. Not here. Not to people we know.

An epidemic, my father said.

And suddenly I went cold. Colder than the breeze that came at us from the tombstones.

Muldoon or something, he had said.

But he knew Mike. He'd known him for years, Mother fed him dinners and lunches, and he once even went on a vacation to the seashore with us.

Muldoon or something.

That's when I thought I was starting to go crazy; that's when I put my arm around Jeanne and held her so tightly she looked up at me and frowned, felt me trembling and held me back. And when it was over and we were walking away, she asked me what was wrong, and I told her.

"So?" she said. "I don't understand."

Neither did I, but it wouldn't let go once it took hold. All day. All night. All the next day, even when Mother said a neighbor saw me walking Jeanne home after school and didn't she tell me not to see her again?

Last night . . . last night was only a few hours ago.

I was lying on my bed, not undressed, just lying there with my hands behind my head and thinking about Jeanne and how Mike wouldn't mind if we got together or something; we'd been best friends, and Jeanne was . . . she was special. Mike knew it. I knew it, and I didn't have to worry with her about what to say or how to act. When I got stupid, she told me; when I did something nice, she told me. Mike wouldn't care. Mike was dead, and God, I missed him.

Then I heard voices downstairs. Arguing. My mother and father in the kitchen, and Father suddenly telling her to quiet down or the boy would hear.

That was my signal. Whenever one of them said that, my ears got sensitive and I turned into a ghost, sneaking out of the room and into the hall, to the head of the stairs and down to the one I knew creaked when you breathed on it. All the lights were out, except over the kitchen table, and all I could see were moving shadows on the hall wall.

"I think," Father said, "it's much too soon. He isn't going to be able to take much more."

Mother was doing something at the stove. Probably baking another pie. "I don't like bad influences, dear."

"She's only a little girl."

"Big enough to cause trouble."

"I don't know. I—"

"Just get your coat, dear. And please watch the noise. I don't want to wake Peggy."

Father's voice changed. "An angel, you know that?

God, I almost cry every time I look at her. She has so much to live for. Not like—"

"I know, dear, I know."

"And when I think about Craig, I could—"

"Your coat, dear. Please."

I backed away from the banister and watched the dark figure that was my father go to the closet and take out his leather jacket, walk back into the kitchen, and say something I couldn't hear. The back door opened, closed, and I sat there with my knees close to my chest, my head turning side to side like something had broken in my neck and I couldn't work it right anymore.

I couldn't really be sure what it was I heard, but it was the tone of their voices that frightened me. So controlled, so sure, and at the same time so threatening that I almost screamed.

Instead, and I don't know why because I was so scared, I crept down the rest of the steps and out the front door, then ran around the side of the house, back toward the shed.

A light was on.

I crouched beside the wall and hugged myself, my teeth chattering so loud I had to put a fist against my jaw to keep from biting my tongue in half.

Then I looked in the window.

Father had turned the chair around and was sitting in it, leaning forward a little and looking at the large wooden crate I had seen the week before. But it was black. So black the light didn't touch it, and when I stared at it long enough I could see right through it, into more blackness, solid dark; and Father was rocking a little now, and I could hear him grunting every so often, rocking, and grunting, shaking his head once and rocking even faster. Grunting. Then, suddenly, he was humming in a high quiet voice, like a song without words, without notes, a child's chant against the dark, driving away the demons until mommy or daddy could come in and save them.

A car drove down our street, its radio loud with rock music.

Humming. Chanting, Parting the black for more black, this time freckled with points of white light.

A window was open in a neighbor's house, and a telephone rang for almost a full minute before someone answered.

Chanting. Rocking. The points beginning to swirl into a dense white cloud whose light was swallowed by the black.

And in the white I saw something that looked like a face.

I blinked quickly because I felt myself crying, felt the tears on my cheeks and I didn't know why. It was stupid. There was some kind of electronic thing in my father's stupid shed, and all that black and all that dead white were making me cry like a stupid little baby.

For a minute, just a minute, I wanted to die.

Father stopped.

The white vanished.

The black faded to normal black, and the wood crate was back.

It was a few seconds before I was able to shake myself into moving around the corner so that, when he came out, whistling to himself, he wouldn't see me. He strolled back to the house with his hands in his pockets, and Mother opened the door for him, nodded, and kissed his cheek.

Then I looked up to the moon, saw the face, and I knew. One thing, then another, and something jumped inside my head and I knew what was going on, and I fell to my knees and put my head in my hands.

Hate is a word I use only about my father, but I know now it's a word both my folks use about me.

It's almost dawn. I've been sitting here so long I'm touched with dew, and I can't move. Not an arm, not a leg, though my teeth stopped chattering a long time ago.

Mike said his big brother was the favorite; Jeanne said it was her two sisters; Tony didn't have anyone; and I have Peggy.

So what can you do about it if you're a parent? You give birth to the kid and you watch it grow up and into a person, and then you decide if you like it or not. Someone you meet that you don't like you don't have to see again, or you can be polite to, or you can ignore. A kid is there all the time—all day, all week, all year, all your life.

It's cold out here.

So what can you do about it if you're a parent and you don't like your kid? What can you do if you don't want him anymore?

It's very cold, and it's dark.

I think . . . I think some parents go from hate to not caring, and that's the worst of all. And if they look right, they can find someone who can see that, see the dark of it, and make it almost alive. Like a cloud, a black cloud that hangs over you in November, telling you it's going to rain but not telling you when. Those kinds of days are the most rotten, and they make you feel rotten, on the outside where it's raw, and on the inside where you wish you could just go away and find a place that has the sun.

If the cloud stays long enough, you don't wait for the next day, or the rain, or the snow—you go on your own, and you never come back.

I didn't call Mike. My father did.

I didn't talk to Tony. My father did.

I wonder if Mr. Falkenberg hated his son?

I keep trying to remember, but I can't. Jesus. I can't remember whose face I saw in that dying white light.

But there's no sense in running.

I won't go back in the house, but there's no sense in running.

I'm just going to wait here, and maybe think of a way to stop it.

But sooner or later, when the sun comes out and the

birds start flying and the kids are off to school and Peggy is laughing with my mother and my father is off to work, a telephone is going to ring.

My father did the magic; my mother told him who to get.

When that telephone rings, somebody is going to tell someone else that another kid is dead.

Oh shit, Jeanne, don't hate me, but I hope that it's you.

REPOSSESSION

by David Campton

English playwright David Campton was born in Leicester on June 5, 1924, where he still makes his home. During World War II Campton served in the Royal Air Force, and afterward he began writing plays as well as pursuing an acting career. He gave up on the latter in 1963 in favor of writing and has since written more than seventy plays in addition to numerous radio and television plays (including a few in collaboration with Sheila Hodgson, who also appears in this collection). Campton's most recent plays include Cards, Cups and Crystal Ball *(about three clairvoyant sisters who foresee one murder and try to prevent another) and* Can You Hear the Music *(about mice succumbing to the temptations of the Pied Piper).*

When he—all too infrequently—turns his talents to short fiction, David Campton exhibits a precise control of language and a sophistication of style which deftly lead the reader to whatever sort of horrors Campton has in mind this time out. Since he has a penchant for dark humor as well as dark fantasy, it's best to watch your step.

The Johnson audit took longer than I anticipated, but I stayed working until it was finished, and was heading for home when a threatened wintery shower materialized. When I drove by the old Marlow factory I was concentrating on the wet road, so the light in the upper window barely registered and I was well past before the oddness struck me. What was a light doing on in a building that had been shut down for years? Was it vandals? Squatters? Should I do anything about possible trespassers?

I could have telephoned the police, but was sure nobody would thank me. With the place scheduled for demolition there was every possibility it might fall down before the bulldozers moved in; so if some benighted soul had found shelter in the ruin, who was I to interfere? Constructed on the forbidding lines of a Victorian workhouse the derelict works offered only marginally better comfort than an exposed doorway. Let whoever was up there stay there.

I continued to speculate on the light, though. Surely all services had been cut off when Marlow's went into liquidation, so the gleam could hardly have been electric. Could a candle so far away have caught my attention through a sleet-spattered windscreen? Not even a hurricane lamp could have been expected to do that, so why had I even considered it? Except that the light forced itself more and more on my attention.

I tried to shrug off the problem, yet found myself musing on alternatives, even with the car locked away and myself sinking into a reclining chair, keeping the chill at bay with a high-proof rum toddy.

In my mind's eye I could see that top window. Clearly now. No rain or sleet to obscure it. Harsh light streaming through. Who or what could be up there?

From the point of view of the waste ground in front of the building, its grim silhouette made even more forbidding by the glow of city lights in the sky behind it, that solitary rectangle, like a single bright eye high above, was almost fascinating enough to make one forget the freezing slush underfoot. Who? Or what?

I came to my senses when I dropped the toddy glass—fortunately empty by now. No, I was not shivering in the shadow of that monument to nineteenth-century economics. I was comfortably established in my own bachelor domain.

In which case why were my feet so cold? Why were my sodden slippers caked with sludge? And why was icy cloth clammy against my legs?

I was as wet as if I had been standing outside, exposed to the wintery weather. Impossible. But there were the dark stains. Had I been so engrossed that I had spilt the contents of my glass? No. Whatever was soaking into my clothes was not hot rum and lemon. I had not moved from my chair, and yet . . .

An accountant is expected to have a logical brain, and logically there was only one thing to be done—change into something warm and dry. The autopilot that guides us through daily routine took over while my thought processes slithered and foundered, trying to come to terms with the patently unbelievable.

If I had not left the house why did my reflection in the wardrobe mirror look as though I had been trudging through fallow fields? There were actually blades of coarse grass sticking to the mud. A dried leaf. A fragment of paper. On slippers that since the day they were bought had never stepped farther than the front door. Half of me wanted to scream "there is something wrong here," the other half laid out clean underwear, peeled off oozing socks and decided a shower was called for.

While not exactly washing my bewilderment away, the hot water was at least soothing. As circulation returned, my numbed mental powers recovered sufficiently for me to take stock of the situation. I had been sitting back indulging—as surely as a man is entitled to after a long day with ledgers—in idle reverie. Something to do with a light, wasn't it? In the old Marlow place. Yes, now I remembered the lighted window. At the top of . . . and the warm water was rinsing away fresh streaks of dirt from my feet.

Later, wrapped in my bathrobe, I took the rum bottle to my empty glass. Such refinements as lemon and hot water were dispensed with. My present state of nerves called for undiluted restorative. When I stopped shaking I tried to consider what might have happened.

Surely such things did *not* happen. A person cannot be here one minute and somewhere quite different the next. Yet what could not have happened seemed to be connected in some way with . . . No! Don't think about the light. That light was part of the—illusion? —delusion?—phenomenon. Comforting word—phenomenon. A word for papering over cracks. Phenomenon can be applied to anything from young Miss Crummles to a light that . . . No, not that light again! Even at the flicker of memory a gust of night wind seemed to ruffle my hair. I must not think about a light in an upper window.

How to keep at bay those insistent, intrusive images? The baleful hulk of the factory . . . Take a swig of neat rum, fierce enough to concentrate attention on tongue and throat . . . with the glowing rectangle . . . More rum . . . like a signal . . . At this rate I should soon be tight, and how much control would be left then? Another tot. The alcohol was taking effect. Even if I happened to think of a lighted window, it would be a blurred window because I was by now experiencing difficulty in focusing on anything; and at last stopped caring about anything . . .

I woke with a head like an echo chamber and a mouth like a sweaty sock. A thin ray of sunlight picked its way through a gap where the living room curtains failed to overlap. I had passed the night in my reclining chair and the empty bottle on my chest explained why. There are few things to be said in favor of a hangover, but at least its demands take precedence over other preoccupations. I was washed, dressed, aspirin-dosed and halfway through my second black coffee before I recollected the light and what had apparently followed.

Perhaps fully dressed in daylight I felt bolder; perhaps the ache behind my eyes left me feeling that nothing worse could happen; at any rate I tried to repeat last night's experience. Nothing happened.

Somehow I could not exactly picture the way the window had appeared in the looming wall. Anyway, everything there would have been different in the stir of morning. My feet remained firmly planted on the kitchen floor. Whatever had (or had not) taken place was over now. Just something to look back on. "A funny thing once happened . . ." becoming dimmed and distorted with time. The detail was blurred already. Ah, well . . .

The day's work was something to be staggered through. Making allowances for impaired concentration, by midday I was almost normal again.

Though I still could not face a meal. Ploughman's cheese-and-pickle at the pub round the corner lacked appeal; as did the alternative little spaghetti place. I suppose I could have worked through the lunch-hour on more coffee, but I felt a need for fresh air. So I took a walk.

The weather had improved and a fitful sun struggled through thin clouds. There was no mysterious inner compulsion and I did not wander in a daze; but I ended my stroll outside the Marlow factory.

It had once been surrounded by rows of inadequate houses, built to accommodate mill-hands as cheaply as possible. Those streets had been swept away in the first stage of a massive slum-clearance project, but Local Authority had not yet raised finance for the second phase; and the inner-city area, flat as a highwayman's heath, had become an urban wilderness. Playground and natural hazard for stray animals and children, it stretched like an abandoned battlefield, strewn with discarded cans, bottles and waste paper, between a rusted chain-link fence and the grimy factory walls.

I had never been so close to the place before, hardly ever having paused to give the eyesore a glance. After all, on that stretch of road a motorist usually concentrates on rush-hour queue-jumpers and the traffic lights ahead. I felt no more than mild curiosity, but I had half an hour to play with before being due back at the office. So I stepped cautiously across a broken section of fencing, and picked my way through the rough grass and tough weeds that sprouted as mangy covering over the broken ground. Underfoot was still spongy after last night's wintery showers, though to a pedestrian mud was the least noxious of the hazards. By the time I reached the factory I needed the piece of sodden newspaper blown against the door for cleaning my shoes.

Wiping away as much of the mess as I could, I leaned against the door. It opened. I might have guessed the lock would have been smashed. Architectural derelicts tend to attract human counterparts.

Technically I suppose I was trespassing too; but there was no one to stop me—or even shout a word of warning. (Notices warding off intending intruders had long since been burned.) Having seen Marlow's monument from the outside, why pass up the chance to look inside? If anyone should ask, I was interested in industrial archeology. I stepped over the threshold and pulled the door shut behind me.

The entrance lobby was small with narrow stairs in one corner. When first built it must have constituted a natural fire hazard: so many employees jammed into so little space; but in old Marlow's heyday human lives were just so much raw material. Such paint as had not peeled off the walls was mostly obscured with dust, cobwebs and handprints. The floor was littered with torn packets and empty bottles—evidence of previous interlopers.

I called "Anyone there?" not so much expecting a reply as seeking the reassurance of my own voice. Silence followed. Feeling bolder I mounted the stairs.

Dim light filtered into the stairwell from above and below—halfway up was particularly dreary—yet at no time did I feel any sense of foreboding. This was merely an abandoned building that had served its purpose and was waiting to be scrapped. At the first landing a corridor stretched to the rear. On one side open doors revealed a work-room extending over most of the first floor. Iron pillars at intervals supported the floor above. Rough outlines indicated where machinery had once been fixed. There were other indications of more recent occupation. I soon had my handkerchief pressed to my nose: at least that kept out the worst of the stench.

It was probably this that drove me up to the top floor. Here the pattern of the floors below was repeated: on one side of the corridor another workroom (mercifully not yet used as a lavatory) and on the other side several closed doors. I opened them one after the other, peering into rooms that had been stores or offices. One still had shelving in place. But the last door along the corridor would not open.

At first I assumed it had jammed. Stains down the walls suggested a roof in need of attention, and damp could have caused the woodwork to swell. However the door resisted all my pushing and after some wasted effort I had to admit that it must be locked. Ridiculous. Why lock up one room in a building as wide open as this?

Given time I could have doubtless thought of half a dozen explanations, but there was no time for putting theories to the test. I had to be on my way back to the office.

There were stairs at the end of this corridor, too. I hoped they might lead down to the ground floor, avoiding the unpleasantness at the end of the first floor work-room.

As I reached the last few steps I thought I heard a slight scuffle. Rats? The notion brought me to a temporary halt. We all have our phobias, and rodents happen to be one of mine. I silently swore for not taking the possibility into account sooner, especially having seen those food wrappings lying about. I froze while all the data I had ever encountered concerning attacks by vermin flickered through my brain. Did they really make instinctively for the groin? Wasn't that why navvies tied the bottoms of their trousers with string?

But a move had to be made one way or the other. As quietly as possible I peeped round the corner to make sure no gray furry beastie was lying in wait for me. There was nothing.

Only a door almost opposite the stairs slowly edging shut.

Rats, no matter now intelligent, do not close doors with excessive caution. A surge of irritation now replaced my instinctive panic, almost reaching the point of equally irrational fury. I had just made a fool of myself and needed to blame somebody. I bounded forward and booted the door with all the force I could muster. The blow was violent enough to thrust the person on the other side across the room; while, thrown off balance by such feeble resistance, I executed a miniature pirouette before steadying myself. A girl, wide-eyed and open-mouthed, sagged against the wall opposite.

My first impression was of tatters and patches. Even her hair was a dirty yellow-and-brown skewbald—not deliberately so, but the result of inexpert dying half grown out. Her clothes were a jumble of rummage— jeans with one knee out, grubby jumper and torn anorak. She obviously belonged in the dump more than I did. I guessed her age as late teens. Young and frightened I suppose she ought to have aroused my sympathy, but affronted dignity crowds out finer feelings. I wasn't sure what sort of figure I was presenting, but I had a suspicion it must have been fairly ridiculous.

We stared at each other without a word. Until she sniveled and whimpered. At least that broke the ice, and I felt free to bawl, "What the hell are you doing here?"

"I ain't done nothing," she whined, like a rabbit appealing to the better nature of a stoat. Not that I ever thought of myself as a predator; but that please-don't-hit-me-when-I'm-down attitude inevitably provokes the opposite effect.

"You realize you're trespassing," I snapped; which was as near as I could ever get to putting the boot in.

"I ain't done nothing," she repeated forlornly.

A badly tied brown paper parcel lay in one corner. Near it on the dusty floor were an unopened can of fizzy drink and a packet of crisps. A half-eaten meat pie appeared to have been dropped when she was disturbed.

"Yours?" I asked unnecessarily.

"I ain't done nothing," she whispered. What else was there to say? She was lunching at home today. As far as she was concerned this bleak hole was home. Temporary accommodation, no doubt, but with the only alternative a doss under one of the nearby canal bridges, who was I to frighten her away?

"Have you been upstairs?"

She shook her head.

"Liar."

"I ain't done nothing." She slid down the wall and sat in an attitude of huddled resignation.

"I've just been upstairs," I said, and left the implication to register. She looked up at me dumbly. The grubby little creature wasn't even intelligent. Her only attraction lay in her vulnerability. Suddenly I wanted to get away without losing too much face.

"Oh, go to hell," I growled, turned abruptly and left her. I may only have imagined she cried, "I ain't done nothing."

Luckily I found a rear door, also unfastened, so I was spared the embarrassment of blundering about looking for an exit. I didn't even look back at the factory, and only hoped nobody spotted me recrossing the waste ground.

A fleeting memory of the girl came between me and my work a couple of times during the afternoon. In particular I recollected that pathetic half pie; but by then I was feeling hungry myself.

I stayed in town for a meal before going home, making up for my missed breakfast and lunch by in-

dulging in a half carafe of plonk: so I passed the old
Marlow factory about the same time as the night before.

It was all dark. At any rate there was now an
explanation of yesterday's light. A girl on the premises
could have been responsible for almost anything. It
occurred to me that the window in question must have
belonged to the locked room. More mystery? Whatever it was had nothing to do with me. By now I had
convinced myself that whatever I may have imagined
last night had been uneasily compounded of overwork,
slight fever and rum. There would be no rum tonight.
In the first place because there would be no need for
it, and in the second place because there was none left
at my place.

All the same I felt that early retirement was called
for. Just an hour perhaps listening to music before a
milky nightcap. There was a cassette already in the
deck waiting for a press of the "play" button. Had I
been listening to Allegri when. . . ? Did it matter? I
could always find pleasure in Allegri. I pressed the
button and sat back at ease.

The soaring treble of the "Miserere" usually has me
feeling that the world is a better place than it is usually
given credit for, and that I am probably a better person than I am generally given credit for. Self-indulgence
maybe, but even an accountant needs some illusions.

Then, as the music took over, a picture began to
form. Yes, I must have been listening to Allegri earlier, because the picture was as before—a lighted window high up on a dark wall. Only this time I seemed
drawn toward the patch of brilliance. Then I was
inside the upper room.

It was as bare as any I had seen in the factory that
day, bare as a monk's cell: but unlike the others these
bare boards had been spotlessly scrubbed and walls
and ceiling freshly whitewashed. There was a man on
his knees in the middle of the floor, his back toward
me, his curling hair and broadcloth coat stark black
against all that white. With head bowed he appeared
to be praying.

Did music alone have the power to suggest all this?

What is more, the figure seemed to be aware that I stood behind him. He raised his head and started to get up without looking round. He did not need to look round. Whoever he might be, he knew who I was.

Then a click as the music ended and the tape-deck switched itself off. Jerked back into my present surroundings I was staring at the mirror on the opposite side of my own room. Potent stuff the Allegri "Miserere" if it could conjure such impressions. I made no attempt to change the tape, but sat on, half under the spell. I did not want to move. I wanted a little time for contemplation.

Had the imagined room been part of the Marlow factory? However intangible, it had seemed more real than any of the others I had seen earlier in the day; just as the dreamed-up man had seemed more vital than the wretched girl I had actually encountered. The white room was the same size and shape as her miserable refuge. I found myself mentally comparing the two . . .

The girl's ground-floor squat for instance—so dimly lit that shapes could barely be made out in it. The slight effulgence from a frosty moon made its way through holes in corrugated sheeting fastened over the window space. The girl lay on the floor, using her paper parcel as a pillow. Her knees were drawn up and her hands tucked underneath her arms, no doubt for some slight protection against the cold. Was she asleep? She sniffed and then coughed. Automatically I stepped back, encountering the door with a slight thud. It must have been just off the latch, clicking as I pushed back.

The girl raised her head. "Who—?" she murmured. "Whosere?" She peered hazily in my direction, then suddenly sat up. I imagine she was about to scream, but I heard nothing.

Why should I? After all, I was sitting in my own chair. I had never left it. But if I had never left it, where had the thick smear of dust on the back of my hand and sleeve come from?

Although the rum was all gone the cupboard yielded the last of a bottle of gin and some abominably sweet sherry, bought long ago for a forgotten female guest.

Mixed in a tumbler they made a nauseating but necessary cocktail. Did I need the drink to help me to think—or to keep me from thinking? I wasted little time on such hair-splitting. I drank.

After a while my teeth stopped chattering and I tried to make connections. Nobody can be in two places at once, can he? Could I? Delirium! If I believed that, I'd soon have myself believing that I could bend forks. I was an accountant, not some fakir. I believed in facts. I had to. Flights of fancy could lead to trouble with the Inland Revenue Department. Normal people do not move across town instantaneously and unaided. So put aside the delusion that I had just returned to the factory.

Likewise the man in the Victorian frock-coat had been no more than a figment of the imagination. Of that I was certain. After all, it was my own imagination. What more natural than to suppose old Marlow had been such a person. Not so old either in the years when the factory had been turning out highly profitable goods for the Africa trade. Ruthless exploitation after a bright start made him a fortune by the time he was my age. About 1850 wasn't it? Hadn't I heard somewhere that skinning workers here and fleecing customers abroad had actually paid for the building of a Nonconformist chapel? How adroitly the solid citizens of that period manipulated their consciences, somehow contriving to serve both God and Mammon. In Marlow's case Mammon appeared to have been the more influential, because there was no trace left of the chapel, while at least the shell of the factory remained. But what part of its begetter lingered with it?

No doubt that had been Marlow kneeling in the bare white sanctum, locked against inquiring eyes. Praying perhaps to be spared the lusts of the flesh.

Not so easy to curb animal instincts when one is master of several hundred souls—and the bodies that come with them. What did they say of him in the workshops? Why did some of the young minxes cock a speculative eye when he passed?

Not that such cattle offered temptation. More dangerous were the timid ones with frightened eyes, trying not to attract attention; because only token resistance was permissible in days when the rule was work or starve and dismissal meant the workhouse or the streets. With the door of the whitewashed room locked there had been prayers and prayers. Neither sort had been answered. Afterward there had been occasional accidents (conveniently bestowed elsewhere) and even a suicide (believing the river better than a bastard). And inevitably agonies of remorse. Never again. Never, never—until the next time. He could no more resist than she—whoever may be next in the whitewashed room. In spite of all his prayers.

How could I be so certain? The man in the black coat turned to face me. It was like looking into the mirror again. His face was mine. There had been bastards, and after three generations who can be sure of his family tree?

I was certain. After all, an accountant ought to be aware of elementary mathematics. The Marlow factory was the lowest common denominator—for me, for him, for the girl. My grandfather had been conceived in that place where the spirit of old vice lingered.

Into which place that fool of a destitute girl had wandered. Whatever remained there wanted her. That helpless attitude, those familiar frightened eyes had roused him—it. Marlow had at least been a man: what was left was no longer human, and she was no more to it than tethered bait for a tiger. What justification did I have for reaching such a conclusion? An accountant is at least able to add up: even after a half-carafe of house wine and a gin-based concoction. There was enough of my great-grandfather's blood in me to know what he/it intended.

I felt I had to warn her. To explain. If absolutely necessary to pay for other lodgings for her. She must not stay where she was. I did not know what the thing in the black broadcloth might attempt, but I did know what it was still capable of. I had looked into its eyes and I knew. The time for prayers was past.

I stumbled out toward my car, even though I suspected I was in no condition to drive. As it happened I did not have to. I was thinking of the room with the blocked window. By now I should have known better . . .

The room was empty, but the door was open. There was a litter of newspaper on the floor. Perhaps she had been trying it as bedding. The paper-wrapped parcel had not been moved. I picked it up. It was very light. I wondered vaguely what she might keep in it. Then she was in the doorway, looking at me.

I found my voice first. "Get out of here," I said.

Her reply was a half-stifled wail. She shook her head, not so much saying "no" as in disbelief at my appearance.

"Get out," I repeated. "Now." Then in frustration at making no progress with the little idiot, shouted, "Get out!" I thrust her parcel toward her, intending her to take it and go. She must have misunderstood the gesture, because she backed into the corridor with a series of short moans. Then she turned and fled empty-handed.

She might so easily have found that rear exit. Instead she scampered up the stairs. I had no choice but to follow her. She had to be brought down. Upstairs in the Marlow factory was no place for her.

The staircase had been dim enough in daylight, by night I was climbing blind, feeling my way along the wall. I knew she was ahead of me by her frightened sobs. At the top of the stairs there was just enough of a gray glow for illumination. She was nowhere to be seen, but could only have ducked into one of the rooms off the corridor or into the empty workspace. As the door to the latter was flung wide I tried that opening first. I was right. She had stepped just inside, and stood with her back pressed against the wall, I suppose silently beseeching that I might not notice. When she saw me she gave a cry that echoed through the building and scuttled to the other end of the workroom.

I might have caught up with her then, but skidded on something repulsive underfoot. While I was recovering my balance she was on her way up the next flight of stairs.

It was then that I began to call to her. "Not up there. For God's sake, not up there." I doubt if my words made any sense to her. They were merely an alarming clamor that she answered with panic-stricken squeaks.

From the light into the dark, and into the light again. Always upward. I was driving her toward the one place where she should not be; but what else could I have done? I had to catch up with her before she reached that upper room.

Its door was open now. The moonlight shining full on that side of the factory spilled from the room into the corridor.

As I emerged, panting at the head of the last flight of stairs, she was already half-way toward the open door. I had given up shouting. I needed the breath. Instead I made cooing and clucking noises as though trying to calm a terrified animal. I remembered with irrational clarity how when a boy I had once picked up a shrew and seen it die of fright on my hand. I think I murmured "There now. There now." But she backed away from me without a word.

Slowly, one step at a time, we edged toward the other end of the passage. Her eyes were wide and unblinking. She sniffed regularly, and the end of her tongue was constantly moistening her lips.

Desperately, I took one stride longer than the others.

"No," she whispered, and increased her backward shuffle.

Abandoning caution I lunged. She fled. She reached

the open door seconds before I could, and it slammed in my face. Like a trap snapping shut, the light was cut off.

For one of those instants that stretch toward eternity I faced the dark panels. Then from inside the room came a feebly despairing wail.

Expecting to encounter the lock, I pushed furiously, but met no resistance and stumbled into his presence. The radiance of the full moon was reflected from the white walls, filling the room with an unearthly brilliance. Black from curling hair to immaculate boots, with only his face a pale oval, he contrasted starkly against the shining background.

She stood trembling between us, repeatedly looking from one to the other—apart from our clothes alike as twins. She was caught between devil and deep.

As he smiled, I realized this was no chance encounter. I had done what I had always been intended to do. Brought her to him.

At least he was on the far side of the room and I was the one between her and the way of escape. I cleared the way to the door and pointed. Words would not come, but at least she could see what I meant. So why didn't the spineless young fool take her chance? Why waver until history repeated itself?

As he moved, as silent and regardless of obstacles as a shadow, I stepped between them. From him I expected the rage of a patriarch denied, from her some final burst of activity. Neither reacted. It was like finding myself in the frozen frame of a film.

At last I seized her by the shoulders and tried to force her toward the door. She resisted me and began to scream. In desperation I began to shake her. Was I trying to shake some sense into her or merely trying to end those rasping shrieks? They stopped when her head flopped loosely from side to side like a rag doll's.

I realized I was supporting her full weight, and lowered her gently to the floor. As I leaned over her, my hands underneath her back, I realized that my arms were not covered by fawn lamb's-wool, but by black broadcloth . . .

Then here I was at my own kitchen door.

So what am I to do now? Tell the authorities what they are likely to find in the old Marlow factory? Why bother? Sooner or later she'll be found, if not by some prying vagrant then by the inevitable demolition crew. Will anything be found then that can be traced back to me?

Does it matter anyway? Something far more important weighs on my mind. You see, he has me too. He uses me. About the time of change in the moon is worst, when those old lusts rage again. There have been no more supernatural trips. No need because he is always with me, part of me.

Every so often attacks are reported in the newspapers. The police repeat that they are following a lead, though that seems to be a routine statement, and so far nobody has knocked on my door.

But what is to become of me?

MERRY MAY

by Ramsey Campbell

Born in Liverpool on January 4, 1946, Ramsey Campbell was 18 when his first collection of horror stories was published by Arkham House, and he hasn't let up since. One wonders whether he might be some sinister counterculture's answer to The Beatles, since he has a fondness for using Liverpool settings for his nastiest tales. Presently Campbell lives with his wife and two children in Merseyside in "an enormous turn-of-the-century house with fifteen rooms or more and a cellar and sundry other good things." Don't look in the cellar.

Ramsey Campbell's latest novel is Ancient Images, *originally entitled* The Dead Hunt *(Campbell's titles seem always to change upon publication). Two recent collections are* Cold Print *and* Scared Stiff, *as well as an English "best of" omnibus. Curiously, Campbell's story in last year's* Year's Best Horror Stories, *"Apples," was to have appeared in an English reprint of* Halloween Horrors, *but a copy editor there rewrote the story from start to finish. Sphere Books pulped the entire edition. No word as to the present whereabouts of the copy editor.*

As Kilbride left the shadow of the house whose top floor he owned, the April sunlight caught him. All along this side of the broad street of tall houses, trees and shrubs were unfurling their foliage minutely. In the years approaching middle age the sight had made him feel renewed, but now it seemed futile, this compulsion to produce tender growth while a late frost lay in wait in the shadows. He bought the morning paper at the corner shop and scanned the personal columns while his car warmed up.

Alone and desperate? Call us now before you do anything else . . . There were several messages from H, but none to J for Jack. Deep down he must have known there wouldn't be, for he hadn't placed a message for weeks. During their nine months together, he and Heather had placed messages whenever either of them had had to go away, and the day when that had felt less like an act of love to him than a compulsion had been the beginning of the end of their relationship. The thought of compulsion reminded him of the buds opening moistly all around him, and he remembered Heather's vulva, gaping pinkly wider and wider. The stirring of his penis at the memory depressed and angered him. He crumpled the newspaper and swung the car away from the curb, deeper into Manchester.

He parked in his space outside the Northern College of Music and strode into the lecture hall. So many of his female students reminded him of Heather now, and not only because of their age. How many of them would prove to be talented enough to tour with even an amateur orchestra, as she had? How many would suffer a nervous breakdown, as she had? The eager bright-eyed faces dismayed him: they'd drain him of all the knowledge and insight he could communicate, and want more. Maybe he should see himself as sunlight to their budding, but he felt more like the compost as he climbed onto the stage.

"Sonata form in contemporary music . . ." He'd given the lecture a dozen times or more, yet all at once he seemed to have no thoughts. He stumbled through the introduction and made for the piano, too quickly. As he sat down to play an example there wasn't a note of living music in his head except his own, his thoughts for the slow movement of his symphony. He hadn't played that music to anyone but Heather. He remembered her dark eyes widening, encouraging him or yearning for him to succeed, and his fingers clutched at the keys, hammered out the opening bars. He'd reached the second subject before he dared glance at his students. They were staring blankly at him, at the music.

Surely they were reacting to its unfamiliarity; or could it be too demanding or too esoteric in its language? Not until a student near the back of the hall yawned behind her hand did it occur to Kilbride that they were simply bored. At once the music sounded intolerably banal, a few bits of secondhand material arranged in childishly clever patterns. He rushed through the recapitulation and stood up as if he were pushing the piano away from him, and felt so desperate to talk positively about music that he began another lecture, taking the first movement of Beethoven's *Ninth* to demonstrate the processes of symphonic breakdown and renewal. As the students grew more visibly impatient he felt as if he'd lost all his grasp of music, even when he realized that he'd already given them this lecture. "Sorry, I know you've heard it all before," he said with an attempt at lightness.

It was his only lecture that Friday. He couldn't face his colleagues, not when the loss of Heather seemed to be catching up with him all at once. There was a concert at the Free Trade Hall, but by the time he'd driven through the lunchtime traffic clogged with roadworks, the prospect of Brahms and early Schoenberg seemed to have nothing to do with him. Perhaps he was realizing at last how little he had to do with music. He drove on, past the Renaissance arcades of the Hall, past some witches dancing about for a camera crew outside the television studios, back home to Salford.

The road led him over the dark waters of the Irwell and under a gloomy bridge to the near edge of Salford. He had to stop for traffic lights, so sharply that the crumpled newspaper rustled. He wondered suddenly if as well as searching for a sign of Heather he'd been furtively alert for someone to replace her. He made himself look away from the paper, where his gaze was resting leadenly, and met the eyes of a woman who was waiting by the traffic lights.

Something in her look beneath her heavy silvered eyelids made his penis raise its head. She wasn't crossing the road, just standing under the red light, drumming silver fingernails on her hip in the tight black glossy skirt. Her face was small and pert beneath studiedly shaggy red hair that overhung the collar of her fur jacket. "Going my way?" he imagined her saying, and then, before he knew he meant to, he reached across the passenger seat and rolled the window down.

At once he felt absurd, aghast at himself. But she stepped toward the car, a guarded smile on her lips. "Which way are you going?" he said just loud enough for her to hear.

"Whichever way you want, love."

Now that she was close he saw that she was more heavily made up than he'd realized. He felt guilty, vulnerable, excited. He fumbled for the catch on the door and watched her slip into the passenger seat, her fishnet thighs brushing together. He had to clear his throat before he could ask "How much?"

"Thirty for the usual, more for specials. I won't be hurt, but I'll give you some discipline if that's what you like."

"That won't be necessary, thank you."

"Only asking, love," she said primly, shrugging at his curtness. "I reckon you'll still want to go to my place."

She directed him through Salford, to a back street near Peel Park. At least this wasn't happening in Manchester itself, where the chief constable was a lay preacher, where booksellers were sent to jail for selling books like *Scared Stiff* and the police had seized *The Big Red One* on videocassette because the title was suggestive, yet he couldn't quite believe that it was happening at all. Children with scraped knees played in the middle of the street under clotheslines stretched from house to house; when at first they wouldn't get out of the way, Kilbride was too embarrassed to sound his horn. Women in brick passages through pairs of terraced houses stared at him and muttered among themselves as he parked the car and followed the silvered woman into her house.

Beyond the pink front door a staircase led upward, but she opened a door to the left of the stairs and let him into the front room. This was wedge-shaped, half of an already small room that had been divided diagonally by a partition. A sofa stood at the broad end, under the window, facing a television and videorecorder at the other. "This is it, love," the woman said. "Don't be shy, come in."

Kilbride made himself step forward and close the door behind him. The pelt of dark red wallpaper made the room seem even smaller. Presumably there was a kitchen beyond the partition, for a smell of boiled sprouts hung in the air. The sense of invading someone else's domesticity aggravated his panic. "Relax now, love, you're safe with me," the woman murmured as she drew the curtains and deftly pulled out the rest of the sofa to make it into a bed.

He watched numbly while she unfolded a red blanket that was draped over the back of the sofa and spread it over the bed. He could just leave, he wasn't obliged to stay—but when she patted the bed, he seemed only able to sit beside her while she kicked off her shoes and hitched up her skirt to roll down her stockings. "Want to watch a video to get you in the mood?" she suggested.

"No, that isn't . . ." The room seemed to be growing smaller and hotter, which intensified the smell of sprouts. He watched her peel off the second stocking, but then the shouts of children made him glance nervously behind him at the curtains. She gave him an unexpected lopsided smile. "I know what *you* want," she said in the tone of a motherly waitress offering a child a cream cake. "You should've said."

She lifted a red curtain that had disguised an opening in the partition and disappeared behind it. Kilbride dug out his wallet hastily, though an inflamed part of his mind was urging him just to leave, and hunted for thirty pounds. The best he could do was twenty-seven or forty. He was damned if he would pay more than he'd been quoted. He crumpled the twenty-seven in his fist as she came back into the room.

She'd dressed up as a schoolgirl in gymslip and knee socks. "Thought as much," she said coyly. As she reached for the money she put one foot on the bed, letting her skirt ride up provocatively, and he saw that her pubic hair was dyed red, like her hair. The thought of thrusting himself into that graying crevice made him choke, red dimness and the smell of sprouts swelling in his head. He flung himself aside and threw the money behind her, to gain himself time. He fumbled open the inner door, then the outer, and fled into the street.

It was deserted. The women must have called in their children in case they overheard him and their neighbor. She'd thought when he glanced at the window that the children were attracting him, he thought furiously. He stalked to his car and drove away without looking back. What made it worse was that her instincts hadn't been entirely wrong, for now he found himself obsessively imagining Heather dressed as a schoolgirl. Once he had to stop the car in order to drag at the crotch of his clothes and give his stiffening penis room. Only the fear of crashing the car allowed him to interrupt the fantasy and drive home. He parked haphazardly, limped groaning upstairs to his flat, dashed into the bathroom and came violently before he could even masturbate.

It gave him no pleasure, it was too like being helpless. His penis remained pointlessly erect, until he was tempted to shove it under the cold tap, to get rid of his unfulfilling lust that was happier with fantasy than reality. Its lack of any purpose he could share or even admit to himself appalled him. At least now that it was satisfied, it wouldn't hinder his music.

He brewed himself a pot of strong coffee and took the manuscript books full of his score to the piano. He leafed through them, hoping for a spark of pleasure, then he played through them. When he came to the end he slammed his elbows on the keyboard and buried his face in his hands while the discord died away.

He thought of playing some Ravel to revive his pianistic technique, or listening to a favorite record, Monteverdi or Tallis, whose remoteness he found moving and inspiring. But now early music seemed out of date, later music seemed overblown or arid. He'd felt that way at Heather's age, but then his impatience had made him creative: he'd completed several movements for piano. Couldn't he feel that way again? He stared at the final page of his symphony, Kilbride's Unfinished, The Indistinguishable, Symphony No. -1, Symphony of a Thousand Cuts, not so much a chamber symphony as a pisspot symphony. . . . Twilight gathered in the room, and the notes on the staves began to wriggle like sperm. When it was too dark to see he played through the entire score from memory. The notes seemed to pile up around him like the dust of decades. He reached out blindly for the score and tore the pages one by one into tiny pieces.

He sat for hours in the dark, experiencing no emotion at all. He seemed to be seeing himself clearly at last, a middle-aged nonentity with a yen for women half his age or even younger, a musical pundit with no ability to compose music, no right to talk about those who had. No wonder Heather's parents had forbidden him to visit her or call her. He'd needed her admiration to help him fend off the moment when he confronted himself, he realized. The longer he sat in the dark, the more afraid he was to turn on the light and see how alone he was. He flung himself at the lightswitch, grabbed handfuls of the torn pages and stuffed them into the kitchen bin. "Pathetic," he snarled, at them or at himself.

It was past midnight, he saw. He would never be able to sleep: the notes of his symphony were gathering in his head, a cumulative discord. There was nowhere to go for company at this hour except night-clubs, to meet people as lonely and sleepless as himself. But he could talk to someone, he realized, someone who wouldn't see his face or know anything about him. He tiptoed downstairs into the chilly windswept night and snatched the newspaper out of the car.

Alone and desperate? Call us now before you do anything else . . . The organization was called Renewal of Life, with a phone number on the far side of Manchester. The distance made him feel safer. If he didn't like what he heard at first he needn't even answer.

The phone rang for so long that he began to think he had a wrong number. Or perhaps they were busy helping people more desperate than he. That made him feel unreasonably selfish, but he'd swallowed so much self-knowledge today that the insight seemed less than a footnote. He was clinging stubbornly to the receiver when the ringing broke off halfway through a phrase, and a female voice said "Yes?"

She sounded as if she'd just woken up. It *was* a wrong number, Kilbride thought wildly, and felt compelled to let her know that it was. "Renewal of Life?" he stammered.

"Yes, it is." Her voice was louder, as if she was wakening further, or trying to. "What can we do for you?"

She must have nodded off at her post, he thought. That made her seem more human, but not necessarily more reassuring. "I—I don't know."

"You've got to do something for me first and then I'll tell you."

She sounded fully awake now. Some of what he'd taken for drowsiness might have been something else, still there in her voice: a hint of lazy coyness that could have implied a sexual promise. "What is it?" he said warily.

"Swear you won't hang up on me."

"All right, I swear." He waited for her to tell him what was being offered, then felt absurd, embarrassed into talking. "I don't know what I was expecting when I called your number. I'm just at a low ebb, that's all, male menopause and all that. Just taking stock of myself and not finding much. Maybe this call wasn't such a good idea. Maybe I need someone who's known me for a while to show me if there's anything I missed about myself."

"Well, tell me about yourself then." When he was silent she said quickly, "At least tell me where you are."

"Manchester."

"Alone in the big city. That can't be doing you any good. What you need is a few days in the country, away from everything. You ought to come here, you'd like it. Yes, why don't you? You'd be here for the dawn."

He was beginning to wonder how young she was. He felt touched and amused by her inexpertness, yet the hint of an underlying promise seemed stronger than ever. "Just like that?" he said laughing. "I can't do that. I'm working tomorrow."

"Come on Saturday, then. You don't want to be alone at the weekend, not the way you're feeling. Get away from all the streets and factories and pollution and see May in with us."

Sunday was May Day. He was tempted to go wherever she was inviting him—not the area to which the telephone number referred, apparently. "What sort of organization are you, exactly?"

"We just want to keep life going. That's what you wanted when you rang." She sounded almost offended, and younger than ever. "You wouldn't have to tell us anything about yourself you didn't want to or join in anything you didn't like the sound of."

Perhaps because he was talking to her in the middle of the night, that sounded unambiguously sexual. "If I decide to take you up on that I can call you then, can't I?"

"Yes, and then I'll give you directions. Call me even if you think you don't want to, all right? Swear."

"I swear," Kilbride said, unexpectedly glad to have committed himself, and could think of nothing else to say except, "Good night." As soon as he'd replaced the receiver he realized that he should have found out her name. He felt suddenly exhausted, pleasantly so, and crawled into bed. He imagined her having been in bed while she was talking to him, then he saw her as a tall slim schoolgirl with a short skirt and long bare thighs and Heather's face. That gave him a pang of guilt, but the next moment he was asleep.

The morning paper was full of oppression and doom. He scanned the personal columns while he waited for his car engine to rouse itself. He no longer expected to find a message from Heather, but there was no sign of the Renewal of Life either.

That was his day for teaching pianistic technique. Some of his students played as if passion could replace technique, others played so carefully it seemed they were determined not to own up to emotion. He was able to show them where they were going wrong without growing impatient with them or the job, and their respect for him seemed to have returned. Perhaps on Tuesday he'd feel renewed enough to teach his other classes enthusiastically, he thought, wondering if the printers had omitted the Renewal of Life from today's paper by accident.

One student lingered at the end of the last class. "Would you give me your opinion of this?" She blushed as she sat down to play, and he realized she'd composed the piece herself. It sounded like a study of her favorite composers—cascades of Debussy, outbursts of Liszt, a token tinkle of Messiaen—but there was something of herself too, unexpected harmonic ideas, a kind of aural punning. He remarked on all that, and she went out smiling with her boy friend, an uninspired violinist who was blushing now on her behalf. She had a future, Kilbride thought, flattered that she'd wanted his opinion. Maybe someday he'd be cited as having encouraged her at the start of her career.

A red sky was flaring over the turrets and gables of Manchester. Was he really planning to drive somewhere out there beyond the sunset? The more he recalled the phone conversation, the more dreamlike it seemed. He drove home and made sure he had yesterday's paper, and thought of calling the number at once—but the voice had said Saturday, and to call now seemed like tempting fate. The success of the day's teaching had dampened his adventurousness; he felt unexpectedly satisfied. When he went to bed he had no idea if he would phone at all.

Birdsong wakened him as the sky began to pale. He lay there feeling lazy as the dawn. He needn't decide yet about the weekend, it was too early—and then he realized that it wasn't, not at all. He wriggled out of bed and dialed the number he'd left beside the phone. Before he could even hear the bell at the other end a voice said, "Renewal of Life."

It was brisker than last time. It had the same trace of a Lancashire accent, the broad vowels, but Kilbride wasn't sure if it was the same voice. "I promised to call you today," he said.

"We've been waiting. We're looking forward to having you. You are coming, aren't you?"

Perhaps the voice sounded different only because she had clearly not just woken up. "Are you some kind of religious organization?" he said.

She laughed as if she knew he was joking. "You won't have to join in anything unless you want to, but whatever you enjoy, you'll find it here."

She could scarcely be more explicit without risking prosecution, he thought. "Tell me how to get to you," he said, all at once fully awake.

Her directions would take him into Lancashire. He bathed and dressed quickly, fueled the car and set out, wondering if her route was meant to take him through the streets and factories and pollution the first call had deplored. Beyond the city center streets of small shops went on for miles, giving way at last to long high almost featureless mills, to warehouses that made him think of terraced streets whose side openings had been bricked up. Their shadows shrank back into them as the sun rose, but he felt as if he would never be out of the narrow streets under the grubby sky.

At last the road began to climb beyond the crowding towns. Lush green fields spread around him, shrinking pools shone through the half-drowned grass. The grimy clouds were washed clean and hung along the horizon, and then the sky was clear. He drove for miles without meeting another car on the road. He was alone with the last day of April, the leaves opening more confidently, hovering in swarms in all the trees.

Half an hour or so into the countryside he began to wonder how much farther his destination was. "Drive until you get to the Jack in the Green," she'd said, "and ask for us." He'd taken that to be a pub, or was it a location or a monument? Even if he never found it, the sense of renewal he had already derived from the day in the open would be worth the journey. The road was climbing again, between banks of ferns almost as large as he was. He'd find a vantage point and stop for a few minutes, he thought, and then the road led over a crest and showed him the factory below.

The sight was as unexpected as it was disagreeable. At least the factory was disused, he saw as the car sped down the slope. All the windows in the long dull-red facade had fallen in, and so had part of the roof. Once there had been several chimneys, but only one remained, and even that was wobbling. When he stared at it, it appeared to shift further. He had to strain his eyes, for something like a mist hung above the factory, a darkening of the air, a blurring of outlines. The chimney looked softened, as did all the window openings. That must be an effect of the air here in the valley—the air smelled bad, a cold, slightly rotten stench—but the sight made him feel quiverish, particularly around his groin. He trod hard on the accelerator, to be out from among the drab wilting fields.

The car raced up into the sunlight. He blinked the dazzle out of his eyes and saw the village below him, on the far side of the crest from the factory. A few streets of limestone cottages led off the main road and sloped down to a village green overlooked by an inn and a small church. Several hundred yards beyond the green, a forest climbed the rising slopes. Compared with the sagging outlines of the ruin, the clarity of the sunlit cottages and their flowery gardens was almost too intense. His chest tightened as he drove past them to the green.

He parked near the inn and stared at its sign, the Jack in the Green, a jovial figure clothed and capped with grass. He hadn't felt so nervous since stage fright had seized him at his first recital. When he stepped out of the car, the slam of the door unnerved him. A dog barked, a second dog answered, but there was no other sound, not even of children. He felt as if the entire village was waiting to see what he would do.

A tall slim tree lay on the green. Presumably it was to be a maypole, for an axe gleamed near it in the grass, but its branches had still to be lopped. Whoever had carried it here might be in the inn, he thought, and turned toward the building. A woman was watching him from the doorway.

She sauntered forward as his gaze met hers. She was tall and moderately plump, with a broad friendly face, large gray eyes, a small nose, a wide very pink mouth. As she came up to him, the tip of her tongue flickered over her lips. "Looking for someone?" she said.

"Someone I spoke to this morning."

She smiled and raised her eyebrows. Her large breasts rose and fell under the clinging green dress that reached just below her knees. He smelled her perfume, wild and sweet. "Was it you?" he said.

"Would you like it to be?"

He would happily have said yes, except that he wondered what choices he might be rejecting. He felt his face redden, and then she touched his wrist with one cool hand. "No need to decide yet. When you're ready. You can stay at the Jack if you like, or with us."

"Us?"

"Father'll be out dancing."

He couldn't help feeling that she meant to reassure him. There was an awkward pause until she said, "You're wondering what you're supposed to do."

"Well, yes."

"Anything you like. Relax, look around, go for a walk. Tomorrow's the big day. Have some lunch or a drink. Do you want to work up an appetite?"

"By all means."

"Come over here then and earn yourself a free lunch."

Could he have been secretly dreaming that she meant to take him home now? He followed her to the maypole, laughing inwardly and rather wildly at himself. "See what you can do about stripping that," she said, "while I bring you a drink. Beer all right?"

"Fine," he said, reflecting that working on the maypole would be a small price to pay for what he was sure he'd been led to expect. "By the way, what's your name?"

"Sadie." With just the faintest straightening of her smile she added, "Mrs. Thomas."

She could be divorced or a widow. He picked up the axe, to stop himself brooding. It was lighter than he expected, but very sharp. When he grasped a branch at random and chopped experimentally at it, he was able to sever it with two blows.

"Not bad for a music teacher," he murmured, and set to work systematically, starting at the thin end of the tree. Perhaps he should have begun at the other, for after the first dozen or so branches the lopping grew harder. By the time Sadie Thomas brought him a pint of strong ale, his arms were beginning to ache. As she crossed the green to him he looked up, wiping sweat from his forehead in a gesture he regretted immediately, and found that he had an audience, several men sitting on a bench outside the inn.

They were Kilbride's age, or younger. He couldn't quite tell, for their faces looked slack, blurred by indolence—pensioned off, he thought, and remembered the factory. Nor could he read their expressions, which might be hostile or simply blank. He was tempted to step back from the maypole and offer them the job—it was their village, after all—but then two of them mopped their foreheads deliberately, and he wondered if they were mocking him. He chopped furiously at the tree, and didn't look up until he'd severed the last branch.

A burst of applause, which might have been meant ironically, greeted his laying down the axe. He felt suddenly that the phone conversations and the rest of it had been a joke at his expense. Then Sadie Thomas squatted by him, her green skirt unveiling her strong thighs, and took his hands to help him up. "You've earned all you can eat. Come in the Jack, or sit out if you like."

All the men stood up in case he wanted to sit on the bench. Some looked resentful, but all the same, they obviously felt he had the right. "I'll sit outside," he said, and wondered why the men exchanged glances as they moved into the inn.

He was soon to learn why. A muscular woman with cropped gray hair brought out a table which she placed in front of him and loaded with a plateful of cheese, a loaf and a knife and another tankard of ale, and then Sadie came to him. "When you're done eating, would you do one more thing for us?"

His arms were trembling from stripping the maypole; he was only just able to handle the knife. "Nothing strenuous this time," she said reassuringly. "We just need a judge, someone who isn't from around here. You've only to sit and choose."

"All right," Kilbride said, then felt as if his willingness to please had got the better of him. "What am I judging?"

She gave him a coy look that reminded him of the promise he thought he'd heard in the telephone voice. "Ah, that'd be telling."

Perhaps the promise would be broken if he asked too many questions, especially in public. It still excited him enough to be worth his suffering some uncertainty, not least over how many of the villagers were involved in the Renewal of Life. His hands steadied as he finished off the cheese, and he craned to watch Sadie as she hurried into the village, to the small schoolhouse in the next street. He realized what they must want him to judge at this time of the year as the young girls come marching from the school and onto the green.

They lined up in front of the supine maypole and faced him, their hands clasped in front of their stomachs. Some gazed challengingly at him, but most were shy, or meant to seem so. He couldn't tell if they knew that besides casting their willowy shadows toward him, the sun was shining through their uniforms, displaying silhouettes of their bodies. "Go closer if you like," Sadie said in his ear.

He stood up before his stiffening penis could hinder him, and stroke awkwardly toward the girls. They were thirteen or fourteen years old, the usual age for a May Queen, but some of them looked disconcertingly mature. He had to halt a few yards short of them, for while embarrassment was keeping his penis more or less under control, every step rubbed its rampant tip against his flies. Groaning under his breath, he tried to look only at their faces. Even that didn't subdue him, for one girl had turned her head partly away from him and was regarding him through her long dark eyelashes in a way that made him intensely aware of her handfuls of breasts, her long silhouetted legs. "This one," he said in a loud hoarse voice, and stretched out a shaky hand to her.

When she stepped forward he was afraid she would take his hand in front of all of them. But she walked past him, flashing him a sidelong smile, as the line of young girls broke up, some looking relieved, some petulant. Kilbride pretended to gaze across the green until his penis subsided. When he turned, he found that several dozen people had gathered while he was judging.

The girl he'd chosen had joined Sadie. Belatedly he saw how alike they were. Even more disconcerting than that and silent arrival of the villagers was the expression he glimpsed on Sadie's face as she glanced at her daughter, an expression that seemed to combine pride with a hint of dismay. The schoolgirls were dispersing in groups, murmuring and giggling. Some of the villagers came forward to thank Kilbride, so hesitantly that he wasn't sure what he was being thanked for; the few men who did so behaved as if they'd been prodded into approaching him. Close up their faces looked flabbier than ever, almost sexless.

Sadie turned back from leading away her daughter to point along the street behind the inn. "You are staying with us, aren't you? We're at number three. Dinner's at seven. What are you going to do in the meantime?"

"Walk, I should think. Find my way around."

"Make yourself at home," said a stocky bespectacled woman, and her ringleted stooping companion added, "Anything you want, just ask."

He wanted to think, though perhaps not too deeply. He sat on the bench as the shadows of the forest crept toward the green. He was beginning to think he knew why he'd been brought here, but wasn't he just indulging a fantasy he was able at last to admit to himself? He stood up abruptly, having thought of a question he needed to ask.

The inn was locked, and presumably he wasn't meant to go to Sadie's before seven. He strolled through the village in the afternoon light, flowers in the small packed gardens glowing sullenly. People gossiping outside the cottages hushed as he approached, then greeted him heartily. He couldn't ask them. Even gazing in the window of the only shop, a corner cottage whose front room was a general store, he felt ill at ease.

He was nearly back at his starting point after ten minutes' stroll when he noticed the surgery, a cottage with a doctor's brass plaque on the gatepost, in the same row as Sadie's. The neat wizened gnomish man who was killing insects on a rockery with precise bursts from a spray bottle must be the doctor. He straightened up as Kilbride hesitated at the gate. "Is there something I can do for you?" he said in a thin high voice.

"Are you part of the Renewal of Life?"

"I certainly hope so."

Kilbride felt absurd, though the doctor didn't seem to be mocking him. "I mean, are all of you here in the village part of that?"

"We're a very close community." The doctor gave a final lethal squirt and stood up. "So don't feel you aren't welcome if anyone seems unfriendly."

That was surely a cue for the question, if Kilbride could frame it carefully enough. "Am I on my own? That's to say, was anyone else asked to come here this weekend?"

The doctor looked straight at him, pale eyes gleaming. "You're the one."

"Thank you," Kilbride said and moved away, feeling lightheaded. Passing the church, where a stone face with leaves sprouting from its mouth and ears grinned from beneath the steep roof, he strolled toward the woods. The doctor's reply had seemed unequivocal, but questions began to swarm in Kilbride's mind as he wandered through the fading light and shade. Whether because he felt like an outsider or was expected to be quite the opposite, he skulked under the trees until he saw the inn door open. As he returned to the village, a hint of the stench from the factory met him.

The bar was snug and darkly paneled. The flames of a log fire danced in reflections on the walls, where photographs of Morris dancers hung under the low beams. Kilbride sat and drank and eventually chatted to two slow men. At seven he made his way to Sadie Thomas' house, and realized that he couldn't remember a word of the conversation at the pub.

Sadie's cottage had a red front door that held a knocker in its brass teeth. When Kilbride knocked, a man came to the door. He was taller and bulkier than Kilbride, with a sullen almost circular face. A patchy mustache straggled above his drooping lips. He stared with faint resentment at the suitcase Kilbride had brought from the car. "Just in time," he muttered, and as an afterthought before Kilbride could step over the threshold, "Bob Thomas."

When he stuck out his hand Kilbride made to shake it, but the man was reaching for the suitcase. He carried it up the steep cramped stairs, then stumped down to usher Kilbride into the dining kitchen, a bright room the width of the house, its walls printed with patterns of blossoms. Sadie and her daughter were sitting at a round table whose top was a single slice of oak. They smiled at Kilbride, the daughter more shyly, and Sadie dug a ladle into a steaming earthenware pot. "Sit there," Bob Thomas said gruffly when Kilbride made to let him have the best remaining chair.

Sadie heaped his plate with hotpot, mutton stewed with potatoes, and he set about eating as soon as seemed polite, to cover the awkwardness they were clearly all feeling. "Good meat," he said.

"Not from around here," Sadie said as if it was important for him to know.

"Because of the factory, you mean?"

"Aye, the factory," Bob Thomas said with unexpected fierceness. "You know about that, do you?"

"Only what I gathered over the phone—I mean, when I was told to get away from factories."

Bob Thomas gazed at him and fingered his mustache as if he were trying to conjure more of it into existence. Kilbride froze inside himself, wondering if he'd said too much. "Daddy doesn't like to talk about the factory," the daughter murmured as she raised her fork delicately to her lips, "because of what it did to him and all the men."

"Margery!"

Kilbride couldn't have imagined that a father could make his child's name sound so like a curse. Margery flinched and gazed at the ceiling, and Kilbride was searching for a way to save the conversation when Margery said, "Did you notice?"

She was talking to him. Following her gaze, he saw that the rounded beam overhead seemed more decorative than supportive. "It's a maypole," he realized.

"Last year's."

"She sounded prouder than he could account for. "You believe in keeping traditions alive, then," he said to Bob Thomas.

"They'll keep theirselves alive whatever I believe in, I reckon."

"I mean," Kilbride floundered on, "that's why you stay here, why you don't move away."

Bob Thomas took a deep breath and stared furiously at nothing. "We stay here because family lived here. The factory came when we needed the work. Him who owned it was from here, so we thought he was doing us a kindness, but he poisoned us instead. We found work up the road and closed him down. Poisoned we may be, we'll not be driven out on top of it. We'll do what we have to to keep place alive."

It was clearly an unusually sustained speech for him, and it invited no response. Kilbride was left wondering if any of it referred to himself. Sadie and her daughter kept up the conversation during the rest of the meal, and Kilbride listened intently, to their voices rather than to their words. "Father isn't like this really, it's just the time of year. Don't let him put you off staying," Sadie said to Kilbride as she cleared away the plates.

"Swear you won't," Margery added.

He did so at once, because now he was sure he'd spoken to her on the phone at least the first time. Bob Thomas lowered his head bull-like, but said nothing. His inertia seemed to sink into the house; there was little to say, and less to do—the Thomases had neither a television nor a radio, not even a telephone as far as Kilbride could see. He went up to his bedroom as soon as he reasonably could.

He stood for a while at the window that was let into the low ceiling, which followed the angle of the roof, and watched the moon rise over the woods. When he tired of that he lay on the bed in the small green room and wished he'd brought something to read. He was loath to go out of the room again, in case he met Bob Thomas. Eventually he ventured to the bathroom and then retired to bed, to watch an elongating lozenge of moonlight inch down the wall above his feet. He was asleep before it reached him.

At first he thought the voices were calling him, dozens of voices just outside his room. They belonged to all the girls who had paraded for his judgment on the green, and now they were here to collect a consolation prize. They must be crowded together on the steep staircase—he'd have no chance of escaping until they had all had a turn, even if he wanted to. Besides, his penis was swelling so uncontrollably that he was helpless; already it was thicker than his leg, and still growing. If he didn't answer the voices the girls would crowd into the room and fall on him, but he was unable to make any sound at all. Then he realized that they couldn't be calling him, because nobody in the village knew his name.

The shock wakened him. The voices were still calling. He shoved himself into a sitting position, almost banging his head on the ceiling, and peered wildly about. The voices weren't calling to him, nor were they in the house. He swung his feet off the bed, wincing as a floorboard creaked, and gazed out of the window.

The moon was almost full. At first it seemed to show him only slopes coated with moonlight. Nothing moved except a few slow cows in a field. Not only the cows but the field were exactly the color of the moon. The woods looked carved out of ivory, so still that the shifting of branches sent a shiver through him. Then he saw that the trees which were stirring were too far apart for a wind to be moving them.

He raised the window and craned out to see. He

stared at the edge of the woods until the trunks began to flicker with his staring. The voices were in the woods, he was sure. Soon he glimpsed movement in the midst of the trees, on a hillock that rose above the canopy of branches. Two figures, a man and a woman, appeared there hand in hand. They embraced and kissed, and at last their heads separated, peering about at the voices. The next moment they disappeared back into the woods.

They were early, Kilbride thought dreamily. They ought to wait until the eleventh, May Day of the old calendar, the first day of the Celtic summer. In those days they would be blowing horns as well as calling to one another, to ensure that nobody got lost as they broke branches and decorated them with hawthorn flowers. Couples would fall silent if they wanted to be left alone. He wondered suddenly whether he was meant to be out there—whether they would be calling him if they knew his name.

He opened the bedroom door stealthily and tiptoed onto the tiny landing. The doors of the other bedrooms were ajar. His heart quickened as he paced to the first and looked in. Both rooms were empty. He was alone in the cottage, and he suspected that he might be alone in the village.

Surely he was meant to be in the woods. Perhaps tradition forbade anyone to come and waken him, perhaps he had to be wakened by the calling in the trees. He closed his bedroom window against the stench that seeped down from the factory, then he dressed and hurried downstairs.

The front door wasn't locked. Kilbride closed it gently behind him and made for the pavement, which was tarred with shadow. Less than a minute's walk through the deserted village took him into the open, by the church. Though only the stone face with leaves in its ears and mouth seemed to be watching him, he felt vulnerable in the moonlight as he strode across the green, past the supine maypole, and into the field that was bordered by the woods. Once he started, for another stone face with vegetation dangling from its mouth was staring at him over a gate, but it was a cow. All the way from the cottage to the woods, he heard voices calling under the moon.

He hesitated at the edge of the trees, where the shadow of a cloud crept over bleached knuckly roots. The nearest voices were deep in the woods. Kilbride made his way among the trees, his feet sinking into leaf-mold. He stopped and held his breath whenever he trod on a twig, however muffled the sound was, or whenever he glimpsed movement among the pale trunks etched intricately with darkness. All the same, he nearly stumbled over the couple in the secluded glade, having taken them for moving shadows.

Kilbride dodged behind a tree and covered his mouth while his breathing grew calmer. He didn't want to watch the couple, but he dared not move until he could measure his paces. The woman's skirt was pushed above her waist, the man's trousers were around his ankles; Kilbride could see neither of their faces. The man was tearing at the mossy ground with his hands as his buttocks pumped wildly. Then his shoulders sagged, and the woman's hands cupped his face in a comforting gesture. The man recommenced thrusting at her, more and more desperately, and Kilbride was suddenly convinced that they were Bob and Sadie Thomas. But the man's head jerked back, his face distorted with frustration, and Kilbride saw that he was no more than twenty years old.

In that moment a good deal became clear to Kilbride. What was happening in the woods wasn't so much a celebration of Spring as a desperate ritual. Now he saw how total the effect of the pollution by the factory had been, and he realized that he hadn't seen or heard any young children in the village. He hid behind the tree, his face throbbing with embarrassment, and tip-toed away as soon as he thought he could do so unnoticed. All the way out of the woods he was afraid of intruding on another scene like the one he'd witnessed. He was halfway across the moonlit field, and almost running for fear that someone would see him and suspect that he knew, when he realized fully what they must expect of him.

He stood in the shadow of the inn to think. He could fetch his suitcase and drive away while there was nobody to stop him—but why should he fear that they would? On the contrary, the men seemed anxious to see the last of him. He wouldn't be driven out, he promised himself. It wasn't just that he'd been invited, it was that someone needed him. All the same, back in the green bedroom he lay awake for hours, wondering when they would send for him, listening to the distant voices calling in the dark. They sounded plaintive to him now, almost hopeless. It was close to dawn before he fell asleep.

This time his dreams weren't sexual. He was at a piano in an empty echoing concert hall, his fingers ranging deftly over the keys, drawing music from them that he'd never heard before, music calm as a lingering sunset then powerful as a mountain storm. The hands on the keys were his hands as a young man, he saw. He looked for pen and paper, but there was none. He'd remember the music until he could write it down, he told himself. He must remember, because this music was the whole point of his life. Then a spotlight blazed into his eyes, which jerked open, and the dream and the music were gone.

It was the sun, shining through the window in the roof. He turned away from it and tried to grasp the dream. Sunlight groped over his back and displayed itself on the wall in front of him. Eventually he gave up straining, in the hope that the memory would return unbidden. The silence made itself felt then. Though it must be midday at least, the village was silent except for the lowing of a cow and the jingle of bells. The sound of bells drew him to the window.

The maypole was erect in the middle of the green. The villagers were standing about on the grass. The young women wore short white dresses, and garlands in their hair. Half a dozen Morris dancers in uniform—

knee-breeches, clogs, bracelets of bells at their wrists—
stood near the inn, drinking beer. At the far side of
the green were two empty seats. Kilbride blinked sleep-
ily toward these, and then he realized that one of them
must be his—that the whole village was waiting for
him.

They might have wakened him, then. Presumably
they had no special costume for him. He bathed hastily, dressed and hurried out. As he reached the green,
the villagers turned almost in unison to him.

The Morris man who came over to him proved to be
Bob Thomas. Kilbride found the sight of him in costume disconcerting in a variety of ways. "Ready, are
you?" Bob Thomas said gruffly. "Come on, sit you
down." He led Kilbride to the left-hand of the chairs,
both of which were made of new wood nailed together
somewhat roughly. As soon as Kilbride was seated,
two of the garlanded girls approached him with arm-
fuls of vines, wrapping them around his body and then
around his limbs, which they left free to move, to his
relief. Then Margery came forward alone and sat by
him.

She wasn't wearing much under the long white dress.
As she passed in front of him, shyly averting her eyes,
her nipples and the shadows around them appeared
clearly through the linen. Kilbride gave her a smile
which was meant to reassure her but which he suspected might look lecherous. He turned away as the
girls approached once more, bearing a crown composed of blossoms on a wiry frame, which they placed
on Margery's head.

The festivities began then, and Kilbride was able to
devote himself to watching. When Sadie Thomas
brought him and Margery a trayful of small cakes, he
found he was ravenous. The more he ate, the stranger
and more appealing the taste seemed: a mixture of
meat, apple, onion, thyme, rosemary, sugar and another herbal taste he couldn't put a name to. Margery
ate a token cake and left the rest for him.

The young girls danced around the maypole, holding onto ribbons that dangled from the tip. The patterns of the dance and the intricate weaving of the ribbons gradually elaborated themselves in Kilbride's mind, a kind of crystallizing of the display on the green, the grass reaching for the sunlight, the dazzling white dresses exposing glimpses of bare thighs, the girls glancing at himself and Margery with expressions he was less and less sure of. How long had they been dancing? It felt like hours to him and yet no time at all, as though the spring sunlight had caught the day and wouldn't let it go.

At last the girls unweaved the final pattern, and the Morris dancers strode onto the green. Bob Thomas wasn't the leader, Kilbride saw, feeling unaccountably relieved. The men lined up face to face in two rows and began to dance slowly and deliberately, brandishing decorated staves two feet long, which they rapped together at intervals. The patterns of their turns and confrontations seemed even more intricate than the maypole dance; the muscularity of the dancing made his penis feel thickened, though it wasn't erect. The paths the dancers described were solidifying in his mind, strengthening him. He realized quite calmly that the cakes had been drugged.

The shadows of the Morris men grew longer as he watched, shadows that merged and parted and leapt toward the audience of villagers on the far side of the green. Shouldn't shadows be the opposite of what was casting them? he thought, and seemed unable to look away from them until the question was resolved. He was still pondering when the dancing ended. The shadows appeared to continue dancing for a moment longer. Then the Morris men clashed their staves together and danced away toward the nearest field.

Kilbride watched bemused as all the males of the village followed them. Several boys and young men glared at him, and he realized that his time was near. Led by the Morris dancers, the men and boys disappeared over the slope toward a green sunset. The jingling of bells faded, and then there was only the sound of birdsong in the woods behind him.

He supposed he ought to turn to Margery, but his head was enormous and cumbersome. He gazed at the dimming of the green, which felt like peace, imperceptibly growing. His awareness that Sadie and another woman were approaching wasn't enough to make him lift his head. When they took hold of his arms he rose stiffly to his feet and stood by the chair, his body aching from having sat so long, while they unwound the vines from him. Then they led him away from Margery, past the maypole and its willowy garlands, past the clods the Morris dancers' heels had torn out of the ground. The women beside the green parted as he reached them, their faces expressionless, and he saw that Sadie and her companion were leading him to the church.

They led him through the small bare porch and opened the inner door. Beyond the empty pews the altar was heaped with flowers. A few yards in front of the altar, a mattress and pillows lay on the stone floor. The women ushered Kilbride to the mattress and lowered him onto it, so gently that he felt he was sinking like an airborne seed. They walked away from him side by side without looking back, and closed the doors behind them.

The narrow pointed windows darkened gradually as he lay waiting. The outlines of pews sank into the gathering dark. The last movements he'd seen, the women's buttocks swaying as they retreated down the aisle, filled his mind and his penis. His erection felt large as the dark, yet not at all peremptory. He had almost forgotten where he was and why he was waiting when he heard the porch door open.

The inner door opened immediately after. He could just see the night outside, shaped by the farther doorway. Against the outer darkness stood two figures in white dresses. Their heads touched to whisper, and then the slimmer figure ventured hesitantly forward.

Kilbride pushed himself easily to his feet and went to meet her. He hadn't reached her when her companion stepped back and closed the inner door. A moment later the porch door closed. Kilbride paced forward, feeling his way along the ends of pews, and as he gained the last he made out the white dress glimmering in front of him. He reached out and took her hand.

He felt her stiffen so as not to flinch, heard her draw a shaky breath. Then she relaxed, or made herself relax, and let him lead her toward the altar. Though the dark had virtually blinded him, his other senses were unusually acute; the warmth of her flesh seemed to course into him through her hand; her scent, more delicate than Sadie's, seemed overwhelming. He hardly needed to touch the pews to find his way back to the mattress. Once there he pushed her gently down on it and knelt beside her. The next moment she reached clumsily for him.

Her hands groped over his penis, fumbled at his flies. He stroked her hair, which was soft and electric, to soothe her, slow her down, but she dragged at his clothes all the more urgently. She'd eaten one of the cakes, he remembered; it might well have been aphrodisiac. He wriggled out of his clothes and left them on the stone floor, then he found her again in the dark.

Her hands closed around his swelling penis, her nervous fingers traced its length. He stroked her narrow shoulders, ran his hands down her slim body, over her firm buttocks, which tensed as his hands slid down her thighs and back up under her dress. She raised herself so that he could pull the dress over her head, then her hands returned to his penis, more confidently. When he stroked her buttocks, which were clad in thin nylon, she moaned under her breath.

As soon as he began to ease her knickers down she pulled them off and kicked them away, then grabbed his hand and closed her thighs around it. He ran his thumb through her wiry pubic bush, and her thighs opened wide to him. The lips of her sex closed over his fingers, gulping them moistly, more and more greedily, and then she curled herself catlike and took his penis in her mouth.

As her tongue flickered over the tip his erection grew suddenly urgent. His penis felt like pleasure incarnate, pleasure so intense it made the darkness blaze and throb behind his eyes. He put one hand under her chin to raise her head. Before he could move she climbed over him and lowered herself onto his penis, thrust him deep into her.

He couldn't tell if her cry expressed pain or pleasure: perhaps both. She pressed herself fiercely against him as her body grasped his penis moistly, sucking him deeper. Despite the urgency, each crescendo of sensation was longer and slower and more lingering. Her arms began to tremble with supporting herself above him, and he rolled her over and plunged himself as deep as he could. When he came, it seemed to last forever. He was intensely aware of her and of the church around them, and the slow flowering of himself seemed an act of worship of both.

As he dwindled within her, sensations fading slowly as a fire, he felt capable of embracing the world. All at once the path of his life, leading through it to this moment, grew clear to him. He viewed it with amused tolerance, even the music in his dream, which he remembered now. It wasn't that good, he saw, but it might be worth transcribing. Just now this sense of all-embracing peace was enough.

Or almost enough, for the girl was shivering. He could see the outline of her face now, in the moonlight that had begun to seep through the narrow windows. He lay beside her, his penis still in her, and stroked her face. "It was the first time for Renewal of Life too, wasn't it? I hope it achieves what it was meant to. I just want to tell you that I've never experienced anything like it, ever. Thank you, Margery."

He must be speaking more loudly then he intended, for his voice was echoing. He thought that was why she jerked away from him, lifted herself clear and fled along the glimmering aisle—and then he realized what he'd done to make her flee. He'd used her name, he'd betrayed that he knew who she was. They would never let him go now.

The notion of dying at this point in his life was unexpectedly calming. He felt as if he'd achieved the best he was capable of. He dressed unhurriedly and paced along the aisle, through stripes of moonlight. As he stepped into the darkness of the porch he heard a muffled sobbing outside the church. He hoped it wasn't Margery. He grasped the iron ring and opened the outer door.

The moon was high above the green. From the porch it looked impaled by the rearing maypole. The sound of renewed sobbing made him turn toward the inn. Several women had gathered outside, and in their midst was Margery, weeping behind her hands. Someone had draped a black coat over her white dress. Sadie Thomas glanced at Kilbride, regret and resignation and a hint of sympathy on her face, as the Morris men who had been waiting outside the church moved toward him.

Bob Thomas was leading them. For the first time Kilbride saw power in his eyes, though the man's face was expressionless. All the men had taken off their bracelets of bells, but they still carried the decorated staves two feet long they'd used in the dance. Their clogs made no sound on the grass. As Bob Thomas raised his stave above his head Kilbride closed his eyes and hoped it would be the last thing he would see or feel.

The first blow caught him across the shoulders. He gritted his teeth, squeezed his eyes tighter, prayed that the next blow wouldn't miss. But the stave struck him across his upper arm, agonizingly. He opened his teary eyes in protest and saw that the women had gone. He turned to Bob Thomas, to try belatedly to reason with him, and read on the man's face that they didn't mean to kill him—not yet, at any rate.

They began to beat Kilbride systematically, driving him away from the church, heading him off when he tried to dodge toward his car. He fled toward the woods, his bruised body aching like an open wound. With their clogs they wouldn't be able to keep up with him, he told himself, and once he was far enough out of reach he could double back to the car. But they drove him into the woods, where he tripped over roots in the dark. Soon he was limping desperately. When he saw that they were herding him toward a hut beside a glade he lurched aside, but they caught him at once. One shoved a stave between his legs and felled him in the glade.

Kilbride struggled around on the soft damp ground to face them. He was suddenly afraid that they meant to stamp him to death with their clogs, especially when four of them seized his arms and legs. As Bob Thomas stooped to him, jowls dangling, Kilbride realized that someone had followed the chase, a small figure in the shadows at the edge of the glade. "Never experienced anything like it, haven't you?" Bob Thomas muttered. "You've not experienced the half of what you're going to, my bucko."

Kilbride tried to wrench himself free as he heard metallic sounds in the shadows, saw the glint of a knife. Bob Thomas moved aside as the doctor came forward, carrying his bag. He might never have seen Kilbride before, his wizened face was so impassive. "Our women make us feel small but our friend here won't, I reckon," Bob Thomas said and stood up, rubbing his hands. "We'll feed him and nurse him and keep him hidden safe, and comes Old May Day we'll have our own Queen of the May."

THE TOUCH

by Wayne Allen Sallee

Wayne Allen Sallee is the main maniac of the small press horror field with, at latest count (his), 552 poems and short stories accepted for publication. His work seems to appear in virtually all of the current array of small press horror publications, as well as in countless literary magazines and outlaw poetry journals. Even granted that much of this involves short poems, it's an astonishing track record— the more so considering that Sallee was born on September 19, 1959 and has had relatively few years to get things rolling. A Chicago native, Sallee continues to lurk in the Windy City, where his current projects include a novel entitled The Holy Terror, *a 179-line poem entitled* Narcopolis, *and a stab at his autobiography,* Living Like the Fugitive.

The man who looked exactly like Rifkin, the crooked lawyer from the old Barney Miller show, scowled at Downs from his table next to the stage. When Downs returned the stare, the fat man stabbed violently at the bridge of his plastic-framed glasses, pushing them farther up his pudgy nose. Both arms of the glasses were held in place by black electrical tape. The fat man sat hunched over in his chair, three empty beer bottles lined up next to the one he was currently working on, his legs wrapped around the stubby chair legs so that his feet were nearly touching. The man looked like a fat seal minus the whiskers.

The house lights dimmed slightly as a new girl stepped onto the stage from behind a battered Peavy amplifier. Downs did not know her name because this was the first time he had come to The Touch. Downs always remembered the names of the girls at the places he'd been before. He didn't know why. Once, Downs had read a story about a serial killer talking to his unsuspecting next victim in a bar very much like this one, bragging that he always remembered people's eyes. The man the killer had met, who was drunk, did not know the killer was talking about his victims.

Downs always remembered the girls' names. He wondered if that was wrong.

The girl on stage danced to a song called "Rosanna." Maybe that was her name. Sometimes they would play songs like that. Downs knew that most girls played cassettes with dance mixes that they chose themselves. And that they would often play a song like The Knack's "My Sharona" or even Jan & Dean's "Linda." One time a black girl in one of the bars on Rush Street had danced to Little Richard's "Lucille." Now that had been a pip.

The song ended and the girl placed her left palm against the print-smudged mirror. She balanced herself as she took off her panties. Her panties were black.

Downs raised his empty bottle to signal the woman behind the bar to bring him another. The girl on stage was wearing a knee-length black negligee with butterfly patterns across it. One of the secretaries in the building where Downs worked wore pantyhose with the same pattern. The negligee was see-through and that was the reasoning behind taking her panties off after only one song. The girl knew that many men liked this better than seeing her prance in a g-string and garters. The other girls did that, and Downs knew that the quicker the girl on stage could arouse the men in the audience, the better chance she had of making more bucks. The girl's pubic hair was shaved slightly.

The waitress, scrawny and ugly, came to his table, setting the seven ounce Budweiser and a glass down noisily. Downs gave her a five. She asked if he would like to give her a tip and Downs pretended not to hear. She turned away, purposely upsetting the table and nearly causing the beer to spill.

Downs grabbed the bottle and took a long pull, drinking half. He pushed the glass aside. You can never be too sure in a place like this. The song ended and an unenthusiastic few clapped for all of three seconds.

One of the girls walked between Downs and the stage, the lone green light above the stage creating a slight aura around her, illuminating the blonde hairs on her arms.

She tried avoiding the man at the first table—the fat guy who had been giving Downs dirty looks—but came close enough for him to take a meaty swipe at her tush. The girl said a few words to him, but Downs couldn't make out what they were because of the music. The fat man cursed her loudly. His tone was slurred and coarse. The girl looked back toward the doors, toward the bouncers.

Maybe that was why the fat man had been glaring at him before. Maybe he was jealous or pissed that the girls had gone to Downs' table and not his own. And the guy looked as if he came in here often. Actually, only one girl had been to Downs' table in the hour he'd been at the lounge.

Her name was Crystal. At least, that was what she called herself. She had been dancing on the stage when Downs had first arrived.

Crystal's hair was bleached blonde and shoulder length. Downs could see the black roots when she bent closer to him. Her eyes were brown and she wore just enough makeup to keep her from looking like a mannequin. Crystal's lips were thin and Downs thought

that they looked that way because she spent a lot of
time fighting back tears.

When she smiled, Downs saw that her teeth were
perfect and white, but with a gap between the two
front teeth. This did not make her look bad.

Downs had seen a girl in Las Vegas who had been
gap-toothed, when he went there in January. She called
herself Raven, and, unlike the girls here in Chicago,
she did not have a bit of cellulite anywhere on her
body. The bar was the Palomino, run by an old guy
who looked like Captain Kangaroo, located on the old
Strip across from Jerry's Double Nuggett. Drinks were
two bucks and there was a variety of beer brands.
Downs had seen a girl on Rush Street who was a
dancer and had a caesarean scar across her stomach.

The first thing Crystal asked him when she sat down
was why he was wearing bands across his upper arms.
Everybody Downs met eventually asked him about his
armbands, especially now, in May, when he wore short-
sleeved shirts. Usually, the guys who didn't know just
thought they were sweatbands for exercising. It was
the girls who always voiced the question.

Downs had slight cerebral palsy. He had been wearing the bands since early 1985. The bands were held
together with Velcro, so that they were easily adjusted. Thin rubber balls within the fabric created
pressure points to help stop the pain. The doctor who
prescribed the bands said "alleviate" the pain. Downs
said *stop* the pain. A girlfriend of one of his room-
mates remarked that the bands weren't too noticeable.
Downs had said, oh yes, the bands were a big hit on
Oak Street Beach.

Downs simply told Crystal that the bands helped
strengthen his arms, not caring if saying that made the
girl think him macho. Considering where he was, Downs
didn't give a good goddamn what anybody thought.

He was in a two-bit clip joint on Front Street in
Fallon Ridge, Illinois on a Friday night drinking five-
dollar Buds in two gulps apiece. The only thing that
would make things any better, Downs thought sarcas-

tically, would be when the scrawny waitress started serving four-dollar Jolly Good colas after midnight. So the hell with what the girl thought. And the hell with what the fat man in front thought. The hell with what everybody in the whole goddamn world thought.

Crystal, who looked all of nineteen, with a kind of cheerful exuberance not shared by Chicago hookers, whose faces were often dulled by age or by drugs, or by repeated beatings from their Broadway and Leland pimps, or by constant harassment by the plainclothes detectives of the Belmont-Cragin district house for any reason whatsoever, even crossing in the middle of the street, Crystal, whose sharp jawline and thin lips etched by private tears when the lights went down and the dancing stopped, Crystal the hooker sitting at Downs' table, Crystal's eyes lit up as she realized she had what she thought was something in common with the guy that was sitting next to her, the guy fate had had a field day with.

Crystal told Downs that she once had a dog that was epileptic. Downs loved it, absolutely loved it! He was talking to a hooker about her crippled *dog*. This was simply wonderful.

The dog had always been having seizures and Crystal wanted to know if Downs' disease was, like, the same thing. He told her that it was not the same thing. Downs had known a girl in college who had epilepsy. She was twenty-four when, during a bad seizure in the middle of the night, her head smashed into the corner of her bureau. She bled to death. The actor William Holden died the same way. From a self-inflicted head wound. Only he was drunk.

Crystal then asked Downs if his hands and his arms were good enough to feel her breasts. If Downs would buy her a twelve dollar tom collins glass of ginger ale from the scrawny waitress waiting, vulture-like, in the shadows behind the bar, he could do just that. Feel her breasts. Touch the fabric of her blouse. Her white blouse with red stripes on the sleeves, matching her tight shorts. Downs could inadvertantly cop a feel from a dozen different women on any crowded day in the Loop. He could do this for free.

Downs could have said something clever like, "I'm on a budget," but he just told Crystal no, he wasn't interested. He wasn't even paying much attention as she left the table. Downs repressed the urge to say something nasty about her dog of bygone days.

The fat man at the first table motioned to Crystal and patted the empty chair next to him. She ignored him, walking past the table with her head in the air, crossing across the length of the bar to a door at the far end of the room. As she opened the door, Downs spotted a poster of Bruce Springsteen and a huge blue sign that said ALL EMPLOYEES MUST WASH HANDS BEFORE RETURNING TO WORK. He snuffled a laugh at that.

Then the door shut and that was the last of Crystal the nineteen-year-old blonde hooker from the safe suburbs of Chicago.

Downs stared into the mouth of his beer bottle for several minutes. He was sick of killing time with his life. He was sick of hiding behind the lame excuse that his cerebral palsy was keeping him from being more successful. What was he doing sitting here in this dive? He couldn't even justify things by being mildly buzzed.

A song by Alan Parsons Project broke the stillness as a new girl took the stage. *Eye In The Sky*. Downs had tried dancing to this song with a girl he met at Gingerman's on Division Street a few weeks back. She had pretended to spot an old friend in the crowd and had left Downs on the pastel-colored neon stage like a flaming fool. *"I am the maker of rules, the keeper of fools, I can cheat you blind . . ."*

The girl on stage had a face that was okay, but her body had seen better days. She didn't seem to care enough to dance, as if dancing would draw attention to her looks. Downs thought that maybe she had kids to support or something.

The fat man started in on her immediately; Downs had wondered when the heckling would begin. There was always heckling. It made sense that the fat man would be the first to start. Downs figured that the woman was below the fat man's tastes and deserved to be ridiculed. At least the others in the bar had encouraged the fat man further. Uneasily, Downs scanned the tables around him. About ten guys, all fairly young, had come in since the last time Downs had bothered to look, several beers ago. Four of the guys, at two separate tables, were wearing softball jerseys, red on blue, that advertised the Tapped-Out Lounge in beautiful, downtown Berwyn.

The fat man was telling the girl on stage that, as a deputy sheriff for Cook County, he should run her in on account of excessive ugliness.

So *that* explained it. The bouncers weren't doing anything about that fat slug because, if it was true that he was a deputy, he could probably give them quite a bit of heat. Downs had recently read a story in the Tribune about the lousy procedures the state had in the hiring of their deputies. Virtually anybody could be eligible.

The fat man was absolutely degrading the woman on stage. He spoke of what kinds of animals would avoid having sex with her. He said that if he were to have sex with her, he'd probably have to pull her scabs off first. The fat man spoke very loudly and did not laugh at his own outbursts. He wasn't a heckler, Downs decided. He was being a prick because he was in a position to get away with it.

Downs thought that the fat man was taking things too far. He decided it was time to leave, and pushed away from the table.

Taking one last look at the girl, Downs saw her head lowered, her hips undulating listlessly. Downs walked between the tables to the bathroom, his hands in his pockets.

The bathroom was dimly lit, the lone ceiling bulb flickering every other second, it seemed. There was one bowl, no stalls or urinals: the deluxe suite. There were quite a few misses at the bowl. Downs read some of the graffitti on the walls as he urinated. The usual "For a Good Time, Call . . ."; DOWN WITH KHOMEINI (when the *hell* did they scrub these walls down last, if ever?); Cassady 8-11-82; another admonition: AT LEAST THE TOILET SEATS IN THIS JOINT GO DOWN ON YOU FOR FREE; a few other mindless scribbles. Against the far wall, an ancient machine advertised a LOVE KIT or a RIBBED TINGLER for two quarters.

Downs zipped up and passed the bouncers on his way out the front door. The two men, both built as all bouncers are built, looking like they were made out of solid lead and suffering from perpetual hemorrhoids, were discussing the off-duty deputy up front. The older of the two, who resembled a Bears quarterback from the late '70's, told the other that something had to be done.

Then Downs was out in the early May night. It was about two a.m., he figured. A strong breeze came from the quarry across the lot; Downs smelled salt. A random sports page blew up from the quarry and was plastered against the surrounding chain link fence. Cans of Budweiser and Miller High Life were piled against the fence. The streetlamps on Front Street glittered against the gold of the Miller cans.

The Touch was at the corner of Front Street and Summit Avenue, the first strip joint/clip joint along a half-mile stretch of Fallon Ridge known as Sin Strip. The salt quarry, closed nights since the last of the Midwest snowstorms was long past, ran parallel behind Summit, a residential street dotted with gas stations and convenience marts. There was always controversy about Sin Strip in the local papers.

Downs started a slow walk toward the RTA terminal several blocks away. The bus would be coming soon. He heard voices behind him, muffled by the walls of the lounge. Downs stepped back into the shadows.

The two bouncers were dragging the fat man out of the doorway with much difficulty. The fat man's face was very red, and he looked like he was about to explode. As the front door bounced twice against the frame before shutting, Downs heard "Rosanna" playing again.

"All I want to do when I wake up in the morning . . ."

The fat man struggled violently and Downs thought that he might have been handcuffed, as he could not see the fat man's hands. His feet kicked at the gravel helplessly. Sworls of white dust hung heavily in the air.

One of the bouncers lost his balance slightly and the fat man moved away from him toward the roof. The other bouncer hit the fat man squarely in the right ear, drawing blood, and the fat man fell forward against the hood of a red Buick. His hands *were* handcuffed.

Both bouncers kicked the fat man repeatedly, in the back, in the neck, everywhere. Falling to the lot, the man's body was kicked toward the fence surrounding the quarry.

The fat man rolled over and over, his blue windbreaker slapping against his exposed, bloodied face, his eyes shut in pain and terror, his mouth saying wordlessly over and over I'm a cop I'm a cop I'm a cop

and then his body hit the chain-link fence

(every time one of the Cubs hits one over the fence, it's a Tru-Link fence . . . for beauty, privacy, security)

his whole body jiggling like a jello mold as it stopped amid the beer cans and weeds at the fence's base. One bouncer kicked him in the crotch. The other kicked him in the teeth. The blood was black and splattered the Miller High Life cans. Downs thought of their new ad slogan—Miller: Purity You Can See. A mad thought.

Though it was in the 50's, with none of the humidity summer would bring, Downs was very warm indeed. His underarms were soaked and a thin line of sweat ran down his spine to his buttocks. That winter, at the AKA on Broadway, Downs had spilled his Seagram's down the back of a Mexican girl's dress and she had been super-pissed. Downs figured that his drink had ended up right where his sweat was now.

Downs looked across the street and saw a jovial Rusty Jones shaking hands with Mr. Goodwrench. He knew all along what the men were going to do, and the sudden realization shocked him.

The bouncers had the fat deputy up above their heads now, nearly to the top of the barbed wire fence. Their flexed muscles resembled tree roots. The fat man's shirt was pulled up around his neck. His right nipple was hanging off. He was whimpering. Then— heave, now—he was half over the fence.

The lights on Front Street showed everything. The barbed wire pierced the fat man's skin in half a dozen places. The blood on his chest was like paint squeezed from tubes.

Another push and he was over. Incredibly, the man's belt buckle caught on the fence and the deputy hung suspended on the opposite side of the fence, several hundred feet above the ground. He seemed to be a warped version of a guy on a weight inverter in the Chicago Health & Racquet Club commercials.

It took three hard kicks from the bouncers to shake him off. Looking at the deputy's lips in these last seconds, you'd think he was praying.

He hit something on the way down. It sounded like a tree branch. Then a muffled crack as he hit bottom. The sound echoed like it had been a basketball bouncing in a vacant lot. The two bouncers simply turned and went back inside the bar, each allowing themselves one quick look at the result of their handiwork. They did not congratulate themselves.

When the lounge door was opened, Downs heard "West End Girls" playing and he remembered exactly where he was. Three sailors walked down Front Street, oblivious to anything that had just occurred.

He had to look. He *had* to.

Downs felt like a ghoul. One foot forward, then the next. If the bouncers saw him, he'd say he was urinating. What would they care? He *had* to look.

He jumped as he kicked a beer can errantly. Touching the fence slowly, as if it might suddenly be electrified, Downs strained to see bottom. He saw only shadows.

After long moments, Downs moved away. The blood on the fence left dark, wet grids on Downs face and hands, but he didn't know this.

He walked to Front Street, and kept walking, past the Club Aphrodite, past the Feline Inn, the Union 76, the Feelie-Meelie, not looking back until The Touch was just an ugly spot in the background.

Downs did not know what he was going to do next.

MOVING DAY

by R. Chetwynd-Hayes

R. Chetwynd-Hayes ranks as one of England's finest practitioners of the art of horror fiction, both as author and as editor. Born in Isleworth, Middlesex on May 30, 1919, Chetwynd-Hayes made his first sale in 1954 and since then has written more than twenty-five novels and collections of short stories in addition to editing some twenty-five horror anthologies. While Chetwynd-Hayes writes more in line with the traditional horror tale than do many of the younger English writers, his prose displays a crisp sophistication and, often, a macabre sense of humor to prove that the author is a major stylist in his own right.

Two of his many books have been filmed: From Beyond the Grave *(1973) and* The Monster Club *(1981). His most recent books include* Dracula's Children *and* The House of Dracula—*these two being an outrageous family history of the descendants of Dracula's three wives—as well as* Tales from the Hidden World *and* Clavering Nightmare. *While R. Chetwynd-Hayes has remained virtually unknown in the United States these many years, this unfortunate lapse is now being rectified by Tor Books, who have recently reprinted* The Grange *(U.K. title,* The King's Ghost*) and* Tales from the Other Side. *Hope to see more.*

I went to live with my aunts just before my thirty-fifth birthday.

In fact they were my great-aunts, being the three sisters of my maternal grandmother. The eldest Edith was ninety-eight, the middle one Matilda eighty-seven, the youngest Edna eighty-five. My grandmother had rather let the side down by dying at the ridiculously youthful age of eighty-one. Perhaps the fact she was the only one to marry had something to do with that. As I was the only living relative and in consequence the sole heir to whatever estate they eventually left, moving in with them was not such a bad idea. At least so I thought at the time. I would be able to keep an eye on what would one day be my property and make certain that no kindly person tried to ease his or her way into their wills. It has been known to happen.

I had not been in that large, musty, over-furnished and damp-haunted house a week, before I realized the three sisters were—at the very best—looked upon as eccentrics in the neighborhood and even feared.

Certainly from the very first I had to admit there was an oddness about them that was hard to define. Something to do with the way they walked. A kind of quick-glance-over-the-shoulder-shuffle. Then their pre-occupation with the local churchyard was out of the ordinary.

The only people they seemed to know were there. In the churchyard.

The table talk I endured on my first night put me off the really excellent food. Edna was cook and a very good one she was too.

Edith waved a fork at me and said: "When you move, David, you want to make certain all is ready. The furniture ordered, the box chosen, the wordage composed."

I smiled gently, assuming old age had muddled her poor old brain. "But, Auntie, dear, I have just moved. Moved from my bachelor flat into your nice house."

A genteel titter ran round the table and Edna poked me playfully in the ribs with a dessert spoon. "You silly boy! We mean when you move into your permanent home. The cozy little nest in the churchyard."

I made an interesting noise, then tried to adjust my outlook to the exceptionally unusual. "I see. Be prepared for anything? Eh?"

"He's quite sensible," Edna informed Edith. "So many young people these days are apt to treat *moving* with unseemly levity."

"Takes after his granddad," Matilda maintained. "In fact Alfred—did you know, David, that was your grandfather's name?—moved twenty-five years ago last Christmas. He said, 'Make certain the lad—you—knows what's what.' And I said, 'You never need fear about that, Alfred.' "

"Only the other day," Edith stressed, tapping a knife handle on the table, "you forgot to mention Alfred said that only the other day."

"I hadn't forgotten," Matilda protested, "I just hadn't got round to it. At the same time as I was going to mention the lovely surprise we've planned for David's birthday."

Edith shook her head reproachfully. "Now, you've spoilt it all, Matilda. The fact he now knows a lovely surprise is planned for his birthday, means it will only be half a lovely surprise. He may even guess what it is. If you have a failing, Matilda, it is talking out of turn. Gladys Foot, who you may remember *moved* in 1932, said the same thing only yesterday. 'Matilda will talk out of turn,' she said. 'She even told me when I was going to *move*, and I didn't want to know until a day after the event.' "

Matilda dabbed her eyes with a black-edged handkerchief. "I mean well, Edith. I'm sure dear David won't give the matter of a lovely surprise on his birthday another thought, until he learns what it is on the great day, which I believe is the day after tomorrow."

Edith hastened to console. "Don't take on so, dear. I mean I only correct you for your own good. Have a glass of Mortuary 51. It will cheer you up."

I may as well point out that Mortuary 51 was a

rather bad sherry and had nothing to do with a mortuary, but they had churchyard-funeral titles for almost everything. I mean the pepperbox was an earth-sprinkler, potatoes—corpoties, spoons—grave-diggers and any kind of soup or gravy, churchyard bouillon.

When I was escorted to my bedroom by Edna, she assured me that: "The bed shrouds were changed this morning."

I lay awake for most of the night trying to understand how this death-related mania had come into being. Possibly their longevity and the fact everyone they had known had died, might have had something to do with it. In the very beginning I mean.

My thirty-fifth birthday will never be forgotten.

To begin I found three black-edged cards propped up against a toast rack on the breakfast table. The goodwill messages were I am certain unique in birthday greeting history.

Three times thirty-five is one hundred and five,
    Then you should no longer be alive.
With luck this could be the last birthday.
        And that's all we have to say.

From your loving aunties Edith, Edna and Matilda and all those who have *moved*.

But no present. No lovely surprise.

I had to assume it was the birthday tea that was planned for five o'clock. But I was wrong.

After lunch I was ordered to put on my best suit, polish my shoes and comb my hair, because we were going visiting. The aunts put on black satin dresses, black straw hats, and black button-up boots. Then we all set out, walked the entire length of the High Street, watched I swear by the entire population of the village. Then we turned into a narrow lane, picked our way over puddles, pushed open—or rather Edna did—a low gate and entered the churchyard.

Edith called out, "Hullo, everybody. Don't worry

about us. Won't be long," then led us along weed-infested paths until we came to that part of the church-yard where those who had reaped a reasonably rich harvest during their day in the earthly vineyard slept the long sleep. Or so I assumed. Marble angels stood guard over miniature flower gardens. Granite head-stones proclaimed the virtues of those who rested under marble chips. We stopped at a strip of closely clipped grass, into which at regular intervals had been inserted round lead plaques, all bearing black numbers: 14, 15, 16, 17.

Edna took an envelope from her handbag. "You see, dear, we have purchased our permanent homes. Here are three deeds which state that plot 14 belongs to Edith, plot 15 belongs to Matilda and plot 16 belongs to me. Eventually we will move into our plots, but you may be sure leave them now and again to see how you are getting on."

There was really no answer for that one, so I kept quiet and displayed more interest in the empty plots than I actually felt. Then Edna produced the fourth deed.

"Now, dear, we come to your lovely birthday surprise. We have all clubbed together and bought you plot 17. You too now own your permanent home. What have you to say about that?"

All three looked at me with such an air of joyful expectancy, I just had to express delight—near ecstasy—happy surprise, even if it did mean gabbling insane nonsense.

"How can I thank you—something I've always wanted—I will treasure it for as long as I live—and longer. I can't wait to get into it . . ."

"We had thought," Matilda said, "of tying a greetings present card to the plot number, but Edith thought it wouldn't be respectful. Now, Edna, make the presentation in the proper way."

Edna straightened up and stood rather like a soldier at attention, the little slip of paper in her hand. It was in fact a receipt for five pounds. She raised her voice until it was in danger of dissolving into a rasping croak.

"I hereby bestow on my beloved, great-nephew David Greenfield the deeds of his permanent home, trusting he will lie in it with credit to his noble *moved-on* ones."

I accepted the "deeds" and said thank you very much several times, having exhausted my fund of grateful words in the acceptance speech.

Then we all sang the first verse of "Abide with Me" before starting the tramp back to the village, bestowing words of farewell onto most of the graves as we went. I became acutely aware of the considerable crowd that had collected just beyond the churchyard wall, some of which gave gratuitous advice that included, "Why don't yer stay there?," "Dig hard and hearty and bed down," "Set up house there," "Yer all dead, why don't yer lie down?"

However all this came to an abrupt end when Matilda pointed two rigid fingers at the crowd and chanted in a shrill voice:

On ye all the evil eye.
By Beldaza ye all die.
If ye not gone in one mo.
Or before I wriggle big toe.

And they all went. Running, jumping, pushing, gasping; I have never before or since seen a crowd that included quite a number of elderly people move so fast, or with such agility.

Edna sighed deeply. "What a shame, sisters, we have to frighten people so much. I'd much rather be friendly and explain all about *moving* over a cup of tea and a condensed milk sandwich."

"The price of being special," Edith explained.

"The curse of being upper," Matilda agreed.

"I do hope we don't have to become too drastic," Edna had the last word. "People should only *move* when it's right and proper."

*   *   *

Two weeks later Edith was taken ill.

Not exactly ill, rather taken faint. She wilted and took to her bed and I slowly became aware that the house was being invaded.

Sort of.

Matilda and Edna accentuated their quick-glance-over-one-shoulder shuffle, only the quick glance was not so quick anymore. There was an awful lot of whispering too. I couldn't catch all of it, but what I did seemed very ordinary. "How are you, dear? Doesn't seem a year since you *moved*. Yes, time does fly. Shouldn't be long now before your Tom starts turning up his toes . . ."

Another thing. I began to take quick glances over my shoulder, for there was the distinct impression that someone was standing way back and a quick turning of the head enabled me to catch the merest glimpse of him. Not sufficient to register any details, but enough to send a cold shiver down my spine.

As time passed—three days or more—impressions began to set into near certainties. I distinctly saw the back of a woman attired in a polka dot muslin dress disappear round the corner of the landing, which led to Edith's bedroom. When I turned the same corner some ten seconds later there was no one in sight. I peeped into Aunt Edith's bedroom, she was lying still with hands crossed, but otherwise the room was empty.

Twice I was awakened in the middle of the night by cold lips kissing my forehead. Once by cold fingers gently caressing my throat. When I complained to Matilda and Edna next morning, both giggled and Matilda said, "Martha Longbridge always had an affectionate nature," and Edna added, "Daphne is so mischievous."

I asked, "Who are Martha and Daphne?" and they both gave me a pitying smile, before Edna replied:

"Two old friends who *moved* a long time ago."

I did not dare ask any more questions.

Three weeks after Edith had been taken faint, she

died. At least I would have said she died, the two remaining sisters insisted she had merely prepared herself for *moving*. Not *moved* you understand. Stopped breathing so as to *prepare* for *moving*.

The funeral took place three days later and was a very sparse affair. The coffin was pushed to the churchyard on a hand bier—rather like a costermonger's barrow—and the clergyman was not encouraged to linger once he had galloped his way through the burial service. A deep grave had been dug in plot 14 and Edith's cheap pine coffin was lowered into it, then the earth shoveled back in and piled up as an untidy hump, which Edna crowned by a jam jar containing three marigolds. One from each of us. Then we went home to roast beef, Yorkshire pudding, roast potatoes (corpoties), Brussels sprouts and rich churchyard bouillon, followed by apple pie and custard.

The house ceased to be invaded. The unseen guests merely settled in.

By that I mean I only occasionally felt the urge to glance quickly over the left shoulder, but really had the heebies when I woke up and found something very cold in bed with me. According to Edna, this was Susan Cornwall who had been—and presumably still was—very lustful. Needless to say she had *moved* a long time ago.

But the two sisters became very preoccupied and rarely seemed to have time to spare for me. The word *moving* became commonplace.

"We'll talk about that, dear, after the *moving*."

"Come and see me after the *moving*, dear."

And when I asked what *moving* entailed, I was told: "You'll know afterward, dear."

May I belatedly explain that all three sisters had always looked elderly, but more due to dress and deportment than physical appearance. Edith of course had looked the older because she was and ninety-eight is a burden of years to carry about. The other two were fairly tall and gaunt, but could easily be taken for ladies in their middle to late sixties.

That was before Edith died.

The interval that separated Edith's death and her *moving* seemed to age them dreadfully. From lean they became emaciated. Eyes sank, teeth were bared in the likeness of a maniac's grin, bones became merely a framework to support brown wrinkled skin. This deterioration was explained by Edna in the following words:

"We both give a bit, dear, so as to make a whole. One day you will have to give for both of us."

The atmosphere both in the house and in the village was pretty grim, and after the episode of my waking to find something very cold in bed with me, I did begin to entertain ideas about moving out, but—greed is a great courage maker. I found I was one hundred and twenty-five thousand pounds the richer by Edith's death and I stood to gain twice as much when the other two sisters *moved*, so I prayed for the preservation of my sanity and stood firm if not steady.

I suppose it must have been two weeks after the funeral when I began to realize that the vicar was hanging around the street in which the house stood, and could sometimes be seen taking a long time to tie up a shoelace on the other side of the road, ready to bolt should either of the great-aunts appear, but succumb to an attack of nods, winks and head jerking whenever I put foot over the front doorstep.

His name was Humphrey Mondale, tall, thin and bald; a twisted stick of a man, who jerked in a forwardly direction rather than walked, and looked even more eccentric than the two remaining sisters. It was he who had galloped through the burial service on the occasion of Edith's funeral. I kept well clear of him.

But one morning he sprang out on me from the passage that ran between the post office and the public library and had a numbing grip on my left arm before I could get away.

I think he either suffered from chronic catarrh or a perpetual bad head cold, for he spoke with a thick voice and sometimes blurred his syllables.

"Must twalk," he insisted, his head jerking from side to side on his thin neck, so I was reminded of a ventriloquist's dummy when the head is pushed up too high. "Nephoo . . . yes?"

I said I was the nephew of the two maiden ladies who lived in Moss House, but he did not allow me to finish.

"Twying to contact you for deys. Must stop *moving*. Turrible effect on local people. No one come to church for years. Churchyard shunned. Bishop won't lesson."

I am one of those people who have a low sales' resistance and once buttonholed find it very difficult to get away. The fellow insisted I go with him to the vicarage and what is more hung on to me like grim death to make certain I did. There a female counterpart of himself—plus an untidy mop of gray hair—was introduced as his sister. She gave me a strange look, crossed her two thumbs and said: "Not me as a good Christian woman, you don't," then ran into a small kitchen, from which she presently emerged carrying two mugs of weak tea.

Mr Mondale pulled me into a room he called his den—tired old armchairs, a battered desk, plus for some reason the smell of stale urine and green water.

I sank into a chair which instantly groaned and tried to do something dreadful to me with a broken spring. We didn't say a great deal until his sister had served the weak tea, but I then managed to muster some indignant resolution and asked:

"What is all this about, Mr Mondale? You dragged me in off the street, without so much as by your leave."

The tea must have done something for his cold for his speech delivery improved.

"Distant member of the family myself, you know. Otherwise I'd have been moved long ago. You know the village is terrified of your aunts. Fear takes many forms. That scene by the churchyard the other day was one. But one day the aunts will really let rip—and then I'd hate to thunk what would happen. Particularly after a *moving*."

Curiosity got the better of irritation and I leaned forward to ask the all important question:

"What the hell—beg pardon—is this *moving*? They won't tell me a thing. I thought they meant the actual moment of death, or even possibly the funeral. But apparently there's something more."

The vicar leaned back in his chair and yawned at the ceiling in an effort to emphasize there was indeed more. Much more.

"Good . . . good Guard, yes. My word yes. It's the *moving* which upsets the village and will in time bring the newspaper people—especially that Sunday lot—beating a trail to our doors. Fortunately it takes place at night and most people close their curtains and try to ignore what's going on. Two years ago a foolhardy youth did come out and *saw*. He hasn't spoken since and has dreadful fits of the shakes to this day."

I dragged my chair forward. "But . . . but . . . what did he *see*?"

The Reverend Mr Mondale put out a hand. It was not particularly clean and the nails needed trimming.

"Does that member shake?"

"No."

"Would you say that is a steady hand with not a tremor about it?"

"I would indeed."

"Surely that is evidence enough that I have never been such a fool as to peer through parted curtains when your aunts and *that which is with them* pass the house."

"Then you don't know?"

He jerked his head forward twice, his bad cold losing out to the strong emotion that now held his entire body in a masterly grip.

"I can surmise, sir. I am not the only one who has had the merest glimpse of those who sometimes stray back from the grave and pay a social call on your aunts. Unfortunately churchyards have become associated with certain supernatural nastiness in the public mind. Can it be wondered at, that if at times, in some particular locality, the seeds of that nastiness come to full fruition? Eh?"

I felt a need to confess, share a fear that up to that moment I had not been aware existed.

"There's a nasty atmosphere in the house. Things lurking behind the left shoulder—something cold in the bed—cold fingers on the throat, whispers in the dark."

The vicar raised both hands, then let them fall back on to the desk with a kind of soggy thump. "Ah! Then it was not imagination! I have seen white faces with runny eyes looking down from the upper windows! There is only one answer. That house must be razed to the ground and the ground itself sewn with salt."

"Look here, I'm going to inherit that house!"

"Could you live there after the remaining aunts have *moved*?"

"No, I'd sell it. Good development land."

Now the vicar raised his eyes ceilingward. "There is no piercing the armor of the mercenary ungodly."

I rose. "Thank you for all you have *not* told me."

I became more unhappy as the days passed, even more so when told Aunt Edith's *moving* day would be the coming Thursday.

Thursday has always been my unlucky day, I will probably die on a Thursday—and be *moved* the following Thursday.

Edna laid a loving hand on my shoulder. "We say day, dear, in fact it's night. Between eleven and twelve in the evening. The best time. The pub has turned out and all honest people are tucked up in bed. Others!" She shook her head, then tucked her chin in. "Others must take the consequences if they see that which they shouldn't. After all, *moving* is strictly a family affair."

For the last three days I went for long walks and turned into an opposite direction whenever I saw the Reverend Mondale, for he had now taken to pushing notes through the letter box begging me to burn the house down before the dreaded event, stating that if I didn't, he would, an item of information I felt duty bound to pass on to the aunts.

Edna tut-tutted and Matilda sighed deeply. "He was always a trial even as a boy. Edna, we can't have Edith upset and besides this house is home for the entire family. There's no help for it . . ."

Edna nodded slowly. "A visit from Cousin Judith."

"You think that will be sufficient?" Matilda asked with some anxiety.

"Of course. You may remember the year the church-yard was flooded with the overflow from the chemical works?"

"I most certainly do. A disgrace."

"Well, Cousin Judith has never been quite the same since. She is really in no fit state to visit anyone. Especially a nervous clergyman."

I had no more trouble from the Reverend Humphrey Mondale. He was found wandering the downs counting his fingers and expressing great surprise that they were all there. His sister was seen dancing naked on the village green singing a tuneless dirge that accompanied words that ran something like this.

She ain't got no fingers or toes,
Her ears have gone, so has her nose,
One leg's turned green, the other blue,
And both feet are nailed to a horse's shoe.

I actually prayed I would never see Cousin Judith.

The great day dawned clear and bright. Far across the downs a dog barked—always far away—and nearer to hand a cock crowed and set in motion a series of other sounds that included my two great-aunts calling out, "Happy moving day, Edith," which was acknowledged by the door of Edith's room slamming all by itself. Well, it must have done. There was no one near it at the time and not so much as a breath of wind.

When I looked out of the window I saw a small

army of cats running down the center of the road, making for the downs. I was afterward informed they all collected on top of a mound called locally the Giant's Grave, where they howled and spat for most of the day and part of the following night. You can't ignore the fact that cats have a lot of know-how.

The aunts were very busy all day. They took three baths—I only one. Edna baked lots of little round loaves, which she laid out all over the house. And believe me—they all disappeared. Then I was given the job of collecting large bunches of dandelions; they were mashed into a pulp in the kitchen sink, then boiled in the jam-making saucepan, before being ladled into saucers, which were also laid out all over the house.

And you really must believe me again—every single one was licked clean as Oliver Twist's gruel bowl.

But come sunset and the action hotted up.

Edna and Matilda put on long black robes, gray veils which had the effect of giving their faces a ghost like appearance, then inspecting me who was wearing the same black suit I'd worn at Edith's funeral.

"You look very nice, dear," Edna commented. "Doesn't he, Matilda?"

Matilda nodded. At least I think she did. It was hard to tell what she was doing under that veil. "Yes. But I think he looks more handsome with his hair brushed back. Parted he reminds me of that assistant in the shoe shop who once laid a familiar hand on Edith's ankle."

Then all three of us sat in the lounge exchanging small talk while waiting for the sun to set. Aunt Edna said she had not known such warm weather since dear Mary-Lou *moved*, and Aunt Matilda expressed a hope that the threatened rain would hold off until Edith was nicely settled.

Presently I got tired of sitting and listening to their old voices and after excusing myself wandered out into the garden. Two young lads who had been keeping watch over the back wall, dropped out of sight while one shouted. "He's got his funeral suit on! It must be tonight!" Shortly afterward I heard a vast amount of door shutting and the locking of windows.

I looked upon a glorious sunset, but even as I watched little fat black clouds came drifting in from the east and set about demolishing that lovely scene, warning all who could read the message that night would soon position its platoons in both city and countryside.

Aunt Edna called from the kitchen doorway:

"Soon be time, David dear," and indeed it was time to go indoors and face the horrors of unreality.

Both sisters had donned something more than a long black robe and a gray veil. A complete new personality that hinted at an odd kind of professionalism. I cannot, try as I may, explain how this was so, save I had the impression they were drawing upon an enormous fund of experience, that normally would be locked away in some dark recess of their brains.

I was pushed gently into the hall and made to face the stairs; Edna to my left and Matilda to my right. Both looked up the stairs with a kind of pathetic expectancy, before Edna called out in a quavering voice:

"It's time, Edith dear. It's your *moving* time."

I waited, not really expecting anything particular to happen, but right deep down knowing it would.

Edith's bedroom door creaked open. The creaking was very drawn out as though someone with not too much strength to spare was pulling the door open very slowly.

The creaking stopped. The heavy footsteps began.

Edith-sized in granite—those were the words that flashed across my brain. Thump-thump-thump. The ceiling below must have trembled and possibly sent down a little shower of plaster. Very, very heavy footsteps that moved very, very slowly. They came out even more slowly on to the landing—and Edith emerged into view.

My first impression—white—white—white—with black pupilless eyes that moved. Moved all the time. I think there may have been a tiny spot of light dead center, but I can't swear to that, for I was not just frightened—I was one babbling mass of trembling, trouser-pissing, stomach-heaving terror. That thing—Edith—she—it—was white plastic marble. Take a statue of a woman in a long white robe, then give it movement, but with no expression on the face at all, save for those moving black eyes, and maybe the merest suggestion of a smile etched round the mouth—and you may—just may have some inkling of what that apparition looked like.

Only it was no apparition, or if it was, a damned solid one.

One dead white hand gripped the banister rail, then thump-thump down the stairs, with the two sisters shouting encouragement.

"Come on, Edith dear . . . that's right . . . don't worry about chipping the paint, David can put that right tomorrow morning. Pick your feet up, won't do to have you tumbling down like Cousin Jane did."

She thumped-thumped down those stairs and as she came nearer I began to notice little details, like the tiny mole under her left eye, only now it too was dead white, and the rather nice lock of hair that used to dangle over her forehead; now it really did looked like brilliantly carved marble. And—yes—it did seem as if the ghost of a smile was etched round her mouth.

I had the impression it took quite an effort to step down into the hall, for she took some time to lower the left bare foot on to the fitted carpet, then hung on to the banister rail while she brought the right down to join it.

In fact I believe some kind of restorative—not rest—non-action was required, a standing still interval, when the only movement was continuously rolling black, pupilless eyes.

Presently Edna nudged me. "David! What are you thinking about, dear? Give your Auntie Edith a nice kiss."

God of my fathers—forgive me and save at least a

remnant of my sanity—I BLOODY WELL DID IT. I kissed that cold horror and MY LIPS STUCK TO HER CHEEK. She was so cold my lips froze on contact and I left a strip of flesh behind when I pulled my mouth free. The two sisters looked at me reproachfully and Edna pushed a wad of tissues into my hand with a muttered: "Blood on the carpet!" then wiped what I had left behind from Edith's cheek. You know, even in the midst of that body and brain numbing terror I still felt that I had blotted my copybook for kissing Aunt Edith too hard and messing up the hall carpet.

Edith went into action again. Very slowly along the hall, a careful walk over the front doorstep, then down the garden path to the front gate. We lined up on the pavement.

Edith in front. She was the pace setter. Edna next. Then Matilda with me bringing up a very reluctant rear. As we progressed down the High Street a gurgling scream came from a window over the butcher's shop, before a bright red curtain quivered and fell away, as though some falling body were clinging to it.

Matilda shook her head sadly. "Peepers weepers. There's always one who just won't learn."

After a while, when I had recovered sufficiently to think of something other than my own terror, I noticed that out here in the open Edith shone. Or glimmered whitely. When the moon slid behind a cloud bank she positively glowed. Like illuminated snow.

But she did look fearsome. I could well understand that someone who wasn't family and had not been acclimatized by degrees, giving vent to a howling scream just prior to slipping down into the pit of madness.

The cats on the Giant's Grave were letting rip now and the dogs seemed determined not to be outdone, and believe you me there is no sound more hideous on this earth than the united howls of a hundred or more cats and dogs.

We left the village behind and Edna and Matilda began to sing "Home Sweet Home" and the way they sang it, I could hardly tell the difference between their din and that made by the cats and dogs.

The churchyard lane was full of potholes and I wondered what would happen if Edith were to stumble and fall flat on her white cold face, but fortunately that did not happen, although I almost knocked Matilda over when I tripped on a ruddy great stone.

We moved into the churchyard and eventually came to the mound of earth that covered all that I recognized as Edith's earthly remains.

Now comes the awful part.

Edith stood beside her grave and stared at the old church, rolling those dreadful black eyes and rather giving the impression she wasn't all that keen about doing whatever came next. Edna whispered, "You move in, dear. Can't leave you standing here. The locals just wouldn't understand. And when the sun comes up, dear, you'll catch your death of heat."

I shook my head quite violently when Matilda said to me, "Can't you give your Auntie Edith a little shove, dear? That's all she needs to get her going."

But Edith at length got herself going. Trod into the loose soil, pounded it down and ploughed her way up and in until she stood on the very peak of the mound, her feet covered with earth, her eyes rolling like black marbles.

The sisters expressed encouragement by clapping black-gloved hands together and saying, "Well done, dear. Oh, very well done." Then: "Down you go, dear. Down you go."

Grand-Aunt Edith began to vaporize.

She did. She did.

First the head began to dissolve into white, seething vapor. Then the neck went all floppy before running into the torso. After that the process speeded up. Arms sort of exploded into vapor, only there wasn't any sound. Torso collapsed, Vapor dropped around the legs as if to hide them from vulgar gaze. Then the entire mess sank into the grave and disappeared from view.

Edith had finally *moved*.

The two sisters lowered their heads and called out in low sweet voices: "Bye-bye, dear. See you on Sunday."

I can't be sure but I think that's the way vampires are born, but for what now passes for my peace of mind I'm not suggesting that Great-Aunt Edith became a vampire. If she had I am certain someone in the village would have mentioned it.

Before we left the churchyard, the moon being by now quite bright, they insisted we visit my empty plot. My grave to be. Edna looked at it, while Matilda looked at me. I think they both spoke together.

"To think that one day you will *move* into here! How thrilled you must be."

But the final chilly twist came on the way home. We all three walked abreast. Edna on my left, Matilda to my right. Suddenly Edna looked back and expelled her breath as a deep sigh of annoyance.

"It is really too bad," she said.

I looked back. A column of vapor about five feet six high was drifting down the middle of the road. Matilda stamped her foot.

"No, dear, not until Sunday. You really musn't follow us. Go back."

Both sisters advanced toward the column making shooing sounds.

I ran toward the railway station.

OK, I passed up two hundred thousand pounds, but money is not everything.

LA NUIT DES CHIENS

by Leslie Halliwell

Born in Bolton in 1929, Leslie Halliwell presently makes his home in Surrey—when he isn't making buying trips to Hollywood or just globe-trotting in general. Since 1968 Halliwell has been program buyer for the entire ITV network in England, and more recently for Channel 4, where his nostalgic season of films from the golden age of movies has won wide approval. He is well known in England for his books on television and film, including Halliwell's Filmgoer's Companion, Halliwell's Film Guide, Halliwell's Television Companion, Halliwell's Teleguide, Halliwell's Hundred, *and* Halliwell's Harvest.

Aside from his love for films, Leslie Halliwell has a deep interest in ghost stories—a genre in which he feels the cinema has never truly done justice. Recently Halliwell has taken to writing horror fiction of his own, in moods which range from M.R. James to Roald Dahl to dark humor. His first such collection, The Ghost of Sherlock Holmes, *has been followed by a second,* A Demon Close Behind. *Halliwell has also recently published a novel,* Return to Shangri-La *(a sequel to* Lost Horizon*), and he is preparing two more collections of ghostly tales,* A Demon on the Stair *and* A Demon at the Window.

"*Près du château illuminé?*" asked the concierge. "*Ah, oui*, á Malchâteau. You 'ad better not go there to-night, monsieur. *C'est la nuit des chiens.* I suggest to you per'aps . . ."

Leonard Haskins allowed the man to book a table for five at a restaurant he had never heard of along the main road to Menton, but he was not happy about it. His days at the Monte Carlo market were few enough for him not to take chances on restaurants. Both his wife and his chairman would expect him to have pulled something out of the hat, and at least two of the restaurants in Malchâteau were commended in Michelin. Besides, the Coca Cola boys were paying, so they had to be satisfied too. It was a shame. From the hotel steps you could see the old castle high across the bay, rising out of the immemorial mountainside to which the entire village seemed to cling: that is often the way with these ancient villages of the Alpes Maritimes, with their damp smells and impossibly stepped streets.

Once in his youth Leonard had climbed up to the castle, which was ruined and less remarkable than its village; he remembered that in one of the bars he had drunk more Ricard than was good for his stomach. He had certainly preferred Malchâteau to St Paul de Vence, because it was less commercialized. Still, since he spoke only a few words of French, and the hotel staff refused to speak clear English, there was no point in trying to argue; and in any case it couldn't be less than a tolerable evening, because Bruce Meredith and Tom Vernon were pleasant chaps who would lay on a comfortable car and expensive wine to ease the burdens of conversation. All they had asked Leonard to do was choose the location, and he felt he had let them down. Well, Pinocchio might be better than he feared: the concierge of a four-star hotel was supposed to know about things like that. But it was annoying all the same. What was that the man had said about a night of dogs? Some local festival, presumably, that closed the whole village to casual visitors. Might have been interesting at that.

They met at eight and clambered into a capacious Volvo. The evening was cool for Monte Carlo, but the whole of Europe had felt that particular winter more than most. Everything began well. The salesfolk were old friends. Bernard Poskitt, Leonard's new Chairman, was clearly disposed to enjoy himself. Even Leonard's wife Rosalie was clearly looking forward with pleasure to what might have been a mere duty evening. But they soon came to a setback: the *maître d'* at Pinocchio had never heard of them—the concierge must have called the wrong restaurant—and the place was *absolument complet*.

Though the mistake was not his fault, Leonard felt bound somehow to set things right. By now, all the restaurants along the millionaires' coast would be full of his friends and colleagues. High on the hills, though, matters should be different. He suggested a voyage of discovery, starting at the modernistic hotel Vistaero, which overhangs the *Haute Corniche* like a pile of white matchboxes. If that disappointed, there were modest eating places in La Turbie; the group might hopefully be amused by their lack of presumption. And if all else failed, they could double back to the Grill at the Hôtel de Paris, which was open till midnight.

In less time than it takes to tell they were speeding east along the coast road, looking for a left turn which would take them into the hills. The first one they found had a sign for Vistaero, and also one for Malchâteau; indeed, after less than five miles of uphill bends they found themselves rounding a curve immediately below the modestly floodlit castle of the ancient community. On impulse Leonard suggested a quick tour of the village: they could always turn back if the crowds were too thick, and the restaurants might not be full after all. The plan was agreed, but when a sharp turn to the right carried them swiftly up the steepest hill of the evening, and brought them within two minutes into the lower part of Malchâteau itself, whatever festivities constituted the night of the dogs seemed to be over; at any rate, not a human being was to be seen on the dark streets.

It was a mystery indeed. Cars were parked, and lights were on within some of the old houses, but all doors were firmly shut. "Take the next sharp right," said Leonard. "It runs you up to a sort of square with a view of the coast." Bruce stepped on the accelerator and proved this prediction to be true; but the upper *place* was just as deserted as the lower. Cars crowded the little area, and he parked with difficulty in the only possible space, so that the party could stretch its legs and see the view. This they were all delighted to do, but the mystery of Malchâteau deepened. Even the little café, *La Grotte*, was firmly closed, and no sound of radio, television, or other entertainment came from within. The deserted area formed a strange contrast with the distant lights of the Monte Carlo shore.

"It's eerie," said Rosalie, and the men agreed.

"Whatever festivities are taking place here tonight," said Bernard, "are taking place indoors. The village is as empty as a film set after dark."

"Perhaps it *is* a film set," suggested Tom: "we could hire it and stage a new version of *Dracula*." Leonard was promptly cast as the count, with Bernard as Van Helsing, but after that, imagination faltered. And then it transpired that the village was not quite empty after all. A strange pattering sound from an alley to the right turned out to herald a large dog carrying in its mouth a foot-long piece of squashed plastic which might have once been a skittle from a child's set but was now firmly the dog's plaything. The animal dashed it to the ground at Bruce's feet, then bounded back and forth until the gentle American picked up the object and hurled it down the street. The dog, a large breed which in the darkness looked like an Irish wolfhound with a French coiffure, had clearly intended this, for the object was retrieved and the action repeated. Twice was enough for Bruce, but the dog wanted more; when more was not forthcoming, it put its feet up on Bruce's shoulders, and bit his ear.

The bite may not have been intended, but teeth certainly came into contact with the side of Bruce's face, and scratched his ear lobe quite badly, so that it bled all over his collar. After that, the dog was firmly sent packing, and everyone made suggestions, thinking vaguely of rabies; but the only remedy to hand was some menthol lip salve which had lain long in Rosalie's handbag, and that had to do. Afterward Bruce waved away the various expressions of sympathy with a shrug of apparent composure, but one could tell that for him the evening was ruined: he made no more jokes. "Hadn't we better do something about finding a restaurant?" he asked.

Tom had become separated from the group and was studying a notice high on the wall below a lamp bracket. "Wait a minute," he said. "Here's one that says it's open *toutes les nuits*. Nothing about dog night being excluded. And there's an arrow and a walking sign. Eighty-four rue du Château. La Maitresse des Chiens, it's called. My word, aren't they doggy around here?"

"Let's try it," said Bruce crisply. "A concierge is wrong once, he can be wrong twice." The arrow pointed through a narrow space between domestic buildings, and less than twenty yards on the other side Leonard found steps clearly labeled rue du Château. Steep they were, and, from a recent icy snap, full of grit which acted like miniature ball bearings and made progress a slippery business. It was a short but wearying climb, and Leonard was not cheered when he looked back and saw in the shadows at least four large dogs silently following them up the steps. But very shortly, on the right under an arch, there came in view a small illuminated sign for the restaurant they sought; and the door when opened revealed an empty but delightfully welcoming and well-warmed double chamber with stone walls and arches. From under one of the latter there emerged an elegant though sallow Frenchwoman in her fifties. She issued a rather formal welcome, and said that she would be pleased to offer all of her specialties, none of which took very long in the cooking.

It was a satisfying, candlelit, impeccably served meal, though the industry gossip was more subdued than usual. They all began with *soupe aux truffes en croûte*, and were then divided between *fillet au poivre* and *mostelle à l'anglaise*. It was a puzzle where the food was cooked—some of it seemed to be brought in from the street—but there was certainly nobody to serve it but madame, who produced each dish with style but seemed disinclined for conversation. Leonard's French, as has been said, was fragmentary, but he did once make an effort by pointing on the menu to the name of the establishment and asking: *"Ou sont les chiens? Au dehors?"*

"Oui," she said with a strange thoughtful smile. *"Tous. Au dehors."*

"They are at that," said Bernard, who was just returning from *la toilette*. "All outside. Dozens of them, milling about. I could see through the front window. Frankly I don't understand what's going on, but they seem quiet enough."

Eventually the coffee was drunk and the bill paid. Leonard had finished off with a *marc de Provence*, but still felt unaccountably chilled as he stepped into the night air, and Rosalie shivered audibly as she slipped into the gray coat he was holding for her. "Now, don't anybody break a leg going down those steps," he said. "It's dark and treacherous out here. And my God, there seems to be a dog in every doorway, watching us. Must be walkey-walkey time in Malchâteau!"

The dogs however were not troublesome at this point: only their dimly seen red eyes were disturbing. It was the darkness that was worrying: the main street lights seemed to have been switched off, leaving only a few faint pools of illumination. At one point Tom turned back to ask *madame* for help, but not only had she gone inside, the entire restaurant was now in sudden darkness.

"I have the distinct feeling," said Bernard, "that she only opened up for our benefit, though don't ask me how she knew we were coming."

"The dogs told her, of course," said Rosalie; "or perhaps the whole village is like Brigadoon, and only comes to life once in a hundred years."

Leonard could not be amused by the conversation: he was too aware that an increasingly large number of dogs was silently following them down the steps, and in imagination he felt the savage amusement of the beasts at the group's clumsy, hesitant progress. Absolute concentration on the next step was essential, and, probably for this reason, they realized too late that they had gone down more steps than they came up. Bernard and Rosalie were by this time far ahead of the others, and Tom called to them as loudly as he could without raising the village: "Stay where you are: I'm going back to find the turning." The distant faint clatter of Rosalie's heels came to a halt as Tom bounded back up the steps, followed by Bruce and Leonard, who was relieved to see that no dogs now blocked their path. The narrow alleyway between the two houses was quickly found: it had been missed because the bright light over it had been turned off, making the alley look more private than public. The square on the other side of it, however, still had its meager share of illumination, and Bruce was clearly relieved to find that his hired car was intact. Leonard was less happy. "Look at the doorways," he said. They did, and perceived dimly in each the eyes of at least one dog.

"I'm beginning not to like this," said Bruce. "Let's get out of here. Are the others coming up?"

"No," said Tom. "Shall I go down?"

"Better do something. Reassure them at least. If they've found a way to the main road, go down with them and we'll pick you up. We'll wait five minutes first in case you come back."

"Right." Tom clattered off along the pebbles, and then the sound died away.

Bruce lit a cigarette, glancing around him the while, and threw it away after a couple of puffs. "Get in the car," he said to Leonard. "I'll turn it round." Even after he had done so, the rest of the five minutes seemed endless, but at last, with a final look toward the gap through which Tom had disappeared, he switched the car into action and said, "Right. Obviously they've all gone on down. We're off."

It was the work of less than a minute to drive down to the lower car park, but nowhere along the road to the T-junction was a human being to be seen. "They can't have come out further on, surely," muttered Bruce. "We'd better go back, God damn it." At the junction he just managed a three-point turn and headed back for the upper *place*, which however proved as empty as when they left it. No human beings, anyway: just the dogs. Leonard glanced at his luminous watch and was disconcerted to find that the time was five minutes to midnight. "What do we do now?" he muttered. "Wherever they are they're going to be cold and lonely, and it's starting to drizzle."

Bruce swore to himself. "You stay here and I'll chase down the steps after them." Leonard felt that this was an insufficiently detailed arrangement, but Bruce was already out of the car and running off in the same direction as Tom, leaving not only engine and lights on but his door open. Left alone, Leonard found the engine noise encouraging, but decided to open his passenger door and stand in the fresh air. As he did so, the lights inside *La Grotte* went out, along with every light in the square except those on the car. And a distant clock began to strike twelve. "This is silly," thought Leonard to himself, beginning to feel like the last little nigger boy. But reality struck back instantly in the sound of a horrid choking cry, which might have come from almost any animal including one of his friends. Without thinking of any possible danger, he propelled himself over to the viewing platform and gazed down at the dark lower streets of the village. "Who's there?" he called. "Where are you, Bruce?"

"Coming back," came a welcome reply. "But what the hell was that cry?"

It was a rhetorical question, and Leonard was almost too relieved to answer, especially when he heard another familiar voice from the opposite direction: "Is that you, Leonard? We're near the lower car park." So Bernard was safe, and Rosalie too. "We'll come and get you," Leonard called back. "Wait two minutes." He shook his head incredulously: they would all laugh about this on the way home. Bruce's steps were nearer now, and predictably slower as the steps got steeper. "Might as well sit in the car," thought Leonard; but as he made his move to do so, the entire *place* came alive with dogs. Hairy dogs, smooth dogs, big dogs and small dogs, but all snarling dogs with sharp teeth, hurling themselves in his direction. He closed the door on his side easily enough, but the driver's door was something else, and he got his hand badly gashed in the attempt before using his cane to hook onto the open half window and slam the door shut. At the first attempt he seemed to close the metal on a paw; at any rate a large animal ran squealing down the street. Simultaneously, in the car headlights, he saw the breathless figure of Bruce running toward him.

It was a valiant effort, but too late. Bruce was clearly exhausted from the steps, and he was still ten yards from the car when he was overcome by snarling canines which leaped at him from all sides until he sank under a quivering mountain of them. His cries of agony were more prolonged than Leonard would have liked, but mercifully stopped at last, just as Leonard dropped into the driver's seat and propelled the car forward. The howling animals scattered, and there was nothing now to be seen of Bruce except an unrecognizable shape being dragged off by the last of them. A shape that had once worn a blue striped suit . . .

The car had a sunshine roof. Almost demented by what he had witnessed, Leonard opened it, stood on the seat and cried for help. But now there was no one within earshot to respond except the dogs, several of which snarled ominously from the shadows. He dropped again into the driver's seat and switched on full headlights, which only illuminated the shiny pool of blood where Bruce had last been seen. Three desperate turns brought him to the slope at the foot of which he urgently hoped and desired to find Rosalie and Bernard intact, since they had left the village proper before the holocaust began . . . and there they were indeed, picked up by his headlights as they sheltered from the drizzle against the back wall of a primitive bus shelter. Both seemed in good order, though Rosalie was on the verge of hysterics because of the terrible sounds which had assailed her ears from the upper *place*. To their questions, Leonard could only shake his head: it was too early even to try to explain what had happened to Bruce. And as for Tom, he presumably was still wandering the cobbled streets . . . unless the night of the dogs had been his last, too.

Leonard bundled the rescued pair into the back seat of the Volvo and zoomed once more up the hill, though when he arrived in the *place* he was careful to turn his headlights away from the blood. He had found a torch in the glove compartment, and when it revealed no sign of dogs he and Bernard ventured as far as the terrace to call once more for Tom. There was no reply; but nor was any window in Malchâteau opened in protest at this desecration of the small hours of night.

An official investigation was the only possibility which remained, but the local gendarmes, when summoned from the little station on the coast road, showed some reluctance to come up to the village at all. When prevailed upon to do so with a few guns and flashlights, their wary patrol of the steep narrow streets produced no conclusive discovery of Tom unless one counted, in a back alley under the cliff, one black shoe with part of a foot in it, such a fragment as may sometimes be left by a partly satisfied animal when its feast is disturbed. From the upper *place*, torn strips of the blue serge suit were also recovered. This was hysteria time for Leonard and Bernard as well as for Rosalie, but two hours later, as they sat huddled and dazed in the old gendarmerie, Leonard was sufficiently strengthened by cups of hot chocolate to take down from a shelf an old book called *Villages Perchés des Alpes-Maritimes*. Looking up Malchâteau, he found the following passage, given here in translation:

It is said that in medieval times the villagers kept savage dogs with whose help they waylaid and killed solitary travelers for their money and valuables. The dogs were bred for the purpose by a certain Madame Béjard who also kept a local restaurant, renamed *La Maitresse des Chiens*. Here, it was alleged, the remains of the victims often turned up in the *ragout*. The woman was executed in 1823, but to the villagers, whose fortunes seemed to turn for the better as a result of her activities (the notoriety attracting many tourists) she remained something of a heroine; and so for many years, no doubt with tongue in cheek, one winter night in each year has been reserved in her honor. Though a local by-law has long prevented dogs from being kept in the village (the chief intention being to prevent fouling of the narrow streets) and the restaurant itself was torn down a hundred years ago by incensed descendants of the victims, few who know the legend would venture alone on that night into the alleys of Malchâteau.

Leonard thought suddenly of the *steak au poivre*, and went off to be sick.

ECHOES FROM THE ABBEY

by Sheila Hodgson

As a rule I would have completed making my selections for The Year's Best Horror Stories by Christmas each year. This time, however, I was laid low for weeks by a memorably nasty flu bug, all of which delayed my mailing out permissions requests until the very last minute. So, on January 25 I wrote to Sheila Hodgson at her former address, and I quickly received her answer, dated January 30: "It was pure luck that I got your letter at all—we moved house six months ago and there is nobody living at our previous address! Fortunately (well, not really) the place was damaged in the hurricane we suffered last October, so we went back to Hove to oversee the repairs and found your contract lying in the hall." Perhaps "Echoes from the Abbey" was fated to appear in this book.

London-born Sheila Hodgson began her career in the theater before joining the BBC in 1960 as a staff writer. Six years later she turned free lance, writing for both commercial television and the BBC in addition to working extensively for radio. While she has also published short stories and a novel, fans of this genre will be most interested in a series of radio plays she wrote based upon story ideas suggested by M. R. James in his essay, "Stories I Have Tried to Write." "Echoes from the Abbey" is one of these *inventive efforts, and this story was originally written as a radio play, which was broadcast on BBC Radio 4 on November 21, 1984. As an added novelty, M. R. James himself takes center stage here.*

I have always held that friendship is the chief thing, friendship ranks first among the uncertain pleasures of this world. I have been fortunate in my friends, but acquaintances—ah, that is an altogether different matter! The casual meeting, the mumbled introduction, the name that all too often fails to reach my ear and if it does will convey nothing to me when I come face to face with the owner some days later. Horrible! Horrible! Moreover memory can play abominable tricks; it is not that I don't remember faces, I feel quite positive that I do. Not so long ago I had a letter from Canada, a graduate who declared he had met me at the May Day ball in 1893; he was apparently in England on a visit and expressed a great desire to see me again. Now I could have sworn I knew the gentleman, a medievalist and scholar of some talent. I made haste to send a cordial invitation. It was only when a wretched little humbug bounced into my chambers, all hairy beard and smiles, that I realized I had confused him with somebody else; why, I remembered this fellow and would have gone to considerable lengths to avoid him. Too late! Alas, too late! Since then I have exercised caution when dealing with any correspondent who claims to be an old acquaintance; the question is not Do they remember me—I will not dispute the recollection of others—but Do I remember them?

Arthur Layton. He wrote in flowing compliment underlining several of the words, a practice I deplore; he informed me that he had risen to become headmaster of some obscure private school and attributed his success entirely to my early tuition.

Arthur Layton?

Memory, when prodded, obliged with a faded impression of a young man, somewhat nervous, given to overstretching his limited ability. Yes, yes. Arthur Layton. I must confess I had not given the fellow another thought from that day to this; his letter seemed quite unreasonably cordial, good heavens, he invited me to visit him just before Christmas! He urged me to accept in black ink with more copious underlinings; he hinted at some mystery and promised lavish entertainment; the handwriting positively shook with anxiety and need. The pages were on their way to my waste paper basket, I had already formulated a polite refusal when, needing to prepare the envelope, I glanced at the address. Medborough Academy For Young Gentlemen, near Medborough Abbey.

Odd. I am frequently amused by the part played in our lives by coincidence. As chance would have it I had recently undertaken to write a series of articles on English Abbeys, and Medborough. . . ? A ruin as far as I could recall, a little-known enclosed order of monks had lived there and vanished entirely after the Suppression of the Monasteries. It might yield a couple of paragraphs; possibly I could sketch any points of architectural interest. I made my way to the college library and what I found there was so very curious . . .

But I anticipate. Suffice it to say that I redrafted my letter to Mr. Arthur Layton; I accepted his kind invitation, and on a day of quite unparalleled nastiness I descended from the train at Medborough Halt. A thin sleet hissed across the roof of the station and the landscape appeared to be soaked in mist.

There was nobody there.

I would certainly have gone straight home had the only train not left. I could see no cab or indeed any kind of conveyance, there were no railway staff visible and the waiting room proved to be locked. After rattling foolishly at the doorknob and shouting to the empty air, I grabbed my valise and set off down the road; fortunately the Abbey tower showed clear against the skyline, and at a little distance I perceived a squat building which must surely be the Academy For Young Gentlemen. My natural indignation made me step out at a good speed. I occupied myself by composing a speech; upon my word, this was a shabby way to treat a guest, to abandon him in the middle of winter at a strange railway station. After a while the sleet abated, by the time I drew level with the Abbey the mist had drained away into the ground and the ruins stood in wet blocks around me.

There was really very little left. A single finely vaulted bay which promised to reward investigation, some excellent late Perpendicular work, the traces of a cloister. I put down my baggage and made a detour; it might be sensible to discover what was or was not worthy of attention before the light went. I drew my cloak tight against the chill and smiled, the action reminding me briefly of my goddaughter. On seeing me for the first time in the garment, she had exclaimed, "Would you mind if I called you Black Mouse?" I assured her I should be honored; and remained Black Mouse to the end of the chapter. Still smiling at the recollection I picked my way among the masonry, and received a most disagreeable impression.

I was being watched.

It is hard to say what primeval instinct warns a man on such occasions. I could see nothing and hear no sound, yet I became most horribly aware of eyes following my every movement, an almost physical sensation in the small of my back. Robbers? Inconceivable. A tramp, sheltering among the arches. . . ? I paused—swung round—and surprised him.

A small boy, sitting high up on a ledge. My immediate concern was that the child might fall; I cried out loud:

"Boy! Come down at once! What are you doing there? Come down!"

He continued to stare at me with an expression of blank terror as if beholding some monstrous ghost, so I called to him again.

"This is not safe! Come here, you little imp!"

His voice reached me in a gasp barely audible above the wind.

"Are you one of *them*. . . ?" whispered the boy;

and tumbled backward in frantic alarm. He stumbled and picked himself up and disappeared among the tombstones—running, running, running.

Oh dear me. The young can be singularly irritating; I can cope with only a certain amount of unreason. I turned in some annoyance and made my way to the Medborough Academy, determined to rebuke my host and demand an explanation.

The man was not there. Mrs. Layton received me in a babble of apology; I gathered her husband had gone to meet the wrong train, I have no idea why. She fed me buttered toast and prattled by the fireside; at least they kept a good fire; a moth-eaten tiger rug lay on the floor concealing or rather failing to conceal a bare patch in the carpet; the furniture had seen better days but not, I fear, recently. The lady herself wore bangles, earrings, and thin ginger hair twisted into frizzy curls; she talked incessantly and seemed relieved when the door opened and Arthur Layton clattered in at last.

"Ah, Dr. James, do forgive me, I thought the Cambridge train arrived at four-ten, how very stupid, what appalling weather, have you had tea?"

He stood gabbling like his wife; I studied him, ah yes, I did remember the gentleman. The years had simply accentuated the eager smile, the semaphoring hands, the bulging eyes fixed on mine; he had looked the same in 1894 when he arrived in my chambers demanding to know, in tones of mounting hysteria, why his examination results had been so unaccountably bad. Then as now I lacked the courage to tell him the truth; I heard myself uttering conventional lies and assuring him I had enjoyed my walk from the station and was delighted to renew his acquaintance.

It had been a great mistake to come.

How great became apparent shortly after Mrs. Layton left us. I gathered she had private means; not to put too fine a point on it he had used her money to set up the Medborough Academy For Young Gentlemen. Well, well. That explained one mystery; I had indeed wondered how such a person had ever risen to be headmaster of anything. No matter. I wished him well, he was an amiable creature and entitled to do the best he could for himself. But worse was to follow; while offering me a small sherry he grew pink around the ears and said:

"Dr. James. It occurred to me. Forgive the liberty. I thought perhaps—as a friend—an old acquaintance. Would you care to mention Medborough Academy to any parents you meet at Cambridge? I should be most appreciative—grateful—and perhaps a small paragraph in your house magazine?"

I confess I felt outraged. One should not be over-sensitive, but I became conscious of being manipulated for private and possibly undesirable ends. It was a piece of impertinence, I had to frame my answer carefully; I had no wish to hurt the man but in all conscience . . .

"It would be highly improper, Layton! Oh come, come! Surely you realize! I really must decline to do anything of the sort. I have absolutely no knowledge of your school."

"You will be staying at least a week! You can form your own opinion!"

"While the place is empty? No, no, no. May we drop the subject, please, it can only embarrass both of us. Oh dear me. Good heavens. I fear you have invited me to Medborough on a false assumption; this is most unfortunate . . ."

At which juncture the door opened and a small boy peered in. I recognised him instantly; if he recognised me he showed no sign of it. Arthur Layton leapt to his feet, exclaiming:

"Harley! Good, yes, let me introduce you to Dr. James. Harley has been left with us for the Christmas holidays. His parents are in Hyderabad," he added, as if confiding some deplorable social gaffe. The boy shifted his feet, muttered "Sir" to the carpet and was understood to say that Dinner was ready. I wondered at the lack of a maid servant; during the meal it occurred to me that perhaps they had no cook either, the food being quite inexcusably bad. Layton kept up a running monologue on the problems that beset him, the shortage of teachers, the expense of the new gymnasium, the irrational demands of parents and a general tendency not to pay his fees on time. His wife echoed each complaint with little wails of her own, the boy ate in silence and I contented myself with those courteous grunts which pass for conversation on such occasions. As soon as I decently could I pleaded fatigue and the need to unpack, Mrs. Layton vanished into the kitchen, the child Harley skidded upstairs and I left Layton himself in a deep melancholy, stabbing at the fire with a cast iron poker.

At about two in the morning I woke from uneasy slumber to a sound of wild female shrieks. In that curious half-dreaming state my first conscious thought was: Ah, they have maids after all; then I struggled from bed, groped for my dressing gown and went out into the passage to investigate. A disheveled creature who I subsequently discovered was called Gladys rushed past me howling, "Oh sir, we can't find him, oh sir, he's been murdered in his bed!"

Before I could point out the basic absurdity of this statement Layton came down the stairway, he looked dazed and on seeing me stopped short, clutching at the bannister.

"James. I had no idea you were awake."

I remarked that it would be somewhat difficult to sleep through the general uproar.

"The boy is missing!"

"Good heavens."

"He must be found! We are responsible for the child! If there's been some frightful accident and his parents hear of it . . ."

It took several minutes to calm the man. I gathered he had discovered the situation by accident; on his way to the bathroom he noticed Harley's bedroom door ajar and the bed empty. As they had already searched the house I proposed to put my clothes on and help in a search of the grounds; by now it was half past two and bitter cold. On emerging into a glittering night (oh dear me, it had been snowing as well), I saw most of the household rampaging up and down alternately shrieking to the boy and shrieking to one another.

"Harley! Harley! Harley!"

Memory stirred at the back of my sleepy brain. A small figure balanced on a stone ledge. I left them to it and made my way across the frozen grass to the ruins of Medborough Abbey. It seemed to me that my hypothesis was quite as likely as any other. The ground proved treacherous, slippery with ice and potholed by neglect; twice I skidded, saving myself only by a wild clutch at a bush; once I tripped on a broken tombstone and nearly fell flat on my face, which would most certainly have broken my glasses if not my ankle. Jagged pillars cut the sky, slabs of masonry lay tilted at crazy angles, a net of hoar frost had been flung over everything and a thin wind hissed along the north transept. As I stepped between the boulders I could hear the wind. Surely it must be imagination that turned the sound into voices?

Does-he-know-he-must-not-know-he-surely-knows!
Does-he-know-he-must-not-know-he-surely-knows!

Whispering. Innumerable voices whispering among the ruin of the chapter house, and now they grew louder and now they grew ever clearer and more close.

Will-he-come-he-must-not-come-He-comes-he-comes!
Will-he-come-he-must-not-come-He-comes-he-comes!

As if a company of people were stealthily approaching, a muttering group of men . . .

Then the wind changed direction, and high above the chorus I heard Layton shouting that the boy had been found.

Sleepwalking, it appeared. He had wandered out of the house in his sleep and no harm done. Well, well. I returned to my bed and got precious little rest myself. My mind kept puzzling over the voices; they reminded me of a curious incident when I was at Eton. One of the pupils there was given to talking in his sleep, and I had noticed how, when this happened, the entire dormitory would begin to toss and turn and murmur until the whole room filled with a strange babbling sound. Odd. Being quite unable to close my eyes again I got up and spent the rest of the night studying the notes I had made on Medborough Abbey. It seemed the monks were allowed to talk together for one hour every day in a particular room set aside for the purpose, and very reasonably named the Talking Room. I amused myself by wondering if my voices had been some weird echo from the past, a recreation of a conversation long gone.

It was far more likely to be the wind.

I extinguished the gas and went back to bed.

Now, I had every intention of making some courteous excuse the next day and leaving; I found both the house and the company depressing and quite beyond anything I could do to help, alas. The unfortunate Layton had my sympathy but I could imagine no way of saving his Academy For Young Gentlemen; the whole enterprise had been foolhardy to a degree. I opened my mouth to frame a suitable apology to Mrs. Layton, to ask what time the next train left for Cambridge . . . and was forestalled by my host bursting into the breakfast room clutching a metal object.

"James! My dear James! How very fortunate, thank goodness you're here, I really have no idea what to do. It's extraordinary, inexplicable; I have questioned the boy of course, I have demanded an explanation, I can get no sense out of him at all. Bless my soul, what am I going to do?" He dropped the object on the table causing milk to spill from the jug and spread slowly across the tablecloth. Mrs. Layton uttered a little squeal while I . . . I looked at the thing.

It was a crucifix. A rather large crucifix, stained and

dented by age but quite possibly made of gold. I blinked. So did Mrs. Layton.

"Good gracious me."

"The housemaid found it in his bed! Hidden in that wretched boy's bed!"

I do not pretend to any expert knowledge of church antiques but it did seem a most curious discovery. I said as much and went with him to question the child. Our enquiries were not helped by the headmaster's hysterical insistence on "the truth, the truth, tell me the truth, Harley!", and Harley's defiance, a kind of timid obstinacy. He backed against the wall, he gazed fixedly at his boots; finally he declared:

"Well, he must have left it there."

"Who *left* it, Harley?"

"I think he was a monk!" said Harley, and burst into tears. When we succeeded in checking the flood there emerged through choking sobs a tale of bad dreams, moonlight, and a figure standing by the end of his bed.

"A ghost?" sneered Layton in tones that would have done credit to an actor at the Lyceum; he had a most unfortunate tendency to use theatrical gestures and intonations, a habit which ought not to have detracted from one's belief in his sincerity. But did. "I suppose this monk gibbered, rattled bones, and threatened you!"

"No," said Harley faintly. "He just looked rather surprised at finding me there."

"After which he vanished through the wall, no doubt!"

"I don't know what he did, sir! Honestly! I was hiding under the bedclothes."

"I will not listen to these impudent lies! How dare you, boy, your parents shall be informed, oh yes, they shall be told of your behavior. Where did you get the crucifix?"

"I didn't! It's nothing to do with me!"

"Liar!"

We were making no progress whatsoever and the

situation seemed to me to be getting out of hand. I stepped between the two and asked, "Why do you believe it was a monk, Harley?"

"Because the Abbey is haunted." A sniff. He wiped his nose. "Everybody knows the Abbey is haunted."

"The Abbey is not haunted!" shrieked Layton, quite beside himself with rage. "Go to your room, you wretched child! You will stay there and you will have no luncheon; would you try to deceive Dr. James; have you no honesty, no respect?"

Harley fled and Layton grumbled all the way back to the breakfast table, mostly on the subject of mendacious boys, the disobedience of the rising generation and the damage any rumors—however false—of ghostly apparitions could do to the school.

"I have enough troubles," he said somberly, and said no more for the remainder of the meal.

But I was sufficiently curious to seek out young Harley and ask for a more detailed account of his adventure. He struck me as a commonplace and rather timid person, unlikely to have invented the tale for the sake of notoriety; a theory much favored by Mrs. Layton who hinted the whole thing had been fabricated in a juvenile attempt to grab at our attention.

I did not think Harley wanted our attention.

In an effort to put the boy at his ease I chattered on about the Abbey, the enclosed order of monks, the place set aside for conversation and known as the Talking Room. This last roused him.

"Oh, I know where that is. I've heard them."

A flat statement. I could get no more and I would have dismissed it except for a memory which stirred in my own mind.

Does-he-know-he-must-not-know-he-surely-knows!

Strange. An illusion! Had we both had the same illusion?

It would do no harm to stay for another couple of days. I occupied the morning by sketching various parts of the Abbey; most of it appeared to be late Norman work and I particularly admired the south cloister. From time to time I would stop and listen. I could hear nothing save the faint movement of grass. Presently to my considerable annoyance it began to snow.

Over luncheon (to which young Harley had not been summoned; my host set great price on the consistency of his threats), Mrs. Layton leaned across the table and, trailing her sleeve in the soup, said:

"Do tell me, Dr. James, is much known about the history of Medborough Abbey? I mean, could there actually be a ghost or anything horrid like that?"

Her husband gave a snort of irritation and tore his roll in half, I consulted my recollections and produced the only story likely to entertain her.

"Well, now. There is a legend, I believe. It appears that during the Suppression of the Monasteries the monks plotted to save their precious silver and gold by the simple device of setting fire to the Abbey, having first removed the valuables; the purpose being to declare them lost in the ensuing blaze. They kept the plan secret from their Abbot. I regret to tell you he came upon them suddenly one day in the Talking Room and discovered everything."

"Good gracious! So they abandoned the plot?"

"No, no. The good Abbot, on overhearing their scheme, endorsed the idea of arson as both practical and prudent and gave it his blessing."

"So they burned the Abbey down. . . ? On purpose. . . ?"

"This is just hearsay," muttered Layton.

"My dear Layton, all history is merely hearsay, and written evidence often a record of other men's lies. I give you the tale for what it is worth."

"But how fascinating! What happened to the silver and gold?"

"I have no idea."

"I suppose the monks took it away. . . ?"

"We shall never know, Mrs. Layton. Unfortunately

Henry the King regarded both the fire and the monks with grave suspicion and they were hanged."

She gave the expected little squeal, her husband changed the subject and the meal ground to its indigestible end. As we left the table he indicated the crucifix now standing on the sideboard and murmured:

"Could that possibly be. . . ? James? Could it?"

I replied truthfully that I could not possibly tell, it would need to be dated by an expert in such things and I considered the notion unlikely in the extreme. But he lingered in the dining room after we had gone and a backward glance showed him polishing the relic vigorously with his table napkin.

The broken night had left me fatigued, I retired to my bedroom and was shaken from sleep by a ragged chorus of carol singers, apparently directly beneath my window. "God rest you merry, gentlemen, may nothing you dismay!" Upon my soul. I had been trying to rest, I was dismayed; still, we were within a week of Christmas and one should be charitable at the festive season. I opened the window meaning to throw a coin down and was mildly surprised to see three rough-looking men below. On hearing the noise they looked up and for some reason burst into raucous laughter. The next moment the front door opened and Layton came out; his appearance triggered another burst of laughter and more singing.

"God rest you, merry gentlemen, may nothing you dismay!"

They clustered round the headmaster; instead of receiving a suitable tip they were presenting him with some object, they were giving him—of all things!—a Christmas cracker. "Happy Christmas!" I cried, tossing down my contribution.

Layton stepped back and gazed up at me with the most extraordinary expression on his face; really, one would have said the man was frightened. Yet he knew I was there! As I watched, trying to make sense of his reaction, Mrs. Layton trotted down the steps, noticed the cracker in his hand and seized it. Her voice shrilled up through the cold air—a cracker, how delightful, why, they had not had crackers for years; how clever of the visitors to guess there was a child in the house! At this the carol singers backed away down the path laughing uncontrollably, Mrs. Layton squealed that she found the cold quite unendurable and retreated into the house taking the cracker with her. She waved it gaily as she went.

As for Layton . . . He stood there; and if he had seen young Harley's monk he could not have looked more shaken.

A curious scene. I shut the window and went back to bed.

Whatever their financial difficulties, Mrs. Layton had made a most determined effort to provide Christmas fare and an atmosphere of Yuletide jollity. We sat down that night to goose and plum pudding, the room had been decked with sprigs of evergreen and a pile of crackers occupied the center of the table, where they were in imminent danger of being set alight by the candles. Red crinkly paper, silver foil—she must have decided to supplement the gift; one cracker would have looked distinctly odd. Young Harley had evidently been forgiven; still, he seemed downcast, he concentrated on his food and made no attempt to respond to Mrs. Layton's playful jokes, while Layton, I regret to say, concentrated on the wine and was drinking altogether too much of it. From time to time he eyed the center decoration. I confess to a certain interest myself; one of them might indeed be the cracker handed in at the door, impossible to say which. So Layton drank and Mrs. Layton prattled, the boy ate and the crucifix winked on the sideboard. It had been polished to great advantage.

The meal commenced at half past six; by eight o'clock my host appeared slightly drunk, his wife's hair was coming down while Harley looked sick, no doubt from an excess of sugar plums. The maid Gladys served coffee. Mrs. Layton suddenly made a little grab at the heap crying "Crackers! Crackers!" Her action scattered the things in all directions, I noticed her husband fumbling through them with a shaking hand, and if he could identify that one particular cracker it was more than I could do. Courtesy demanded I join in the gaiety; we pulled crackers, we read appalling jokes to each other and laughed quite immoderately. There were snaps and mottoes and paper hats which perched uneasily upon our adult heads. I gathered this performance was for the benefit of the boy, who was most certainly not enjoying it. He leaned forward obediently, urged on by Mrs. Layton. As the snap exploded with a small "plop" and the red casing tore apart, something fell to the table between them. Arthur Layton snatched it up.

"That's mine!" protested Harley.

"Arthur, don't be naughty, that was our cracker!"

He continued to stare at the scrap of paper in his hand.

"Arthur? Is it a joke? Oh, do tell us, what have you got there, a motto or a riddle? I love riddles, don't you love riddles, Dr. James?"

I nodded. The puzzle occupying my mind at that moment was why the headmaster should look so inexplicably alarmed. He recovered almost instantly, muttering words to the effect that the contents were unsuitable for juvenile ears; he stuffed the paper into his pocket and reached for the wine decanter. For some time after, he sat in a morose silence and kept glancing at the clock. Presently, and possibly because she had noticed the direction of his eyes, Mrs. Layton turned to Harley and cried merrily, "Bedtime! Bedtime!"

I began to rise from the table myself; and was astonished to hear Layton exclaim: "NO!".

He pushed the chair back. His eyes were quite unnaturally bright and his manner really very odd. It occurred to me that the man had had far too much to drink.

"We must celebrate!" He leaned on the chair for

support. "We have an honored guest, we have Dr. James with us; he is an authority—an authority on Medievalism." He stumbled over the word. "He wants to see the Abbey. Come along, come along, we must show him the Abbey."

"Not at this time of night, Arthur!"

Her wail was echoed by my own protest; I had no desire to be dragged out into the winter air, I am subject to colds. He ignored us both, and staggered toward the door, both arms flailing.

"Tomorrow we might be snowed up. It won't do. Tomorrow will be too late."

We chased after him, raising every sensible objection; the whole idea of visiting the ruins was ludicrous, out of the question . . . But he was already in the hall shouting for the staff, calling for lanterns, and urging us to put on warm overcoats. I drew Mrs. Layton aside and begged her to get her husband to bed. She was in tears and totally ineffective, she clutched at my arm and entreated me not to leave them; the scene grew further confused as young Harley shot out of the dining room shrieking that the Abbey was haunted and he wouldn't go. So far from helping the situation, this goaded Layton into further and even more grotesque action; he vanished from the hall and reappeared carrying the crucifix, he shouted defiance: the Abbey was not haunted, there were no ghosts, and he would not suffer his school to be destroyed by vicious rumors and malicious invention!

In the end we wrapped ourselves in outer clothing and trailed after him; he had succeeded by now in raising the entire household. We crossed the grass in ragged procession, clinging on to one another to avoid slipping on the frozen ground. I have never seen a more absurd undertaking. Arriving among the ruins it became apparent that Mr. Layton (who did not believe in ghosts) had come there with the intention of exorcising them. He placed the crucifix on a ledge and began to intone prayers of doubtful authenticity and quite horrid ferocity, calling on the Lord to strike his enemies dead; he insisted on our small group—Mrs. Layton, the boy, the maid Gladys, the cook—responding to his exhortations. And very strange we must have looked, gathered together in the shadow of the north transept, the lantern flickering in the wind. I listened: among Layton's outbursts I managed to identify lines from the terrible 109th Psalm. "Destroy mine enemy! Set thou a wicked man over him and let Satan stand at his right hand!" Something pressed against my side; I became conscious of Harley cowering up against me and realized that he was listening too.

But for something else.

"Can you hear them?" he whispered.

I feigned ignorance; one should not needlessly alarm the young, and besides I could hear nothing save Layton's voice raised in prayer, our own mumbled Amens, and a rustling . . .

A whispering?

A dry murmur from beyond the arch.

At that moment Layton shouted to heaven for justice, Mrs. Layton squealed, the cook jumped sideways, knocked over the lantern and the light went out. There was a certain amount of confused scuffling in the dark; by some malign chance the moon took that moment to vanish behind a surge of billowing cloud.

I became conscious of a strong smell of burning.

And then beyond all hope of pretense or concealment I heard them—they came from the chapter house, they rushed upon us through the shattered pillars of the nave, and the chorus grew and swelled and became a monstrous roar.

Save-us-save-us-save-us-save-us-save-us!
Save-us-save-us-save-us-save-us-save-us!
SAVE-US-SAVE-US-SAVE-US!

On a sleepless night it can haunt me still. There arose from the ruins a kind of spiraling vapor, a mist that wavered and took form and swept along the north transept; the most appalling stench hit our nostrils, we scattered and fled in all directions and still the Thing swept on. My last impression was of a series of gaping mouths set in folds of dirty linen.

It lasted perhaps ten seconds. It ended, leaving only a faint murmur beyond the columns, the noise of Gladys weeping, and an all-pervading reek of decay. We calmed the women to the best of our ability, Mrs. Layton's terror subsiding quite fast into a shrill abuse. We discovered the path and thought at first the moon must have reappeared, for the horizon seemed flooded with light. But Harley cried that the whole sky was changing color, and as we turned the reason became dreadfully apparent.

The school was on fire.

Round blobs erupted from the roof, they sprouted like so many black toadstools from the gable and rose and spread in puff-ball smoke. Lurid streaks of flame shot up between them and flared and sank again. The maid Gladys screamed "Oh my God," Layton stood as if nailed to the ground, his wife called out—absurdly, ludicrously!—"Help, help, help!" Then we all began to run.

I have nothing but praise for the fire service. They arrived within forty minutes, they struggled with great courage to control the blaze; but the fact remains that there had been a fatal delay owing to the number of emergencies over the Christmas holiday, the dangerous state of the roads due to the weather, and our own failure to alert them at once. I have a confused memory of ladders, hose pipes, men clambering along the parapet and a solitary figure which appeared at a window and threw a tiger-skin rug onto the lawn, where it lay grinning among the debris. As for the rest—Why—shouts, screaming, the hiss of water and the crash of falling masonry. At one point I came upon Layton staring wild-eyed at the chaos.

"I fear they have come too late," I said.

"Yes," he replied. "They can do nothing now."

Next day the cold swept back, refreezing the snow which had melted in the heat, forming strange patterns on the ground, twisting curves and lines and rivulets of ice between the blackened walls. And so I left them side by side: the ancient ruin of the Abbey and the present wreck of Medborough Academy For Young Gentlemen.

Two months after the disaster, Arthur Layton called on me at Cambridge. He seemed in low spirits, understandably. He sat drinking whiskey and bewailing his fate; he had moved his family into lodgings, he had written to the parents of one hundred children, and had arranged for some distant cousin to collect the luckless Harley. Life held nothing but misery and confusion. I offered conventional sympathy and more whiskey; the fellow appeared positively distraught, pacing backward and forward, and waving his arms in the old remembered semaphoring gesture. I had to stop him sitting down again upon my cat. Presently he leaned forward and whispered:

"James. I am in serious difficulties."

Well, yes. One would have supposed as much, given the facts. Moreover I could not imagine why the man was whispering; we were quite alone and the door to my chambers shut. He glanced at it, then at the window, then he dropped his voice even lower and said:

"The insurance company have refused to pay me."

Certain rather horrid suspicions began to form in my mind.

"Oh dear me."

"A minor problem! Of no significance! They seem to find it odd that everybody had left the building before it went up in flames. Now, you and I know, Dr. James, we were playing a harmless Christmas game! Amusing the staff! Why, anything might start a fire at Christmas time—candles falling from the tree, a log rolling out onto the carpet, I can think of a dozen reasons."

I felt reasonably sure he could.

"It's utterly monstrous to suggest . . . James, James, you were there! You can bear witness that we went to the Abbey because we had celebrated rather too well;

we were merry, we needed fresh air, we decided to take a walk. The maids came with us because it was the festive season, peace to all men; I *believe* in a democratic society!" cried Layton. "We are brothers under the skin!"

He had certainly made sure everybody got out. On my first arrival at Medborough Abbey I had been indignant, I had resented his suggestion that I might advertise his college; it seemed to me I was being manipulated. My feelings then were as nothing to my emotions now.

"Layton. Are you telling me you are suspected of having started the fire yourself?"

The cat got up and prudently removed itself to a distance.

"It's ludicrous! Absurd! Not that I blame them, no, no, obviously they have to be cautious. But I must have the money, James! I must! If you will just speak for me—explain the situation—a man of your reputation and standing should have no trouble persuading them."

"I see."

Alas, I did see, and all too clearly.

"Could you oblige me? If you would be so very kind and write a suitable letter to the insurance company?"

"No," I said. I might have had more sympathy for the man but for his blatant attempt to use me, to exploit an early acquaintance.

"But Dr. James . . ."

I opened the door. Embarrassment, distress, and a degree of justifiable annoyance gave too much edge to my voice.

"I am very sorry. I fear I must absolutely decline to have any part in this business."

Do you blame me? It was fraud: plain, clumsy and criminal.

He stood, the color flooding into his cheeks; then he gathered up his coat and left without looking at me. I could hear the bells ringing across the court as he went.

I never saw Arthur Layton again. He wrote to me once; a wild incoherent epistle concerning Medborough Abbey. The monks' treasure, wrote Layton; when they fired the Abbey where did they hide the treasure? The crucifix. I did remember the crucifix; in the general alarm of that night the crucifix had vanished, but was it possible, did I not think it probable the crucifix had formed part of their horde? And surely, surely if there had been one object there might be others: a chalice, candelabra, gold or silver plate; now where in my considered opinion would such valuables have been concealed? Where should he start digging?

I had no opinion on the subject. My view of the thing had been altogether too brief; in any event it struck me as infinitely more likely that the monks' possessions were scattered throughout England, and as for the folly of digging through the Medborough ruins—I replied in terms of gentle discouragement.

He never answered. I opened my newspaper one morning to read the unhappy news that the schoolmaster had been found dead near Medborough Abbey, apparently of a heart attack. I would have written to his wife but was quite unable to discover her address. Whether the man had indeed been engaged on some frantic treasure hunt, whether he met again the whispering brothers and saw again their gaping faces, we shall never know.

VISITORS

by Jack Dann

*Born in Johnson City, New York on February
15, 1945, Jack Dann presently lives with his wife in
Binghamton, New York in "an old Greek Revival,
which could fit the Third Regiment." Dann has written or edited more than twenty-one books to date,
some of them in collaboration with Gardner Dozois.
Recent books include his mainstream novel,* Counting Coup, *and an anthology of stories concerned
with the Vietnam War,* In the Fields of Fire, *edited
with his wife, Jeanne Van Buren Dann.*

*Jack Dann's stories often exemplify what Charles
L. Grant calls "quiet horror"—a sense of melancholy and unease devoid of bloody chainsaws and
exploding heads. Noted fantasy critic, E. F. Bleiler,
commenting on Dann's story, "Tattoos," in* The
Year's Best Horror Stories: Series XV, *wrote that it
"has suggestions of Chagall and Isaac Bashevis
Singer." Not bad company for a writer.*

After Mr. Benjamin died, he came back to Charlie's
room for a visit. He was a tall man, taken down to the
bone by cancer. His face had a grayish cast; and his
thick white hair, of which he had been so obviously
proud, had thinned. But he was still handsome even as
he stood before Charlie's bed. He was sharp-featured,
although his mouth was full, which softened the effect

of his piercing, pale blue eyes; he wore white silk pajamas and a turquoise robe, and was as poised and stiff as an ancient emperor.

"They closed all the doors again," Charlie said to Mr. Benjamin—they always closed the doors to the patients' rooms when they had to wheel a corpse through the hallway.

"I guess they did," Mr. Benjamin said, and he sat down in the cushioned chair beside Charlie's bed. He usually came for a visit before bedtime; it was part of his nightly ritual.

But here he was, and it was mid-afternoon.

Sunlight flooded through a tripartite window into the large high-ceilinged room, magnifying the swirling dust motes that filled the room like snow in a crystal Christmas scene paperweight. The slate-gray ceiling above was barrel-vaulted and although cracked and broken and discolored, the plaster was worked into intricate patterns of entwined tendrils. A marble fireplace was closed off with a sheet of metal, and there was an ancient mahogany grandfather clock ticking in the corner. The hospital had once been a manor, built in the eighteen hundreds by the wealthiest man in the state; its style was Irish gothic, and every room contained the doric columns and scrolled foliage that was a trademark of the house.

"I wonder who died?" Charlie asked.

Mr. Benjamin smiled sadly and stretched his long legs out under Charlie's bed.

Charlie was fifteen and had had an erection before Mr. Benjamin came into the room, for he was thinking about the nurses, imagining how they would look undressed. Although Charlie's best friend had been laid, Charlie was still a virgin; but he looked older than he was and had even convinced his best friend that he, too, had popped the cork. He had been feeling a bit better these last few days. He had not even been able to think about sex before; there was only pain and drugs, and even with the drugs he could feel the pain. All the drugs did were let him investigate its shape; Charlie had discovered that pain had shape and color; it was like an animal that lived and moved inside him.

"How are you feeling today?" Mr. Benjamin asked.

"Pretty good," Charlie said, although the pain was returning and he was due for another shot. "How about you?"

Mr. Benjamin laughed. Then he asked. "Where's Rosie?" Rosie was Charlie's private nurse. Charlie's father was well-to-do and had insisted on round-the-clock private nurses for his son. But Charlie didn't want private nurses or a private room; in fact, he would have preferred a regular double-room and a roommate, which would have been much less expensive; and if Charlie had another setback, his roommate would be able to call for a nurse for him. Charlie had been deathly ill: he had developed peritonitis from a simple appendectomy, and his stomach was still hugely distended. Drainage tubes were sunk deeply into his incisions, and they smelled putrid. He had lost over thirty pounds.

Charlie seemed to be slipping in and out of a dream; it was just the Demerol working through his system.

"Rosie's off today," he said after a long pause. He had been dreaming of whiteness, but he could hear clearly through the dream. He came fully awake and said, "I love her, but it's such a relief not to have her banging everything around and dropping things to make sure I don't fall asleep. The regular nurses have been in a lot, and I got two backrubs." He grinned at Mr. Benjamin. It was a game he played with Mr. Benjamin: who could win the most points in wooing the nurses. One night, when Charlie had been well enough to walk across the hall and visit Mr. Benjamin, he found him in bed with two nurses. Mr. Benjamin had a grin on his face, as if he had just won the game forevermore. The nurses, of course, were just playing along.

Mr. Benjamin leaned back in the chair. It was a bright, sunny day, and the light hurt Charlie's eyes when he stared out the window for too long. Perhaps it was an effect of the Demerol, but Mr. Benjamin just seemed . . . not quite defined, as if his long fingers and strong face were made out of the same dustmotes that filled the air and the room.

"Is your wife coming over today?" Charlie asked. "It's Wednesday." Charlie was in on Mr. Benjamin's secret: two women came to visit him religiously. His mistress, a beautiful young woman with long red hair, on Tuesdays and Thursdays; and his wife, who wasn't beautiful, but who must have been once, and who was about the same age as Mr. Benjamin, came every Monday, Wednesday, Friday, and Sunday. His friends came to see him on Saturday, but not his women.

"No, not today," Mr. Benjamin said.

"That's too bad."

And just then one of the nurses came into the room. She was one of the old hands, and she said hello to Charlie, fluffed up his pillow, took his temperature, and gave him a shot all the while she talked, but it was small-talk. The nurse ignored Mr. Benjamin, as she tore away the bandages that covered the drainage tubes in Charlie's stomach. Then she pulled out the tubes, which didn't hurt Charlie, and cleaned them. After she had reinserted the tubes—two into the right side of his abdomen, one into the left—and replaced the bandages, she hung another clear plastic bag of saline solution on the metal pole beside the bed and adjusted the rate of fluid that dripped into the vein in Charlie's right wrist.

"Who died?" Charlie asked her, wishing one of the pretty nurses'-aides had been sent in, or had at least accompanied her.

She sat down on the bed and rubbed Charlie's legs. He had lost so much weight that they were the size his arms had once been. This nurse was one of Charlie's favorites, even though she was old—she could have been fifty or sixty-five, it was difficult to tell. She had a wide, fleshy face, a small nose, and perfect, capped teeth. "You'll have to know anyway," she said without looking up at him. "It was Mr. Benjamin. I know how close you felt to him, and I'm so very sorry, but as you know he was in a lot of pain. This is the best thing for the poor man, you've got to try to believe that. He's in a happier place now."

Charlie was going to tell her she was crazy, that he was right here, and had a mistress and a wife and an architect job to go back to and that it was all bullshit about a happier place, but he just nodded and turned toward Mr. Benjamin. She made a fuss over Charlie, who was ignoring her, and finally left. "Are you sure you'll be okay?" she asked.

Charlie nodded. His mouth felt dry; the Demerol would soon kick in. "Yeah, I'll be fine." Then, turning back to Mr. Benjamin, he asked, "Are you really dead?"

Mr. Benjamin nodded. "I suppose I am."

"You don't look dead."

"I don't feel dead. My goddamn legs are still aching and itching like hell."

Charlie's face felt numb. "Why are you in here if you're dead?"

"How the hell should I know. There are worse places I can think of. I just got out of bed and walked in here, same way as I always do."

"Are you going to stay?"

"For a while. Do you mind?"

Charlie just shook his head and took comfort, as he always did, in Mr. Benjamin's presence. But then the man in the next room started screaming again, praying to God to relieve him of his pain, begging and whining and whimpering and waking up the other patients.

It was difficult to rest with all that commotion going on.

The Demerol came upon him like a high-tide of anesthesia. It soaked into him and everything in the hospital room turned white, as if the molding and wall panels and ceiling scrollwork and inlaid marble chimney piece were carved out of purest snow. He dreamed of winter and castles and books he had read when he was a child. He was inside a cloud, his thoughts drifting, linking laterally, as he dreamed of chalk and snow and barium, of whitewash and bleach, of silver and frost and whipped cream, of angels and sand, of girls as white as his Demerol highs, chalky and naked with long white hair and pale lips, long and thin and small breasted, open and wet and cold, cold as snow, cold as his icicle erection, cold as his thoughts of glacially slow coitus.

He woke up shivering in a dark room, sweat drying on his goosebumped skin. Gray shadows crawled across the room, a result of traffic on the street below.

Mr. Benjamin was still sitting beside the bed.

"Have you been here all this time?" Charlie asked. It was late. The nurses had turned out the lights in his room, and the hallway was quiet. If he listened carefully and held his breath, he could hear the snoring and moaning of other patients between the tickings of the clock. His mouth was parched, and he reached for the water tumbler. It sat on his nineteen-fifties style nighttable, which also contained the remote control unit that turned the television on and off and also allowed him to buzz the nurse's station. He poured some icewater into a paper cup. "You look more . . . real," Charlie said.

"What do you mean?" Mr. Benjamin asked.

"I dunno, you looked kinda weak before."

"Well, I'm feeling better now. My legs stopped itching, and they only ache a little bit now. I can stand it, at least. How about you?"

"I feel like crap again," Charlie said. "I thought I was getting better." The pain in his stomach was intense and stabbing; it hadn't been this bad in a long time. "And I know that old fat Mrs. Campbell isn't going to give me another shot until I start screaming and moaning like the guy across the hall."

Charlie's night-nurse thought he was becoming too dependent on painkillers.

"He's getting worse," Mr. Benjamin said.

"Who?" Charlie asked.

"The guy across the hall, Mr. Ladd. Rosie told me he'd had most of his stomach removed."

"I just wish he would stop crying and begging for the pain to go away. I can't stand it. He makes such a racket. There's something pitiful about it. And he's not the only one who's in pain around here."

"Well, who knows, maybe he can cut a deal," Mr. Benjamin said.

"You're not dead," Charlie said.

Mr. Benjamin shrugged.

"I thought you said you had all kinds of contracts to build new buildings and stuff. You said you wanted to work until you dropped dead, that you wanted to travel and all. And what about Miss Anthony . . . and your wife?"

"It's all gone," Mr. Benjamin said.

"Doesn't it bother you?"

"I don't know," he said, surprised. "I don't really feel anything much about it. Maybe a little sad. But I guess not even that."

"Tell me what it's like to be dead."

"I don't know. The same as being alive, I would suppose, except my legs feel better."

"You're not dead," Charlie said.

"I'll take your word for it, Charlie."

Charlie became worse during the night. He used the speaker in the nighttable to call Mrs. Campbell for a shot, but she told him he wasn't due for another hour. He tried to argue with her, he kept calling her, but she ignored him. He listened to the clock on the wall and turned this way and that, trying to find a comfortable position. Goddamn her, Charlie thought, and he tried to count himself to sleep. If he could fall asleep for just a little while, it would then be time for his shot.

Goddamn it hurts. . . .

And Mr. Ladd across the hall started screaming and whining and trying to make a deal with God again. Charlie gritted his teeth and tried to pretend that the room was turning white, and that he was numb and frozen, made of blue ice. Ice: the absence of pain.

"Mr. Benjamin, are you still there?" Charlie asked.

But there was no answer.

Finally, it was time for his shot, and Charlie slept, drifting through cold spaces defined by the slow ticking of the clock.

Although it was four in the morning and everyone was asleep, the nurses and orderlies ritually closed the doors, as they always did, when they wheeled a corpse down the hallway.

Charlie was awake and feeling fine when Mr. Benjamin brought Mr. Ladd into the room; the pain was isolated and the metallic taste of the drugs was strong in his mouth. Mr. Ladd appeared nervous. He was in his sixties, and bald. He was thin, emaciated-looking, and his skin was blemished with age-marks.

"Our friend here hasn't quite gotten used to being dead," Mr. Benjamin said to Charlie. "I found him wandering around the hallway. You mind if he stays a while?"

"I dunno," Charlie said, although he didn't want the old man in his room. "What's he going to do here?"

"Same thing you're doing. Same thing I'm doing."

Mr. Ladd didn't even acknowledge Charlie. He looked around the room, his head making quick, jerky motions; then he walked across the room, sat down on the stained cushion of the windowseat, and looked down into the street.

"At least your pain's gone," Mr. Benjamin called to him, but the old man just stared out the window, as if he hadn't heard him. "How about you?" Mr. Benjamin asked Charlie.

"I'm okay, I guess," but then someone else came into the room. A middle-aged woman in a blue bathrobe. She exchanged greetings with Mr. Benjamin and walked over to the window. "You know her?" Charlie asked.

"Yeah, I sat with her some yesterday and tonight she was real bad. But I guess you can't win. I left Mr. Ladd to be with her. Now they're both here." Mr. Benjamin smiled. "I feel like a goddamned Florence Nightingale."

But Charlie had fallen asleep.

He awoke to bright sunlight. His condition had deteriorated further, for now he had an oxygen tube breathing icy air into one nostril, while in the other was a tube that passed down his esophagus and into his stomach. His private nurse Rosie was in the room, moving about, looking starched and efficient and upset. His mother sat beside the bed, leaning toward him, staring at him intently, as if she could think him well. Her small, delicate face seemed old to him, and her dyed jet-black hair looked as coarse and artificial as a cheap wig. But both his mother and Rosie seemed insubstantial, as if *they* were becoming ghosts. His mother blocked out most of the light coming through the windows, but some of it seemed to pass through her, as if she were a cloud shaped like a woman that was floating across the sun. Her voice, which was usually high and piercing, was like a whisper; and her touch felt dry, like leaves brushing against his skin. He suddenly felt sorry for his mother. She loved him, he supposed, but he felt so removed from her. He probably felt like Mr. Benjamin did when he died. Just a little sad.

Charlie just wished that everyone would leave. He looked toward the light, and saw Mr. Benjamin, Mr. Ladd, and the woman who had walked into his room last night standing near the window. He called for Mr. Benjamin; neither Rosie nor his mother seemed to understand what he was saying.

"Mr. Benjamin?"

His mother said something to Rosie, who also said something to Charlie, but Charlie couldn't understand either of them. Their voices sounded far away; it was like listening to static on the radio, and only being able to make out a word here or there. It was as if Rosie and his mother were becoming ghosts, and the visitors, who were already dead, were gaining substance and reality.

"Yes?" Mr. Benjamin said as he walked over to the bed and stood beside Charlie's mother. "I'm afraid you've had a bit of a setback."

"What are they still doing here?" Charlie asked, meaning Mr. Ladd and the woman who had come into his room last night.

"Same thing I am," said Mr. Benjamin.

"Okay, what are *you* doing here?"

"Making sure you won't be alone."

Charlie closed his eyes.

Perhaps his mother sensed the presence of the visitors, too, for she suddenly began to cry.

Charlie's mother stayed for the rest of the day. She talked about Charlie's father, as if nothing was going wrong with their marriage, as if she could simply ignore the other dark haired woman who had come into her husband's life. Charlie knew about Laura, the other woman; but he had learned a lot about such things from watching Mr. Benjamin's wife and mistress come and go every week. He supposed it was just the way adults behaved. He couldn't stand to see his mother hurt, yet he couldn't get angry with his father. He felt somehow neutral about the whole thing.

She sat and talked to Charlie as she drank cup after cup of black coffee. She would nod off to sleep for a few minutes at a time and then awaken with a jolt. At five she took her dinner on a plastic tray beside Charlie's bed. Charlie couldn't eat; he was being fed intravenously. He slept fitfully, cried out in pain, received a shot, and lived in whiteness for a while. When he was on the Demerol, his mother and Rosie would all but disappear, yet he would be able to see Mr. Benjamin and the visitors. But Mr. Benjamin wouldn't talk much to him when his mother or hospital personnel were in the room.

Finally, Rosie's shift was over. Rosie tried to talk Charlie's mother into leaving with her, but it was no use. She insisted on staying. Mrs. Campbell, the night nurse, talked with Charlie's mother for a while, and then left the room, as she always did. Charlie would need a shot soon.

His mother held his hand and kept leaning over him, brushing her face against his, kissing him. She talked, but Charlie could barely hear or feel her.

Charlie came awake with a jolt; it was as if he had fallen out of the bed. He was sweaty and could taste something bitter in his mouth. The drugs were still working, but the pain was returning, gaining strength. It was an animal tearing at his stomach. Only a shot and the numbing chill of white sleep could calm it down . . . for a time.

"Hello," said a young woman standing by the bed beside Mr. Benjamin. She had straight, shoulder-length dark brown hair, a heart-shaped face, blue eyes set a bit too widely apart, a small, upturned nose, and full, but colorless lips. She looked tiny, perhaps five feet one, if that, and seemed very shy.

"Hello," Charlie replied, surprised. He felt awkward and looked over to Mr. Benjamin, who smiled. It was dark again. He turned toward the spot where his mother had been sitting, but he couldn't tell if she was still there. He could only hear the clock and the sound of leaves rustling that he imagined might be his mother's voice. The room was dimly lit, and there seemed to be a shadow, a slight flutter of movement, around the chair. Except for the visitors, the hospital seemed empty and devoid of doctors, nurses, orderlies, aides, and candystripers. Charlie felt numb and cold. The air in the room was visible . . . was white as cirrus clouds and seemed to radiate its own wan light.

"This is Katherine," Mr. Benjamin said. "She's new here, and a bit disoriented, I think." Katherine seemed to be concentrating on the foot of the bed and avoiding eye contact with Charlie. But Charlie noticed that she didn't seem as real, as corporal, somehow, as Mr. Benjamin. Perhaps she wasn't dead long enough. That would take some time. "I'll step aside and give you a chance to win this time," Mr. Benjamin continued.

Charlie blushed. Mr. Benjamin walked to the other side of the room to be with the other visitors.

"How did you die?" Charlie asked Katherine.

She just shook her head, a slight, quick motion.

"Do you feel all right?" he asked. "Are you scared or anything?"

"I just feel alone," she said in almost a whisper.

"Well, you got Mr. Benjamin," Charlie said.

She smiled sadly. "Yeah, I guess." She sat down on the bed. Her robe was slightly opened and Charlie could see a hint of her cleavage. "Are you dying?" she asked.

That took him by surprise, although as soon as she said it, he realized that it shouldn't have. "I dunno. I've just been sick."

"Do you want to live?"

"Yeah, I guess so. Wouldn't you?"

"It feels kinda the same," she said, "only—"

"Only what?"

"I don't know, it's hard to explain. Just alone, like I said. You seem out of focus, sort of," she said. She touched his hand tentatively, and Charlie could feel only a slight pressure and a cool sensation. Charlie held her hand. It was an impulsive move, but she didn't resist. Her hand felt somehow papery, and Charlie had the feeling that he could press his fingers right through her flesh with but little resistance. She leaned toward him, resting against him. It felt like the cool touch of fresh sheets. She seemed weightless. "Thank you," she whispered.

He curled up against her, put his arm around her waist and rested his hand on her leg. He remembered taking long baths and letting his arms float in the water. Although the water would buoy them up, it also felt as if he was straining against gravity. That's what it felt like to touch Katherine.

Charlie wanted this to last; it was perfect. He felt the pain in his stomach, but it was far away. Someone else was groaning under its weight.

They watched visitors file into the room. Each one looking disoriented and out of focus. Each one walking across to the other side, to the window, to be with the others, who began to seem as tangible and fleshy as Charlie.

Charlie tried to ignore them. He pulled the sheets over himself . . . and Katherine. He pressed himself as closely as he could to her, and she allowed him to kiss and fondle her.

As everything turned white, numbed by another shot given to him by a ghost, his nurse, Charlie dreamed that he was making love to Katherine.

It was cool and quiet, a wet dream of death.

At dawn Mr. Benjamin called Charlie to leave. The room was empty; the last of the other visitors had just left without a footfall. Mr. Benjamin looked preternaturally real, as if every line of his face, every feature had been etched into perfect stone. Katherine rose from the bed and stood beside Mr. Benjamin, her robe tightly pulled around her. She, too, looked real and solid, more alive than any of the shadows flitting through the halls and skulking about his room: the nurses and aides and orderlies. Charlie found it difficult to breathe; it was as if he had to suck every breath from a straw.

"Why are you leaving?" Charlie asked, his voice raspy; but his words were glottals and gutturals, sighs and croakings.

"It's time. Are you coming?"

"I can't. I'm sick."

"Just get up. Leave what's in the bed," Mr. Benjamin said impatiently, as if dying was not a terribly important or difficult thing to do.

Katherine reached for his hand, and her flesh was firm and real and strong. "I can see you very clearly now," she said. "Come on."

But someone moved in the chair beside Charlie. A shadow, more of a negative space. Charlie tried to make it out. Into a soft focus came the outlines of a woman, his mother. But she was a wraith. Yet he could make her out, could make out her voice, which sounded as distant as a train lowing through the other side of town. She was talking about his younger brother Stephen and the sunflowers behind the house that had grown over six feet tall. The sunflowers always made Charlie feel sad, for they signaled the end of summer and the beginning of school. He could feel the warm, sweaty touch of her hand on his face, touching his forehead, which was the way his mother had always checked his temperature.

"I love you, Charlie," she said, her voice papery. "Everything's going to be all right for all of us. And you're going to get well soon. I promise. . . ."

Katherine's hand slipped away, and then Charlie felt the warm, almost hot, touch of his mother's hand upon his own. She clutched his fingers as if she knew she might be losing him, and in the distance, Charlie could hear that train sound: now the sound of his mother crying. And he remembered the rich and wonderful smells that permeated her tiny kitchen when she was making soup; he could see everything in that room: the radio on the red painted shelves, the china bric-a-brac, the red and black electric cat clock on the wall that had a plastic tail and eyes that moved back and forth; and he remembered his grandmother, who always brought him a gift when she visited; and he could almost hear the voices of his friends, as if they were all passing between classes; he remembered kissing Laurie, his first girlfriend, and how he had tried unsuccessfully to feel her up behind her house near the river; and even with his eyes closed he could clearly see his little brother, who always followed him around like a duck, and his gray-haired, distant father who was always "working"; he remembered the time he and his brother hid near the top of the red carpeted stairs and watched the adults milling around and drink-

ing and laughing and kissing each other at a New
Year's Eve party, and how his father had awakened
him and his brother at four o'clock in the morning on
New Year's day so they could eat eggs and toast and
home fries with him and Mom in the kitchen; he
remembered going to Atlantic City for two weeks in
the summer, the boardwalk hot and crowded and gritty
with sand, the girls in bikinis and clogs, their skin
tanned and hair sun-bleached; he remembered that his
mother always tanned quickly, and she looked so young
that everyone thought she was his girlfriend when they
went shopping along the boardwalk; and suddenly that
time came alive, and he could smell salt water taffy
and taste cotton candy and snow cones that would
immediately start to melt in the blazing, life-giving
sun.

Charlie could feel himself lifting, floating; yet another part of him was solid, fleshy, heavy with blood
and bone and memory.

He thought of Katherine, of her coolness, the touch
of her pale lips and icy breasts . . . and then his
mother came into focus: age-lines, black hair, shadows
under frightened hazel eyes—his eyes.

And her touch was as strong as Katherine's.

He floated between them . . . caught.

Soon he would have to decide.

THE BELLFOUNDER'S WIFE

by A. F. Kidd

A. F. Kidd, better known to her friends as Chico, was born on April 21, 1953 in Nottingham and currently resides in Middlesex. Kidd read law at King's College, London, but her interests in writing, drawing, and cinema pushed a law career aside, and at last word she was working as an advertising copywriter. Both artist and author, Kidd has written several stories and illustrated others for Rosemary Pardoe's Haunted Library publications and elsewhere. She has also written and illustrated two small chapbooks of her own stories, Change & Decay and In and Out of the Belfry. These stories are very much in the English ghost story tradition, and most of them are associated with campanology, in which she is keenly interested.

Perhaps I'd best let A. F. Kidd explain: "Campanology—the English art of change-ringing—is practiced on bells hung on wheels with ropes hanging down in a circle so that the order in which the bells sound can be changed at each pull of the rope. (Hence, 'change-ringing.') It can be done on any number of bells from four to twelve, to set patterns known as 'methods.' There are a great many of these, each officially recognized one having its own particular name." Well, you get the idea.

If you want to know how I got this white streak in my hair, I'll tell you.

Some years ago I was commissioned to illustrate a series of booklets on Royal Arms in English churches, a chance I rather jumped at because it meant I could combine a bit of tower-grabbing with my work. Strictly speaking, I didn't *need* to visit every single church (nor would I have got much work done if I had)—but show any ringer a bunch of towers, all with bells, clustered together in one area, and the temptation is irresistible.

On my travels in one part of the country I couldn't help but become aware that a rather prolific family of bellfounders had been active during the eighteenth and early nineteenth centuries. Time and again appeared the names William Merrilees, Joshua Merrilees, and, most frequently, Abraham of that ilk; and it was not a name I had ever noticed before.

They seemed proud of their work, too, this family. On one bell I saw the inscription

> North, South, Easte, Weste,
> Merrilees bells is alwaies beste.

And on another

> When a bell a Maiden be
> Know twas cast by Merrilee.

Well, my curiosity was aroused: indeed, I have always found bells fascinating. They are the greatest instruments man has made, and whether they speak for the glory of God or for the glory of the peal-ringer, each single one has its own mystery, and its own majesty. And the folk who founded them were imbued with a glamour in my mind. Where only Whitechapel and Loughborough now remain, yet their heritage is great, and strange, and intriguing. Who *were* the Bilbies, who Agnes le Belyetere? And who, indeed, these founders whose names I now saw, time and again?

I admit it: those long-dead Merrilees had captured

my imagination. Unfortunately, no one seemed to know anything about them, nor could they suggest any avenues of inquiry.

Until I came to the village of Lacey Magna. I love village names: I can stare at maps for ages. This one caught my eye for no more reason than that; so I looked it up in *Dove* and found it had six bells, tenor 13 cwt, and that I could arrive on practice night, if I left that day.

It was a misty January day, raw with chill: the air was like tin. Frost had spread fronds over the windows of my car, and took ten minutes to scrape off. Buildings, hedges, trees, were humps of nothingness, less substantial than the fog which masked them. Black ice hid itself on the roads, and the grass of the verges was clustered so thick with crystals they looked like the inside of a freezer.

I was listening to a tape in the car—it was the Brandenburg Concertos—and it suddenly struck me how absolutely extraordinary it was to be moving along in a machine propelled by an internal combustion engine while hearing sounds which had first been heard in the eighteenth century. Maybe, I thought, this is what ghosts are: a re-creation, by some strange science, of people or things which had once lived or happened. The image of the paranormal as some kind of supernatural video-tape made me smile, and the day became a little brighter for that.

Naturally I had needed no further encouragement to book a room at the pub in Lacey Magna—the "Five Bells" it was called, since they do not tend to augment inn signs—nor to sit in its bar, that evening, with an ear cocked to the church of St. Dunstan. Beside me, an open fire shed its pungent scent into the room, and little, jerky flames began to eat into the logs.

As soon as I heard the bells start to go up, I went outside. The exterior of the pub (Tudor, with infills of brick in a dog'stooth pattern) was dimly lit; a feeble streetlamp outside the lychgate made a pale halo in the mist; and that was it. Lacey Magna might never

have heard of electricity, otherwise. Yews loomed fog-
gily, more sensed than seen; underfoot, mud had turned
to frosty ridges which turned my ankles. That night
the air was still, and clear, and sharp cold, and the
church tower seemed a very far thing indeed: the
uttermost farthing, I thought, remembering a line at
random.

Sometimes it can be a very curious experience, entering a strange churchyard in pitch darkness. There is
some kind of atavism there, I think: it does not inspire
fear, except the fear of tripping over a tombstone and
falling flat on your face; but there is, sometimes, an
eerie kind of awe. The fog had that strange shining
quality you get when there is no other illumination—
having its own glow, a kind of dark light, if you know
what I mean. It seemed to affect my eyes oddly: I kept
thinking I saw queer dullish patches in the night, as if
it had faded in places—but only out of the corners of
my eyes: I could not look directly at them, for they
seemed to slide away.

I was relieved to find a dark studded door which
opened when I turned its big cold handle, and which
gave onto a worn spiral stone staircase. Rounds began
above me and quickly gave way to changes—I haven't
the ear to identify methods, but it was some kind of
Doubles, quite well struck, and the bells had a mellow
tone to them which was utterly charming. They sang
like angels; or as near as we can ever come to the
music of the spheres. I had, and have, never heard
anything quite so harmonious. Plain-song comes close,
sometimes, and parts of the chorale in Beethoven's
Ninth; but these depend on the singers and are therefore too transient for comparison, for every rendition
must be different.

The door to the ringing chamber was ajar, so I was
able to sidle in. Two men who were not ringing smiled
briefly at me.

"Single," said the conductor, a short, pleasantly
ugly man with vivid red hair, who resembled nothing
so much as an amiable pig; his arms and shoulders

were big as a blacksmith's. I sat down on a bench of black wood, worn smooth by generations of ringers' bottoms, and took in the ringing chamber. Gold and black sallies, like elongated bees: except for the treble, which was red-white-and-blue. Six small scruffy mats to stop the ropes wearing the worn carpet. A fan-heater valiantly puffing out hot air, like an over-enthusiastic conductor. A table in the center piled high with the usual impedimenta. And the walls were covered, completely covered with peal-boards, old photographs, framed documents, yellowed prints. The place was a feast: there were boards dating from the eighteenth century, nearly the birth of change-ringing. Some had been carefully restored, but others were almost illegible. I looked for a notice about the bells and was delighted: all six had been cast by the Merrilees, five by Abraham in 1782 and the treble by William in 1804.

"Bob," said the conductor, and "This is all," then, shortly afterward, "Stand." I waited for ringing etiquette to take its course, and was surprised when the conductor beamed at me, held out his hand, and introduced himself: "I'm Adam Merrilees. How d'you do?"

I shook his large hand, and said, "How d'you do. Michael Denehey. Are you related to *those* Merrilees?" gesturing toward the notice.

"Not difficult to figure that out," he replied with a grin. "Me, I make clocks. What would you like to ring?—mind, we're not up to Surprise standard here." I was glad to hear this, as neither was I—not by a long way.

"Nowt wrong with Stedman," remarked one elderly gentleman. "Good enough for our forebears, and good enough for us."

"Oh, come on, Jack," retorted someone else. "People've been ringing Surprise methods for a century at least."

"More. Longer than that," began one of the younger ringers. I had the feeling that this was an old argument which had been simmering for some time.

"Stedman will do fine," I said hastily. "Or Plain Bob, or Grandsire." The old man, whose face was purpling, seemed mollified. "All right, Stedman it is," he grunted.

"Which one would you like?" Adam Merrilees asked me.

"Oh, I don't mind," I said. "—Would you mind telling me something about the Merrilees, some time?"

"Sure. Take the fourth, if you like—she's quite well-tempered."

"Would you care to call something, Mr. Denehey?" asked the old boy, Jack, which flustered me. Only my bank manager calls me that.

"Er, no, thanks, I'm afraid I'm not up to that," I said.

"You, then, Adam. Fill in, please. We're not here to stand around gossiping."

"Silly old fool," muttered a girl next to me, uncharitably. I looked at her, and she reddened. She was small and slight, with spiky fair hair; but there was something about her, though, which didn't quite *fit* with her modern appearance. Her face was like those which you sometimes see in Renaissance paintings— not quite Botticelli, but close—and which the Pre-Raphaelites just failed to recapture; but, in retrospect, I think it was, rather, something ancient in her eyes which made her different. Fortunately old Jack seemed to be deaf enough to miss her remark: he was endeavoring, with some impatience but little success, to induce someone to ring the tenor.

After the practice, I discovered that half the ringers were, in fact, Merrilees. Jack, the patriarch, who was such a martinet in the ringing chamber, actually bought me a pint in the "Five Bells." Adam's wife Lesley and their daughter Jane, the girl who had made the disparaging stage-whisper, were the others. Such a proliferation of the family quite overwhelmed me: it was one thing to be fascinated by the exploits of the ancestors— quite another to come face to face with their descendants.

"What was you interested in finding out?" Jack asked me.

"Well—anything about the bell-founding Merrilees. I keep seeing the name, and I'd never heard of them before."

"Not surprising, unless you come from these parts. Irish, are you?—name like Denehey?"

The old man kept unsettling me. "Er—no—I expect my ancestors were."

"William Merrilees was my five-times great grandfather," said Jack. "Joshua, the first bellfounder, was *his* grandfather. He cast his first bell that we know about in 1723, when he was in his early twenties."

"They had their foundry here in Lacey," put in Adam.

"Aye, but that was later. See, there was tin and copper to be had locally—the coast's ten miles away, so they didn't have to go far to get sand—and this valley's full of clay. They had all they needed for their trade right on the doorstep."

"You said—1723? And the bells here are 1780 or something—that's a long time for his home village," I remarked.

"Time for that tale when we come to it," said Jack.

"He'll tell the story his own way," said Lesley Merrilees.

"They were proud of their workmanship," Jack went on, "and with good reason. Merrilees' bells seldom needed chipping or scraping—they was maiden bells, already in tune. William claimed they used a secret ingredient, but I don't know what it was."

"There's the story of the lady who threw a silver coin into the furnace to make a clear ring," young Jane observed. I stole a look at her: she was leaning forward, elbows on the table, an intent expression on her face; though, I thought, she must have heard this story many times. Her eyes were gray as mist. Jack did not seem to relish the interruption.

"That's as may be," he said brusquely. "There's stories like that for any founder you care to name. Abraham said it was all down to their special rituals, the way they prepared and cast the bells."

"What was special about it?" I asked.

"Well, they insisted on absolute silence to get the right note. So they always completed the castings at midnight when the air was at its stillest. And it had to be a full moon, too. And when they traveled away to cast bells, they did the casting in the churchyard—so it would be as silent as the grave."

"That's fascinating," I said, meaning it, picturing it, the black of the night, the glow of the furnace, illuminating those eighteenth-century faces like a de la Tour painting. My imagination almost became lost in the image: I'd have liked to paint it. Jack continued:

"Joshua was asked to cast a ring of bells for St. Dunstan's in 1732. Now he didn't have a proper foundry then, because he dug a pit and set about doing the work in the churchyard. And there was a dreadful accident, and his wife was killed—some say burned to death in the furnace, some by molten bell-metal. It took the spirit out of him: he refused to go on with the job, and St. Dunstan's stayed without bells for nigh on fifty years.

"After Joshua died they asked his son—Abraham, that was—to cast the bells for St. Dunstan's. He did the work, but reluctantly, and that's the back five now. He later said that all the time he was doing the work he was aware of his mother's presence, and that she disapproved. Which I suppose is logical, if ghosts can be logical. What we do know is that *his* son, William, who was a lad of about sixteen at the time, suffered some kind of fit or seizure while the work was being done, and was unable to speak for twenty-two years—though he carried on the family trade well enough, by all accounts.

"Now at the beginning of the last century, William took it into his head to add a sixth bell to St. Dunstan's. No one asked him to do it, he just did the work and asked no payment; and the bell being there, well, it was put in the tower. I don't know the ins and outs. But the long and the short of it is, after that treble bell was hung, William could speak again."

"So the tale has a happy ending," I said.

"Not exactly," said Adam. "It was said after that, that William had 'lost the silence' and the bells he founded were so much trouble to tune that the family firm went out of business."

"Do people ever see the ghost?" I asked curiously.

"The ghost of Joshua's wife is said to walk, yes. But it's not good to see her, young man. Nor should you seek her out."

If I thought Jack was being circumspect, it did not occur to me to quibble. By this time the pub had long since closed its doors, and it must have been due only to some local laxity or respect for the elder Merrilees that they had not been chucked out. The family departed then, and I went upstairs to bed.

I couldn't sleep. The room was hot and stuffy. Brief dreams kept chasing each other between bouts of wakefulness. I smoked a great many cigarettes.

At half past two I gave up the attempt and went to sit by the window. Idly, I drew back one of the curtains and peered out into the darkness; found my breath misted the window, so opened that too.

Now I may have been dreaming, then: may have had my imagination fuelled by old histories and too much beer. But I don't think so.

The fog had dispersed, and the frost-laden air which surged in made me gasp: it was as chill as a glacier. Outside, great evergreens rose, inky shadows on the inky sky, blotting out the brilliant icy stars. My eyes were drawn to the dark under these trees, where I became aware of a phenomenon I had seen before: a pallid patch in the night, as if someone had rubbed a bit of it away.

This time, it appeared to be drawing nearer. I wasn't afraid, only curious, and my interest seemed to be winching it in, like a fish on a line, but without the reluctance.

Gradually, it became clearer. Now it looked like a pale woman in a white, long nightdress: her hair was blonde as barley. Down one side of her body and her arm lay a filmy shadow which took on the appearance of pumice-stone as she neared me. Something was clotted in the pit of my stomach—a sort of anticipation. My heart was beating fiercely. I could see her very clearly: she was white, but not the white of snow, for snow is *only* white, and blue shadow, and unformed outlines; the woman's whiteness was gentle contours, rounded as only the shading of flesh can be. But if there was warmth there, it was not the flow of life.

She was almost close enough to touch, now, and I saw with a sort of fascinated revulsion that the whole of her side and her arm were *boiling*, like milk on a stove, bubbles rising to the surface and bursting. The flesh hissed and simmered, and I felt the heat which radiated from it. Her ruined face drew close to mine; and then she smiled.

All the breath went out of me, as if I had been hit in the heart. It was sweet beyond description—in that smile was all the joy and love and laughter in the world: it was as if the smile and the beauty had gathered themselves into a great fist and thumped me. I fell to my knees, there was no strength left in them. When I raised my head again, she was gone.

If her smile had gathered in all my positive emotions, her departure hit me harder. Now there was so much loss and pain and emptiness in the world that I wanted to die. I couldn't cope with the breadth of that despair: I passed out.

The night was dimming toward dawn when I woke up. Things drawn on the dark were beginning to solidify into chairs and furniture. I was freezing cold and stiff and aching with the loss of the glory; I managed to crawl into bed and pull the covers round me, shivering uncontrollably and as weak as a puppy.

I woke up, late, with chilly feet and a draught down my back, but a hot bath soon cured that; then I breakfasted and went to get my camera and gear out of the car—it's easier to work from photographs on this type of assignment. It was a bright clear morning, but bitterly cold: I was able to see Lacey Magna for the first time, a pleasant village but not picturesque enough to attract too many tourists.

"D'you want a hand with that?" asked a voice, startling me a little. I turned to see Adam Merrilees, a little incongruous in a vast ski-jacket and red moon-boots. "I mean, I presume you got permission to take photos in the church."

"Yes, I phoned the rector."

He picked up one of my cases without any apparent effort, hoisted a light over one shoulder, and headed toward the church. I locked the car and followed, festooned with camera and lenses and feeling unaccountably awkward.

"I'm going up to do a bit of maintenance," Adam said, "but give me a shout when you've finished. There's a peal-board you might find interesting. Ever thought of *doing* something with peal-boards?—you know, making a collection of photos, or something?"

"Yes, I have, actually, but—"

"Well, as I say, give me a yell. I expect you'd like to see the bells, too. Cheers then!"

St. Dunstan's was like the inside of a refrigerator. My two spotlights, which can usually be relied on to heat an enclosed space quite uncomfortably, made no impression. I took a couple of rolls of the Royal Arms, which were, unusually, carved and not painted, then reloaded the car and went to find Adam Merrilees.

He was in the ringing chamber, fiddling with the clock. The room, as most do in daylight, looked shabby; Adam with his bright hair and gaudy pullover (he had discarded the jacket) seemed curiously exotic.

"This was what I wanted to show you," he said, "you being so interested in the family."

It was a small board, one of the unrestored ones, black with age and barely decipherable: the script was crowded in as if the signwriter had not wanted to use up too much space, and the lettering was now little more than bumps on the surface. Peering close, I could just read it: it was not, strictly speaking, a *peal*-board:

In the Tower of Moreton Lacey,
St. Mary the Virgin,
ON THE 14 OF JVNE 1730
Was Rung on Extent of Grandfire Bob Tripples
Being a True *Seven Hundred and Twenty*
By the Following Ringers:
Thos. Bartholomew, Trebble.
Robt. Richards, 2nd.
Josh. Merrileef, 3rd.
Jne. Merrileef, 4th.
Wm. Garfton, 5th.
Geof. Norwich, 7th.
Jn. Harte, Tenor.

"There was Abraham, and William, and here's Joshua," I said. "But who was 'JNE' Merrilees?"

"Ah!" said Adam. "I reckon *that* was Joshua's wife."

"What?" I exclaimed, as my heart seemed to lurch.

"Hm? A lady ringer in 1730, you mean? I've got a theory about that."

Something seemed to be constricting my throat. In my mind's eye I could see a white figure, drifting toward me, her arms outstretched. My breath labored. I shook my head, trying to clear it: the first sharp thuds of a monster headache beat in my temples. I tried to concentrate on what Adam was saying, but it was cold, so cold in that room.

"You see, it can't be *John*, because there's a 'JN' on the tenor, and this is definitely 'JNE'; anyway, we don't know any John Merrilees. But you see, I think Joshua's wife was one of those ladies who didn't like *being* a lady in 1730. You know: like that woman, I've forgotten her name, she disguised herself as a man and joined the Marines—but why else would Joshua's wife have been anywhere near the furnace, to have been burned to death—unless she had insisted in helping Joshua in his work?"

"Adam," I said, "I'm sorry, but my head's got a pneumatic drill in it."

He turned and looked at me, his eyes narrowed. "Are you all right?"

"Yes, I'll be OK—I—I think I'll sit down," I finished lamely, and did so. Adam looked like a ghost: his edges seemed insubstantial, as if yesterday's fog had crept into the room. I started to shiver.

"Come on," said Adam. "Let's get a couple of pints of 'Winter Warmer' down you. Pub's open now."

Well, he got me down the stairs and back to the "Five Bells," and I *did* feel better after a few drinks, sitting by the fire. But that had *scared* me. Had I really seen a ghost, the night before? And if so, why? —Not *who*, but *why*?

Moreton Lacey was in *Dove*: the church was derelict. I found the name on my map, and wondered about driving over; but the day was too cold, flurries of snow were being flung at the windows, like torn paper, my head was still aching—I felt disinclined to go anywhere. Or, really, to think about the Merrilees. It had been difficult enough to get rid of Adam. I did some desultory work on an illustration, but my heart wasn't in it; some time later, I dozed off in a chair.

It was dark when I woke up. I had a crick in my neck, my left arm had gone to sleep, and my head felt stuffed with kapok. The clock said ten to six, so I picked up the *Times* and *Telegraph* and a pen for the crosswords, stuck a book in my pocket, and went to sit in the bar.

None of the Merrilees family came in that evening, but I was quite content with my own company. I was a bit fidgety, but managed to occupy the time, making a leisurely dinner and a half-hearted attempt at the crosswords, and retiring to bed having spoken only to the barman and the middle-aged lady who served the meal.

I still had a headache; the day had been half-wasted, and I hadn't done a great deal, but I was tired, and fell asleep quickly.

If I had thought, or hoped, that I would sleep the night through and be able to leave Lacey Magna refreshed in the morning, I was wrong. At twenty to three I was thoroughly and completely awake, sitting up in bed staring at the darkness, and wondering why I felt so strange. It was as if I were waiting for something, but I hadn't felt so excited since I was ten years old. The dancing butterflies of childhood disturbed my stomach, my breath was short and loud in the silence, and my heart was beating rapidly. I hadn't forgotten the ghost; but I didn't feel as if I were waiting for a ghost.

I felt as if I were waiting for a lover.

Leaning out of the window, I strained my eyes, willing the shadows and the whirling snow to coalesce into a different whiteness. A shiver convulsed me, but it didn't feel like a shiver of cold, despite the icy night.

She drifted into my vision, and my heart leapt. Her warmth misted the night, steaming from her side like smoke.

"Come here," I whispered, voicelessly, staring into pale eyes in a suppurating face, transfixed, waiting for the great smile. My knees were shaking. I gripped the window sill helplessly until she filled my sight: there was nothing in the world except *her*. She reached out to me.

"Oh, warm," she said in a voice like fire, and her face suddenly blazed with joy and delight, bright as a phosphorous flame. I jerked my eyes shut in startled reflex: she burned behind them like lightning.

Something touched my face, then—a cool, scented hand, it felt like. It traced the line of my shoulder, touched my arm; then ran gently through my hair, and was gone.

Ice flooded at me, freezing wind surged round like a sudden blast from the Arctic. My eyes opened wide with the shock of it, and with a great racking breath I realized I was standing in front of an open window in the depths of winter, stark naked and alone, and my hands were frozen to the window sill.

I panicked and tore them loose, leaving skin and flesh behind, though I couldn't feel a thing. There was frost on my fingers. Shuddering with cold, I lurched across the room to the radiator, having enough sense left to drape a towel over it—holding it between my wrists, for my fingers were useless.

Feeling gradually returned, and pain with it, like being slashed with knives of ice. Blood seeped out of my hands and soaked into the towel, but at least it showed me I was alive.

Whether I was about to die from hypothermia was another matter. I was shivering so much my body didn't want to obey me, and my hands throbbed and burned, but I struggled into a haphazard collection of clothes and crawled into bed, wrapping the towel clumsily around my lacerated fingers and palms. Eventually I drifted into a fitful doze.

Some warmth had regenerated when I woke, but I was weak and sick and chilled to the bone. My hands were an utter mess, the towel glued to them with clotted blood, but I didn't feel capable of moving, far less seeing what was under that gory fabric.

However, there was the telephone. On the dial was a note reading "Ring 0 for Room Service" (which meant the landlord's wife with a mug of tea). It was the first time in my life I had approved of a push-button phone: I told them I'd caught a chill and needed a day in bed. The landlord's wife fussed a bit, and brought the expected scalding tea, which did not warm me: the cold was like agony.

I honestly don't know how I got through that day. I'd never been really ill before: the worst had been measles at sixteen, and I don't remember a whole lot about that, except being terribly weak. This time I kept slipping in and out of wild dreams which were both hideous and erotic at the same time—I don't really know whether I was shivering with cold, or terror, or desire. It was frightful. At one stage I remember longing to sleep but not daring to, in case I never woke up; another time I was so desperately cold that I found myself deliriously counting my toes, over and over, just to make sure they hadn't fallen off with frostbite.

But the worst, the very worst, thing was that *she*

had gone. I felt that everything inside me which had ever had meaning had drained away, leaving a hollow, frozen, empty wasteland that nothing could fill.

Or one thing could fill.

What does a haunted man look like? I wondered dully, but was too weak to look in the mirror.

Adam Merrilees showed me. He came in, kindly, to see how I was; took one look and his face blanched.

"You've seen her," he said bleakly. I nodded—it was all I could manage. The tundra inside me was too cold. Adam picked up a mirror from the table and showed me my reflection.

My face had gone gaunt, gray: along the path which a cool finger had traced was a livid red blistering line, and my hair was singed in places. I turned my head painfully and saw the trail of blisters continuing down inside my clothes; as soon as I was aware of it, it began to burn, making me draw my breath in sharply. I stared dispassionately at my hands: the towel had come loose, revealing seeping, raw patches.

"Michael, listen to me," said Adam. "I believe she's a type of vampire. She seems to feed on heat. Body heat—not emotions. She could drain you as completely as any blood-sucking Dracula."

I touched the track of burns, listlessly. It felt very hot to my flayed fingers. "What am I supposed to do?" I said, and it was difficult to get the words out.

"Fight her."

"How?" I didn't want to. I wanted her back.

"Do what William Merrilees did. Give her something hotter," said Adam Merrilees.

I sat by a vast open grate in the house in Bell Lane where the twentieth-century Merrilees lived, and where the eighteenth- and nineteenth-century Merrilees had founded bells and fostered an insatiable desire. The fire in the grate was huge, whole logs, it seemed, piled one on top of the other. On the other side of the kitchen, an Aga stove pumped out great waves of warmth. Despite this, despite overcoat and blankets, I shivered. Only my bandaged hands and the strings of burn on my face and shoulder throbbed with heat. Some of the blisters had burst: under them were more blisters.

Ever since darkness had fallen, drawing shadows in early, Adam had been feeding the fire. The center was, now, probably *literally* as hot as a furnace, and *he* was finding it difficult to sit any nearer than six feet away. From time to time he tried to talk to me, in a low, wounded voice, as though *he* had failed in some way; I hardly replied, first through weakness, then through a growing excitement which was constricting my chest and throat. For I was looking forward to seeing the blanched figure which burned with cold fire: more, I wanted it with increasing desperation as the minutes passed.

Around midnight I removed the blankets, and later the coat. I was growing warm, *physically* warm, as the longing and the anticipation increased.

Adam saw it first, I think. Saw the little flames at the edge of the fire wither. He got to his feet: he seemed to be moving very slowly, as if through mercury. I looked into the flames and saw their fiery center *sucked* into blackness which spread outward from the core until the whole blazing mass was cold gray and white ash.

She arose from the center of the grate, powder falling off her which seconds before had been the heart of an inferno. She had absorbed the fire, and it was not enough for her.

I stood up. *I* was blazing now, the longing was pure heat inside me, aching, desperate for her to smile again, that smile of joy incarnate. Dimly, I was aware that Adam had stopped on the other side of the fireplace and that his mouth was working.

Her side and her face were seething. She crackled.

"So much warmth," she whispered. "But not enough." And reached out her hand to me, as her destroyed lips smiled again and I was lost once more in an overwhelming, staggering rush of delight.

She put her hand on my chest, and I felt my skin start to burn through my jumper, through my shirt. I put out my arms to embrace her, seeing little runnels of her flesh like wax spilling off her at the same time, around and down from that sweet, sweet smile; but all there was in me was desire.

Adam's voice, strained and unrecognisable, broke into my trance. He was yelling something—I couldn't tell what. I saw his brawny arm rise and fall: she glowed; she was lambent; and then she was gone, and suddenly the pressure inside me too was gone and I fell to the floor as if all my strings had been cut.

It was Jack Merrilees who found us first, followed by Jane and Lesley: though I never found out what, if anything, Adam had said to them. Adam and I were lying either side of a long furrow of scorch, burned four inches deep in the stone kitchen floor. His arm was seared with a burn like the track of a lightning strike, and I was in a worse state. Jane gave me some water: I drank about three pints.

When I felt able to speak, I croaked at Adam—even my throat felt scorched—"What did you do?"

"I . . . applied . . . the final . . . straw," he said, his voice as painful as mine, and pointed stiffly to a small fused lump of bright metal on the blackened floor. "I hit her . . . with the poker . . . from the Aga." He paused again, and swallowed. "It acted . . . like . . . a lightning conductor."

"She's gone," said Jack, with a touch of sadness. "Gone for good now, I think. I also think," he added, more sternly, "that you might have done my family a favor, Mr. Denehey."

"Please don't call me that," I said, with some difficulty.

"Pardon?"

"Only my bank manager calls me that."

"You nearly paid more than you ever paid into your bank," said Jack Merrilees, quietly, looking at me.

"We didn't . . . know," added Adam, looking slightly embarrassed.

I thought for a moment. "Did you ever feel it—the loss and the emptiness, when she left?"

"No," said Jack; Adam shook his head. "No. You had the desire, which we never had. It seems you acted as a—catalyst, I think the word is. A channel for the cold fire."

A burned channel, I thought. And my hair grew back white where she had touched it.

You may be surprised to learn that I went back to Lacey Magna. Something pulled me back: a fair Renaissance face with the eyes of a ghost. I married Jane Merrilees last year, not long after Jack died (at the respectable age of eighty-nine). Adam doesn't ring very much any more, though he seems content with his lot, and I don't attend the practice every week. For one thing, Jane, who runs them now, has got the band up to five-spliced now, which is way beyond me; for another, my hands get sore after I've been ringing for any length of time—though I'm lucky: I can wield pen and pencil still; my occupation's not gone.

Only sometimes, when I happen to wake in the dead hour of a winter night, and look at Jane asleep with moonlight on her face and her pale hair fanned out, I sense a shadow growing there: a shadow like mottled stone all down one side; and then my hands draw and ache, and the old burn on my scalp grows warm.

Of course, it might be my imagination. But, somehow, I don't think so.

THE SCAR

by Dennis Etchison

Now, with twenty-five years of professional writing under his belt, Dennis Etchison has grudgingly become recognized by editors and publishers as one of the horror genre's foremost writers and thinkers. But then, that's something readers have known all along. So, why did it take so long for the people who move their lips when they read to catch on? For one thing, Etchison is not enormously prolific—not to count his screenplays and movie novelizations. Aside from that, Etchison has worked almost exclusively in short fiction, with his first major novel, Darkside, *coming out in 1986. Primarily though, Etchison's fiction sort of falls between the cracks of genre labels. Disturbed editors riffle in confusion through his manuscripts, searching for rotting zombies, demonic children, or any handle upon which to grasp to explain the uneasy impact of his fiction. A mood of paranoid urgency isn't easy to label, or to forget.*

Born in Stockton, California on March 30, 1943, Dennis Etchison currently lives in Los Angeles—there keeping close to the movie scene, which is his major interest after championship wrestling. He is presently at work on a number of screenplays; is awaiting publication of the third Scream/Press collection of his short stories, The Blood Kiss; *is hard at work on his stories for a forthcoming* Night Visions *volume*

from Dark Harvest; editing Masters of Darkness
III; *is planning a new anthology,* Double Edge, *to
follow his tremendously successful* Cutting Edge.
Keeps him off the streets, and that's just as well.

This time they were walking a divided highway, the
toes of their shoes powdered white with gravel dust.
The little girl ran ahead, skipping eagerly along the
shoulder, while her mother lagged back to keep pace
with the man.

"Mind the trucks," called the woman, barely raising
her voice. Soon the girl would be able to take care of
herself; that was her hope. She turned to him, showing
the good side of her face. "Do you see one yet?"

He lifted his chin and squinted.

She followed his gaze to the other side of the highway. There, squatting in the haze beyond the over-
pass, was a Weenie Wigwam Fast Food Restaurant.

"Thank God," she said. She thought of the Chinese
Smorgasbord, the Beef Bowl, the Thai Take-Out and
the many others they had seen already. She added,
"This one will be all right, won't it?"

It was the edge of the town, RV dealerships and
fleet sales on one side of the road, family diners and
budget motels on the other. Overloaded station wag-
ons and moving vans laden with freight hammered the
asphalt, bringing thunder to the gray twilight. Without
breaking stride the man leaned down to scoop up a
handful of gravel, then skimmed stones between the
little girl's thin legs and into the ditch; he held onto
one last piece, a sharp quartz chip, and deposited it in
his jacket pocket.

"Maybe," he said.

"Aren't you sure?"

He did not answer.

"Well," she said, "let's try it. Laura will be hungry,
I know."

She hurried to catch the little girl at the crossing.
When she turned back, the man was handling an empty
beer bottle from the roadside. She looked away. As he

moved up to join them, zippering the front of his service jacket, the woman forced a smile, as if she had not seen.

In the parking lot, the man took their hands. A heavy tanker geared down and pounded the curve, bucking and hissing away behind them. As it passed, the driver sounded his horn at the traffic. The sudden blast, so near that it rattled her spine, seemed to release her from a bad dream. She laced her fingers more securely with his and swung her arm out and back and out again, hardly feeling the weight of his hand between them.

"This is a nice place," she said, already reading a banner for the all-day breakfast special. "I'm glad we waited. Aren't you glad, Laura?"

"Can I ride the horse?" asked the little girl.

The woman looked at the sculpted gray-and-white Indian pinto, its blanket saddle worn down to the fiberglass. There were no other children waiting at the machine. She let go of his hand and dug in her purse for a coin.

"I don't see why not," she said.

The little girl broke away.

He came to a stop, his empty hands opening and closing.

"Just one ride," the woman said quickly. "And then you come right inside, hear?"

On the other side of the glass, couples moved between tables. A few had children, some Laura's age. Families, she thought. She wished that the three of them could go inside together.

Laura's pony began to wobble and pitch. But the man was not watching. He stood there with his chin up, his nostrils flared, like an animal waiting for a sign. His hands continued to flex.

"I'll see about a table," she said when he did not move to open the door.

A moment later she glanced outside and saw him

examining a piece of brick that had come loose from the front of the restaurant. He turned it over and over.

The menus came. They sat reading them in a corner booth, under crossed tomahawks. The food items were named in keeping with the native American motif, suggesting that the burgers and the several varieties of hot dogs had been invented by hunters and gatherers. Bleary travelers hunched over creased roadmaps, gulping coffee and estimating mileage, their eyes stark in the chill fluorescent lighting.

"What would you like, Laura?" asked the woman.

"Peanut butter and jelly sandwich."

"Do they have that?"

"And a vanilla milkshake."

The woman sighed.

"And Wampum Pancakes. Papoose-size."

She opened her purse and counted the money. She blinked and looked at the man.

He got up and went over to the silverware station.

"What's he doing?" said the little girl.

"Never mind," said the woman. "His knife and fork must be dirty."

He came back and sat down.

"And Buffalo Fries," said the little girl.

The woman studied him. "Is it still okay?" she asked.

"What?" he said.

She waited, but now he was busy observing the customers. She gave up and returned to the menu. It was difficult for her to choose, not knowing what he would order. "I'll just have a small dinner salad," she said at last.

The others in the restaurant kept to themselves. A man with a sample case ate a piece of pecan pie and scanned the local newspaper. A young couple fed their baby apple juice from a bottle. A take-away order was picked up at the counter, then carried out to a Winnebago. Soft, vaguely familiar music lilted from wall speakers designed to look like tom-toms, muffling the clink of cups and the murmur of private conversations.

"Want to go to the bathroom," said the little girl.

"In a minute, baby," the woman told her. A waitress in an imitation buckskin mini-dress was coming this way.

The little girl squirmed. "Mom-*my!*"

The waitress was almost here, carrying a pitcher and glasses of water on a tray.

The woman looked at the man.

Finally he leaned back and opened his hands on the table.

"Could you order for us?" she asked carefully.

He nodded.

In the rest room, she reapplied makeup to one side of her face, then added another layer to be sure. At a certain angle the deformity did not show at all, she told herself. Besides, he had not looked at her, really looked at her in a long time; perhaps he had forgotten. She practiced a smile in the mirror until it was almost natural. She waited for her daughter to finish, then led her back to the dining room.

"Where is he?" said the little girl.

The woman tensed, the smile freezing on her lips. He was not at the table. The food on the placemats was untouched.

"Go sit down," she told the little girl. "Now."

Then she saw him, his jacket with the embroidered patches and the narrow map like a dragon on the back. He was on the far side of the room, under a framed bow and arrow display.

She touched his arm. He turned too swiftly, bending his legs, his feet apart. Then he saw who it was.

"Hi," she said. Her throat was so dry that her voice cracked. "Come on, before your food gets cold."

As she walked him to the table, she was aware of eyes on them.

"I had a bow and arrow," he said. "I could pick a

sentry out of a tree at a hundred yards. Just like that. No sound."

She did not know what to say. She never did. She gave him plenty of room before sitting down between him and the little girl. That put her on his other side, so that he would be able to see the bad part of her face. She tried not to think about it.

He had only coffee and a small sandwich. It took him a while to start on it. Always travel light, he had told her once. She picked at her salad. The people at the other tables stopped looking and resumed their meals.

"Where's my food?" asked the little girl.

"In front of you," said the woman. "Now eat and keep quiet."

"Where's my pancakes?"

"You don't need pancakes."

"I do, too!"

"Hush. You've got enough." Without turning her face the woman said to the man, "How's your sandwich?"

Out of the corner of her eye she noticed that he was hesitating between bites, listening to the sounds of the room. She paused, trying to hear what he heard. There was the music, the undercurrent of voices, the occasional ratcheting of the cash register. The swelling traffic outside. The chink of dishes in the kitchen, as faint as rain on a tin roof. Nothing else.

"Mommy, I didn't get my Buffalo Fries."

"I know, Laura. Next time."

"When?"

Tomorrow? she thought. "All right," she said, "I'll get them to go. You can take them with you."

"Where?"

She realized she did not know the answer. She felt a tightening in her face and a dull ache in her throat so that she could not eat. Don't let me cry, she thought. I don't want her to see. This is the best we can do—can't she understand?

Now his head turned toward the kitchen.

From behind the door came distant clatter as plates were stacked, the squeak of wet glasses, the metallic clicking of flatware, the high good humor of unseen cooks and dishwashers. The steel door vibrated on its hinges.

He stopped chewing.

She saw him check the room one more time: the sharply-angled tables, the crisp bills left for tips, the half-eaten dinners hardening into waste, the full bellies and taut belts and bright new clothing, too bright under the harsh fixtures as night fell, shuttering the windows with leaden darkness. Somewhere outside headlights gathered as vehicles jammed the turnoff, stabbing the glass like approaching searchlights.

He put down his sandwich.

The steel door trembled, then swung wide.

A shiny cart rolled into the dining room, pushed by a busboy in a clean white uniform. He said something over his shoulder to the kitchen crew, rapid-fire words in a language she did not understand. The cooks and dishwashers roared back at his joke. She saw the tone of their skin, the stocky, muscular bodies behind the aprons. The door flapped shut. The cart was coming this way.

He spat out a mouthful of food as though afraid that he had been poisoned.

"It's okay," she said. "See? They're Mexicans, that's all. . . ."

He ignored her and reached inside his jacket. She saw the emblems from his Asian tour of duty. But there were also patches from Tegucigalpa and Managua and the fighting that had gone on there. She had never noticed these before. Her eyes went wide.

The busboy came to their booth.

Under the table, the man took something from his pants pocket and set it beside him on the seat. Then he took something else from the other side. Then his fists closed against his knees.

"Can I have a bite?" said the little girl. She started to reach for the uneaten part of his sandwich.

"Laura!" said the woman.

"Well, he doesn't want it, does he?"

The man looked at her. His face was utterly without expression. The woman held her breath.

"Excuse," said the busboy.

The man turned his head back. It seemed to take a very long time. She watched, unable to stop any of this from happening.

When the man did not say anything, the busboy tried to take his plate away.

A fork came up from below, glinted, then arced down in a blur, pinning the brown hand to the table.

The boy cried out and swung wildly with his other hand.

The man reached under his jacket again and brought a beer bottle down on the boy's head. The boy folded, his scalp splitting under the lank black hair and pumping blood. Then the cart and chairs went flying as the man stood and grabbed for the tomahawks on the wall. But they were only plastic. He tossed them aside and went over the table.

A waitress stepped into his path, holding her palms out. Then she was down and he was in the middle of the room. The salesman stood up, long enough to take half a brick in the face. Then the manager and the man with the baby got in the way. A sharp stone came out, and a lockback knife, and then a water pitcher shattered, the fragments carrying gouts of flesh to the floor.

The woman covered her little girl as more bodies fell and the room became red.

He was going for the bow and arrow, she realized.

Sirens screamed, cutting through the clot of traffic. There was not much time. She crossed the parking lot, carrying the little girl toward the Winnebago. A retired couple peered through the windshield, trying to see. The child kicked until the woman had to put her down.

"Go. Get in right now and go with them before—"

"Are you going, too?"

"Baby, I can't. I can't take care of you anymore. It isn't safe. Don't you understand?"

"Want to stay with you!"

"Can we be of assistance?" said the elderly man, rolling down his window.

She knelt and gripped the little girl's arms. "I don't know where to go," she said. "I can't figure it out by myself." She lifted her hair away from the side of her face. "Look at me! I was born this way. No one else would want to help us. But it's not too late for you."

The little girl's eyes overflowed.

The woman pressed the child to her. "Please," she said, "it's not that I want to leave you . . ."

"We heard noises," said the elderly woman. "What happened?"

Tall legs stepped in front of the camper, blocking the way.

"Nothing," said the man. His jacket was torn and spattered. He pulled the woman and the little girl to their feet. "Come on."

He took them around to the back of the lot, then through a break in the fence and into a dark field, as red lights coverged on the restaurant. They did not look back. They came to the other side of the field and then they were crossing the frontage road to a maze of residential streets. They turned in a different direction at every corner, a random route that no one would be able to follow. After a mile or so they were out again and back to the divided highway, walking rapidly along in the ditch.

"This isn't the way," said the little girl.

The woman took the little girl's hand and drew her close. They would have to leave their things at the motel and move on again, she knew. Maybe they would catch a ride with one of the truckers on the interstate, though it was hard to get anyone to stop for three. She did not know where they would sleep this time; there wasn't enough left in her purse for another room.

"Hush, now." She kissed the top of her daughter's head and put an arm around her. "Want me to carry you?"

"I'm not a baby," said the little girl.

"No," said the woman, "you're not. . . ."

They walked on. The night lengthened. After a while the stars came out, cold and impossibly distant.

MARTYR WITHOUT CANON

by t. Winter-Damon

t. Winter-Damon is a poet from Tucson, Arizona whose work is a splendid example of the spontaneous generation of new writing talent within the small press field. Multitalented, he has published fiction, poetry, texts and illustrations here and in Europe—appearing in such publications as Bad Haircut Quarterly, New Blood, Back Brain Recluse, Poet's Corner, Opossum Holler, Tarot, The Rhysling Anthology, Haunts, Fantasy Tales, Ice River, *and many, many more. Don't look for these at your supermarket newsstand, however.*

Baptize me with the wanton venom of your serpent
   kisses!
Thrust your thorns of pleasure deep into my skull!
Hammer your rusted spikes into my outstretched palms,
                     My Courtesans of Darkness!
Transfix my feet into an *entrechat* of frostbite-searing
   rapture
Rack me high upon the Tree of Pain
—Let Passion's roses bloom upon my chastened
   nakedness

                              in bright profusion
—Let the winnowing winds flay me to the twisted
   shape

                              of your desire

251

—Let my screams of silence echo in the arid canyons
                              of your mercy
Sedduce me with the hollow promise of your empty
   chalice
Moisten the fevered leather of my lips with your soaked
   sponge
                              of vinegar and brine
Inhale the poppy fragrance of my fear that trickles in
   chill rivulets
                        of feather-tonguing torment
—Let the ravens feast upon the tainted colors
                              of my soul
—Let the flies crust black and emerald upon the bud-
   ding blossoms
                        of my transformation
—Let the Dark Dreams swirl like incense smoke from
   out this flesh
              emancipated from its chains of Reason!
This wickerwork of bone no longer claims me . . .
Rack me high upon the Tree of Pain
   Where Herakles in his masque of Everyman still
   strains—
      unable to escape the spasms of his ravished logic.

all quivers to the violet howl to steel wolves of
electric desolation & Van Gogh & Janis J. & Goya
slash the sky of amethyst with brush-strokes frantic.
unremitting. manic. & the shadows scream in jagged
lines of desperation, & the howl of violet stirs the
coals of arctic flame into a crematory blast that
chars the pinkest clouds into gray ash. & from out
of Golgotha erupt the arcs of blinding blackness
like a wildly vacillating pendulum. like a metronome
of epileptic tic/tic/ticking . . . obsidian in shattered
curves of razor. ripples of deadly beauty.
   . . . black/yellow/red. black/yellow/red. black/yellow/
red . . . like smoke rings of silken venom. & the coral
snake like Ouroboros slithers through the tunnels of per-
ception. Rimbaud & Jim of The Doors & Baudelaire.

& the Seps shall share the tonguing of my ardor in French kisses of necrotic splendor. & below the violet blades of grass we writhe in visions of abandon. (do not hunger yet to drink my sins! grind not the gruel of *bool keban*! the maize shall rot before my steeping! even now i stride!). & i shall feast upon the dragon's flesh to know the fullness of the barrow. to savor the secrets of the mound. & i shall swill deep trenchers of his black & fiery liquor. & i shall bathe my flesh-that-is-no-longer-flesh in torrents of his steaming essence. (& *i shall toast the blood elixer*!)

Flow the sacred wine of madness!
—ORPHEUS—
Madness of wine! Sacred the flow!
& Blind Lemon Jefferson & Balder & James Joyce. & glaciers & waterfalls of molten indigo geyser up into the carbon void where once the planets & the constellations reeled in fiery rituals of birth & death prolonged in seconds of eroding diamond. pinpricks & chrysanthemums. & irises of indigo of shattered glass of repetitions of the first expression & echoes of steel & gut reaction. rhythms of indigo equation. & the audience applauds with white-gloved hands of flogging hunger & the flowers of the belladonna blossom rising like velvet curtains from the stage of dramas & tragedy. & the Sorceror of cruel angular. frenetic. oyster-eyed. like the psychopompos escaped from the asylum. & he breathes. he breathes the meanings of meaningless. the Navel of Limbo. he breathes & gestures with exaggeration. & the brush flows sepia upon the canvas . . . & Faust & Gretchen & their analyst the angel of the light invites them to the couch. & the brush flows sepia upon the canvas . . .
& Heinrich von Kleist & Sid Vicious & de Nerval. & the gift of liberated second sight. & beneath a black sun the exiled prince of Aurelia wanders. & the prince in exile wanders through the twisting shadows of the lamppost forest. & Sex Pistols. &

the queen of amazons/ the lioness of snowy wastes.
& her hounds bay at the stony moon. & her guest
(baptized in frigid waters) races forever second to
the tortoise. & her feast of red roses. & The Last
Supper . . . & the phoenix revels in the flame. &
Isis & her sacred cobra. & Carnea jingles tempt-
ingly her keys . . .

RACK ME HIGH UPON THE TREE OF PAIN
UNLOCK THE GATES OF UNDERWORLD

Lenny Bruce & Crimes of Passion & Apollinaire. &
images in ultraviolet. delusions/nihilist/phantom/peacock
. . . the one-eyed god . . . moonshadow/arabesques/
mouths shrieking/minarets/mooncrimson . . . the one-
eyed god . . . fissures yawning like dissolute pariah
priests. & beggars belching coffin stench. brimstone.
fermented bile . . . the one-eyed god . . . silk/satin/
velvet/serpent & sparrow/chinchilla/leather/lace . . .
the ebon horse . . .
& i wander a forest bare-limbed as bone. where feath-
erless birds sing voiceless songs . . .
 RACK ME HIGH UPON THE TREE OF PAIN
Capture my vagrant flesh within your brazen bell!
Beat upon it with your hammers of sensation. Drum
forth the clamor of the Joyous Damned! Rupture these
fragile tympani with ringing madness. Until i only hear
the iridescent whispers of the evernight!

Gouge out my eyes! Your shafts of mistletoe shall
blind me. Until i only see the roaring colors of the
evernight!

Corrupt my tongue with maggots' lust! Until i only
taste quicksilver/acid/liquor . . .
                              Until i only taste the sap

of the moon-plant/resin of the wise. Until I only
speak in syllables of scoured bone! in syllables of
evernight . . .

Baptize me with the wanton venom of your serpent
    kisses—
Thrust your thorns of pleasure deep into my skull—
Hammer your rusted spikes into my outstretched palms,
                My Courtesans of Darkness—
Transfix my feet into an *entrechat* of frostbite-searing
    rapture—

RACK ME HIGH UPON THE TREE OF PAIN.

THE THIN PEOPLE

by Brian Lumley

*Born in Horden, Durham on December 2, 1937,
Brian Lumley joined the army at age 21 and served
twenty-two years in Berlin and Cyprus among other
postings. Retired from the army, he writes full time
now and lives with his wife, Dorothy, in Devon. At
conventions Lumley has been known to share a bottle of brandy with other late-night program partici-
pants, and he's a good man to have on your side if a
fight erupts afterward in the bar.*

*In addition to numerous short stories, Brian Lumley
has published some twenty-five books—most recently,* Necroscope II. *Many of his earlier books—*
The Caller of the Black, The Burrowers Beneath,
Beneath the Moors, The Transition of Titus Crow—
*were rooted in Lovecraft's Cthulhu Mythos, and while
he has not abandoned this interest, Lumley's recent
novels—*Psychomech, Necroscope—*have been ambitious delvings into more contemporary horrors. A
case in point is "The Thin People"—certainly not a
Cthulhu Mythos story. However, after reading this I
intend to examine closely the next bottle of brandy
Lumley offers to share.*

1

Funny place, Barrows Hill. Not *Barrow's* Hill, no.
Barrows without the apostrophe. For instance: you

won't find it on any map. You'll find maps whose borders approach it, whose corners impinge, however slightly, upon it, but in general it seems that cartographers avoid it. It's too far out from the center for the tubes, hasn't got a main-line station, has lost much of its integrity by virtue of all the infernal demolition and reconstruction going on around and within it. But it's still there. Buses run to and from, and the older folk who live there still call it Barrows Hill.

When I went to live there in the late '70s I hated the place. There was a sense of senility, of inherent idiocy about it. A damp sort of place. Even under a hot summer sun, damp. You could feel blisters of fungus rising even under the freshest paint. Not that the place got painted very much. Not that I saw, anyway. No, for it was like somewhere out of Lovecraft: decaying, diseased, inbred.

Barrows Hill. I didn't stay long, a few months. Too long, really. It gave you the feeling that if you delayed, if you stood still for just one extra moment, then that it would grow up over you and you'd become a part of it. There are some old, old places in London, and I reckoned Barrows Hill was of the oldest. I also reckoned it for its *genius loci*; like it was a focal point for secret things. Or perhaps not a focal point, for that might suggest a radiation—a spreading outward—and as I've said, Barrows Hill was ingrown. The last bastion of the strange old things of London. Things like the thin people. The very tall, very thin people.

Now nobody—but nobody *anywhere*—is ever going to believe me about the thin people, which is one of the two reasons I'm not afraid to tell this story. The other is that I don't live there anymore. But when I did . . .

I suspect now, that quite a few people—ordinary people, that is—knew about them. They wouldn't admit it, that's all, and probably still won't. And since all of the ones who'd know live on Barrows Hill, I really can't say I blame 'em. There was one old lad lived there, however, who knew *and* talked about them. To me. Since he had a bit of a reputation (to be frank, they called him "Balmy Bill of Barrows Hill") I didn't pay a deal of attention at first. I mean, who would?

Barrows Hill had a pub, a couple of pubs, but the one most frequented was "The Railway." A hangover from a time when there really was a railway, I supposed. A couple of years ago there had been another, a serious rival to "The Railway" for a little while, when someone converted an old block into a fairly modern pub. But it didn't last. Whoever owned the place might have known something, but probably not. Or he wouldn't have been so stupid as to call his place "The Thin Man!" It was only open for a week or two before burning down to the ground.

But that was before my time and the only reason I make mention of pubs, and particularly "The Railway," is because that's where I met Balmy Bill. He was there because of his disease, alcoholism, and I was there because of mine, heartsickness—which, running at a high fever, showed all signs of mutating pretty soon into Bill's problem. In short, I was hitting the bottle.

Now this is all incidental information, of course, and I don't intend to go into it other than to say it was our problems brought us together. As unlikely a friendship as any you might imagine. But Balmy Bill was good at listening, and I was good at buying booze. And so we were good company.

One night, however, when I ran out of money, I made the mistake of inviting him back to my place. (My place—hah! A bed, a loo and a typewriter; a poky little place up some wooden stairs, like a penthouse kennel; oh, yes, and a bonus in the shape of a cupboard converted to a shower.) But I had a couple bottles of beer back there and a half-bottle of gin, and when I'd finished crying on Balmy Bill's shoulder it wouldn't be far for me to fall into bed. What did surprise me was how hard it was to get him back there. He started complaining the moment we left the bar—or rather, as soon as he saw which way we were headed.

"Up the Larches? You live up there, off Barchington Road? Yes, I remember you told me. Well, and maybe I'll just stay in the pub a while after all. I mean, if you live right up *there*—well, it's out of my way, isn't it?"

"Out of your way? It's a ten minute walk, that's all! I thought you were thirsty?"

"Thirsty I am—always! Balmy I'm not—they only say I am 'cos they're frightened to listen to me."

"They?"

"People!" he snapped, sounding unaccustomedly sober. Then, as if to change the subject: "A half-bottle of gin, you said?"

"That's right, Gordon's. But if you want to get back on down to 'The Railway' . . ."

"No, no, we're half-way there now," he grumbled, hurrying along beside me, almost taking my arm in his nervousness. "And anyway, it's a nice bright night tonight. They're not much for light nights."

"They?" I asked again.

"People!" Despite his short, bowed legs, he was half a pace ahead of me. "The thin people." But where his first word had been a snarl, his last three were whispered, so that I almost missed them entirely.

Then we were up Larches Avenue—*the* Larches as Balmy Bill had it—and closing fast on twenty-two, and suddenly it was very quiet. Only the scrape of dry, blown leaves on the pavement. Autumn, and the trees half-naked. Moonlight falling through webs of high, black, brittle branches.

"Plenty of moon," said Bill, his voice hushed. "Thank God—in whom I really don't believe—for that. But *no street lights*! You see that? Bulbs all missing. That's them."

"Them?" I caught his elbow, turning him into my gateway—if there'd been a gate. There wasn't, just the post, which served as my landmark whenever I'd had a skinful.

"Them, yes!" he snapped, staring at me as I turned my key in the lock. "Damn young fool!"

And so up the creaky stairs to my little cave of solitude, and Balmy Bill shivering despite the closeness of the night and warmth of the place, which leeched a lot of its heat from the houses on both sides, and from the flat below, whose elderly lady occupier couldn't seem to live in anything other than an oven; and in through my own door, into the "living" room, where Bill closed the curtains across the jutting bay windows as if he'd lived there all of his life. But not before he'd peered out into the night street, his eyes darting this way and that, round and bright in his lined, booze-desiccated face.

Balmy, yes. Well, maybe he was and maybe he wasn't. "Gin," I said, passing him the bottle and a glass. "But go easy, yes? I like a nip myself, you know."

"A nip? A nip? Huh! If I lived here I'd need more than a nip. This is the middle of it, this is. The very middle!"

"Oh?" I grinned. "Myself, I had it figured for the living end!"

He paced the floor for a few moments—three paces there, three back—across the protesting boards of my tiny room, before pointing an almost accusing finger at me. "Chirpy tonight, aren't you? Full of beans!"

"You think so?" Yes, he was right. I did feel a bit brighter. "Maybe I'm over it, eh?"

He sat down beside me. "I certainly hope so, you daft young sod! And now maybe you'll pay some attention to my warnings and get yourself a place well away from here."

"Your warnings? Have you been warning me, then?" It dawned on me that he had, for several weeks, but I'd been too wrapped up in my own misery to pay him much heed. And who would? After all, he was Balmy Bill.

" 'Course I have!" he snapped. "About them bloody—"

"—Thin people," I finished it for him. "Yes, I remember now."

"Well?"

"Eh?"

"Are you or aren't you?"

"I'm listening, yes."

"No, no, *no*! Are you or aren't you going to find yourself new lodgings?"

"When I can afford it, yes."

"You're in danger here, you know. They don't like strangers. Strangers change things, and they're against that. They don't like anything strange, nothing new. They're a dying breed, I fancy, but while they're here they'll keep things the way they like 'em."

"Okay," I sighed. "This time I really am listening. You want to start at the beginning?"

He answered my sigh with one of his own, shook his head impatiently. "Daft young bugger! If I didn't like you I wouldn't bother. But all right, for your own good, one last time . . . just listen and I'll tell you what I know. It's not much, but it's the last warning you'll get . . ."

2

"Best thing ever happened for 'em must have been the lampposts, I reckon."

"Dogs!" I raised my eyebrows.

He glared at me and jumped to his feet. "Right, that's it, I'm off!"

"Oh, sit down, sit down!" I calmed him. "Here, fill your glass again. And I promise I'll try not to interrupt."

"Lampposts!" he snapped, his brows black as thunder. But he sat and took the drink. "Yes, for they imitate them, see? And thin, they can hide behind them. Why, they can stand so still that on a dark night you wouldn't know the difference! Can you imagine that, eh? Hiding behind or imitating a lamppost!"

I tried to imagine it, but: "Not really," I had to admit. Now, however, my levity was becoming a bit forced. There was something about his intensity—the way his limbs shook in a manner other than alcoholic—which was getting through to me. "Why should they hide?"

"Freaks! Wouldn't you hide? A handful of them, millions of us. We'd hound 'em out, kill 'em off!"

"So why don't we?"

" 'Cos we're all smart young buggers like you, that's why! 'Cos we don't *believe* in 'em."

"But you do."

Bill nodded, his three or four day growth of hair quivering on jowls and upper lip. "Seen 'em," he said, "and seen . . . *evidence* of them."

"And they're real people? I mean, you know, human? Just like me and you, except . . . thin?"

"And tall. Oh—*tall!*"

"Tall?" I frowned. "Thin and tall. How tall? Not as tall as—"

"Lampposts," he nodded, "yes. Not during the day, mind you, only at night. At night they—" (he looked uncomfortable, as if it had suddenly dawned on him how crazy this all must sound) "—they sort of, well, kind of *unfold* themselves."

I thought about it, nodded. "They unfold themselves. Yes, I see."

"No, you don't see," his voice was flat, cold, angry now. "But you will, if you hang around here long enough."

"Where do they live," I asked, "these tall, thin people?"

"In thin houses," he answered, matter-of-factly.

"Thin houses?"

"Sure! Are you telling me you haven't noticed the thin houses? Why, this place of yours very nearly qualifies! Thin houses, yes. Places where normal people wouldn't dream of setting up. There's half-a-dozen such in Barchington, and a couple right here in the Larches!" He shuddered and I bent to turn on an extra bar in my electric fire.

"Not cold, mate," Bill told me then. "Hell no!

Enough booze in me to keep me warm. But I shudder every time I think of 'em. I mean, what *do* they do?"

"Where do they work, you mean?"

"Work?" he shook his head. "No, they don't work. Probably do a bit of tea-leafing. Burglary, you know. Oh, they'd get in anywhere, the thin people. But what do they *do*?"

I shrugged.

"I mean, me and you, we watch telly, play cards, chase the birds, read the paper. But them . . ."

It was on the tip of my tongue to suggest maybe they go into the woods and frighten owls, but suddenly I didn't feel half so flippant. "You said you'd seen them?"

"Seen 'em sure enough, once or twice," he confirmed. "And weird! One, I remember, came out of his thin house—thin house in Barchington, I could show you it sometime in daylight. Me, I was behind a hedge sleeping it off. Don't ask me how I got there, drunk as a lord! Anyway, something woke me up.

"Down at its bottom the hedge was thin where cats come through. It was night and the council men had been round during the day putting bulbs in the street lights, so the place was all lit up. And directly opposite, there's this thin house and its door slowly opening; and out comes this bloke into the night, half of him yellow from the lamplight and half black in shadow. See, right there in front of the thin house is a street lamp.

"But this chap looks normal enough, you know? A bit stiff in his movements: he sort of moves jerky, like them contortionists who hook their feet over their shoulders and walk on their hands. Anyway, he looks up and down the street, and he's obviously satisfied no one's there. Then—

"—He slips back a little into the shadows until he comes up against the wall of his house, and he—unfolds!

"I see the light glinting down one edge of him, see it suddenly split into two edges at the bottom, sort of hinged at the top. And the split widens until he stands in the dark there like a big pair of dividers. And then one half swings up until it forms a straight line, perpendicular—and now he's ten feet tall. Then the same again, only this time the division takes place in the middle. Like . . . like a joiner's wooden three-foot ruler, with hinges so he can open it up, you know?"

I nodded, fascinated despite myself. "And that's how they're built, eh? I mean, well, hinged?"

"Hell, no!" he snorted. "You can fold your arms on their elbows, can't you? Or your legs on their knees? You can bend from the waist and touch your toes? Well I sure can! Their joints may be a little different from ours, that's all—maybe like the joints of certain insects. Or maybe not. I mean, their science is different from ours, too. Perhaps they fold and unfold themselves the same way they do it to other things—except it doesn't do them any harm. I dunno . . ."

"What?" I asked, puzzled. "What other things do they fold?"

"I'll get to that later," he told me darkly, shivering. "Where was I?"

"There he was," I answered, "all fifteen foot of him, standing in the shadows. Then—?"

"A car comes along the street, sudden like!" Bill grabbed my arm.

"Wow!" I jumped. "He's in trouble, right?"

Balmy Bill shook his head. "No way. The car's lights are on full, but that doesn't trouble the thin man. He's not stupid. The car goes by, lighting up the walls with its beam, and where the thin man stood in shadows against the wall of his thin house—"

"Yes?"

"A drainpipe, all black and shiny!"

I sat back. "Pretty smart."

"You better believe they're smart. Then, when it's dark again, out he steps. And *that's* something to see! Those giant strides—but quick, almost a flicker. Blink your eyes and he's moved—and between each movement his legs coming together as he pauses, and nothing to see but a pole. Up to the lamppost he goes, seems almost to melt into it, hides behind it. And *plink!*—out goes the light. After that . . . in ten minutes he had the whole street black as night in a coalmine. And yours truly lying there in somebody's garden, scared and shivering and dying to throw up."

"And that was it?"

Balmy Bill gulped, tossed back his gin and poured himself another. His eyes were huge now, skin white where it showed through his whiskers. "God, no—that wasn't it—there was more! See, I figured later that I must have got myself drunk deliberately that time— so's to go up there and spy on 'em. Oh, I now that sounds crazy now, but you know what it's like when you're drunk mindless. Jesus, these days I can't *get* drunk! But these were early days I'm telling you about."

"So what happened next?"

"Next—he's coming back down the street! I can hear him: *click*, pause . . . *click*, pause . . . *click*, pause, stilting it along the pavement—and I can see him in my mind's eye, doing his impression of a lamppost with every pause. And suddenly I get this feeling, and I sneak a look around. I mean, the frontage of this garden I'm in is so tiny, and the house behind me is—"

I saw it coming. "Jesus!"

"A thin house," he confirmed it, "right!"

"So now *you* were in trouble."

He shrugged, licked his lips, trembled a little. "I was lucky, I suppose. I squeezed myself into the hedge, lay still as death. And *click*, pause . . . *click*, pause, getting closer all the time. And then, behind me, for I'd turned my face away—the slow creaking as the door of the thin house swung open! And the second thin person coming out and, I imagine, unfolding him or herself, and the two of 'em standing there for a moment, and me near dead of fright."

"And?"

"*Click-click*, pause; *click-click*, pause; *click-click*— and away they go. God only knows where they went, or what they did, but me?—I gave 'em ten minutes' start and then got up, and ran, and stumbled, and forced my rubbery legs to carry me right out of there. And I haven't been back. Why, this is the closest I've been to Barchington since that night, and too close by far!"

I waited for a moment but he seemed done. Finally I nodded. "Well, that's a good story, Bill, and—"

"I'm not finished!" he snapped. "And it's not just a story . . ."

"There's more?"

"Evidence," he whispered. "The evidence of your own clever-bugger eyes!"

I waited.

"Go to the window," said Bill, "and peep out through the curtains. Go on, do it."

I did.

"See anything funny?"

I shook my head.

"Blind as a bat!" he snorted. "Look at the street lights—or the absence of lights. I showed you once tonight. They've nicked all the bulbs."

"Kids," I shrugged. "Hooligans. Vandals."

"Huh!" Bill sneered. "Hooligans, here? Unheard of, Vandals? You're joking! What's to vandalize? And when did you last see kids playing in these streets, eh?"

He was right. "But a few missing light bulbs aren't hard evidence," I said.

"All *right*!" he pushed his face close and wrinkled his nose at me. "Hard evidence, then." And he began to tell me the final part of his story . . .

3

"Cars!" Balmy Bill snapped, in that abrupt way of his. "They can't bear them. Can't say I blame 'em much, not on that one. I hate the noisy, dirty, clattering things myself. But tell me: have you noticed anything a bit queer—about cars, I mean—in these parts?"

I considered for a moment, replied: "Not a hell of a lot of them."

"Right!" He was pleased. "On the rest of the Hill, nose to tail. Every street overflowing. 'Specially at night when people are in the pubs or watching the telly. But here? Round Barchington and the Larches and a couple of other streets in this neighborhood? Not a one to be seen!"

"Not true," I said. "There are two cars in this very street. Right now. Look out the window and you should be able to see them."

"Bollocks!" said Bill.

"Pardon?"

"Bollocks!" he gratefully repeated. "Them's not *cars*! Rusting old bangers. Spoke-wheels and all. Twenty, thirty years they've been trundling about. The thin people are *used* to them. It's the big shiny new ones they don't like. And so, if you park your car up here overnight—trouble!"

"Trouble?" But here I was deliberately playing dumb. Here I knew what he meant well enough. I'd seen it for myself: the occasional shiny car, left overnight, standing there the next morning with its tires slashed, windows smashed, lamps kicked in.

He could see it in my face. "You know what I mean, all right. Listen, couple of years ago there was a flash Harry type from the city used to come up here. There was a barmaid he fancied in 'The Railway' —and she was taking all he could give her. Anyway, he was flash, you know? One of the gang lads and a rising star. And a flash car to go with it. Bullet-proof windows, hooded lamps, reinforced panels—the lot. Like a bloody tank, it was. But—" Bill sighed.

"He used to park it up here, right?"

He nodded. "Thing was, you couldn't threaten him. You know what I mean? Some people you can threaten, some you shouldn't threaten, and some you mustn't He was one you mustn't. Trouble is, so are the thin people."

"So what happened?"

"When they slashed his tires, he lobbed bricks through the windows. And he had a knowing way with him. He tossed 'em through thin house windows. Then one night he parked down on the corner of Barchington. Next morning—they'd drilled holes right through the plate, all over the car. After that—he didn't come back for a week or so. When he did come back . . . well, he must've been pretty mad."

"What did he do?"

"Threw something else—something that made a bang! A damn big one! You've seen that thin, derelict shell on the corner of Barchington? Oh, it was him, sure enough, and he got it right, too. A thin house. Anybody in there, they were goners. And *that* did it!"

"They got him?"

"They got his car! He parked up one night, went down to 'The Railway,' when the bar closed, took his lady-love back to her place, and in the morning—"

"They'd wrecked it—his car, I mean."

"Wrecked it? Oh, yes, they'd done that. They'd *folded* it!"

"Come again?"

"Folded it!" he snapped. "Their funny science. Eighteen inches each way, it was. A cube of folded metal. No broken glass, no split seams, no splintered plastic. Folded all neat and tidy. An eighteen-inch cube."

"They'd put it through a crusher, surely?" I was incredulous.

"Nope—folded."

"Impossible!"

"Not to them. Their funny science."

"So what did he do about it?"

"Eh? Do? He looked at it, and he thought, 'What if I'd been sitting *in* the bloody thing?' Do? He did what I would do, what you would do. He went away. We never did see him again."

The half-bottle was empty. We reached for the beers. And after a long pull I said: "You can kip here if you want, on the floor. I'll toss a blanket over you."

"Thanks," said Balmy Bill, "but no thanks. When

the beer's gone I'm gone. I wouldn't stay up here to save my soul. Besides, I've a bottle of my own back home."

"Sly old sod!" I said.

"Daft young bugger!" he answered without malice. And twenty minutes later I let him out. Then I crossed to the windows and looked out at him, at the street all silver in moonlight.

He stood at the gate (where it should be) swaying a bit and waving up at me, saying his thanks and farewell. Then he started off down the street.

It was quiet out there, motionless. One of those nights when even the trees don't move. Everything frozen, despite the fact that it wasn't nearly cold. I watched Balmy Bill out of sight, craning my neck to see him go, and—

"Across the road, three lampposts—where there should only be two! The one on the left was okay, and the one to the far right. But the one in the middle? I never had seen that one before. I blinked bleary eyes, gasped, blinked again. Only *two* lampposts!

Stinking drunk—drunk as a skunk—utterly boggled!

I laughed as I tottered from the window, switched off the light, staggered into my bedroom. The balmy old bastard had really had me going. I'd really started to believe. And now the booze was making me see double—or something. Well, just as long as it was lampposts and not pink elephants! Or thin people! And I went to bed laughing.

. . . But I wasn't laughing the next morning.

Not after they found him, old Balmy Bill of Barrows Hill. Not after they called me to identify him.

"Their funny science," he'd called it. The way they folded things. And Jesus, they'd folded him, too. Right down into an eighteen-inch cube. Ribs and bones and skin and muscles—the lot. Nothing broken, you understand, just folded. No blood or guts or anything nasty—nastier by far *because* there was nothing.

And they'd dumped him in a garbage-skip at the end of the street. The couple of local youths who found him weren't even sure what they'd found, until they spotted his face on one side of the cube. But I won't go into that . . .

Well, I moved out of there just as soon as I could—do you blame me?—since then I've done a lot of thinking about it. Fact is, I haven't thought of much else.

And I suppose old Bill was right. At least I hope so. Things he'd told me earlier, when I was only half listening. About them being the last of their sort, and Barrows Hill being the place they've chosen to sort of fade away in, like a thin person's "elephant's graveyard," you know?

Anyway, there are no thin people here, and no thin houses. Vandals aplenty, and so many cars you can't count, but nothing out of the ordinary.

Lampposts, yes, and posts to hold up the telephone wires, of course. Lots of them. But they don't bother me anymore.

See, I know *exactly* how many lampposts there are. And I know exactly *where* they are, every last one of them. And God help the man ever plants a new one without telling me first!

FAT FACE

by Michael Shea

Michael Shea's books include A Quest for Simbilis, Nifft the Lean, The Color Out of Time, *as well as his recent Arkham House collection,* Polyphemus. *Born in Los Angeles in 1946, Shea currently lives with his wife and two kids in the hinterlands of Windsor, California. Shea is an unpredictable writer, capable of superior pastiches of Jack Vance or of H. P. Lovecraft and of generating nastiness all of his own, as in his celebrated novella, "The Autopsy."*

"Fat Face" is a Cthulhu Mythos story treated in contemporary terms. Michael Shea enjoys writing in this sub-genre, despite the fact that all too many amateurish excesses here have made it difficult to find serious markets. In defense, Shea maintains: "HPL had one of the essences of good horror down pat—that endlessly drawing-aside of a transparent veil from an already-known horror. The pantomime of disclosure—Revelation constantly looms at hand, only to withdraw penultimately, whisked away by the narrator's impossibly lucid and eloquent obtuseness." Well, I guess. "Fat Face" was published as a limited edition chapbook, and it's my pleasure to unveil it to a wider audience.

"They were infamous, nightmare scupltures, even when telling of age-old, by-gone things; for Shoggoths

273

and their work ought not to be seen by human
beings, nor portrayed by any beings . . ."
                        At The Mountains of Madness
                        by Howard Phillips Lovecraft

When Patti started working from the lobby of the
Parnassus Hotel again, it was clear she was liked from
the way the other girls joked her, and unobtrusively
took it easy on her for the first few weeks, while she
got to feel steadier. She was deeply relieved to be
back.

She had been doing four nights a weeks at The
Encounter, a massage parlor. Her man was part-owner,
and he insisted that this schedule was to her advantage, because it was "strictly a hand-job operation,"
and the physical demands on her were lighter than
with street-work. Patti would certainly have agreed
that the work was lighter—if it hadn't been for the
robberies and killings. The last of these had been the
cause of her breakdown, and though she never admit-
ted this to her man, he had no doubt sensed the truth,
for he had let her go back to the Parnassus, and told
her she could pay him half-rate for the next few weeks,
till she was feeling steady again.

In her first weeks at the massage parlor, she had
known with all but certainty of two other clients—not
hers—who had taken one-way drives from The Encounter up into the Hollywood Hills. These incidents wore,
still, a thin, merciful veil of doubt. It was the third one
which passed too nearly for her to face away from it.

From the moment of his coming in, unwillingly she
felt spring up in her the conviction that the customer
was a perfect victim: physically soft, small, fatly
walleted, more then half-drunk, out-of-state. She
learned his name when her man studied his wallet
thoroughly on the pretext of checking his credit cards,
and the man's permitting of this liberty revealed how
fuddled he was. She walked ahead swinging her bottom, and he stumbled after, down the hall to a massage

room, and she could almost feel in her own head the ugly calculations clicking in her man's

The massage room was tiny. It had a not-infrequently-puked-on carpet, and a table. As she stood there, pounding firmly on him under the towel, trying to concentrate on her rhythmn exclusively, a gross, black cockroach ran boldly across the carpet. Afterward, she was willing to believe she had hallucinated, so strange was the thing she remembered. The bug, half as big as her hand, had stopped at midfloor and *stared* at her, and she in that instant had seen clearly and looked deep into the inhuman little black-bead eyes, and known that the man she was just then firing off into the towel was going to die later that night. There would be a grim, half-slurred conversation in some gully under the stars, there would be perhaps a long signing of travelers checks payable to the fictitious name on a certain set of false I.D. cards, and then the top of the plump man's head would be blown off.

Patti was a lazy girl who lazily wanted things to be nice, but was very good at adjusting to things that were not nice at all, if somebody strong really insisted on them. This, however, struck her with a terror that made her legs feel rubbery under her. Her man met her in the hall and sent her home before the mark had finished dressing inside. The body was found in three days and given scarcely two paragraphs in the paper. Patti was already half sick with alcohol and insomnia by the time she read them, and that night she took some pills which she was lucky enough to have pumped out of her an hour or so later.

But if her life-patterns offered any one best antidote for her cold, crippling fear, it was working out of the Parnassus. Some of her sweet-bitter apprentice years had been spent here or near it, and the lobby's fat, shabby red furniture still showed a girl to advantage, to the busy streets beyond the plate-glass windows.

The big, dowdy hotel stood in the porno heartland of Hollywood. It was a district of neon, and snarled traffic on narrow, overparked streets engineered back in the thirties. It offered a girl a host of strolling and lounging places good for pick-ups, and in fact most of the girls who spent time at the Parnassus spent as much or more of each night at other places too.

But Patti liked to work with minimum cruising. Too much walking put her in mind of the more painful recollections from her amateur years—the alley beatings, the cheats who humped and dumped and drove off fast, the quick, sticky douches with a shook-up Coca-Cola taken between trash-bins in back of a market. . . . All the deskmen at the Parnassus were fairly unextortionate. They levied an income-related tax, demanded only that a reasonable protocol govern use of the lobby, and made a small number of rooms available for the hookers' use. Patti worked the nearest bus stops from time to time, or went to the Dunk-o-Rama to sit over coffee and borrow many napkins and much sugar from single male customers, but primarily she worked the Parnassus, catching the eyes of the drivers who slowed to turn at the intersection, and strolling out when she noticed one starting to circle and trying to catch her eye. She usually took her tricks to the Bridgeport, or the Azteca Arms, which were more specifically devoted to this phase of the trade than the Parnassus was.

The virtual exemption of her home base from the ultimate sexual trafficking suited Patti to the ground. It aided a certain sunny sentimentalism with which she was apt to regard the "little community" that she and her colleagues were, after all, long-term members of. Because of these views, and also, perhaps, because she came from a rural hamlet, her friends called her Hometown.

And though they could always get her to laugh at her own notions, it still comforted her—for instance—to greet the man at the drug store with cordial remarks on the traffic or the smog. The man, bald and thin-mustached, never did more than grin at her with timid greed and scorn. The douches, deodorizers and fra-

grances she bought from him so steadily had preju-
diced him, and guaranteed his misreading of her folksy
genialities.

Or she would josh the various pimply employees at
the Dunk-O-Rama in a similar spirit, saying things
like, "They sure got you working, don't they?" or, of
the tax, "The old Governor's got to have his bite,
doesn't he?" When asked how she wanted her coffee,
she always answered with neighborly amplitude: "Well,
let's see—I guess I'm in the mood for cream today."
These things, coming from a vamp-eyed brunette in
her twenties, wearing a halter top, short-shorts and
Grecian sandals, disposed the adolescent counter-hops
more to sullen leers than to answering warmth. Yet
she remained persistent in her fantasies. She even
greeted Arnold, the smudged, moronic vendor at the
corner newsstand, by name—this in spite of an all too
lively and gurgling responsiveness on his part.

Now, in her recuperation, Patti took an added comfort from this vein of sentiment. This gave her sisterhood much to rally her about in their generally
affectionate recognition that she was much shaken and
needed some feedback and some steadying. A particular source of hilarity for them was Patti's revival of
interest in Fat Face, whom she always insisted was
their friendliest "neighbor" in their "local community."

An old ten-story office building stood on the corner
across the street from the Parnassus. As is not uncom-
mon in L.A., the simple, box-shaped structure bore
ornate cement freize-work on its facade, and all along
the pseudo-architraves capping the pseudo-pillars of
the building sides. Such freizes always have exotic
cliches as their theme—they are an echo of DeMille's
Hollywood. The one across from the Parnassus had a
Mesopotamian theme—ziggurat-shaped finials crown-
ing the pseudo-pillars, and murals of wrenched pro-
files, curly-bearded figures with bulging calves.

A different observer from Patti would have judged
the building *schlock*, but effective for all that, striking
the viewer with a subtle sense of alien portent. Patti

seldom looked higher than its fourth floor, where the usually open window of Fat Face's office was.

His appeared to be the only lively businesses maintained in that building. He ran two, and their mere combination could still set people cackling in the lobby of the Parnassus: a hydrotherapy clinic, and a pet refuge.

The building's dusty directory listed other offices. But the only people seen entering were unmistakably Fat Face's—all halting or ungainly, most toiling along on some shiny prosthetic or other.

Fat Face himself was often at his window—a dear, ruddy, bald countenance beaming, as often as not, avuncularly down on the hookers in the lobby across the street. His bubble-baldness was the object of much lewd humor among the girls and the pimps. Fat Face was much waved-at in sarcasm, whereat he always smiled a crinkly smile that seemed to understand and not to mind. Patti, when she sometimes waved, did so with pretty sincerity.

But she had to laugh at him too. He seemed destined to be comic. His patients were generally a waddling, pachydermous lot, shabbily and baggily dressed. They often compounded the impact of their grotesqueness by arriving in number for what must have been group sessions. And, as if more were needed, they often arrived with stray dogs and cats in tow. That the animals were not their own was made ludicrously plain by the beasts' struggles with leash or carrying cage. The doctor obviously recruited his patients to the support of his stray clinic, exploiting their dependency with a charitable unscrupulousness. For it seemed that the clinic had to be an altruistic work. It supported several collection vans, and leafleted widely—even bought cheap radio spots. The bulletins implored telephone notification of strays wherever observed. Patti had fondly pocketed one of the leaflets:

Help us Help!
Let our aid reach these unfortunate

creatures.
Nourished, spayed, medicated,
They may have a better chance
for health and life!

This generosity of feeling in Fat Face did not prevent his being talked of over in the lobby of the Parnassus, where great goiter-rubbing, water-splashing orgies were raucously hypothesised, with Fat Face flourishing whips and baby-oil, while cries of "rub my blubber!" filled the air. At such times Patti was impelled to leave the lobby, because it felt like betrayal to be laughing so hard at the goodly man.

Indeed, in her convalescent mellowness, much augmented by Valium, she had started to fantasize going up to his office, pulling the blinds, and ravishing him at his desk. She imagined him lonely and horny. Perhaps he had nursed his wife through a long illness and she had at last expired gently. . . . He would be so grateful!

This fancy took on such a quality of yearning that it alarmed Patti. Although she was a good and well-adapted hooker, she was, outside her trade's rituals of exchange, very shy in her dealing with people. She was not forward in these emotional matters, and she felt her longing to *be* forward as an impulse in some way alien to her, put upon her. Nonetheless, the sweet promptings retained a fascination, and she was kept swinging between these poles of feeling, to the point where she felt she had to talk about them. Late one afternoon she dragged Sheri, her best friend, out of the lobby and into a bar a couple blocks away. Sheri would keep confidence, but on first hearing the matter, she was as facetious as Patti had foreseen.

"Jesus, Patti," she said. "If the rest of him's as fat as his face it'd be like humping a hill!"

"So you pile only superstars? I mean, so what if he's fat? Try and think how *nice* it would be for him!"

"I bet he'd blush till his whole head looked like an eggplant. Then, if there was just a slit in the top, like

Melanie was saying—" Sheri had to break off and hold herself as she laughed. She had already done some drinking earlier in the afternoon. Patti called for another double and exerted herself to catch up, and meanwhile she harped on her theme to Sheri and tried to get her serious attention:

"I mean I've been working out of the Parnassus— what? Maybe three years now? No, four! Four years. I'm part of these people's community—the druggist, Arnold, Fat Face—and yet we never do anything to show it. There's no getting-together. We're just faces. I mean like Fat Face—I couldn't even *call* him that!"

"So let's go look in the directory of his building!"

Patti was about to answer when, behind the bar, she saw a big roach scamper across a rubber mat and disappear under the baseboard. She remembered the plump body in the towel, and remembered—as a thing actually seen—the slug-fragmented skull.

Sheri quickly noted the chill on her friend. She ordered more drinks and set to work on the idea of a jolly expedition, that very hour, over to Fat Face's office. And when Patti's stomach had thawed out again, she took up the project with grateful humor, and eagerly joined her friend's hilarity, trading bawdy suppositions of the outcome.

They lingered over yet a further round of drinks and at length barged, laughing, out into the late-afternoon streets. The gold-drenched sidewalks swarmed, the pavements were jammed with rumbling motors. Jaunty and loud, the girls sauntered back to their intersection, and crossed over to the old building. Its heavy oak-and-glass doors were pneumatically stiff, and cost them a stagger to force open. But when they swung shut, it was swiftly, with a deep click, and they sealed out the streetsound with amazing, abrupt completeness. The glass was dirty and it put a sulfurous glaze on the already surreal copper of the declining sun's light outside. Suddenly it might be Mars or Jupiter out beyond those doors, and they themselves stood within a great dim stillness that might have matched the feeling of a real Mesopotamian ruin, out on some starlit desert. The images were alien to Patti's thought—startling intrusions in a mental voice not precisely her own. Sheri gave a comic shiver but otherwise made no acknowledgment of similar feelings. She merrily cursed the old elevators with a hand-written out-of-order sign affixed to their switchplate by yellowed scotch tape, and then gigglingly led the way up the green-carpeted stairs, up which a rubber corridor mat ran that gave Patti murky imaginings of scuffed, supple, reptilian skin. She struggled up the stairs after her skylarking friend, gaping with amazement at the spirit of gaiety which had so utterly deserted her own thoughts at the instant of those doors' closing.

At the first two landings they peeked down the halls at similar vistas: green-carpeted corridors of frosted-glass doors with rich brass knobs. Bulbs burned miserly few, and in those corridors Patti sensed, with piercing vividness, the feeling of *kept* silence. It was not a void silence, but a full one, made by presences not stirring.

Patti's dread was so fierce and gratuitous, she wondered if it was a freak of pills and booze. She desperately wanted to stop her friend and retreat with her, but she couldn't find the breath or the words to broach her crazy panic. Sheri leapt triumphantly onto the fourth-floor landing and bowed Patti into the corridor.

Every door they passed bore the clinic's rubric and referred the passer to the room at the end of the hall, and every step Patti took toward that door sharpened the kick of panic in her stomach. They'd gotten scarcely halfway down the hallway when she reached her limit, and knew that no imaginable compulsion could make her go nearer to that room, Sheri tugged at her, and rallied her, but finally abandoned her and tiptoed hilariously up to the door, trying to do a parody of Patti's sudden fear.

She didn't knock, to Patti's relief. She took out her notepad, and mirthfully scrawled a moderately long message. She folded the note, tucked it under the door, and ran back to Patti.

When they reached the last flight of stairs, Patti dared speech. She scolded Sheri about the note.

"Did you think I was trying to steal him?" Sheri taunted, "giving him my address?" She alluded to a time, at a crowded party, when Patti had given Sheri a note to pass to a potential john, and Sheri had tampered with it and brought the trick to her own apartment. Patti was shocked at the possibility of such a trick, before discarding the idea as exceeding even Sheri's quirkishness.

"Did you hear any music up there?" Patti asked as they stepped out on the street. Coming into the noise outside was a blessed relief—breaking out into air and the color, as if surfacing from the long, crushing still-ness of a deep drowning. But even in this sweet rush she could call up clearly a weird, piping tune—scarcely a tune really, more an eerie melodic ramble—which had come into her mind as they hurried down the slick-rubbered flights of stairs. What bothered her as much as the strange feeling of the music was the way in which she had received it. It seemed to her that she had not *heard* it, but rather *remembered* it—suddenly and vividly—though she hadn't the trace of an idea now where she might have heard it before. Sheri's answer confirmed her thought:

"Music? Baby, there wasn't a sound up there! Wasn't it kind of spooky?" Her mood stayed giddy and Patti gladly fell in with it. They went to another bar they liked and drank for an hour or so—slowly, keeping a gloss on things, feeling humorous and excited like schoolgirls on a trip together. At length they decided to go to the Parnassus, find somebody with a car and scare up a cruising party.

As they crossed to the hotel Sheri surprised Patti by throwing a look at the old office building and giving a shrug that may have been half shudder. "Jesus. It was like being under the ocean or something in there, wasn't it, Patti?"

This echo of her own dread made Patti look again at her friend. Then Arnold, the vendor, stepped out from the newsstand and blocked their way.

The uncharacteristic aggressiveness gave Patti a nasty twinge. Arnold was unlovely. There was a babyish fatness and a redness about every part of him. His scanty red hair alternately suggested infancy or feeble age, and his one eyeless socket, with its weepy red folds of baggy lid, made his whole face look as if screwed up to cry. Over all his red, ambling softness there was a bright blackish glaze of inveterate filth. And, moronic though his manner was most of the time, Patti now felt a cunning about him, something sly and corrupt. The cretinous, wet-mouthed face he now thrust close to the girls seemed, somehow, to be that of a grease-painted conman, not an imbecile. As if it were a sour fog that surrounded the newsman, fear entered Patti's nostrils, and dampened the skin of her arms. Arnold raised his hand. Pinched between his smudgy thumb and knuckle were an envelope and a fifty-dollar bill.

"A man said to read this, Patti!" Arnold's childish intonation now struck Patti as an affectation, like his dirtiness, part of a chosen disguise.

"He said the money was to pay you to read it. It's a trick! He gave me twenty dollars!" Arnold giggled. The sense of cold-blooded deception in the man made Patti's voice shake when she questioned him about the man who'd given him the commission. He remembered nothing, an arm and a voice in a dark car that pulled up and sped off.

"Well, how is she supposed to read it?" Sheri prodded. "Should she be by a window? Should she wear anything special?"

But Arnold had no more to tell them, and Patti willingly gave up on him to escape the revulsion he so unexpectedly roused in her.

They went into the lobby with the letter, but such was its strangeness—so engrossingly lurid were the fleeting images that came clear for them—that they ended taking it back to the bar, getting a booth, and working over it with the aid of whiskey and lively surroundings. The document was in the form of an unsigned letter which covered two pages in a lucid, cursive script of bizarre elegance, and which ran thus:

Dear Girls:

How does a Shoggoth lord go wooing? You do not even guess enough to ask! Then let it be asked and answered for you. As it is written: *"The Shoggoth lord stumbleth unto his belusted, lo, he cometh heavily unto her, upon alien feet. From the sunless sea, from under the mountains of ice, cometh the mighty Shoggoth lord unto her."*

Dear, dear girls! Where is this place the Shoggothoi come from? In your tender, sensual ignorance you might well lack the power to be astonished by the prodigious gulfs of Space and Time this question probes. But let it once more be asked and answered for you. Thus has the answer been written:

"Shun the gulf beneath the peaks,
The caverned ocean black as night,
Where star-spawned gods made their retreat
From the slowly freezing world of light.

For even star-spawn may grow weak,
While what has been its slave gains strength;
Even star-spawn's will may break,
While slaves feed on their lords at length."

Sweet harlots! Darling, heedless trollops! You cannot imagine the Shoggoth lord's mastery of shapes! His race has bred smaller since modern men last met with it. Oh, but the Shoggoth lords are limber now! Supremest polymorphs—though what they are beneath all else, is Horror itself.

But how is it they press their loving suit? What do they murmur to her they hotly crave? You must

know that the Shoggoth craves her fat with panic—
full of the psychic juices of despair. Therefore he
taunts her with their ineluctable union; therefore he
pipes and flutes to her his bold, seductive lyric,
while he vows with a burning glare in his myriad
eyes that she'll be his. Thus he sings:

"Your veil shall be the wash of blood
That dims and drowns your dying eyes.
You'll have for bridesmaids Pain and Dread,
For vows, you'll jabber blasphemies.
My scalding flesh will be your gown,
And Agony your bridal song.
You shall both be my bread
And, senses reeling, watch me fed.

O maids, prepare her swiftly!
Speedily her loins unlace!
Her tender paps annoint,
And bare unto my seething face!"

Thus, dear girls, he ballads and rondelays his
belusted, thus he waltzes her spirit through dark,
empty halls of expectation, of always-harkening Horror, until the dance has reached that last, closed
room of consummation!

As many times as the girls flung these pages onto the
table, they picked them up again after short hesitation.
Both Sheri and Patty were very marginal readers, but
the flashes of coherent imagery in the letter kept them
coming back to the murky parts, trying to pick the lock
of their meaning. They held menace even in their very
calligraphy, whose baroque, barbed elegance seemed
sardonic and alien. The mere sonority of some of the
obscure passages evoked vivid images, a sense of murky
submersion in benthic pressures of fearful expectation,
while unseen giants abided in the dark nearby.

It put Patti in a goosefleshy melancholy, but of real
fear it raised little, even though it meant that some

out-to-lunch hurt-freak had quite possibly singled her and Sheri out. The letter held as much creepy entertainment for her as it did threat. The ones really into letter writing were much less likely to be real doers. Besides that, it was a very easy fifty dollars.

She was the more surprised, then, at Sheri's sudden, jagged confession of paranoia. She had been biting back panic for some time, it appeared, and Patti was sure that even as she spoke she was holding back more than she told. She was afraid to go home alone.

"All this bullshit," she pointed at the letter, "it's spooked me, Patti, I can't explain it. I got the bleep scared out of me, girl. Come on, we can sleep in the same bed, just like slumber parties in school, Patti. I just don't want to face walking into my living room tonight and turning on the light."

"Sure you can sleep over! But no kicking, right?"

"Oh, that was only because I had that dream!" Sheri shrilled. She was so happy and relieved it was pitiful, and Patti found herself developing an answering chill that made her glad of the company.

They got some sloe gin and some vodka and some bags of ice and bottles of Seven-Up. They got several bags of chips and puffs and cookies and candy bars, and repaired with their purchases to Patti's place.

She had a small cottage in a four-cottage court, with very old people living in the other three units. The girls shoved the bed into the corner so they could prop pillows against all the walls to lean back on. They turned on the radio, and the tv, and got out the phone book, and started making joke calls to people with funny names while eating, drinking, smoking, watching, listening and bantering each other.

Their consciousness outlasted their provisions, but not by long. Soon, back to back, they slept, bathed and laved by the gently burbling soundwash, and the ash-gray light of the pulsing images.

They woke to a day that was sunny, windy and smogless. They rose at high, glorious noon, and walked to a coffee shop for breakfast. The breeze was combing buttery light into the waxen fronds of the palms, while the Hollywood Hills seemed most opulently brocaded—under the sky's flawless blue—with the silver-green of sagebrush and sumach.

As they ravened breakfast, they plotted borrowing a car and taking a drive. Then Sheri's man walked in. She waved him over brightly, but Patti was sure she was as disappointed as herself. Rudy took a chair long enough to inform Sheri how lucky she was he'd run into her, since he'd been trying to find her. He had something important for her that afternoon. Contemptuously he snatched up the bill and paid for both girls. Sheri left in tow, and gave Patti a rueful wave from the door.

Patti's appetite left her. She dawdled over coffee, and stepped at last, unwillingly, out into the day's polychrome splendor. Its very clarity took on a sinister quality of remorselessness. Behold, the whole world and all its children moved under the glaring sun's brutal, endless revelation. Nothing could hide. Not in this world . . . though of course there were other worlds, where beings lie hidden immemorially. . . .

She shivered as if something had crawled across her. The thoughts had passed through her, but were not hers. She sat on a bus-stop bench and tightly crossed her arms as if to get a literal hold on herself. The strange thoughts, by their feeling, she knew instinctively to be echoes raised somehow by what they had read last night. Away with them, then! The creep had had more than his money's worth of reading from her already, and now she would forget those unclean pages. As for her depression, it was a freakish sadness caused by the spoiling of her holiday with Sheri, and it was silly to give in to it.

Thus she rallied herself, and got to her feet. She walked a few blocks without aim, somewhat stiff and resolute. At length the sunlight and her natural health of body had healed her mood, and she fell into a pleasant veering ramble down miles of Hollywood residential streets, relishing the cheap cuteness of the houses, and the lushness of their long-planted trees and gardens.

Almost she left the entire city. A happy, rushing sense of her freedom grew upon her and she suddenly pointed out to herself that she had nearly four hundred dollars in her purse. She came within an ace of swaggering into a Greyhound station with two quickly packed suitcases, and buying a ticket either to San Diego or Santa Barbara, whichever had the earliest departure time. With brave suddenness to simplify her life and remove it, at a stroke, from the evil that had seemed to haunt it recently. . . .

It was her laziness that, in the end, made her veer away from the decision—her dislike of its necessary but inherently tedious details: the bus ride, looking for an apartment, looking for a job. As an alternative to such dull preliminaries, the endless interest and familiarity of Hollywood took on renewed allure.

She would stay then. The knowledge didn't dull her sense of freedom. Her feet felt confident, at home upon these shady, root-buckled sidewalks. She strode happily, looking on her life with new detachment and ease. Such paranoias she'd been having! They seemed now as fogs that her newly freshened spirit could scatter at a breath.

She had turned onto a still, green block that was venerably overhung by great old peppertrees, and she'd walked well into it before she realized that the freeway had cut it off at the far end. An arrow indicated a narrow egress to the right, however, so she kept walking. Several houses ahead, a very large man in overalls appeared, dragging a huge German shepherd across the lawn.

Patti saw a new, brown van parked by the curb, and recognized it and the man at once. The vehicle was one of two belonging to Fat Face's stray refuge, and the man was one of his two full-time collectors.

He had the struggling brute by the neck with a noosed stick. He stopped and looked at Patti with some intensity as she approached. The vine-drowned cottage whose lawn he stood on was dark, tight-shut, and seemed deserted—as did the entire block—and it struck Patti that the man might have spotted the dog by chance, and might now be *thinking* it hers. She smiled and shook her head as she came up.

"He's not mine! I don't even *live* around here!"

Something in the way her own words echoed down the stillness of the street gave Patti a pang. She was sure they had made the collector's eyes narrow. He was tall, round and smooth, with a face of his employer's type, though not as jovial. He was severely club footed and bloat-legged on the left, as well as being inordinately bellied, all things which the coveralls lent a merciful vagueness. The green baseball cap he wore somehow completed the look of ill balance and slow wit that the man wore.

But as she got nearer, already wanting to turn and run the other way, she received a shocking impression of strength in the uncouth figure. The man had paused in a half-turn and was partly crouched—not a position of firm leverage. The dog—whose paws and muzzle showed some Bernard—weighed at least 170, and it resisted violently—yet scarcely stirred the heavy arms. Patti edged to one side of the walk, pretending a wariness of the dog which its helplessness made droll, and moved to pass. The collector's hand, as if absently, pressed down on the noose. The beast's head seemed to swell, its struggles grew more galvanic and constricted by extreme distress. And while thus smoothly he began throttling the beast, the collector cast a glance up and down the block, and stepped into Patti's path, effortlessly dragging the animal with him.

They stood face to face, very near. The ugly mathematics of peril swiftly clicked in her brain: the mass, the force, the time—all were sufficient. The next couple of moments could finish her. With a jerk he could kill the dog, drop it, seize her and thrust her into the van. Indeed, the dog was at the very point of death. The collector began to smile nastily and his breath came—foul and oddly cold—gusting against her face.

Then something began to happen to his eyes. They were rolling up, like a man's when he's coming—but they didn't roll white—they were rolling up a jet black—two glossy obsidian globes eclipsing from below the watery blue ones. Her lungs began to gather air to scream. A taxi-cab swung onto the street.

The collector's grip eased on the half-unconscious dog. He stood blinking furiously, and it seemed he could not unwind his bulky body from the menacing tension it had taken on. He stood, still frozen on the very threshold of assault, and the cold foulness still gusted from him with the labor of his breathing. In another instant Patti's reflexes fired and she was released with a leap from the curb out into the street, but there was time enough before for her to have the thought she *knew* that stench the blinking gargoyle breathed.

And then she was in the cab. The driver sullenly informed her of her luck in catching him on his special shortcut to a freeway on-ramp. She looked at him as if he'd spoken in a foreign tongue. More gently he asked her destination, and without thought she answered: "The Greyhound station."

Flight. With sweet, simple motion to cancel Hollywood, and its walking ghosts of murder, and its lurking plunderers of the body, and its nasty, nameless scribblers of letters whose pleasure it was to defile the mind with nightmares. But of course, she must pack. She re-routed the driver to her apartment.

This involved a doubling-back which took them across the street of her encounter. The van was still parked by the curb, but neither collector nor dog were in sight. Oddly, the van seemed to be moving slightly, rocking as if with interior movement of fitful vigor. Her look was brief, from a half block's distance, but in the shady stillness the subtle tremoring made a vivid impression.

Then she bethought herself of Fat Face. She could report the collector to him! That just and genial face instantly quelled all the horror attaching to the collector's uglier one. What, after all, had happened? A creepy, disabled type with some eye infection had been dangerously tempted to rape her, and she had lucked out. That last fact was grounds for celebration, while all that was strong and avuncular in the good doctor's expression promised that she would be vigorously protected from further danger at the same hands. She even smiled to imagine the interview: her pretty embarrassment, the intimate topic, her warmly expressed girlish gratitude. It could become the tender seduction of her fantasy.

So she re-routed the driver again—not without first giving him a ten-dollar tip in advance—to the boulevard. There she walked a while, savoring the sunlight, and lunched opulently, and went to two different double-bills, one right after the other.

But her mood could have been better. She kept remembering the collector. It was not his grotesqueness that nagged at her so much as a fugitive familiarity in the whole aura of him. His chill, malignant presence was like a gust out of some *place* obscurely known to her. What dream of her own, now lost to her, had shown her that world of dread and wonder and colossal age which now she caught—and knew—the scent of, in this man? The thought was easy to shake off as a freak of mood, but it was insistent in its return, like a fly that kept landing on her, and after the movies, feeling groggy and cold in the dusk, she called Sheri.

Her friend had just got home, exhausted from a multiple trick, and wearing a few bruises from a talk with Rudy afterward.

"Why don't I come over, Share? Hey?"

"Naw, Patti. I'm wrung out, girl. You feel OK?"

"Sure. So get to sleep then."

"Naw, hey now—you come over if you want to, Patti. I'm just gonna be dead to the world is all."

"Whaddya mean? If you're tired you're tired and I'll catch you later. So long." She could hear, but not change the anger and disappointment in her own voice. It told her, when she'd hung up but remained staring at the phone, how close to the territory of Fear she still stood. Full night had surrounded her glass booth. Against the fresh, purple dark, all the street's scribbly neon squirmed and swam, like sea-things of blue and rose and gold, bannering and twisting cryptically over the drowned pavements.

And, almost as though she expected watery death, Patti could not, for a moment, step from the booth out onto those pavements. Their lethal, cold strangeness lay, if not undersea, then surely in an alien, poisonous atmosphere that would scorch her lungs. For a ridiculous moment, her body defied her will. Then she set her sights on a bar half a block distant. She plunged from the booth and grimly made for that haven.

Some three hours later, no longer cold, Patti was walking to Sheri's. It was a weeknight and the stillness of the residential streets was not unpleasant. The tree-crowded streetlamps shed a light that was lovely with its whiskey gloss. The street names on their little banners of blue metal had a comic flavor to her tongue and she called out each as it came into view.

Sheri, after all, had said to come over. The petty cruelty of waking her seemed, to Patti, under the genial excuse of the alcohol, merely prankish. So she sauntered through sleeping Hollywood, knowing the nightwalker's exhilaration of being awake in a dormant world.

Sheri lived in a stucco cottage that was a bit tackier than Patti's, though larger, each cottage possessing a little driveway and a garage in back. And though there was a light on in the livingroom, it was up the driveway that Patti went, deciding, with sudden impishness, to spook her friend. She crept round the rear corner, and stole up to the screened window of Sheri's bedroom, meaning to make noises through a crack if one had been left open.

The window was in fact fully raised, though a blind was drawn within. Even as Patti leaned close, she heard movement inside the darkened room. In the next instant a gust of breeze came up and pushed back the blind within.

Sheri was on her back in the bed and somebody was on top of her, so that all Patti could see of her was her arms and her face, which stared round-eyed at the ceiling as she was rocked again and again on the bed. Patti viewed that surging, grappling labor for two instants, no more, and retreated, almost staggering, in a primitive reflex of shame more deep-lying in her than any of the sophistications of her adult professional life.

Shame and a weird, childish glee. She hurried out to the sidewalk. Her head rang, and she felt giggly and frightened to a degree that managed to astonish her even through her liquor. What was with her? She'd been paid to watch far grosser things than a simple coupling. On the other hand there had been a foul smell in the bedroom, and there had been a nagging hint of music too, she thought, a faint, unpleasant twisty tune coming from somewhere indefinite. . . .

These vague feelings quickly yielded to the humorous side of the accident. She walked to the nearest main street and found a bar. In it, she killed half an hour with two further doubles and then, reckoning enough time had passed, walked back to Sheri's.

The livingroom light was still on. Patti rang the bell and heard it inside, a rattly probe of noise that raised no stir of response. All at once she felt a light rush of suspicion, like some long-legged insect scuttling daintily up her spine. She felt that, as once before in the last few days, the silence she was hearing concealed a presence, not an absence. But why should this make her begin, ever so slightly, to sweat? It would be Sheri, playing possum. Trying by abruptness to throw off her fear she seized the knob. The door opened and she rushed in, calling:

"Ready or not, one two three!"

Before she was fully in the room, her knees buckled under her, for a fiendish stench filled it. It was a carrion smell, a fierce, damp rankness which bit and pierced the nose. It was so palpable an assault it seemed to crawl all over her—to wriggle through her scalp and stain her flesh as if with brimstone and graveslime.

Clinging still to the doorknob she looked woozily about the room, whose sloppy normality, coming to her as it did through that surreal fetor, struck her almost eerily. Here was the litter of wrappers, magazines and dishes—thickest round the couch—so familiar to her. The tv, on low, was crowned with ashtrays and beercans, while on the couch which it faced a freshly open bag of Fritos lay.

But it was from the bedroom door, partly ajar, that the nearly visible miasma welled most thickly, as from its source. And it would be in the bedroom that Sheri lay. She would be lying dead in its darkness. For, past experience and description though it was, the stench proclaimed that meaning grim and clear: death. Patti turned behind her to take a last clean breath, and stumbled toward the bedroom.

Every girl ran the risk of rough trade. It was an ugly and lonely way to die. With the dark, instinctive knowledge of their sisterhood, Patti knew that it was only laying out and covering up that her friend needed of her now. She shoved inward on the bedroom door, throwing a broken rhomb of light upon the bed.

It and the room were empty—empty save for the near physical mass of the stench. It was upon the bed that the reek fumed and writhed most nastily. The blankets and sheets were drenched with some vile fluid, and pressed into sodden seams and folds. The coupling she had glimpsed and snickered at—what unspeakable species of intercourse had it been? And Sheri's face staring up from under the shadowed form's lascivious rocking—had there been more to read in her expression than the slack-faced shock of sex? Then Patti moaned:

"O Jesus God!"

Sheri *was* in the room. She lay on the floor, mostly under the bed, only her head and shoulders protruding, her face to the ceiling. There was no misreading its now frozen look. It was a face wherein the recognition of Absolute Pain and Fear had dawned, even as death arrived. Dead she surely was. Living muscles did not achieve that utter fixity. Tears jumped up in Patti's eyes. She staggered into the livingroom, fell on the couch and wept. "O Jesus God," she said again, softly now.

She went to the kitchenette and got a dishtowel, tied it around her nose and mouth, and returned to the bedroom. Sheri would not, at least, lie half thrust from sight like a broken toy. Her much-used body would have a shred of that dignity which her life had never granted it. She bent, and hooked her hands under those dear, bare shoulders. She pulled, and, with her pull's excess force, fell backward to the floor. For that which she fell hugging to her breasts needed no such force to move its lightness. It was not Sheri, but a dreadful upper fragment of her, that Patti hugged: Sheri's head and shoulders, one of her arms . . . gone were her fat, funny feet they had used to laugh at, for she ended now in a charred stump of ribcage. As a little girl might clutch some unspeakable doll, Patti lay embracing tightly that which made her scream, and scream again.

Valium. Compazene. Mellaril. Stellazine. Gorgeous technicolored tabs and capsules. Bright-hued pillars holding up the Temple of Rest. Long afternoons of Tuonol and tv; night sweats and quiet, groggy mornings. Patti was in County for more than a week.

She had found all there was to be found of her friend. Dismemberment by acid is a new wrinkle, and Sheri got some press, but in a world of trashbag murders and mass graves uncovered in quiet back yards, even a death like Sheri's could hope for only so much coverage. Patti's bafflement made her call the detectives assigned to the case at least once a day. With gruff tact they heard through her futile rummagings among the things she knew of Sheri's life and background, but soon knew she was helpless to come up with anything material.

She desperately wanted a period of thoughtless rest, but always a vague, unsleeping dread marred her drug-buoyed ease. For she could be waked, even from the glassiest daze, by a sudden sense that the number of people surrounding her was dwindling—that they were, everywhere, stealing off, or vanishing, and that the hospital, and even the city, was growing empty around her.

She put it down to the hospital itself—its constant shifts of bodies, its wheelings in and out on silent gurneys. She obtained a generous scrip for Valium and had herself discharged, hungry for the closer comfort of her friends. A helpful doctor was leaving the building as she did, and gave her a ride. With freakish embarrassment about her trade and her world, Patti had him drop her at a coffee shop some blocks from the Parnassus. When he had driven off, she started walking. The dusk was just fading. It was Saturday night, but it was also the middle of a three-day weekend (as she had learned with surprise from the doctor) and the traffic on both pavement and asphalt was remarkably light.

Somehow it had a small-town-on-Sunday feel, and alarm woke in her and struggled in its heavy Valium shackles, for this was as if the confirmation of her frightening hallucinations. Her fear mounted as she walked. She pictured the Parnassus with an empty lobby, and imagined that she saw the traffic beginning everywhere to turn off the street she walked on, so that in a few moments, it could stretch deserted for a mile either way.

But then she saw the many lively figures through the beloved plateglass windows. She half ran ahead, and as she waited with happy excitement for the light, she saw Fat Face up in his window. He spotted her just when she did him, and beamed and winked. Patti waved and smiled and heaved a deep sigh of relief that nearly brought tears. This was true medicine, not pills, but friendly faces in your home community! Warm feelings and simple neighborliness! She ran forward at the "walk" signal.

There was a snag before she reached the lobby, for Arnold from his wooden cave threw at her as she passed a leer of wet intensity that scared her even as she recognized that some kind of frightened greeting was intended by the grimace. There was such . . . *speculation* in his look. But then she had pushed through the glass doors, and was in the warm ebullience of shouts and hugs and jokes and droll nudges.

It was sweet to bathe in that bright, raucous communion. She had called the desk man that she was coming out, and for a couple of hours various friends whom the word had reached strolled in to greet her. She luxuriated in her pitied celebrity, received little gifts and gave back emotional kisses of thanks.

It ought to have lasted longer, but the night was an odd one. Not much was happening in town, and everybody seemed to have action lined up in Oxnard or Encino or some other bizarre place. A few stayed to work the home grounds, but they caught a subdued air from the place's emptiness at a still-young hour. Patti took a couple more Valium and tried to seem like she was peacefully resting in a lobby chair. To fight her stirrings of unease, she took up the paperback that was among the gifts given her—she hadn't even noticed by whom. It had a horrible face on the cover and was entitled *At The Mountains of Madness*.

If she had not felt the need of some potent distraction, some weighty ballast for her listing spirit, she would never have pieced out the Ciceronian rhythms of the narrative's style. But when, with frightened tenacity, she had waded several pages into the tale, the riverine prose, suddenly limpid, snatched her and bore her upon its flowing clarity. The Valium seemed to perfect her uncanny concentration, and where her vocabulary failed her, she made smooth leaps of inference and always landed square on the necessary meaning.

And so for hours in the slowly emptying lobby that looked out upon the slowly emptying intersection, she wound through the icy territories of the impossible, and down into the gelid, nethermost cellars of all World and Time, where stupendous aeons lay in pictured shards, and massive, sentient forms still stirred, and fed, and mocked the light.

Strangely, she began to find underlinings about two-thirds of the way through. All the marked passages involved references to *shoggoths*. It was a word whose mere sound made Patti's flesh stir. She searched the fly-leaf and inner covers for explanatory inscriptions, but found nothing.

When she laid the book down in the small hours, she sat amid a near-total desertion which she scarcely noticed. Something tugged powerfully at memory, something which memory dreaded to admit. She realized that in reading the tale, she had taken on an obscure, terrible weight. She felt as if impregnated by an injection of tainted knowledge whose grim fruit, an almost physical mass of cryptic threat, lay a-ripening in her now.

She took a third-floor room in the Parnassus for the night, for the simplest effort, like calling a cab, lay under a pall of futility and sourceless menace. She lay back, and her exhausted mind plunged instantly through the rotten flooring of consciousness, straight down into the abyss of dreams.

She dreamed of a city like Hollywood, but the city's walls and pavements were half alive, and they could feel premonitions of something that was drawing near them. All the walls and streets of the city waited in a cold-sweat fear under a blackly overcast sky. She herself, she grasped, was the heart and mind of the city. She lay in its midst, and its vast, cold fear was hers. She lay and somehow she knew the things that were drawing near her giant body. She knew their provenance in huge, blind voids where stood walls older than the present face of earth; she knew their long, cunning toil to reach her own cringing frontiers. Giant worms they were, or jellyfish, or merely great clots of boiling substance. They entered her deserted streets, glidingly converging. She lay like carrion that lives and knows the maggots' assault on it. She lay in her central citadel, herself the morsel they sped toward, piping their lust from foul, corrosive jaws.

She woke late Sunday afternoon, drained and dead of heart. She sat in bed watching a big green fly patiently hammer itself against the pane where the gold light flooded in. Endlessly it fought the impossible, battering with its frail, bejeweled head. With swift fury and pain Patti jumped out of bed and snatched up her blouse. She ran to the window and with her linen bludgeon killed the fly.

Across the street, in a window just one story higher than her own, sat Fat Face. She stood looking back for a moment, embarrassed by her little savagery, but warmed by the way the doctor's smile was filled with gentle understanding, as if he read the anguish the act was born of. She suddenly realized she was wearing only her bra.

His smile grew a shade merrier at her little jolt of awareness, and she knew he understood this too, that this was inadvertence, and not a hooker's come-on.

And so, with a swift excitement, she turned it into coquettry, and applied her blouse daintily to her breasts. She would make her fantasy real and by tenderness would heal the horror that had dogged her life. She pointed to herself with a smile, and then to Fat Face with inquiry. How he beamed then! Did she even see his eyes and lips water? He nodded energetically. With thumb and forefinger she signaled a short interval. As she left the window she noted the arrival, down on the side walk, of a gaggle of hydrotherapy patients, several with leashed strays in tow.

This bothered her, and she washed more slowly than she had meant to. Their arrival not only potentially inconvenienced her interview—it also put her in mind of the collector, and the memory laid a chill on her sexual enthusiasm. She came down slowly to the lobby. It was empty. The streets lay in a Sunday desolation such as only rarely befell this part of the city. Suddenly, all she wanted was a party. To hell with kinky charities. And as she stood at the window, a carful of her friends pulled up to the curb, and waved her to join them.

Almost she went—but then noted that Sheri's sister was in the car. She shuddered at any so near a reminder, and waved them off with a smile. Then she stepped out onto the sidewalk. No. Those patients with their strays had made the building too creepy for her. She turned toward her favorite bar. Arnold darted from his booth and made a grab for her arm.

She was edgy and quick, and jumped away. He seemed to fear leaving the booth's proximity, and came no nearer, but pleaded with her from where he stood:

"Please, Patti! Come here and listen."

Like a thunderbolt, the elusive memory of last night now struck Patti. "Shoggoth" was eerie, and that whole story familiar, because they were precisely what that letter had been all about! She was stunned that she could so utterly put from her mind that lurid document. It had spooked Sheri badly the night before she died. It had come from Arnold—and so had that book! That was the meaning of his look. The red, moronic face glared at her urgently.

"Please, Patti. I've had knowledge. Come here—" He darted forward to catch her arm and she sprang back, again the quicker, with a yelp. Arnold, thus drawn from the screening of his booth, froze fearfully. Patti looked up, and thrilled to find Fat Face looking down—not in amity, but in wrath upon Arnold. The newsman gaped, and mumbled apologetically, as if to the sidewalk: "No. I said nothing. I only *hinted*. . . ." Joyfully Patti sprang across the street and in moments was flying up those stairs she had climbed once before with such reluctance.

The oppression she had first found in these muted corridors was not gone from them—the quality of dread in some manner belonged to them—but she outran it. She moved too quickly in her sunny fantasy to be overtaken by that heaviness. She ran down the fourth-floor hall, and at the door where Sheri had knelt giggling and she had balked, she seized the knob and knocked simultaneously with pushing her way in, so impetuous was her rush toward benign sanity. There Fat Face sat at a big desk by the window she'd always known him through. He was even grosser-legged and more bloat-bellied than his patients. It gave her a funny shock that did not change her amorous designs.

He wore a commodious doctor's smock and slacks. His shoes were bulky, black, and orthopedically braced. Such a body less enkindled by warm spirit might have repelled. His, surmounted by the kindly beacon of his smile, seemed only grandfatherly, afflicted, dear. From somewhere there came, echoing as in a large, enclosed space, a noise of agitated water and of animals—strangely conjoined. But Fat Face was speaking:

"My dear," he said, not yet rising, "you make an old, old fellow very, very happy!" His voice was a marvel which sent half-lustful gooseflesh down her spine. It was an uncanny voice, reedy and wavering and shot with flutelike notes of silver purity, sinfully melodious. That voice knew seductions, quite possibly, that Patti had never dreamed of. She was speechless, and spread her arms in tender self-presentation.

He leapt to his feet, and the surging pep with which his great bulk moved sent a new thrill down the lightning-rod of her nerves. On pachydermous legs he leapt spry as a cat to a door behind his desk, and bowed her through. The noise of animals and churning water gusted fresher from the doorway. Perplexed, she entered.

The room contained only a huge bowl-shaped hydrotherapy tub. Its walls were blank cement, save one, which was a bank of shuttered windows through which the drenched clamor was pouring. She finally conquered disbelief and realized a fact she had been struggling with all along: those dozens of canine garglings,

and cat shrieks, were sounds of agony and distress.
Not hospital sounds. Torture chamber sounds. The
door boomed shut with a strikingly ponderous sound
followed by a sharp click. Fat Face, energetically un-
buttoning his smock, said:

"Go ahead and peek out, sweet, heedless trollop! O
yes, O yes, O yes—soon we'll *all* dine on lovely flesh—
men and women, not paltry vermin!" Patti gaped at
the lurid musicality of his speech, struggling to receive
its meaning. The doctor was shucking his trousers. It
appeared that he wore a complex rubber suit, heavily
strapped and buckled, under his clothes. Dazed, Patti
opened a shutter and looked out.

She saw a huge indoor pool, as the sounds had suggested, but not of the sane shape and bright chlori-
nated blue she expected. It was a huge slime-black
grotto that opened below her, bordered by rude, sea-
bearded rocks of cyclopean size. The sooty, viscous
broth of its waters boiled with bulging elephantine
shapes. . . .

From those shapes, when she had grasped them, she
tore her eyes with desperate speed, long instants too
late for her sanity. Nightmare ought not to be so
simply *there* before her, so dizzyingly adjacent to Reality. That the shapes should be such seething plasms,
such cunning, titan maggots as she had dreamed of,
this was just half the horror. The other half was the
human head that decorated each of those boiling
multimorphs, a comic excrescence from the nightmare
mess—this and the rain of panicked beasts that fell
from cagework above the pool and became in their
frenzies both the toys and the food of the pulpy
abominations.

She turned slack-mouthed to Fat Face. He stood by
the great empty tub working at the big system of
buckles on his chest. "Do you understand, my dear?
Please try! Your horror will improve your tang. *Your
veil shall be the wash of blood that dims and drowns
your dying eyes*. . . . You see, we find it easier to hold
most of the shape with suits like these. We could

mimic the entire body, but far more effort and concentration would be required."

He gave a last pull and the row of buckles split crisply open. Ropy purple gelatin gushed from his suitfront into the tub. Patti ran to the door, which had no knob. As she tore her nails against it and screamed, she remembered the fly at the window, and heard Fat Face continue behind her:

"So we just imitate the head, and we never dissolve it, not to risk resuming it faultily and waking suspicions. Please struggle!"

She looked back and saw huge palps, like dreadful comic phalluses, spring from the tub of slime that now boiled with movement. She screamed.

"Oh, yes!" fluted the Fat Face that now bobbed on the purple simmer. Patti's arms smoked where the palps took them. She was plucked from the floor as light as a struggling roach might be. "Oh, yes, dear girl—*you'll have for bridesmaids Pain and dread, for vows you'll jabber blasphemies* . . ." As he brought her to hang above the cauldron of his acid body, she saw his eyes roll jet black. He lowered her feet into himself. A last time before shock took her, Patti threw the feeble tool of her voice against the massive walls. She kicked as her feet sank into the scorching gelatin, kicked till her shoes dissolved, till her feet and ankles spread nebulae of liquefying flesh within the shoggoth lord's greedy substance. Then her kicking slowed, and she sank more deeply in. . . .

DAW

Welcome to DAW's Gallery of Ghoulish Delights!

HOUSE SHUDDERS
Martin H. Greenberg and Charles G. Waugh, editors
  Fiendish tales about haunted houses!
☐ UE2223 $3.50

HUNGER FOR HORROR
Robert H. Adams, Martin H. Greenberg, and Pamela Crippen Adams, editors
  A devilish stew of horror from the master terror chefs!
☐ UE2266 $3.50

RED JACK
Martin H. Greenberg, Charles G. Waugh, and Frank D. McSherry, Jr., editors
  The 100th anniversary collection of Jack the Ripper tales!
☐ UE2315 $3.95

VAMPS
Martin H. Greenberg and Charles G. Waugh, editors
  A spine-tingling collection featuring those long-toothed ladies of the night—female vampires!
☐ UE2190 $3.50

THE YEAR'S BEST HORROR STORIES
Karl Edward Wagner, editor
  ☐ Series IX   UE2159—$2.95
  ☐ Series X   UE2160—$2.95
  ☐ Series XI   UE2161—$2.95
  ☐ Series XIV   UE2156—$3.50
  ☐ Series XV   UE2226—$3.50
  ☐ Series XVI   UE2300—$3.95